He was still standing there, poleaxed by the sight of her, when he heard the galloping tattoo of hoof beats gaining, gaining, finally pulling to a stop with a churn and spray of mud.

He turned his head to see his brother, George. They'd raced here cross-country, but George's mount had refused at a stone wall, leaving him to find the long way around.

Constantine hailed his sibling. "George, I'm in love."

"Ha!" His brother leaned forward to pat his horse's gleaming neck. "You wouldn't know love if it leaped up and bit you on the arse."

Constantine tilted his head, considering. "You could be right. Let's go inside and see if we can find her."

"One of the most compelling heroes I've read in years."
—Anna Campbell, author of *Midnight's Wild Passion*

Heiress in Love

CHRISTINA BROOKE

St. Martin's Paperbacks

This is a work of fiction. All of the characters, organizations, and events portrayed in this novel are either products of the author's imagination or are used fictitiously.

HEIRESS IN LOVE

Copyright © 2011 by Christina Brooke.
Excerpt from *Mad About the Earl* copyright © 2011 by Christina Brooke.

For information address St. Martin's Press, 175 Fifth Avenue, New York, NY 10010.

ISBN: 978-0-312-53412-7

Printed in the United States of America

St. Martin's Paperbacks edition / July 2011

St. Martin's Paperbacks are published by St. Martin's Press, 175 Fifth Avenue, New York, NY 10010.

10 9 8 7 6 5 4 3 2 1

For Jamie, with all my love

ACKNOWLEDGMENTS

Publishing is a labor of love and I am fortunate to work with people whose passion for great stories inspires me and encourages me every day.

Monique Patterson, thank you for your energy and skill and your commitment to making my books shine. To Holly Blanck and the rest of the amazing team at St. Martin's, I'm so appreciative of all the work that goes into getting my books to the shelves. Thank you, all.

To my brilliant agent, Helen Breitwieser, thank you for your guidance and support and for all the things you do that go above and beyond expectations. I love working with you.

K and D, there is so very much to thank you for, from your killer plotting and critiquing skills to your loyalty and friendship, all of which are very precious to me.

To my family and friends, thank you for putting up with all of my craziness and for helping me when the going gets tough. I love you all.

PROLOGUE

Y ou found her. After all this time."

The low-pitched feminine voice made the Duke of Montford turn. A lady, magnificent in old gold and diamonds, stood behind him, as out of place as he was in the wholesome austerity of the nursery wing.

"Yes," he said.

He caught a glimmer of maternal softening about the strong, elegant lines of Lady Arden's face as she contemplated the sleeping girl. Then she transferred her shrewd gaze to his.

"Dauntry's child?"

Montford inclined his head. Very few were aware of this little girl's existence, but his companion knew he'd been searching high and low for Lady Jane Westruther.

He shouldn't be surprised that Lady Arden would take a keen interest in the girl. The woman could sniff out an unattached heiress from a mile away.

This particular heiress had been lost for eight years. Her mother had run away from Lord Dauntry's grand estate within a week of the babe's birth, taking the child with her.

Perhaps Lady Dauntry had feared her cruel husband's ire at the babe's sex, or perhaps she'd fallen prey to a malady that sometimes affected women after the birth of a child.

Her lord had not bothered to look for her. From all Montford could discover, she'd died of rheumatic fever within months of making her escape.

Jonathon Westruther, Earl of Dauntry, had broken his neck in a hunting accident, leaving his only daughter under Montford's guardianship. It was a common enough arrangement; as head of the House of Westruther, Montford was named guardian to many children in this large and illustrious family. This was particularly the case where the child stood to inherit a family estate or a fortune that might require Montford's expertise and judgment.

Sadly, Montford had acquired quite a collection of these wealthy orphans.

A tribe of children to his name and still no wife . . . Who'd have thought? Sometimes, he felt a hundred and he hadn't yet reached his thirtieth year.

He glanced at his companion, all glittering elegance, her honey-brown hair gilded by candlelight. She'd followed him up here, God knew to what purpose. He wasn't even sure why he'd come, why he'd needed to see to the child in the middle of his own ball.

Suddenly, Montford felt a trifle foolish. He'd hired a battalion of servants to care for Lady Jane Westruther, after all. One of them, a nursemaid, slept in the adjoining chamber within earshot in case her charge should wake up. He wasn't needed here.

Gesturing for Lady Arden to precede him from the nursery, Montford couldn't resist one last glance over his shoulder. The thin little girl lay with one small hand tucked under her cheek, her rosebud lips slightly parted and quivering with each breath, the fear in her eyes now shuttered beneath gently curving lids.

Fury welled inside him at the source of that fear. Fury, however, was an unprofitable emotion in the circumstances. With swift, ruthless efficiency, he'd destroyed the culprits who'd worked her like a slave in that squalid boardinghouse. She was safe now.

Yet, he couldn't conquer the fear in those large gray eyes as easily as he'd vanquished the villains charged with her care. He wasn't sure he knew how.

Turning away, Montford bowed and offered his arm to Lady Arden. She placed her gloved hand lightly upon it. As they moved through the doorway, he caught a waft of her scent. Understated, complicated, alluring. Much like the lady who wore it.

After a thoughtful pause, she spoke. "That little poppet is a considerable heiress if she is Dauntry's child. I shall want her for Frederick Black. Roxdale's son, you know."

Montford masked his surprise at her directness. Lady Arden was legendary among the *ton* for her prescience and subtlety. "My lady, you know as well as I that this conversation is inappropriate. We must proceed through the proper channels."

Her fingers flexed against his arm. "*Proper* channels! The Ministry of Marriage has become a veritable hotbed of *impropriety*, and you know it. DeVere has voted against every proposal I've made this year."

"DeVere is merely peeved because you are immune to his dubious charms," he replied.

Emotion flitted over her face, and it bothered him that he couldn't decipher it. Perhaps he'd be obliged to pay deVere a visit.

"I want assurances from you that I will get a fair hearing," she persisted.

Montford bit back an acid retort. Why did he find her single-mindedness so irksome? She knew little of the girl's sorry history, after all.

He reminded himself that *he* had founded the aptly nick-named Ministry of Marriage; had only himself to blame for the power struggles that climbed to their peak each Season. In Lady Arden's shoes, he'd be equally eager to win such a prize as the little girl upstairs for a scion of his own dynasty.

Montford bowed. "Of course, any match you propose

will receive due consideration. I am rather a stickler for the rules, you know."

"Particularly when the rules are of your making," she observed dryly. "Very well, if the Ministry approves, I shall have Lady Jane Westruther for the future Lord Roxdale. An excellent match."

Indeed it would be, on paper. He'd need to further his acquaintance with Roxdale to be sure.

They neared the ballroom, where the babble of the crowd swelled over the strains of a quadrille and spilled out into the corridor. Lady Arden swept him a curtsy and turned to go in.

Montford placed his hand on her arm, staying her. "We will speak of this in good time, my lady." He hesitated. "As the girl's guardian, it behooves me to choose her husband carefully."

Lady Arden's brown eyes widened until every one of her dark eyelashes seemed picked out against the ivory of her skin. Did she divine the peculiar importance to him of this little girl? He trusted she did not. As the head of a noble house with countless eligible unmarrieds dangling from the branches of its family tree, as a man who sincerely believed love had no place in the business of marriage, he couldn't afford to show weakness. He couldn't afford to admit the truth: for once, he didn't give a damn about the Ministry of Marriage.

He just wanted to see a frightened little girl smile.

CHAPTER ONE

THE COTSWOLDS, ENGLAND, SPRING, 1814

The newly widowed Jane, Lady Roxdale, stood at the window of her private sitting room, staring out at the scene below.

Carriage upon carriage, some draped in black crêpe, some emblazoned with noble coats of arms, choked the rush-strewn drive that wound up to the house. Like a train of shiny black beetles, they shuffled between ornate wrought-iron gates, marched through an avenue of oaks, then paused beneath the portico to disgorge mourners.

Their pace was slow, respectful, inexorable. And Jane could not wait for them all to depart as slowly and respectfully as they'd come.

She pressed trembling fingertips to the windowpane. How soon? How soon must she leave her home?

Not hers anymore. *His.*

Constantine Black. Her husband's cousin and heir. The scoundrel who had not even bestirred himself to appear at his kinsman's funeral.

If he couldn't summon sufficient proper feeling to appear today, was she not right to fear for the estate? But then, the new Lord Roxdale was reputed to be glittering and wild, a philanderer, a drunkard, a gamester, with no thought in his head save the next faro bank, the next wench, the next bottle of wine.

He would run through his new fortune, just as he'd squandered the funds he'd inherited from his father. That would take time, of course, even for an inveterate gamester such as Constantine Black.

The Lazenby estate was vast, bolstered by the spectacular dowry Jane had brought to her marriage. *Her* family's money would fund this wastrel's dissipation, while she was cast out of her home. The utter, galling unfairness of it! If only . . .

If only she'd borne an heir, this disaster could have been averted.

Her throat ached with a sudden rush of sadness. If only Luke were the son of her body as well as the son of her heart.

Outside, sullen drizzle turned to rain, spattering those barouches and landaus, tapping at her fingertips through the windowpane. Footmen with umbrellas emerged to rescue the mourners inside the stalled vehicles and shepherd them into the house.

Jane let the curtain fall and closed her eyes. Constantine Black would plunder the legacy that had dropped like a ripe whore into his lap. She'd no power to stop him. None.

A jolt of awareness made her eyes snap open. Something must have alerted her. Not a sound, for the rain and the thick panes of glass muffled noise from the outside. More an atmosphere. She fingered the gauzy curtain aside and peered out again to see a flurry, a veritable commotion below.

A man. Yes, a man on a white horse, thundering down the lawn alongside the drive, streaking past all those black beetles like a shooting star through the night.

She couldn't see his face, merely gained the impression of broad shoulders, muscular thighs hugging the horse's flanks, and a daredevil billow and furl to his cloak as it streamed out behind.

He reined in where the bottleneck of carriages made passage to the shelter of the portico impossible. The big, milk-white stallion stood quiescent, magnificent, as the gentleman dismounted in a graceful slide.

The newcomer swept off his hat and bowed to the mourners, who were undoubtedly agog but too well-bred to show it. Black curls tousled and damped in the wet breeze.

He stilled. His big shoulders lifted slightly, as if invisible fingers pinched his nape.

Then he turned. And looked up. At her.

Their gazes met, and the distance between them seemed to vanish in a dizzying flash. Somnolent eyes openly stared at her, heavy-lidded, insolent, a touch quizzical.

Jane's lips parted. Her heart pounded against her ribs. She had to remind herself to breathe.

A sudden smile tugged at the corner of his mouth, then grew in a dazzle of white teeth. It seared through the black pall over her soul like a bolt of summer lightning. She felt it down to the soles of her feet, that blinding warmth, that tingling joy. Bit back an answering gleam that seemed drawn from deep within.

The stranger's smile faded. His eyes narrowed to an intent, purposeful regard. Jane's lungs burned as if she breathed smoke, not air. But she kept looking, looking, powerless to wrench her gaze from his.

Heavens, but she'd never seen such a man before. By rights, vice ought to be ugly in its incarnation, but *he* . . . It must be true that the devil looked after his own.

Constantine Black. The new Lord Roxdale. Who else could it be? A hard flutter struck up in her chest, like the wings of a finch trapped behind glass. She took a hurried step back from the window, let the curtain swing shut.

Moments throbbed by in silence before Jane collected herself, straightened her spine. She would not cower and blush before that tricked-out scoundrel, with his loose-limbed charm and his careless strength and his swagger. She disapproved of him utterly. He would not beguile *her*.

"Aunt Jane, Aunt Jane, Aunt *Jane*!"

The series of jubilant yells made her spin around with a

betraying flush. A six-year-old boy flew helter-skelter toward her before skidding to a halt.

"Did you *see* him?" Luke's brown eyes shone as he glanced toward the window, then gazed eagerly up into her face. "The most magnificent beast!"

Jane's thoughts instantly reverted to the dark-haired gentleman.

Her color deepened. "Why, I . . . Oh!" She let out a shaky laugh. Of course! Luke meant the gentleman's horse, not the man himself. "Yes, darling. I did, indeed. A most handsome creature."

Luke dragged a chair to the window and clambered onto it. Pushing the curtain aside, he peered out of the window.

Jane stayed where she was.

"I've never seen a stallion that color before." Luke craned his neck, the better to view this prime piece of horseflesh. "What do you think he is, an Arab or Welsh? Maybe he's too big to be an Arab. He must be seventeen hands, at least!"

"Why don't you run down and find out?" she suggested. "I'm sure the gentleman's groom won't mind if you go and look. But *only* looking, mind," she warned. "That horse is far too large for you to ride."

Luke turned to regard her with a speculative gleam in his big brown eyes.

Jane held out her hand. "Promise?"

His mouth twisted with reluctance. "Oh, very well."

Solemnly, he gripped her hand in his smaller one and pumped her arm in a firm shake. "Word of a gentleman."

Using her hand for balance, Luke jumped down from the chair. She thought he'd take himself off then, but he lingered, his shoulders drooping a little.

"When do we have to leave here, Aunt Jane?"

Surprised at the abrupt change of subject, Jane hesitated. "Oh, not for a little while yet, I expect." Lazenby Hall was the only home Luke had known since he'd been brought here as an orphaned babe. The last thing Frederick had wanted was to be saddled with his kinsman's child, but Jane refused to be gainsaid. From the moment Luke held out his chubby arms to her, Jane had been his slave. She'd do anything to keep him safe.

"I don't see why we can't stay," he muttered, lowering his gaze so that his long, black lashes shadowed his cheeks. "It's not as if there isn't room."

"Thirty-seven of them, to be exact," she agreed lightly. And that was just the bedchambers.

"Thirty-seven rooms and *he* can't spare us a measly two." Luke kicked at the chair leg with the toe of his leather half-boot.

Jane touched her fingertips to his cheek. "I know it seems hard, but this is the new baron's house now. It doesn't belong to us anymore."

"But what will he *do* here, living all alone? I should think he'd want us to stay, don't you, to keep him company? Lady Cecily says I'm *excellent* company, you know."

Laughing a little, Jane ruffled his hair. "The new baron would be privileged to have us, in fact," she agreed. "But I'm afraid we must go, for all that."

Jane repressed a sigh. Lazenby Hall had been her home since she married Frederick at seventeen. Now that she had to leave it, she felt adrift, her spirits more depressed than she would ever admit to Luke. The Lazenby estate and the welfare of its people were no longer her responsibility. She was powerless to help them, much as she longed to do so.

And indeed, she was more fortunate than many women in her situation. Upon her marriage, her guardian, the Duke of Montford, had ensured that her jointure was more than generous. She could live independently if she chose, set up a household of her own.

Besides, she had Luke, and that was the most important thing.

She said to him, "Speaking of excellent company, I have a splendid plan, one I think you will like. You and I shall make our home at Harcourt, with the Duke of Montford and Lady Cecily and Lady Rosamund. Won't that be fun? We'll show you all our old haunts, and there'll be other children there to play with, too."

His dark brows knitted. "But all my friends are here."

Jane's heart ached for him. "Well, perhaps we might come back to visit them." A rash promise, but she'd do anything to make the change in his circumstances less painful.

She made herself sound cheerful. "In the meantime, there is a *very* fine horse awaiting your attention. Why don't you go down to the kitchens for a carrot or an apple to take to him? And if you're lucky, Cook might spare a jam tart or two for you."

Luke brightened instantly at the mention of food. "I need my sketchbook, too. I'll come back later and tell you all about him," he promised.

"I shall look forward to it."

Luke shot off in the direction of the kitchens, barely pausing to bow and pant out a greeting to Rosamund, who narrowly missed colliding with him in the doorway.

Rosamund raised her eyebrows at Jane.

"There's a horse," said Jane, on a note of explanation.

"Oh!" Rosamund laughed. "How is one poor female to compete with that?"

"I'm so *glad* to see you." Jane threw her arms around her cousin and hugged her close. "Thank you for coming. I couldn't face all this without you."

She drew back and held Rosamund's hands in hers. Though the two of them had grown up together, each time they met, Rosamund's stunning fair beauty struck Jane anew.

"There's quite a crowd downstairs." Rosamund's deep blue eyes held affection and concern. "Cecily and Beckenham are eager to see you, too."

She lifted a hand and gently tucked one of Jane's curls behind her ear. "What are you doing up here all alone, Goosey?"

Jane smiled at the childhood nickname. She took a deep breath. "Gathering my courage."

Her mind flew to that lone horseman. He was downstairs . . . somewhere, among the throng. The notion made her lungs seize and her pulse quicken. What was the matter with her?

"The duke grows impatient," said Rosamund. "You'd best come down."

Jane's nerves stretched taut as violin strings. Reading the will. Relatives and acquaintances come to gawk and speculate. How she loathed being the center of attention, the focus of every eye.

She needed all her courage today. To face the mourners, yes, but also to deal with the Duke of Montford. His Grace would have plans for her. Plans she'd refuse to countenance this time.

Freedom. The lure of it was like an outstretched hand, beckoning across an abyss. The terror of it was an open-mawed monster, slavering to consume her flesh and spit out her bones.

Rosamund's voice was firm. "Come on, old thing. I know you hate crushes but you must be there to hear the will read."

"Yes. I suppose I must." Besides, she did so want to see her cobbled-together family. The weight of that desire finally tipped the balance.

Jane moved through the connecting doorway of her sitting room to her bedchamber. She picked up her bonnet from the hat stand where it perched and set the horrid black thing on her head. It hunkered over her auburn curls like a malevolent bird of prey.

Over her shoulder, she said, "I know what the will says. And anyway, the estate is entailed. Everything goes to That Lout."

Rosamund tilted her head. "Do you think he's as handsome as they say?"

Jane gave an uncaring shrug, but the stranger on the white horse dominated her mind's eye. "Far more handsome than is good for him, no doubt. I'd be surprised if there's much substance beneath the surface charm."

Rosamund slanted a glance at her. "You ought to show some respect, Jane. He's head of the family now."

"Not *my* family."

Jane checked her reflection in the mirror above her dressing table, tweaked the delicate ruff of her collar into place. Her complexion was still high; no need to pinch her cheeks to warm them.

She drew a deep breath and linked her arm with Rosamund's. "Very well. Let's go."

"The devil!" Constantine Black stood immobile for the longest time, waiting for that curtain to twitch open. Surely, she'd take pity and reveal herself again.

But women, he'd found, were merciless creatures, so of course she didn't, and of course he was obliged to stand there, rooted to the spot and getting wetter, waiting just in case.

She was . . . luminous. Not like the sun. There was nothing brassy or flashy or even particularly warm about her. She made him think of the subtle gleam of silver, of moonlight.

Tall, slender, yet with a generous, pretty bosom. Darkish hair. It was difficult to tell exactly what color at this distance, in this light. And she'd flattened her lips and stared at him as if he were a worm, unfit to kiss the tips of her fingers.

At the thought of kissing any part of that mysterious female's anatomy, his body heated, in fervent contrast to the cool spring rain.

He was still standing there, poleaxed by the sight of her, when he heard the galloping tattoo of hoofbeats gaining, gaining, finally pulling to a stop with a churn and spray of mud.

He turned his head to see his brother, George. They'd raced here cross-country, but George's mount had refused at a stone wall, leaving him to find the long way around.

Constantine hailed his sibling. "George, I'm in love."

"Ha!" His brother leaned forward to pat his horse's gleaming neck. "You wouldn't know love if it leaped up and bit you on the arse."

Constantine tilted his head, considering. "You could be right. Let's go inside and see if we can find her."

Laughing, George shook his head. They left their horses to a waiting groom and turned toward the house.

A vast pity they'd missed the funeral. Their attendance at a house party in Northumberland had kept them from hearing news of Frederick's death in time. Constantine had only received the tidings upon their arrival in Town. He and George had ridden hell-for-leather but the funeral had concluded by the time they'd arrived at the church.

Given the bitterness of his parting from Frederick all those years ago, he would not have come at all today, but for the note. Among the pile of correspondence awaiting him in his London rooms, he'd discovered a summons from Frederick dated a fortnight before. Frederick must have known the end was near and wished to confer with his heir. Had he even, perhaps, sought some kind of reconciliation?

Something twisted in Constantine's gut. Now, he'd never know.

As they joined the throng that surged through the wide-open front door, Constantine's face settled into a more serious mien. He reminded himself why he'd come today, when he'd rather be almost anywhere else on the planet.

He'd inherited this dear old pile against all expectations. Frederick, dead far too young, before he'd even set up his nursery.

It had been a shock. Yes, a shock.

Poor Frederick. Whispers had it that he'd died *in flagrante,* which made Constantine all the more curious to meet his widow.

Shagged to death. Not a bad way to go. If one must.

Standing head and shoulders over most of the crowd, Constantine searched the female faces. Who was the woman he'd seen looking out the window? She must live in the house, but it couldn't be Lady Roxdale. Surely Frederick's widow would be down here, greeting the mourners, not staring at them from on high like a princess in a tower.

That's what had captivated him, he realized. She'd looked so remote up there, so solitary, so deliciously untouchable. It made him want to strip her and cover her bare skin in openmouthed kisses until she trembled with delight.

Ah, but she'd appeared a virtuous lady, now, hadn't she? The kind who wouldn't lift her skirts if they were on fire. And virtuous ladies, gently bred ladies with spotless reputations, were strictly off-limits for him these days. Had been since that ill-fated affair with Amanda.

As he handed his hat and gloves to a waiting footman, Constantine grimaced. How many people here today would turn their backs on him, pretend he didn't exist?

"Constantine! George!" A strident female voice rising above the murmuring throng brought George to a halt.

Lord, the man had no sense of self-preservation. Constantine kept moving as if he hadn't heard.

He recognized the voice. It belonged to that harridan, that harbinger of doom, his aunt Lady Endicott. The displeasure that throbbed in her tone promised him a dressing-down for something or other; he didn't wait to find out what. He abandoned George to his fate and continued smoothly up the central staircase and out a connecting door.

The door led to a long gallery, where familiar, disapproving faces stared down on him from inside ornate gold frames. Here, the shades of his ancestors roamed.

It was oddly disconcerting to see that nothing had changed. Except for the addition of a new portrait: the late Frederick Black, Lord Roxdale. Looking rather pale and sick, come to think of it, despite the artist's efforts to romanticize.

Constantine stared down the long, narrow room, and the years slid back. He was here again, playing cricket with Frederick on a day such as this, when the pitch was sodden as a marsh and it seemed the rain would never cease.

Frederick had bowled a sweet one and Constantine forgot

where he was, smashing the hard cork ball for six. He still recalled the crack, thump, and roll as it knocked one of the marble busts from its pedestal, chipping their illustrious ancestor's Roman nose. Constantine smiled faintly, picturing his and Frederick's desperate attempts to fix the damage so Frederick's papa wouldn't see it and thrash them both.

The memory of his final interview with Frederick's sire was a painful one. Constantine pushed it away, avoided meeting the kind eyes of the tenth baron's portrait.

He turned back to the likeness of Frederick, his cousin, his friend. Fishing out his brandy flask, he raised it in a toast.

"God bless, old fellow." He drank, and the brandy warmed his throat as it slipped down. "I'll prove you wrong about me. Just see if I don't."

And yet, even as he made that fine resolution, the lady in the window flashed into his mind. He hissed through his teeth, then took another pull of brandy.

Ah, well. He rarely acted on his good intentions when all was said and done.

CHAPTER TWO

As they entered the old music room, Jane glanced at Rosamund. Contrary to her cousin's assurances, the chamber's sole occupant was the Duke of Montford. Where were the others?

The duke rose from the writing desk by the window and crossed the room to greet them.

"Lady Roxdale." The duke made his bow, while Jane sank into a deep curtsy.

Though he'd stood her guardian from the time she was eight until her marriage, Montford always addressed Jane in this formal manner. Was it to distance himself from her? Or perhaps he wished to savor his victory, roll her title on his tongue like fine wine. After all, the duke's strategizing had brought the status and power of Roxdale within his domain.

But with Frederick's sudden death, those riches had slipped through Montford's fingers. The lands, the pedigree, the political influence—everything would pass to Constantine Black, a male heir who was not his kinswoman's child.

Did Montford feel this as keenly as she suspected? One could never tell what he thought by looking at him.

The duke could have been aged anywhere between forty and fifty. He dressed as austerely as a cleric, but the patrician cast to his countenance and the authority in his demeanor proclaimed his rank more clearly than any external trappings. His dark, hooded eyes glittered with intelligence.

"Allow me to express my condolences, my dear," said the duke. "Roxdale's passing has been a shock to us all. He was a good man." He paused. "How do you go on?"

"Well enough, I thank you, Your Grace," returned Jane. He wasn't the slightest bit concerned with either her health or the upheaval inside her. He no more took heed of her thoughts and emotions than a chess master considered the finer feelings of his pawn.

She couldn't resist adding, "Frederick's passing was not such a shock, after all. He had a weak heart. It could have happened at any time."

Montford tilted his head. "Yes, of course. One still finds oneself unprepared for the end, however. You are bearing up well."

The duke studied her keenly. When she was a child, she'd believed wholeheartedly in his ability to read her mind. In adulthood, she'd realized his talent was nothing so magical. He excelled at reading people's faces, their small, telltale gestures, the meaning behind their words, the things they deliberately left unsaid. She took care to keep her own expression neutral and confine her comments to the minimum. Let him deduce from that what he willed.

"What do you plan to do now, Lady Roxdale?" said Montford. Quite as if he'd give her a choice in the matter.

"I shall stay here as long as I'm needed to ensure the household changes hands smoothly. Then I will return to Harcourt. If that is acceptable to you," she added.

The duke nodded, but he wouldn't let the matter pass so easily. "We must speak of the future. But let us first be done with the will."

Montford slid his long fingers into his waistcoat pocket and pulled out a fine gold timepiece. He flicked it open with a frown of annoyance. "Frederick's man of business should be here by now."

"No doubt he's caught in the melee outside," Rosamund interposed. "Several members of Frederick's family have yet to arrive."

"Most notably his heir," commented Jane dryly.

She blinked. Now, there was a thought. Perhaps the gentleman on the big white horse had not been Constantine Black, after all?

A rush of relief made her almost light-headed. Ah, yes, what a fool she'd been to make such an unwarranted assumption! He could have been anyone, couldn't he, that bold, flamboyant rider? Sometimes, her imagination was so vivid it grew legs and ran away with her.

Voices, footsteps, echoed in the corridor outside. "Jane! You *are* here."

Cecily burst into the room and launched herself at Jane in an exuberant embrace that nearly squeezed the breath out of her. "I *told* Becks you would come down, but he said no, on account of your probably being distraught and not wanting us, and I said what rot, for you didn't care the snap of your fingers for Fre— Oh, confound it, there's Montford and he'll be *monstrous* cross with me."

With the aplomb of the utterly shameless, Cecily disengaged herself from Jane and sank into an accomplished curtsy.

"Your Grace." She smiled sunnily up at the duke as she rose.

Not for the first time, Jane marveled that Cecily could get away with such outré behavior. The duke stared down his nose at her, but Cecily merely waggled her brows back at him, her dark eyes brimming with wit and fun.

"Cecily." The warning came from Beckenham, who'd followed her into the room. "I'd be obliged if you would refrain from uttering exactly what is in your head at any given moment."

"Oh, but I don't! You'd be *thoroughly* shocked if I actually spoke my mind, Becks, I assure you."

Beckenham ground his teeth. To the duke, he said, "That chit will have to learn some conduct if she's to come out next year."

Montford smiled thinly. "I've no intention of inflicting

Lady Cecily on an unsuspecting populace without adequate preparation. Rosamund will see to it, won't you, my dear?"

"Yes, indeed, Your Grace." Rosamund's tone was sober, but her eyes twinkled merrily.

"I admire your fortitude," said Beckenham. He scrutinized Cecily from the top of her dark curls to the toes of her slippers. "She'll require intensive training."

Cecily sniffed. "You make me sound like a horse."

"Not at all. I have the utmost respect for horses."

Beckenham turned his head, his stern visage softening. "Jane."

He moved toward her, holding out his hands to clasp hers. She returned the pressure with a quick, affectionate squeeze. Becks always reminded her of a big black bear—so large and warm, but fierce when his fighting instinct was roused.

"Frederick was a good man," he said, unconsciously echoing Montford's less genuine sentiments. "He'll be missed."

She nodded, disengaging herself from his clasp. "Thank you. Yes. He will be missed."

Not *I'll miss him*. No, she would not admit to that.

"Shall we sit?" Rosamund dispelled the moment of awkward tension. Gracefully, she shepherded Jane to a couch and took her own seat beside her.

Dear Rosamund. She showed her support and affection without prying or exclaiming over Frederick's youth or the suddenness of his demise. Jane appreciated that as much as she admired the tranquil, unassuming air that lent gravity to Rosamund's stunning fair beauty. Rosamund made life so much easier for everyone around her. Unlike Jane, who discomfited them with her unexpected directness and her prickles.

Frederick's solicitor hurried in with profuse apologies and a reference to the crush of carriages outside. The duke moved to greet him and conduct him to the desk, where the two men carried on a murmured conversation. The solicitor fluttered pages, gathered them, set them out on the desk in neat stacks.

Beckenham chose a spindle-legged chair beside Rosamund and Jane. He leaned forward, murmuring, "I take it neither Xavier nor Andrew have deigned to show themselves."

Cecily snorted, plumping herself down between Jane and Rosamund. "Of course not. We haven't seen Andrew since he returned from Egypt. Xavier . . ." She shrugged. "Who knows? *I*, for one, don't give a fig."

"Cecily." Rosamund said it quietly, but her gentle admonishment succeeded where Beckenham's growl had not. Cecily subsided, but the mulish set of her pretty lips proclaimed her annoyance with the one member of their family who had always stood apart.

They all fell silent, contemplating the absentees. Jane forgave Andrew; one always did. No matter how much he provoked her, her anger typically crumbled before his charming contrition, his singular ability to find the ironic humor in any situation. Xavier, on the other hand . . . No, she wouldn't want him here.

They'd all grown up under one roof, under the protection of the Duke of Montford. Unusually, Montford had undertaken the custody as well as the guardianship of these particular children; when one knew the Duke of Montford, one ceased to wonder at the reason: he wanted them under his thumb.

The girls were heiresses, the boys titled and landed or next in line for that honor. The duke had deemed it expedient to quarter these significant orphans in one establishment— Harcourt—until he sent the boys to their respective estates.

Xavier and Rosamund were the only true siblings among them, but they were all related, some of them only through several marriages. It was a connection so tenuous as to be barely there at all, yet the bond between them was strong.

The Westruther family was so very old and very large that one cousin had made the history of this proud and powerful dynasty a lifelong study. Similarly, Montford had made it his life's work to increase the wealth and stature of the Westruthers.

Jane wondered where he'd draw the line. Certainly not at marrying her to Frederick with his dicky heart. A heart, moreover, Jane could never have hoped to win.

Would the duke let her go this time? *Hardly.* Not unless she lost all her money on 'Change, or created a scandal of epic proportions.

Oh, she might be legally her own mistress now, but Montford had a way of drawing unsuspecting pawns back into his game. She'd have to remain one step ahead of him to elude his stratagems.

"Ah," Cecily said. "Some new arrivals."

Feather, the butler, appeared, conducting those of the mourners who had some interest in the will into the music room. Ordinarily, the library would have been the proper place for such an occasion but that room had always been Jane's sanctuary. She couldn't yet accustom herself to losing it.

Jane accepted their condolences with polite murmurs of thanks.

The salon was filling rapidly. Gracious, how many were there? The strident tones of a woman with a very tall hat and an equally high opinion of herself rose above the crowd.

Griselda, Countess of Endicott. One of Frederick's aunts. Jane sank down in her chair, but the feeble attempt to escape notice proved useless. Lady Endicott surged toward her, her massive bosom plowing through the crowd like the prow of a ship.

At her approach, the three cousins rose and curtsied.

"Jane!" boomed the lady. "I hope you mean to tell me what you were about, ordering such a shabby coffin for poor Frederick. When the pallbearers took him out to the hearse, I didn't know where to look!"

Jane's cheeks warmed at the attention the countess attracted from the other mourners. "The coffin was exactly as

Frederick ordered it, my lady." A handsome one, too, fashioned of polished mahogany with brass handles. What possible objection could there be?

Jane had learned by now that the countess was bound to criticize whatever one did. She only wished Frederick's aunt had chosen to do so in a less public forum.

Lady Endicott's slightly protuberant brown eyes popped. "Frederick chose that eyesore? What has he to say to anything?" She gave a dismissive wave of her hand. "My dear Jane, Frederick's funeral is none of *his* concern. As his wife, it's your duty to ignore his wishes and do what's best for him. After all those years of marriage, I'd have thought you'd learned *that*."

Jane didn't know what to reply to that speech, so it was fortunate that their neighbor, Mr. Trent, came up at that moment. He greeted them, then smoothly turned to the countess with his most attractive smile. "Ah, Lady Endicott. Resplendent as ever, I see. I believe the reading is about to begin. Shall we?"

All fluttering compliance, the countess took his arm. As Trent led her away, he glanced at Jane over his shoulder. She mouthed *Thank you* to him, and he gave a nod, his lips quirked up a little at the corners.

The small lawyer cleared his throat in a portentous manner. Finally, the reading began.

Its convoluted legal wording made the document impossible to understand, and Jane's attention wandered almost immediately. Of course, the will would contain few surprises. The estate went to Constantine Black—everyone knew that. There were innumerable small legacies to servants, dependants, and relatives. He'd left them the correct amounts, no more. Frederick had been a punctilious but not a particularly generous man.

Memories rose, unbidden, of Frederick before they married, before everything went wrong. Frederick, visiting her at Harcourt on his school holidays, Frederick bringing her sweetmeats, taking her out in his spanking new curricle.

He'd courted her for form's sake. Foolish girl she'd been, she'd read much more into it than he'd intended.

Groomed from childhood to become Frederick's wife, she'd had such hopes for their future together.

Now, there was no future left. He was gone.

She sucked in a shaky breath.

"Jane?" Rosamund whispered, but her voice seemed to echo from miles away.

Jane shook her head. Tears stung the back of her eyes, hot and insistent. Confound it, she'd been determined not to weep for him. *Why* did those memories overset her now?

But she'd blocked these thoughts, these emotions, for too long. Dry-eyed, she'd watched Frederick breathe his last, helped lay him out for the traditional vigil. She'd seen the gleaming coffin carried out of the house and loaded into the hearse and watched it drive away. No ladies allowed at funerals, of course. She hadn't been obliged to endure that.

She'd kept herself busy these last days—organized mourning bands for the servants, rushes for the drive, ordered her widow's weeds, had some old black gowns made over in the meantime.

And now, when she had no privacy for grief, the sobs gathered and clamored, threatening to burst from her chest.

Frederick.

Again, she gasped for breath. Her husband was gone.

She heard Rosamund say, "Open the window, will you, Becks?"

"No," Jane whispered. "Please . . ."

Beckenham glanced from Rosamund to Jane, then strode over to fling the casement wide. A strong gust blew the rain in, and a startled exclamation from a lady nearby made Jane flutter an imploring hand. "It's all right. Truly, I am well."

Don't fuss. Just . . . I need to get out of this room.

Rosamund reached past Cecily and pressed a soft wad of linen and lace into her hand. Jane closed her fingers around it. The sympathy and love implied in that small gesture was too much. Finally, the dam burst, and it all spewed forth in a loud, ugly sob.

Oh, God! Oh, no! She *couldn't*! Not in front of all these people.

A few furtive murmurs swelled into a buzz of conversation. Of course they were talking about her, speculating. She loathed scenes. She despised being the center of attention like this.

A strong, firm hand beneath her elbow lifted Jane to her feet. Her cousin's deep voice rumbled something placating as he guided her through the crowd. Thank God for Beckenham and his air of calm authority. Becks always knew what to say.

Jane covered her face with Rosamund's handkerchief, shutting out their intrusive gazes, the murmurs and whispers, the hiss of avid curiosity. *Poor dear . . . Not surprised she's distraught . . . Perhaps she's with child . . . Well, I heard something rather shocking . . .*

In moments, she found herself in a comfortable armchair in the library. One of the long windows stood open and the chair was drawn up to it so that the fresh breeze cooled her face, scoured her laboring lungs. The terrace outside largely protected the room from the wet, but the dark crimson curtains streamed toward her as the wind blew in.

When the storm of grief had passed, Jane looked up. Beckenham brought her a glass of water and pressed it into her hand.

"Becks." She gave an inelegant sniff as he lifted her bonnet from her head and set it on the desk. "How good you are."

His hard features were drawn in concern. But he needn't worry. The worst was over. Now that she was at liberty to weep all she wanted, the well of tears seemed to have dried up.

"How mortifying," she said, wiping carefully at her cheeks. "I thought I was made of sterner stuff." She filled her lungs with rain-scented air. "I'm so sorry."

"Don't be. There's no shame in showing emotion."

If only he truly believed that. Perhaps then she might help Beckenham ease the burden of his own pain. But she'd learned never to mention it to him, or even speak a certain lady's name in his presence. She sighed. Each of them had their own burden to bear.

Jane sipped the water and handed it back to Beckenham. She laid her head against the chair and attempted a smile to cover her humiliation. "Please, go and rejoin them. I'd like you to be there so you can explain it all to me afterward. I don't trust Montford."

He glanced in the direction of the music room, then back at her. "Shall I ring for your maid?"

"No, don't do that. I'll go up when I'm ready. I want to sit here a while."

He knew her well enough not to press her. With an awkward pat on her shoulder, he strode off, so large and gruff and dependable, so dear. How lucky they all were. No true brother could have done more for them all than Beckenham.

Jane let her eyes drift closed and listened to his footsteps retreat. The click of the door told her she was alone.

She sighed as relief slowly set in. By degrees, the giant hand that squeezed her chest released its grip and her surroundings regained perspective. Her pounding heart slowed to a steady beat. She drifted for a time . . .

Suddenly, Jane wrinkled her nose. What was that? Smoke? Ugh, not the chimneys again! She simply must do something about them.

But she wasn't mistress here anymore.

Jane opened her eyes and a large form filled her vision—or at least, he filled the doorway—dark hair tousled beyond any recognizable style, heavy-lidded eyes trained on her, and a cigarillo clamped between very white teeth.

She gasped. The rider she'd seen from the upstairs window.

Now, he was close enough to reach out and touch. He smiled at her around that horrible cigarillo, Jane realized with dismay. Her heart lurched into a frantic dance.

Jane's mind fixed on the source of that smoke as a drowning woman might clutch at a rope. She shoved Rosamund's handkerchief into her pocket and scowled up at him. "I hope you aren't going to puff on that disgusting thing in here."

The man's green eyes narrowed, observing her for a moment. Then his lips closed around the repellent object. The hollows in his cheeks deepened; the end of the cigarillo glowed amber. Deliberately, he removed the cigarillo from his mouth, tilted his head, and blew smoke upward. The stream of cloudy gray passed between his well-formed lips, lifting, clouding, curling in tendrils to caress the plasterwork.

In that attitude, the slightly stubborn jut of his chin became pronounced. Despite her annoyance at his studied disregard for her wishes, Jane's fascinated gaze traced the strong lines of his throat as they disappeared into a stark white cravat.

The stranger turned and pitched the butt off the terrace in a sailing arc, into the rain.

As if the heavens resented this wanton act, they opened, hurling water down in sheets. The wind gave a ghostly howl. Bloodred curtains billowed around him, and the fanciful image of a devil stepping out of hell popped into her head. The gentleman moved inside and closed the long window behind him, shutting out the storm.

Jane shot from her chair, which brought her within discomfiting distance of the stranger's tall form. He smelled— not unpleasantly—of horse leathers and rain and the exotic hint of Spanish smoke.

They both moved at once, and she fetched up against him in a heady brush of palm to chest, side to muscular thigh. Two large, strong hands gripped her upper arms to steady her. "Whoa, there."

The heat from his palms and fingers seeped into her chilled skin. He seemed even larger than he'd appeared from beneath her window. She had to crane her neck to look up at him and his decided chin.

A sudden fire glinted beneath those lazy eyelids. She expected him to hold her longer, but he unhanded her almost before she'd regained her balance. She took a hasty step backward and the backs of her knees hit her chair.

The stranger smiled, another flash made brighter by the contrasting swarthiness of his face. "No, no! Don't go on my account." His voice, a husky tenor, plucked its way down her spine.

Jane frowned. Who did he think he was? A gentleman did not barge into private rooms without an invitation. "Oh, *I'm* not going anywhere. You'll find the other mourners in the drawing room, sir."

"I know. That's why I'm in the library." The corners of his eyes crinkled. "You don't have the faintest idea who I am, do you?"

She was beginning to think she did. "Of course not. We haven't been introduced." Despising her priggish tone, she turned slightly and picked at the armrest of her chair with fingers that weren't quite steady.

But surely he wasn't . . . He couldn't . . . If the stranger was Roxdale, he'd have attended the will reading, wouldn't he?

Jane pressed her fingers flat, stopping their destructive work. She was always ill at ease with strangers, but this man unsettled her exceedingly.

Before he could speak again, she said, "I don't care who you are. It's improper for us to be here alone together. You must go."

"Must I? But we are getting on so famously." Without a by-your-leave, he reached past her to move her chair from where it blocked his path and stepped farther into the room.

Prowling by bookshelves and globes and maps, he rounded a large drafting table and homed in on the drinks tray that sat, stocked and ready, on the sideboard. He poured himself a brandy from one of the crystal decanters.

She marched after him, blustering. "Just what do you think—"

"It seems I have the advantage." Turning, he wrapped his long fingers around the glass and tilted it toward her. "For I know who you are."

Jane halted. "How could you? You've only just—" *Only just arrived,* she was about to say. But she didn't wish to allude to that handful of electric moments when she'd been trapped in his gaze like a fly in a honey pot.

"Oh, I made a point of finding out," he said softly. "Lady Roxdale."

As he sipped, the corner of his mouth quirked upward. An indentation beside it that scarcely merited the term "dimple" appeared. Jane found herself fascinated with the seductive contours of his lips as he savored the brandy. She shivered, blinked to clear her head. She seemed to be falling under some sort of enchantment.

Then she realized what he'd said. He'd asked about her. Why?

Societal dictates told her to leave the room immediately, rather than bandy ripostes with a complete stranger. They hadn't been introduced and so could have nothing to say to one another. Jane was somewhat a stickler for the rules of polite society . . . when they allowed her to follow her own inclinations.

But this time, her curiosity proved too rampant. Feigning disinterest, she waved a hand toward him. "And you are . . . ?"

A magician. A conjurer. A wizard, binding me with your spell.

He set down his glass and made an elaborate bow. "I suppose I must be Roxdale." A gleam of white teeth. "But you may call me Constantine."

CHAPTER THREE

For an instant, the lady whitened, then a delicious flush bloomed across her cheeks. Her gray eyes stared up at him, caught fire.

"You," she said—and a world of contempt was contained in that one syllable—"are the new baron."

He bowed. "For my sins."

From the flattened lips with which she greeted that remark it was clear that his sins preceded him. Excellent. Now, the widow was offended by his presence in the specific, rather than the general.

With a cynical smile, he retreated to the sideboard and picked up his glass. Cradling it in his palm, he swirled the amber liquid, warming it with the heat of his hand. Perhaps he ought not to have revealed his identity so soon. She'd be sure to put up her guard, perhaps even shun him, as any virtuous, well-bred lady ought to do.

He raised his gaze to those disconcerting gray eyes. "I'm behindhand in offering my condolences. Frederick was a—"

"Good man. Yes." She said it through gritted teeth.

Did she dispute the common opinion of her husband? Though her eyes were a trifle puffy she didn't seem too distraught that Frederick was gone, but you could never tell with English ladies. Some were so astonishingly reticent that one made the mistake of supposing them cold-blooded. When in fact . . .

Curiosity had always been his besetting sin. Or one of them. Constantine leaned his hip against the sideboard and crossed one leg over the other at the ankle. He couldn't sit in her presence until invited, even in what was now his own home.

She spoke first. "How well did you know my husband?"

So, Frederick hadn't mentioned their history. "We were childhood cronies, Frederick and I. But I haven't laid eyes on him in, oh, seven or eight years. As a point of fact, I have no idea whether he was a good man. He was certainly a good friend to me when we were boys."

She tilted her head, considering that. "He was a good friend to me, too. Long ago."

On the last words, her tone turned hollow. Did she damn Frederick with faint praise or pay him the highest compliment? Not an easy thing to discern. The lady's face gave nothing away. Her hands, however, clung and twisted together like two tortured souls.

She was a contradiction, an intrigue. The urge to peel away her layers teased at him.

Dangerous ground, my boy. Despite the risqué talk of her husband's death by copulation—which, if one were honest, could happen to anyone, really—Frederick's widow was undoubtedly a respectable lady, a member of that rarefied class of female with whom the infamous Constantine Black had no right to associate. He ought not to detain her. Imagine what an uproar there'd be over her tête-à-tête with an unrepentant scoundrel like him. On the day of her husband's funeral, no less.

But he was reluctant to leave without discovering more about her; even more reluctant to concede the territory. This library had always been the most pleasant, welcoming room in the house. And it had the added advantage of being one place where the rest of the mourners weren't. Why shouldn't he stay here if he chose? If she found him so objectionable, *she* could leave.

"Do you return to London tonight, my lord, or put up at an inn?" It seemed the lady was curious about him, too.

He paused. There was, he acknowledged, some awkwardness in his situation. He'd ridden to Lazenby with not much thought beyond attending Frederick's funeral. Now, he was here on a completely different footing: lord of the manor. Though he could see by her looks that Lady Roxdale had another label for him: *usurper.*

The thought lent his resolve uncustomary firmness. "I'm staying here."

Her eyes startled wide. "I'm afraid that won't be possible."

"Why not?"

Her lips were far too luscious to be pressed into such uncompromising lines. "The staff haven't been prepared for your arrival."

Constantine smiled. "Oh, I'm not so high in the instep as that. All I require is bed and board."

"You will find that's not how we do things at Lazenby Hall."

When he merely quirked an eyebrow, she tilted her head in the manner of a queen handing down a royal edict. "You must understand that it's not what *you* require that is at issue."

Her pompous tone didn't amuse him as it should. "If I'm the master of this house, what I require is the *only* thing at issue." Now who sounded pompous?

With an impatient flick of her hand, she persisted. "You must consider the sensibilities of your people. They wish to prepare for your arrival, to do the thing properly, to meet their own standards." Her jaw set. "Even if *you* have none."

He blinked. Then he burst out laughing. The muttered addendum was inexcusably rude but she made no bones about offending him.

Well, of course. She was a Westruther by birth, wasn't she? And Westruthers thought themselves above considerations of common courtesy.

His laughter seemed to take her off guard. A puzzled look puckered her brow, as if she couldn't fathom the reason for his mirth. Didn't anyone laugh at her, then? What a pity. It would do her good to be swept off her high horse now and then.

He sobered. Well, if plain speaking was to be the order of the day . . .

"The staff of this house will be obliged to grow accustomed to my habits. I'm erratic. If I want to go somewhere, I go. I don't ask permission or advertise my movements weeks in advance."

And, he wanted to ask, what the devil did she think she had to say in the matter of his household? Callous to remind her she no longer reigned here, so he forbore to mention it. If it hadn't been for Frederick's summons, he would have waited a month or so before intruding on her like this. But he'd be damned if he'd back down now.

She sucked in a breath, and the color flamed in her cheeks in a most becoming fashion. As if the question pained her, she asked, "You *do* mean to stay here tonight, then?"

He bowed. "If that is agreeable to you, ma'am." The statement was a mere sop to politeness. She'd no power to forbid him his own house and she knew it.

Lady Roxdale turned her head away, as if to conceal her expression from him. The dim light from a branch of candles played over her hair, picking out a reddish tint he hadn't noticed before. He followed the trail of a long, errant curl that had slipped free from her coiffure, mentally traced it down her throat, imagined stroking one fingertip along the shadow of her clavicle . . .

Lord, she was a fine-looking woman, even secretive and disapproving, pokered up like a crusty old spinster.

"Jane!"

Constantine swiveled on his heel, surprised. He'd been so absorbed in her, he hadn't noticed the approach of a large, dark-haired man. The fellow strode into the room, then halted at the sight of Constantine.

Lady Roxdale sprang to life as if caught in wrongdoing, speaking quickly in her agitation.

"Oh! Beckenham. May I present Lord Roxdale to you? My lord, the Earl of Beckenham, who is some sort of cousin of mine."

As Constantine returned the earl's bow, he had the distinct impression that he was being sized up. The other man wasn't hostile, precisely. Perhaps wary was more the word.

So, Lord Beckenham hadn't joined the ranks of gentlemen who openly shunned him. He didn't allow himself to feel relief. He didn't give a damn what Beckenham thought, or anyone else.

Of course, the earl was within his rights to expect an explanation for Constantine's presence, alone, with his kinswoman. Strangely, he didn't ask for one.

Instead, he fixed troubled, dark eyes on Constantine. "You didn't attend the reading of Frederick's will."

"No." He hadn't wished to make a public showing of himself, provide more fodder for gossip than there already was.

Beckenham's hands were clasped behind his back. He snapped the back of one hand against the other palm as he paced. "Then you don't know."

Constantine felt a twinge of unease. "Know what?"

The evidence of some internal struggle passed briefly across Beckenham's face. "The most unfortunate—" He broke off, clearing his throat. "But it is not my place to advise you."

Bad news, then. Of course. He ought to have expected something of the sort.

Constantine's jaw firmed. "Your explanation will do for the moment." Better to hear an unvarnished version than a long-winded load of legal drivel Frederick's lawyer would pour in his ear.

Constantine folded his arms and settled back to listen. Inwardly, he shook his head at himself and his foolish optimism. Life always managed to dunk him head-first in the privy the very minute he nourished a hope of rising above the stink.

Jane watched Constantine Black closely, but she failed to detect the least sign of dismay at the somber tenor of Beckenham's words. Of course, such flippancy must be a façade. He couldn't be as uncaring as that. No one could.

But why did Beckenham regard her so gravely? Her jointure was secure. Montford had negotiated it all in the marriage settlements. He'd taken pains to explain every detail to her. One thing you could say for the duke: he didn't underestimate the intelligence of the female sex.

Beckenham glanced around him, then indicated a grouping of chairs by the fireplace in the center of the room. "Shall we sit down?"

Biting her lip, Jane perched on a sofa. Constantine took the armchair opposite, crossing one booted leg over the other, apparently at ease. Beckenham remained standing, gripping the chair back before him, his arms straight, parallel lines of tension.

Beckenham spoke. "First of all, let me say that I think this was badly done of Frederick. Badly done, indeed. Had he asked me I would have counseled against it."

"Against what?" Jane demanded. "Becks, you are talking in riddles. We all know how the estate was left. There's the entail—all of the property goes to the new baron, here—and then there's my jointure and various other legacies."

He shook his head. "Not at all. You see, the estate was only entailed on Frederick. Before his father died, he and Frederick joined together to break the entail. That gave Frederick the full power to dispose of the estate however he wished."

Beckenham fixed his gaze on her. "Barring those other, smaller legacies, Frederick left all of his funds, stocks, bonds, all of his gold to you, Jane. He has made you a very wealthy woman."

Jane felt as if a giant hand had just picked up her world, turned it upside down, and given it a vigorous shake. Her senses reeled; thoughts hurtled around her brain. Of course, she'd expected a handsome jointure. Wealth on this scale was . . . overwhelming.

"The most serious consequence is for the estate," said Beckenham, turning his attention to Constantine. "In short, Frederick has left you, Lord Roxdale, all of the land commonly attached to the title but no funds to maintain the property."

Jane barely heard a strangled oath from Constantine Black. Her stomach gave a sickening lurch. *"What?"* she said. "But he can't do that!"

The estate cost an astronomical sum to run. There were always repairs and rebuilding to be done to the tenants' cottages, new farming equipment and agricultural projects to fund. Not to mention the house. The servants' wages alone . . .

Jane lifted a hand to her mouth, then let it drop. *Oh, Frederick! How could you think I'd want this?*

But of course, he hadn't done this for her. He'd done it to punish Constantine Black.

Constantine folded his arms and settled back in his chair. "Is that all?"

"Unfortunately, no, it's not." Beckenham sighed. "There is a heavy mortgage over the mill property. Mr. Greenslade can give you the finer details, but I believe the debt has been triggered by Frederick's death. You have less than two months to repay the full amount plus interest, or you'll forfeit the mill."

She glanced at Constantine. His beautiful face was set in an emotionless mask but his green eyes glittered with fury. She didn't want him here—she was almost certain she detested him—but her insides clenched in sympathy. He'd have expected to inherit dazzling wealth, not an albatross around his neck.

"Can nothing be done about it?" she asked. At the same

time, Constantine said, "Surely Frederick didn't have the power to strip the estate like that."

Beckenham began to pace again. "I don't know, Roxdale. You'll need your own solicitor's advice on that point. You could, perhaps, mount a legal challenge. But such things can take years—lifetimes—not to mention the crippling legal fees. Not a terribly practical solution."

"And what about Luke?" said Jane. "I assume Frederick provided for him?"

Beckenham blew out a breath. "I'm afraid not. But that's not the worst part."

He rubbed a hand over the back of his neck. "Hell," he muttered. "I don't know how to tell you this."

"What?" she said sharply, rising from her chair. "Tell me what?"

"Frederick consigned Luke to Roxdale's guardianship."

The shock was like a blow to the stomach. Jane sat down abruptly, clutching at the armrest beside her. Her throat closed over. She couldn't seem to catch her breath. Oh, God, had Frederick grown to hate her, after all? Why would he do such a thing?

What sane man could think Constantine Black a proper preceptor for a six-year-old boy? Surely something could be done to save Luke from such a fate.

Denial pounded in her head. "No!" she gasped out. "That—that *scoundrel* is Luke's guardian?"

Constantine was on his feet, glaring down at her. "May I remind you that I'm still in the room, ma'am?" he said icily. His gaze whipped to Beckenham. "Be so good as to explain to me who on earth this Luke is and why I must stand his guardian? That cannot be right."

"I'm afraid so." Beckenham sighed. "Lucas Black is a six-year-old boy. He is some sort of distant relation of Frederick's—and of yours, too, Roxdale. He was brought here as an infant when his parents died and he has lived here ever since."

Jane clearly recalled the first time she'd seen Luke, with

his chubby little legs and his captivating brown eyes and his gummy grin. He'd instantly won her heart. She'd insisted they take him in. If not for her, Frederick would have abandoned the boy.

Desperation lent an edge to her tone. "You cannot have him," she told Constantine. "I'm taking him with me to Harcourt." It was inconceivable that she should be parted from Luke. She'd never dreamed Frederick would do this to them both.

His brows flexed. "Oh, I don't think so," he said coolly. "After all, I hardly know you. How do I know you're a fit and proper person to look after him? I'd be derelict in my duty to allow it." He turned his head to address Beckenham. "I presume my cousin didn't stipulate that Lady Roxdale retain custody of the boy."

Silently, Beckenham shook his head.

Constantine tilted his head, surveying her. "I wonder why."

Fury and pain twisted inside her. She shot out of her chair and paced toward him. "Frederick was mad, that's why! Surely even you must see he was not thinking rationally when he devised his will. The way he left the estate must testify to that. There's nothing for it. You must renounce the office and appoint me in your stead!"

His gaze held hers. "No."

She stared into his eyes, and could not mistake the implacable determination in them. Fear swamped Jane's chest. Would he keep Luke just to spite her? Surely even Constantine Black could not be so callous.

Beckenham cleared his throat. "Having Roxdale here renounce guardianship was my first thought, too, Jane. But it's impossible."

She looked up sharply. "Why?"

"Frederick stipulated a replacement."

"Who?" Jane was ready to do battle with any number of Blacks, if that's what it took to get Luke.

"Lord Endicott."

Constantine gave a crack of sardonic laughter. "That milk-sop! My dear Lady Roxdale, my aunt would never let her namby-pamby son hand the boy over to you."

He was right. Panic tightened its grip on her throat. Endicott was renowned for being securely fastened to his mother's apron strings. Lady Endicott lived to meddle in other people's lives and had more than her fair share of family pride, besides. She would die before allowing her son to relinquish the care of a Black to a Westruther, particularly to Jane.

It seemed the lesser of two evils might be the man standing before her.

But how could she get him to agree to let Luke live with her? And even if she did, what guarantee did she have that he wouldn't exercise his powers as guardian to take Luke away from her in the future?

A guttural cry wrenched from her chest. "I could kill Frederick for this!"

"A more redundant statement would be hard to imagine," said Constantine.

Jane threw him a fulminating glance. She had the deepest, most unladylike urge to hit him.

The corner of his mouth curled. "Go ahead," he said softly.

Oh, but she was tempted. She dragged her gaze from those mocking green eyes to the beautifully curved mouth. Her palm tingled with the urge to slap that half smile from his face.

Moments ticked by in silent challenge before Beckenham pointedly cleared his throat.

Jane shook herself and addressed Constantine, enunciating carefully. "Promise me one thing. Do not inform Luke of your guardianship until we settle this between us. I may not be his guardian, but I know him best. It must be for me to choose the time and manner of telling him the news."

After a moment, Constantine bowed. "As you wish."

Beckenham addressed Constantine. "Might I suggest that

you confer with Mr. Greenslade, Frederick's solicitor? He's waiting on you in the old music room."

"I'll do that." Deliberately, Constantine replaced his near-empty glass on the sideboard and bowed to them both. Jane turned away, too distraught for social niceties.

The crisp click of the library door told her he'd gone.

She raised her eyes to Beckenham. "He *could* grant me custody, couldn't he, even if he continued as guardian? There's no reason he needs to have Luke live with him, is there?"

Surely the blackguard was only being difficult to provoke her. On mature consideration, Constantine would realize he didn't wish to be saddled with the upbringing of a small boy. What would it take to convince him to relinquish Luke to her? Money? She'd give him the full sum of her inheritance if that's what it took.

She licked her lips. "I'll pay him," she said. "I'll hand over the entire fortune if he will grant me custody of Luke."

Beckenham shook his head. "You can't, Jane. The trust Frederick established states plainly that it is for your own maintenance. You cannot simply give the money away. The trustees wouldn't allow it."

Beckenham rubbed his eyes with his thumb and forefinger. He looked so grave, Jane saw hope slipping from her grasp. Her solid, dependable cousin always took care of things. If he thought there was no solution in this case . . .

"However . . ." Beckenham hesitated, then lowered his gaze. "Upon your marriage, your interest in the trust fund would become your husband's property."

The notion slammed into her like a sledgehammer.

"M-marriage?" she repeated faintly. "*Marry* Constantine Black?"

He blew out a breath. "No. Well, of course not. No one could expect you to. It's merely . . . Jane, it would solve all of your problems, and Roxdale's, too, for that matter. Marry him and the estate will be whole again. And you would get Luke."

Stunned, Jane groped for the mantel beside her. Her knees felt watery, as if they wouldn't hold her up. If marriage was the only way she could keep Luke with her . . . Ah, but she'd just escaped wedlock with one man who didn't care the snap of his fingers for her. How could she fling herself into another loveless union?

She was tempted to take Luke and disappear. But how would they live? It wasn't as if she had funds of her own. As Beckenham pointed out, everything was tied up in trusts. Even if she could find a way to support them both, they'd be fugitives. What sort of life could she give Luke then? He'd be better off with Constantine.

Beckenham came to her. He gripped her shoulder. "I am more sorry than I can say that it has come to this. Be assured, I will do everything I can."

Dear Beckenham. But what could he do? She reached up to put her hand over his. "Thank you, Becks. Thank you for telling me."

He waved away her gratitude, his dark eyes concerned. "Montford awaits you in the green saloon," he said gently. "There are important matters to discuss."

She couldn't face the duke now. All he cared about was her inheritance. She couldn't put her mind to such trivialities now. The only thing she wanted was to keep Luke.

"Then His Grace shall continue to wait." All night, if she could manage it.

Beckenham began to persuade her but she fluttered a hand to stop him. "Please, Becks. I . . . I have an awful headache coming on. I cannot deal with the duke now."

He eyed her for a moment, then nodded. "I'll tell him you're indisposed."

Beckenham leaned forward to give her a brotherly kiss on her cheek. "Get some rest. We'll face all this tomorrow."

She nodded, forcing out a grateful smile.

But rest was farthest from her mind. She needed to find a way to keep Luke with her. She needed to think of a plan.

Marriage to Constantine Black? She shuddered. There *had* to be some other way.

"For the hundredth time, George, no!" Constantine held on to his temper, forcing his lips to curve in a smile of amused tolerance.

Why couldn't his noble idiot of a brother accept that selling Broadmere was out of the question? Ordinarily so even-tempered, George could turn mulish when an idea fixed in his head.

George glared at him. "It's the only way you can stop this place from coming to ruin."

Constantine shook his head. "I'd let it all go to hell before I'd sell the family home from under you. What kind of a blackguard do you think I am?" He gave a humorless laugh. "No, don't answer that."

Constantine turned to stare out the window at the sodden landscape. Lazenby was his now. He'd made a promise to himself that this would be his fresh start. He would not begin his stewardship of this estate by losing a major source of income and employment. He'd find a way to save the mill. He must.

But that imperative did not extend to selling the house that had been in their father's family for generations. The house they'd grown up in, where George's family and their mother still lived. The house Constantine hadn't set eyes on since his disgrace.

When the infamous affair with Miss Flockton became known, his father had banished him from Broadmere, vowing to leave the estate to George. A pity the old gentleman had died before he'd had the chance to change his will. As the elder son, Constantine had inherited everything.

Knowing his father's wishes, Constantine considered Broadmere his brother's in all but name. George had proven stubborn, however. He wouldn't let Constantine formally transfer title to the property.

George held out a foolish, selfless hope that Constantine would relent and ignore their father's dying wish. But he never had. He never would. Instead, Constantine had left everything in his brother's capable hands, refusing to draw more from the estate than a younger son's allowance. And he'd never set foot on Broadmere soil again.

Sell Broadmere to save Lazenby? Damn it all, marrying the Ice Maiden would be preferable to that. That's what men in his position did, wasn't it? Form strategic alliances in exchange for bloodlines or money or prestige. Why should he be any different?

But something in him rebelled against the very notion. He'd sacrificed a vast deal to avoid a bad marriage once before. What bitter irony that fate should throw him that lifeline a second time. On this occasion, however, he had more than his own reputation to consider.

"If you don't sell Broadmere, you'll lose the mill," George persisted. "Will you risk the livelihoods of your tenants for your pride?"

Pride? Not a bit of it. The one good thing he'd ever done was to give the family home to George. He'd be damned if he'd mess that up, too.

He set his teeth. "I'll find another way."

George was correct on one point, though. Constantine needed a substantial influx of funds. Immediately.

According to Greenslade, Frederick had mortgaged the Lazenby woolen mill and the surrounding few acres to a northern mill owner called Bronson. Frederick's death triggered the debt, so that both interest and principal—an astronomical sum—fell due within forty-five days. If Constantine couldn't come up with the money in that time, Bronson would foreclose and take ownership of the mill property.

What the hell had Frederick been thinking, mortgaging the mill? He'd put the livelihoods of everyone on the estate at risk. Worse, he'd thrown the whole tangle in Constantine's lap and denied him sufficient income to repay the staggering debt.

Where had the funds Frederick raised against the mill gone? Into the coffers of one Lady Roxdale? Constantine's mouth flattened into a grim line at the thought.

Then there was the question of Lucas Black. In that, the Ice Maiden was correct: how could Frederick be such an idiot as to suppose Constantine a fit guardian for a six-year-old child?

Still, Constantine was far from convinced Lady Roxdale was the proper person to take care of the boy. He hadn't detected anything particularly maternal about her in the course of their acquaintance. Frederick must have had his reasons for not mentioning her when he'd provided for the boy.

George's jaw tightened. "If you would just let me—"

"I need to go over the books and tour the estate," Constantine interrupted. He had no wish to prolong a futile argument. "There must be some way to claw back the money to repay the debt. I have investments in the funds . . ."

He broke off, narrowing his eyes. A number of those investments had yet to mature. If he sold them off now, he might very well make a loss. His investments would never cover a debt that large, though. He might be forced to speculation. George would not approve.

He fixed his gaze on his brother. "I want no more talk of selling Broadmere. I'll instruct my man to draw up the transfer documents as soon as may be."

George banged his fist on the table. "I will not accept your rightful inheritance. Damn it, Constantine! It's our father all over again. You're the living spit of him. You can't see reason, you're so blinded by pride."

Constantine felt George's words like a stab to the gut. No different from his stiff-rumped, unforgiving father, was he? Ordinarily, he'd laugh and let the jagged edge of such a remark glance off his armor. But this was George, his greatest—his only—ally.

From the pain, anger erupted, hot and destructive. With a clear, brutal intention to offend, Constantine curled his lip.

"Brother, you grow even more tedious than our aunt. Go home to your family, George. Let me go my own way."

For a long moment George stood there, his face a study of impotent fury.

Constantine lifted an eyebrow, as if to say, *Well? What are you waiting for?*

With a biting curse, George turned on his heel and strode toward the door. "You can go your own way, all right," he ground out. "You can go straight to hell!"

CHAPTER FOUR

I don't see why you're so upset about coming into an obscenely large fortune," said Cecily. "If I had control over my inheritance, I should be in ecstasies."

Cecily lay on her stomach on Jane's bed, idly swinging her legs in the air. Rosamund perched in the window seat, an unaccustomed frown in her clear blue eyes.

Jane couldn't be still. She wandered restlessly around the room that was not her bedchamber anymore. Much good her inheritance did if she couldn't use it to barter for Luke.

"Think of it, Jane," breathed Cecily. "You are a *wealthy widow*. If I were you, I'd turn myself into a fashionable eccentric and do exactly as I pleased."

"You *are* a fashionable eccentric," Jane said. "Anyway, it's all very well for you. No one turns a hair when you behave outrageously."

Rosamund smiled. "Oh, I expect Cecily will do her duty when the time comes. *We* cannot escape responsibility any more than someone like the duke or Beckenham can. Though I did hope you would have some sort of respite now, Jane. I'm sorry it has come to this."

Surprised, Jane darted a glance at her cousin. But Rosamund couldn't know the extent of Jane's unhappiness in her marriage. She'd never spoken a word of it to anyone, not even to Rosamund and Cecily.

Surely her cousin hadn't guessed? Impossible. Rosamund

was far too guileless, too willing to believe there was good in everyone.

"You should run away," said Cecily. "And while you're about it, you should take us with you."

Rosamund's face lit. "Where would we go, if only we could?"

"Everywhere!" said Cecily. "Paris, Rome, Egypt." She propped her chin in her hands, dark curls bouncing, eyes bright. "Wouldn't it be a brilliant adventure?"

"I should think it would be exceedingly uncomfortable," said Jane. She bit her lip. "And if it were only the estate, it wouldn't be so bad. But there's Luke." She broke off, biting her lip.

Rosamund shook her head. "Frederick knew how much you love Luke. How could he do such a thing?"

"I don't understand it, either." Jane gripped her hands together. "Perhaps he made that condition a long time ago and simply never troubled to change it." She worried at her lip with her teeth. "Or maybe it was more than that. Luke is, after all, a Black, and you know how fiercely proud they are. I wouldn't be at all surprised if Frederick wanted Luke brought up by his own family, regardless of anyone's feelings in the matter."

Least of all Luke's, she thought bitterly. Frederick had scarcely noticed the boy existed.

"You don't mean the scoundrel won't let you keep Luke!" said Cecily.

The injustice of it burned in Jane's chest. "He says he cannot allow it. I might not be a fit and proper person to care for Luke, if you please!"

"Infamous!" said Cecily.

"The obvious course is to marry Constantine Black, is it not?" said Rosamund quietly.

"Marry that—that *lout*?" said Jane. "Beckenham said the same, but . . . oh, Rosamund, I thought at least *you* would understand my feelings."

Rosamund held up a hand. "I would not for the world

condemn you to matrimony with such an arrant rogue as he is reputed to be, but it appears your affairs and his are inextricably tangled. The estate has been decimated by Frederick's actions. He made no financial provision for Luke. Beckenham was most upset about it. He told me there's nothing else for it; for the good of Lazenby, you and Constantine Black must wed."

Cecily said, "She's right, Jane. And more importantly, you could keep Luke."

Panic twisted in Jane's belly. "I can't." She gripped her hands together. "I can't marry him. Not him. Not anyone."

"They say he is devilishly handsome," said Cecily. "That must be some consolation. I mean, if you have to do *It* with someone you don't love, better he be handsome, don't you think?"

Constantine Black's strongly marked features appeared before Jane's mind's eye. No, somehow his spectacular dark looks made the prospect of . . . of *It* . . . worse, not better.

Her panic climbed, threatening to choke her. "I can't. I'm not fit to be a wife."

Sympathy softened Rosamund's face. "Just because you did not bear a child doesn't mean you're not fit to be a wife, Jane."

Oh, but it does, Jane thought. However, she could not bring herself to discuss such an intimate matter, even with Rosamund.

"Besides, the lout's scarcely fit to be a husband, is he?" said Cecily, with her infallible logic.

"I daresay you'd rub along tolerably well," put in Rosamund.

"You could take a *lover.*" Cecily rolled the word around her tongue and gave it a French twist.

Rosamund nodded. "You wouldn't even have to live here if you didn't want to. Or, better yet, you could send him up to Town while you manage things here. I think it sounds like a good arrangement."

No, it sounded appalling. Impossible.

Rosamund reached up to take Jane's hand. She swung it

gently to and fro. "You'd be wise not to dismiss the notion out of hand."

Jane squeezed Rosamund's strong, slim fingers. She sighed. "I never thought to have any say in my own destiny. I regret Frederick's death, of course I do! But . . . marriage to Constantine Black! How could he do this to me?"

Yet, it was out of the question to leave Luke at Lazenby Hall with no one to love him and only a wastrel libertine's example to follow. Even more powerful than the ties of duty, the bonds of love would keep her here if she couldn't take Luke with her. And she simply couldn't remain indefinitely in the household of a libertine like Constantine Black unless she married him. Her reputation would never survive the disgrace.

Rosamund's face was puckered with dismay. Clearly, she considered Jane's fate sealed. A Westruther heiress simply had no choice in matters of matrimony. They'd all accepted it long ago. Even if Jane's widowhood had granted her freedom from such lofty expectations, Frederick's legacy imprisoned her once more.

All that wealth . . . She'd happily see it at the bottom of the Thames.

"I hate Frederick for doing this!" Jane fought back tears of frustration. She would *not* cry again today. "If not for the stupid way he left everything, I could have Luke. We could be free."

"Jane, Jane." Cecily slipped off the bed. "You poor deluded female. You know what Montford is. If not Constantine Black, it would be some other likely candidate as soon as you were done with mourning. At least this way, you'll get what you want, too."

Jane shook her head in denial, but she knew what Cecily said was true. The duke always succeeded in whatever he set out to accomplish. Oh, he wouldn't force her into matrimony. He simply had a way of making it impossible for her to refuse.

Cecily sighed. "Give her the speech, Rosamund."

"You may do it this time," said Rosamund generously. "You're better at it than I."

Cecily smoothed her sleeve. "Well, I fancy I've heard the speech more often than anyone, including Xavier. In fact, I know it better than Montford does. I had to set him straight on the wording last week."

"He's losing his touch," said Rosamund.

"Mmm. Very sad."

Jane scowled. "I don't need the speech. I know my duty. That's why I'm in this mess."

Rosamund and Cecily looked at each other, then both intoned at once, "What do you think it *means* to be a Westruther, Lady Rox—"

"No!" said Jane, half laughing, half incensed at the kind but misguided attempt to lighten the situation. "No speech!"

She pressed finger and thumb to her temples. "You're right. Of course, you're right. I must marry him. It's the only way I can keep Luke. Even if Constantine Black granted me custody, he could take Luke away any time he felt like it. That is simply not acceptable."

Rosamund regarded her anxiously. "Do you think the rogue will agree?"

Jane shrugged a shoulder. "He'd be foolish to ignore the advantages to the match. After all, he needs my money, doesn't he?"

She thought of certain other things Constantine could require of her as his wife. Heat flashed through her body but her stomach churned with sick apprehension.

He was so . . . so *masculine,* so intensely alive.

She ought to be accustomed to an overabundance of male charisma. Her Westruther cousins possessed that kind of magnetism to a ridiculous degree, after all. Yet, on some primal level, Constantine Black alarmed and unsettled her more than anyone she'd ever met. Instinct warned her to set him at a distance, but that would not help her get Luke.

She wiped her suddenly clammy hands on her skirts. "I'll put the proposition to him logically. A marriage of convenience in which each party gets something they want. He'll be a . . . a substitute Frederick, that's all."

Rosamund looked doubtful. "Do you think you ought to be so frank about it, darling? Some gentlemen might take offense."

Better to offend him than give him the upper hand. She strongly suspected it wouldn't take much encouragement for Constantine Black to press home his advantage.

"I'll *try* to be conciliating," she said. "But I daresay it won't be easy."

Ignoring her cousins' skeptical looks, Jane marched over to her escritoire. Fumbling but determined, she opened her desk. Dawing out paper and ink, she sat down and picked up her pen.

"I need to speak to Lord Roxdale before I face the duke in the morning. I shall arrange a parlay."

Constantine eyed his empty glass, then glared at the dregs in the decanter beside him. He'd already called for another bottle, but who was he fooling? There wasn't enough wine in England to make him sufficiently drunk to escape this appalling state of affairs.

He'd quarreled with George, which he almost never did, and offended his aunt, too. Lady Endicott had retired to her bed with a fit of the vapors, so at least she wouldn't trouble him for the next few hours.

A rift with his aunt didn't bother him. She'd made a career out of disapproving of him, after all. Besides, she'd undoubtedly make good her threat to bring the formidable Lady Arden down upon them, so he couldn't feel too repentant about that.

George was a different matter. He was the only one of their family who'd believed in Constantine, when the rest of society turned their backs. George had stood by him in open defiance of their father, who had forbidden all contact with the family's black sheep.

Regret made Constantine hiss through his teeth. Ah, but better to offend George than see him sacrifice his dream on Constantine's behalf.

Dusk had deepened into night, until the silence of this profoundly rural setting pounded in his ears. He hadn't lit candles. Only the flickering firelight provided any illumination or warmth.

Ignoring Lady Roxdale's express wish that he quarter himself elsewhere, he'd commandeered this bedchamber in the east tower, far from her own apartments. It wasn't the master suite—that would have been too brash, even for him—but it was a comfortable, spacious room overlooking a set of formal gardens.

Constantine rose and crossed to the window, which he'd left open. The rain had ceased, for the moment, but storm clouds blanketed the sky, smothering the stars and moon. The quiet had an expectant quality to it, disturbed only by the occasional snap of a twig or thump of a log burning down in the grate. He stared into the thick darkness, seeking answers.

He would have to decide. And soon.

Well, of course it made sense to marry her. Of course it did. She had the money, he the property. Yes, it would all be tidy if they wed. His aunt demanded it; George put forward the sale of Broadmere as the only other solution.

They were probably right.

And yet . . . His pride stuck in his throat whenever he contemplated marrying a woman for her money. Particularly one who so openly despised him.

He'd never met anyone quite like Lady Roxdale. She'd stated her poor opinion of him in no uncertain terms. Clearly, she also believed herself proof against his wicked wiles.

The only vulnerability she'd displayed was when Beckenham had told him about this Luke's guardianship. Was it merely a pious horror that a man of his stamp might corrupt the young boy? Or did she genuinely care for the lad? What would she be prepared to sacrifice on Luke's behalf?

Ordinarily, Constantine would spurn the idea, but he was fast coming to the conclusion that his situation was desperate.

He admired Lady Roxdale's face and figure. He desired her. In fact, nothing would please him more than to tumble the Ice Maiden from her lofty perch and into his bed.

Once more, he thought of her ready blushes, her skin so sleek, so translucent, his fingertips tingled with the desire to stroke it. He wanted to rub against her softness like a cat. He wanted to make her blush again. All over.

But marry her in a bloodless, loveless marriage of convenience? As a last resort, it was preferable only to selling his family home.

The door behind Constantine opened. He swung around to see his valet bearing a fine bottle of burgundy and a new glass on a salver.

"Ah, Priddle. Good timing." More wine to rescue him from such sobering thoughts.

"My lord." The valet left the salver on the table next to Constantine. Priddle uncorked the wine and poured.

It wasn't until he'd taken his first, appreciative sip of the burgundy that Constantine's eye alighted on the screw of paper that also lay on the silver tray.

"What's this?" He plucked it from the salver and untwisted it, spreading it out.

"What's what, my lord?"

Constantine didn't look up. "Never mind."

Priddle was superbly discreet. If the note was from a lady who had no business sending Constantine notes (as this one was), Priddle would treat the missive as if it had powers of invisibility.

Constantine spread the scrap of paper, smoothing it with his thumbs. He could barely make out the elegant scrawl, which was heavily marred by ink blots. Obviously, it had been written in haste and sent immediately. The ink hadn't yet dried. He inspected a smudge on his thumb.

"A clandestine meeting in the chapel. Hmm . . ." He

cocked an eyebrow at his valet. "What do you say to that, Priddle?"

"Not what I would call a setting conducive to dalliance, my lord."

Constantine fingered his chin. "No. And the chapel at Lazenby Hall is particularly gloomy, if my memory serves right. Quite Gothic, in fact." He sighed. "I fear one is more likely to be stabbed than seduced in the Hall chapel."

He ran a fingertip around the rim of his glass. "Ought I to go, do you think? It might be part of a plan to do away with me."

"One must never disappoint a lady, my lord."

"Even on pain of death?"

"I'll get your coat, sir."

"Don't bother." Constantine slipped his stockinged feet into his evening pumps, downed the wine in a couple of mouthfuls and rose.

"My lord!" Priddle's voice rose in consternation. "You cannot go like that!"

Ignoring his valet, Constantine strode out toward the chapel.

When he reached the meeting place, he found it lit by a single branch of candles on the altar. He set his own candle on a side table and peered through the gloom.

She stood with her back to him, as if examining the stained-glass window before her; a useless activity in the evening with no sun to fire its colors to brilliance. If she'd heard his arrival she didn't show it.

He took the opportunity thus presented to study her. The erect posture; the somber dress; the tightly pinned hair—no dishabille, even at this late hour, for Lady Roxdale. Only small wisps of auburn hair at her ears and nape escaped discipline.

How predictable of him to wish to unwind all those tightly bound trappings, to reveal the pulsing, flesh-and-blood woman beneath. Predictable, and quite possibly stupid. Yet, the urge beat strongly in his blood, for all that.

"My lady."

Her neck stiffened. She drew herself up straighter, if that were possible, then turned, her lips parted on a wordless exclamation. Her eyes gleamed pewter; her skin flickered with golden licks of light.

"You summoned?" His bow was all exaggerated courtliness; his voice was a caress.

Lady Roxdale's eyes widened as she assimilated the full magnificence of his silk dressing gown. With an arrogance that seemed bred into Westruthers, she scanned him slowly, from the top of his uncombed curls to the open neck of his shirt, to the buckles of his black evening pumps.

Her gaze met his and cut away. A trick of the light, or did a flush creep into her cheeks? Not for the first time, he marveled at the fine-grained texture of her skin, so translucent and quick to blush.

He had a feeling this interview was about to turn interesting.

Jane sent up a silent prayer for forbearance. The man was impossible! How could she broach a serious matter when he stood there looking so rumpled and unrepentant and flamboyantly gorgeous?

She knew all about the male fashion for dressing gowns of the most exotic design. Frederick had owned a version of the garment Constantine Black wore so carelessly, yet the strong hues in the Chinese silk had not flattered Frederick's pallor.

The garment the new baron wore seemed expressly designed to set off his dark features and olive skin. The riotous swirl of jewel tones emphasized the green of his eyes. A sliver of tanned neck and chest shouted masculinity; the absence of a cravat or a waistcoat to civilize him lent him a reckless, piratical air.

And here she was, wading into shark-infested waters. Her stomach pitched; her hands trembled. Her heart seemed to have slipped its moorings and anchored in her throat.

What was happening to her? She tried to resist, but her disobedient gaze kept homing in on his chest.

"Lady Roxdale?" The amusement in his voice told her he knew exactly the effect he had on her. Her face flooded with heat.

Wrenching her mind from the strength and grace of Constantine Black's clavicles, she muttered, "You could have put a coat on, at least."

One black brow quirked. "My state of dress is the least improper aspect of this meeting. Why the subterfuge? Don't you know I debauch virtuous maidens for breakfast?"

"How you can stand there and boast of your reputation!" she snapped. "I assure you, I am not impressed."

The corner of his mouth lifted. "And yet, here you are."

He let his gaze wander over her, which she supposed was only fair as she'd just ogled him shamelessly.

The glittering regard of those deep green eyes made her feel hot and uncomfortable and more than a little defensive. She itched to cross her arms over her bosom, even though her gown was made up high at the throat. She was half convinced he could see through her layers of clothing to her naked form beneath. He'd tell her what color garters she wore, if only she gave him the chance.

Her face aflame, Jane hurried into speech. "I need to speak with you on a matter of some import, my lord."

"Strange place to choose."

"Neutral territory." She'd selected the chapel because it was the most prosaic atmosphere she could think of. Yet, as soon as he'd entered it, the air of the place hummed with tension. Her senses heightened. The strangest imaginings danced through her head.

Lord, he was like a perambulating furnace—he took this heat with him wherever he went, filled the room with it. They could meet in a factoring house or a lawyer's office or . . . or a cow byre, and still there would be this charge between them.

She forced herself to say something instead of standing

there like a dunce. "I need to speak with you privately before my—before the Duke of Montford does. I might not have the chance tomorrow."

Everyone knew Town beaux didn't rise before noon. Montford required her presence after breakfast. By the time she cornered Constantine Black, the duke would have settled her fate, allowing her no room to maneuver.

Jane twisted her hands together and raised her gaze to his face. "Frederick left the estate in an awful mess."

"I don't see how you are disadvantaged by inheriting a fortune." Constantine folded his arms and leaned back against a marble pillar.

"Don't you?" she said dryly. "Then you don't know my family."

"I know enough." More than he wished to, from the dourness of his tone.

She narrowed her eyes at him, but decided to let the comment pass. After all, she needed his cooperation, didn't she?

"We shouldn't be alone like this, you know," he commented. "What if the duke were to come down to say his prayers?"

She snorted. "Montford has no need for prayers. He thinks he *is* God, after all. In any case, I believe my reputation can withstand a moment's conversation with my husband's cousin."

"By God, aren't you trusting?" He glanced around, and the gold thread in his dressing gown flashed as he moved. "If I were half as black as I'm painted, the surroundings wouldn't stop me from seducing you."

In spite of her resolve not to let him intimidate her, Jane's breathing quickened. Her heart missed a beat, then jumped into her throat.

After a slight struggle, she managed to curl her lip. "Idle threats, my lord. I'm not afraid of you."

"Ah, but that was not a threat." His lips curved as his gaze ran over her. "It was more in the nature of a speculation."

What on earth could he mean by that remark? The

amusement in his expression told her she'd be better off not
finding out.

Jane fought to focus her mind on her original purpose.
"The way the estate has been divided puts us both in a terrible position. My family thinks the only course is for us to
wed."

She waited, but he made no comment. He wouldn't make
this easy for her. She gripped her hands together. "I'm to
meet with the Duke of Montford tomorrow to discuss the
matter."

At first, she'd been terrified the duke would require her
to marry Constantine Black. Now, she was equally terrified
he'd have other plans for her. She could never consent to
leave Luke behind but the duke wouldn't understand that.
His objective was solely to increase the wealth and power of
the Westruther family. Why should he care about one small
boy?

She eyed Constantine, but again, the provoking man said
nothing. He didn't seem surprised by her revelation. Of
course, he'd have to be a fool not to consider their marriage
as a possible solution to the conundrum Frederick had tossed
in their laps. And despite his complete lack of moral fiber,
she sensed Constantine Black was no fool.

She tried to read his face but it was maddeningly expres-
sionless. He seemed determined to make this as difficult as
possible for her.

Only the need to keep Luke made her battle on.

She took a deep breath, flushing with embarrassment.
"Regardless of our . . . *private* feelings, I believe you and I
must marry to make the estate whole again."

There was a startled pause. His eyebrows climbed. "Ah,"
he said softly. "I am honored that so fair and genteel a lady
would condescend to propose marriage to me."

Well, and so he should be! He had every bit as much to
gain as she did by this alliance, didn't he? And nothing at all
to lose. He could take her fortune and play merry hell with
it, continue to pursue his gaming and his mistresses and his

whores and never count the cost. While she struggled to hold her head up and play lady of the manor and pretend her entire world hadn't crumbled around her.

She swallowed hard. "Of course, it would be a marriage of convenience between us. You must not imagine I expect you to alter your . . . habits, in the least."

"My habits?" The words were gently spoken, but there was a dangerous glint in his eye. "How generous of you. I am quite overwhelmed. Deeply flattered, in fact."

The words burst from her before she could check them. "Flattered! You are the last man on earth I would *choose* to marry. But I have no choice, it seems."

Anger blazed across his face, but it was gone in an instant, leaving him smooth-featured and smiling. She wasn't fooled, however. His eyes were hard and brilliant as emeralds.

"Well," he said softly. "That has put me in my place, hasn't it?"

Jane flushed. An apology for her rudeness hovered on the tip of her tongue, but she swallowed it down. Waspishly, she said, "I suppose you think any lady must faint with delight at the thought of wedding you."

"Faint?"

The smile deepened, but it still did not reach his eyes. He strolled toward her, so effortlessly powerful, his large body moving with grace beneath the fluid silk of his dressing gown. "Why, you're practically swooning right now. Look at you, all pokered up and straitlaced with your tight little bun and your high-buttoned collar." He stopped, inches from her. "And all that passion seething underneath."

She tried to slow her breathing, but it ratcheted up a notch with him so near. She smelled the sweetness of wine from his breath. Her gaze snagged on that intriguing line where his lapel met bare skin. The man's sheer masculinity was overpowering.

But she was *not* frightened of him, not at all. The heat that scintillated through her body had nothing to do with fear.

Boldly defiant, she raised her eyes to his. Passion? Ha!

What did he know of her desires? She had no interest in bedding him. None at all.

He held her gaze and reached out to lift a lock of hair that had fallen from the knot at her nape. One broad fingertip brushed the skin at her jaw, leaving hot thrills in its wake. She felt the faint tug at her scalp as he sifted the curling tendril between finger and thumb.

"Soft," he murmured.

A barrage of conflicting emotions assaulted her, confusing her sense of purpose. With a gasp, she pulled away. Jane turned her back on him, desperately groping for her lost composure.

Jane bit her lip, striving to suppress the lingering quivers in her body. No one had ever touched her like that, not even Frederick. It was intimate. Far too intimate. She ought not to have allowed it.

What could Constantine seek to gain by behaving thus? Did he think to frighten her with such tactics? Suddenly, his mocking words about seduction assumed a sinister aspect.

He spoke softly, startling her. "What possessed Frederick to leave it all to you, hmm?"

There was a suggestive note to that husky voice that she didn't like. She had the impression he sized her up as a bed partner. Perhaps he suspected she'd persuaded a fortune out of Frederick in return for spectacular sexual favors.

How ironic.

"Frederick was mad to do it," she managed. "I had nothing to say in the matter or I would have told him so."

Silence.

He didn't believe her.

Jane swallowed, trying to order her thoughts. Luke's happiness was at stake. She couldn't allow Constantine Black to befuddle her with his practiced wiles.

She rounded on him. "Let's be done with this game of cat and mouse, sir. You know what I want. All I care about is keeping Luke with me. If I must marry you to do that, so be it."

"You'd sacrifice your freedom and your fortune for one scrap of a boy?" His tone told her he found that difficult to believe.

Her voice shook. "Luke is like a son to me." He *was* a son to her. She'd fight for him with her last breath.

Clearly, this reprobate before her would never understand the depth of her feelings. It was useless to even try to explain them.

Goaded beyond civility, she fired her words at him like grapeshot. "Will you or will you not marry me?"

Unmoved by the verbal barrage, he unleashed on her the full power of his most charming smile.

"I don't know," he said simply. "I haven't decided."

CHAPTER FIVE

J ane set the candle down at a safe distance from Luke's bed so as not to disturb him. As she peered through the gloom, she realized Luke's eyes were wide open, watching her.

"It's very late," she said softly. "You should be asleep."

"Can't," he whispered back. "You forgot to read me a story."

Oh, dear. "Darling, I'm so sorry. It's been such a busy day."

She hadn't forgotten, not really. But it was late by the time the final guests had left. After that, she'd been obliged to tend to Lady Endicott, who was suffering a fit of the vapors—brought on by her blackguard nephew, no doubt. She'd managed to extricate herself from the countess, only to realize it was an hour past Luke's bedtime.

After her fraught interview with Constantine, she'd stolen away to check on Luke, fully expecting him to be asleep. But the last few days had brought great upheaval in this little boy's world. It was hardly surprising he couldn't settle.

That firmed Jane's determination to say nothing to Luke about Constantine's guardianship until she'd resolved the problem to her satisfaction. Why worry the poor little fellow about it now? Not even Constantine could be so callous as to part them immediately. In the meantime, she'd do her utmost to convince the new baron to fall in with her plans.

Gently, she stroked Luke's curly hair back from his fore-head, then traced his eyebrow with her fingertip. Would reading help him sleep or merely excite him?

"Please?" He did his best to look soulful and failed utterly, the imp. "I *need* to find out what happened to Sir Ninian."

She didn't even try to resist that imploring look. "Very well. But only another ten minutes, mind." Jane crossed to the bookcase to find Sir Ninian's adventures.

"Here we are," she said, drawing out the volume. "Do you remember where we left him?"

"About to be boiled in oil?" said Luke with undisguised relish.

She chuckled. "Ah, that's right." Jane slid her finger along the pages of the book she'd marked with a green ribbon. The spine crackled as she spread the novel open and began to read.

Poor Sir Ninian, indeed! Cecily, the minx, had penned this thrilling tale of derring-do when still in the schoolroom. Sir Ninian Trinian was supposed to be the hero of the tale, yet he was always being rescued by the resourceful and re-doubtable Henrietta Peddlethorpe, the tavernkeeper's daughter. Delighting in Cecily's talent, their cousin Andrew had ordered copies to be printed and bound for all of the cousins.

Realizing that Luke was a little too old for fairy tales now, Jane had scoured the library for books that might interest a boy his age. They were few and far between. Her own collection of romances didn't seem suitable, either.

Then she'd remembered Cecily's mad creations. If anything could interest a boy like Luke in reading for pleasure, those hilarious episodes would do the trick. Jane hadn't read the tales for years, but she soon became as enthralled as Luke. Cecily's gift for storytelling had been evident, even at fifteen.

Glancing at Luke as she read, she saw his eyelids grow heavy. They fluttered a little as he fought sleep. She read on, lowering her voice a little, until at last, Luke's eyelids drifted closed. Jane let her words trail away until Luke's deep breathing told her he slept.

She marked the place with her green ribbon and returned Cecily's book to the shelf.

Bending down to Luke, Jane kissed the delicious, petal-soft roundness of his cheek. His lips curved a little, as if he knew she was there. With a tiny sigh, he snuggled down into the pillow, secure in the instinctive knowledge that he was loved.

Jane's heart filled. Her eyes moistened. The ache in her throat seemed to form a hard, jagged lump.

She would do anything for this child. Anything.

Even if that meant marrying Constantine Black.

Constantine needed a drink. *Another one.* He strode down corridors, through connecting rooms, his breath streaming harshly through his nostrils.

Bloody rabbit warren of a place! He'd been halfway to his bedchamber when he'd remembered the decanters sitting idle in the library. A pity he hadn't also recalled that one needed a map and a compass to navigate the old pile.

Westruthers! Damn them all to hell. So bloody self-righteous, so superior to the rest of the human race—at least in their own estimation. How *dare* Jane Westruther look down her nose at him?

Tomorrow, he'd move into the master apartments and damn her sensibilities. The sooner she left Lazenby Hall, the happier he'd be.

He hissed air through his teeth. More pressing than showing her who was master here was the need to closet himself with all of Frederick's advisers and see if something might be salvaged from this mess.

If he had to sell Broadmere . . . His stride slowed. He struck his fist against his thigh. No. No, his brother should have their father's property. George had the right. There must be another way.

One that didn't involve taking a prudish, opinionated *Westruther* to wife.

Oh, he'd given her a good scare, telling her he hadn't decided whether he'd fall in with her demands. The look on her face would have given him tremendous satisfaction if it hadn't been so damned insulting to his vanity.

And here he'd thought no one had that kind of power anymore. His father, his mother, hell, even Frederick himself, had done their worst. But *she* . . . Why should he care what she thought of him? They'd only just met!

Typical of such a high-and-mighty lady to believe she knew what was best for Luke. Well, Constantine had been appointed the boy's guardian and it was for him alone to decide that. He'd scarcely be discharging his duty by handing the boy over to Lady Roxdale without thoroughly investigating her first.

In any case, if Frederick had wished Luke to remain with Lady Roxdale, why not stipulate that in his will? He must have had his reasons for excluding her. And Constantine would find out what they were.

He'd begin by talking with the boy himself. He'd summon him in the morning, after his ride.

As he walked the length of the corridor, Constantine heard noises from the other side of the door leading into the gallery. Who could it be at this hour? Although he guessed the time not far past eleven, he'd the impression everyone kept sober hours at the Hall.

He opened the door, to hear the scrape and clang of steel and a grunt of effort. His brows twitched together. He moved cautiously into the room, to see the Duke of Montford fencing with another man.

They were well matched, both highly skilled, subtle in their swordplay. The duke's opponent had the advantage in height and reach but still, he did not have the contest all his own way.

In another lifetime, Constantine would have challenged each of them to a bout. Now, he cleared his throat.

There was a fencer's command to halt and the two combatants turned to stare at him, the tips of their foils pointing to the floor.

"Ah, Roxdale," The Duke of Montford said.

Constantine had thought the other man a stranger, at first. Now, he realized who it must be. He hadn't seen Adam Trent for many years. Trent's lands bordered Lazenby to the west. In the old days, he'd been the golden-haired child who'd told tales on Frederick and Constantine and refused to join in their mischief. By his steely-eyed glare, the idiot still held a grudge.

Over his shoulder, the duke murmured a polite dismissal to his opponent. "Will you excuse us, Mr. Trent? Lord Roxdale and I have important matters to discuss."

Never taking his eyes from Constantine's, Trent handed the duke his foil. Then he gathered up his coat and boots, bowed, and left the gallery.

Constantine quirked a brow. "Friendly fellow, ain't he?" He glanced at the door. "I'd no intention of depriving you of a fencing partner. I was just passing through."

"No matter. It grows late. That is . . . would you care to cross swords with me, my lord?" The duke spoke casually, but there was a note in his voice as honed and lethal as a naked blade.

"No, thanks. I don't fence."

The duke sighed as he replaced the foils in their sconces on the wall. "Such a pity that you young men seek only to fight with the most barbarous of weapons. In my day, we showed more finesse."

In fact, Constantine had some skill with a rapier; tonight, he simply chose not to exercise it. There was a difference, but he didn't feel called upon to explain that to the duke. "A very sad state of affairs, indeed. You like to keep your hand in, obviously."

"I do." The duke smiled as he eased his surprisingly muscular frame into his coat. "When you get to my age, it behooves one to have a care for one's health or simply rot away. Gout, heart troubles, more, er, intimate complaints . . ." He smiled and waved a vague hand. "The wages of sin."

"You sound like a deuced parson," said Constantine,

once more wishing for that drink. First penury, then insult added to injury from the Ice Maiden, and now a moralizing duke. Could this day get any worse?

The duke slipped his feet into his evening pumps. "A little close to the bone, perhaps? My apologies. It was not my intention to preach."

Unhurriedly, he tweaked his cuffs into place, a large signet ring flashing on his right hand. "We should speak of the way things have been left." He paused. "I believe I can help you."

Thanks to his nocturnal tryst with the Ice Maiden, Constantine knew exactly what form the duke's assistance would take.

"I wasn't aware that I needed help."

"Then you're a fool." The dark eyes lost any trace of amusement. "You don't have the slightest inkling how much it costs per annum to run this estate, do you?"

Constantine felt his own gaze harden. "I think I could guess."

Montford named sums that would have staggered Constantine if he hadn't braced for the shock. Where the hell was he going to get that kind of money on top of what he owed Bronson?

"Come to the library," said the duke. "We'll have a brandy and discuss the matter."

It wasn't a request. Constantine wanted more than anything to remind the duke that it was his damned house and his bloody brandy, but that would sound churlish. Besides, he wanted that drink.

As they made their way downstairs, Constantine had to curb his usual purposeful walk to match the duke's gentlemanly saunter. "The house is in excellent repair, at least," murmured Montford. "You won't find a better housekeeper in all of England than Lady Roxdale."

Constantine repressed a grimace. Did Montford truly believe that would win him over? "A most efficient young lady," he agreed.

"You could do worse than let her ladyship show you the ropes around here," the duke observed as they entered the library. "Running such a large house requires planning, tact, and, of course—"

"Money." Constantine walked over to the fireplace and threw himself down on a comfortable sofa, laid his arms wide across the top of it. How unsubtle could Montford be? He knew exactly where the duke headed with this, would have known it even without the forewarning from the Ice Maiden.

"Well, yes, there is that." The duke flipped the tails of his black coat and seated himself across from Constantine. "What do you propose to do about it?"

Propose was exactly what he was *not* going to do.

"I'm considering my options," Constantine said coolly.

That was not blunt enough to head off the duke's line of argument, but it was the best he could contrive at the moment. He still reeled from the news Frederick's pernickety solicitor had imparted to him that day. At this juncture, he couldn't find his footing, much less engage in a complicated contredanse with a wily, matchmaking duke.

Montford's hooded dark eyes opened to their widest. "My dear boy. What choice do you have besides marriage?"

Duke be damned! He didn't have to sit here meekly and listen to this. What was Montford still *doing* here, anyway?

After a moment's silent struggle, Constantine answered pleasantly, "Perhaps you haven't heard. I'm not exactly the marrying kind."

The duke smiled and settled further into his chair. What was so bloody amusing?

Clasping his hands, Montford steepled his index fingers together and pressed them to his lips. "Vulgar as it is to speak of such matters, you need a substantial injection of funds, and quickly. You will be fully occupied with the estate, but this house is large and rambling and difficult to run. It needs a chatelaine."

Constantine snorted.

Spreading his hands, the duke said, "Marry an heiress and

your troubles will be over. Roxdale is an old and respected title, even if the name of Constantine Black has been damaged beyond repair. Despite young Frederick's depredations, your lands are in good heart. Believe me, no matchmaking mama will blink at your reputation with all you have to offer."

A bitter taste flooded Constantine's mouth. "Mercenary."

"Necessary," Montford corrected gently. He waved a blasé hand. "It is the way of our world. You ought to marry a lady who understands the way a marriage of convenience works, and then you will be comfortable. Your, er, habits need not change at all."

Why was everyone alluding to his habits tonight? Bloody Westruthers. Thought they could do and say whatever they damned well pleased.

The duke leaned forward. "Would you care for a drink?"

"No. No, I don't think I would." And it was the truth, for the seething mass of fury in Constantine's belly rose like bile to his throat.

He fixed the duke with a glare. "Let's make this plain between us, Your Grace, since all your dancing around the subject makes me dizzy. Under no circumstances will I marry Lady Roxdale."

He hadn't even made that decision yet, but he was too angry to retract it now.

The duke's eyes cooled to the freezing point; his mouth hardened to a flat line of disgust. Constantine actually felt himself flush at his own boorishness. He'd always prided himself on being impervious to criticism, turning off censorial comments with a smile. Why had he allowed the duke to goad him into uttering an unforgivable insult?

Stiffly, he said, "My apologies."

"Is it possible?" the duke wondered. "Can I have heard correctly?" The dark, hooded eyes widened, as if in surprise. "Could you actually suppose I'd want *you* for Lady Roxdale?"

The contempt dripping from that drawling voice burned like acid in Constantine's chest.

"Of course not." Constantine tugged at the lapel of his dressing gown. "I think I will have that drink, after all."

He launched to his feet, but the duke rose also, blocking his path. Montford was no match for his own height, but Constantine was acutely aware of a powerful presence facing him, a cold fury and an implacable will.

So, there it was. And even as Constantine's hand balled into a tight fist out of anger and affront, he knew Montford's scorn was justified.

How could he have thought for one second that his new situation in life might wipe out past sins? How could he have hoped for a fresh start? He'd rather shave off his eyebrows than wed a contrary and malignant chit who clearly thought him the Devil incarnate. Yet, it was galling to realize Montford had never, not for one moment, contemplated him as a candidate for her hand.

The duke said, "Once you comprehend the full catastrophe of your situation, it will be tempting to grasp at the closest straw. But be advised: that course would most definitely be bad for your health."

Constantine drew a deep breath through his nostrils. "Speak plainly, Your Grace. I am done with your riddles."

In a voice soft with concealed venom, the duke said, "All right, then. Allow me to translate: lay one finger on Lady Roxdale and I'll kill you."

Constantine held Montford's gaze for a long, searching moment. Then he said, "If you don't want me to lay more than my fingers on her, tell her to get the hell out of my house."

CHAPTER SIX

Your Grace,

It has come to the notice of several members of the Ministry of Marriage that a significant prize has suddenly fluttered onto the market. Further, that this plump little pigeon resides in your particular dovecote.

The wolves are already circling, as you might imagine, and I have been unable to locate a certain mutual acquaintance who doubtless wishes to pluck your little pigeon without further ado.

Therefore, I must beg your presence at a meeting, soonest. The usual time and place.

Yours, etc.
deVere

Jane walked into the breakfast parlor, where Rosamund and Cecily sat drinking chocolate.

Ordinarily, Jane would have breakfasted long ago, but she was waiting for Constantine Black to return from his ride. She'd risen betimes and sent a message to his chamber to be handed to him when he woke, but he'd somehow given her the slip. In fact, he'd left his bed far earlier than any Town-idling rake could be expected to do.

She still could not fathom how he'd managed to overset her so completely last night. There should have been no heat at all in their discussion. She'd planned a calm, detached business negotiation. Surely any reasonable man must see the advantages of the match.

Instead, he'd made her dizzy and breathless, toppled her off balance with his ridiculously sensual presence and his suggestive taunts. She was horrified whenever she recalled her own rudeness in return. Only later did it occur to her she ought to have enacted the role of feminine compliance, sought to ingratiate herself, as most ladies in her situation would have done. Other ladies would have cooed and simpered and played the helpless damsel in distress.

Granted, she could never lower herself *that* far. But why, oh why, couldn't she learn to bite her tongue?

Determined to repair the damage, she'd sought him out this morning. So far he'd proven elusive. But the rogue had to eat, didn't he? So she'd lie in wait for him here.

"Well?" demanded Cecily. "What happened?"

Jane threw up her hands. "The man is impossible."

"He won't marry you?" said Rosamund.

"He hasn't decided yet." Jane made a face. "Can you believe it?"

"Hasn't decided?" Cecily curled her lip. "He sounds like a wet fish to me."

"Wet fish" was possibly the last term Jane would use to describe Constantine Black. She shook her head. "No, I'm sure he is merely stringing out the suspense to provoke me."

Too late, Jane heard the pettish note in her voice. Deliberately ignoring Rosamund's raised eyebrows, she glanced out the window. Another dismal morning outside. She'd converted this room into a breakfast parlor because of its pleasant aspect, but today there was no sun to be had. Only pewter-gray clouds and a steady patter of rain and the prospect of her interview with the duke looming before her.

In fact, the sole bright spots on her particular horizon were Rosamund and Cecily. They looked elegant this morning in carriage dresses of the very latest mode. Jane thought of her own dark and dismal wardrobe and sighed.

The significance of her cousins' attire suddenly occurred

to her. "Oh, no! Are you leaving us?" She'd not realized they'd be gone so soon.

Rosamund touched her lips with a napkin. "Yes, it appears so. His Grace has urgent business in London and insists on escorting us there at once. Beckenham travels with us as far as Oxford." She stretched her hand out across the table as if to reach for Jane's. "I'm so sorry we couldn't stay longer."

"But you just arrived!" said Jane. "Why won't he let you stay?"

"I'll wager he doesn't trust Lord Roxdale around Rosamund," said Cecily, her dark eyes dancing over the brim of her teacup. "I wish I may at least *see* the bad baron before we go. Tell me, Jane. Did you find him handsome?"

Constantine Black was easily the most splendid piece of manhood she'd seen in her life, but she'd rather die than say so. "Moderately handsome," she allowed. "But *im*moderately obnoxious. I can't deal with him at all."

"Aha!" said Rosamund, blue eyes knowing.

"Aha?" repeated Jane. "What do you mean, 'aha'? Whatever conclusion you are drawing that makes you look so smug, I beg you will put it out of your mind, Rosamund."

"She can't help it," said Cecily. "She's an incurable romantic."

"Marriage will cure her of it soon enough," muttered Jane. The smile fell from Rosamund's face like light from a snuffed candle.

Suddenly, Jane realized what she'd said. Her heart gave a sickened lurch; her insides cringed. She stared at Rosamund, aghast.

How could she have been so unfeeling, so tactless? Rosamund's lot was harder than anyone's, for she loved a gentleman who was not her intended husband. He was a fine, honorable gentleman, a dashing cavalry officer, but not nearly grand enough for a Westruther heiress. The husband Montford had arranged for Rosamund was a very different sort: a big scowling brute of a man whom she could not possibly hope to love.

"Oh, Rosamund," Jane whispered. "I'm sorry. I didn't mean it!"

Rosamund set down her cup with a small click. She offered Jane a polite, social smile that set her at a distance. "Never mind that. What are we to do about you?"

Turning away to hide the pity that must show in her eyes, Jane crossed to the sideboard. Automatically, she lifted a silver lid and ladled a small portion of porridge into a bowl. She plopped a curl of butter into the center and watched it melt, golden tendrils bleeding outward. Then the milk, just a dribble laced around the yellow center.

Perfect. Or it would be, if her appetite hadn't deserted her. Rosamund was the last person in the world she'd wish to wound. She moved back to the table and sat down.

Cecily propped her chin on her hand and stared hard at Jane. "I know. You must captivate him."

Jane wrinkled her nose. "Flirt, do you mean? But I don't know how."

"A few smiles and a little encouragement wouldn't go astray," said Rosamund. "You can be rather forbidding, you know, darling."

Jane scowled. "Constantine Black is as bold as brass. The last thing he needs is encouragement."

"You've tried reason," Cecily pointed out. "Now, it's time for a little persuasion, don't you think?" She sipped her chocolate. "Either that, or simply seduce him."

Jane choked on her porridge. *"What?"*

Cecily shrugged. "You know. Make him compromise you so you have to marry. It happens all the time."

"Me? Seduce *him*? You cannot be serious."

"Of course she is not serious." Rosamund frowned. "Are you, Cecily?"

"I couldn't possibly," said Jane. "I—I wouldn't know where to start."

There was a hint of curiosity in the tilt of Rosamund's head. She'd certainly stare if she knew how many years it had been since Jane shared a man's bed. Well, except that one last time, of course. She repressed a shudder.

"I wouldn't think he's *too* particular, being a rake," mused Cecily.

Before Jane could answer that complimentary remark, a heavy footstep outside preceded the man she'd been waiting for. He filled the doorway, then stepped over the threshold and filled the room.

Constantine Black was a large man, true, and well proportioned with it, as she'd been privileged to note the previous evening. But it was his personality that seemed to expand and ring through the empty space, bounce off the walls.

Jane's stupid heart bounded into her throat.

"Ladies." He bowed with an insouciant grace that somehow made mockery of the formal gesture.

Jane performed the introductions. Cecily's eyes widened. "*You're* the new Roxdale?"

He tilted his head. "That surprises you?"

There was a disquieting glint in the green eyes, but Cecily was undaunted. "I should rather think so! Aren't you some sort of cousin of Frederick's?"

"That's right."

"You are *nothing* alike."

A film of ice seemed to settle over his features. "Ah. Yes, I'm said to take after my mother, in my coloring, at least. Welsh blood, you know. That might explain it."

"She must be very beautiful," said Cecily. She turned her head and directed an accusing gaze at Jane. "*Moderately* handsome? The Lout is a veritable Adonis, Jane!"

Lout?

Three pairs of feminine eyes inspected Constantine.

He resisted the urge to tug at his cravat. Women had often admired his looks, it was true, but he'd never experienced this kind of openly critical analysis from a young lady, let alone three of them, particularly at the breakfast table. Dammit, he could feel embarrassment warm his cheeks.

He smiled, forcing out between his teeth, "Lady Cecily, you're too kind."

Lady Roxdale shrugged, clearly enjoying his discomfiture. "I daresay such things are a matter of personal taste."

"Handsome is as handsome does," said the beautiful blonde quietly. She glanced at Lady Roxdale, then fixed an oddly penetrating blue gaze back on him.

"Oh, I don't know," said Lady Cecily. "A man can be forgiven much if he's that ornamental."

Lady Cecily Westruther was a brat, but a brat with that typical Westruther belief that she could say and do whatever she wished and get away with it. The Ice Maiden, for all she was a stickler for propriety where *he* was concerned, made no effort to silence the girl. Nor did the quieter beauty.

He let none of this simmering resentment show on his face. "I'm happy to meet with your approval, Lady Cecily."

Setting her elbows on the table, Lady Cecily placed her chin in her hands and stared at him. He felt like a prime side of beef being sized up by a butcher. She was clearly wondering which part of him to carve up next.

"Tell me," the girl said. "Is it terribly *thrilling* to be a rake?"

The blonde surprised him by chuckling as she rose from the table. "Enough, Cecily. You will make Lord Roxdale blush and he has not yet eaten his breakfast. Come, we must go up and see to the packing."

She bent to kiss Lady Roxdale's cheek. "We shall be ready to leave in an hour."

Constantine felt the tension in his shoulders ease a little. Their departure couldn't come too soon for him. He bowed again as the ladies left the room.

"My lord, we must speak further about the situation we now find ourselves in," said Lady Roxdale. "I must implore you to consider the advantages of our alliance."

Why did she want this marriage so badly? Was it only out of her sense of duty toward the estate? To Luke? He could well imagine her officious concern about Constantine's influence on the morals of a small boy. He couldn't believe she had any interest in the child beyond a self-righteous intention to meddle.

"I *am* considering the advantages, believe me," he said. "But until I've assessed my financial position, I would prefer to make no promises in that regard."

His conversation with Montford the previous evening had made him seethe with resentment, but he'd been rash in dismissing the notion of marrying Lady Roxdale. A long, punishing ride through the rain this morning had calmed his temper until he'd seen the truth. He could not afford to spurn the solution Lady Roxdale offered out of hand. Not if he wanted to keep the Lazenby estate intact.

He wondered if he ought to warn her how opposed the duke was to the match, but thought better of it. She would find out for herself soon enough. He wondered how much the duke's opinion would sway her. Last night, she'd seemed determined to stand against him but he suspected that wouldn't be easy.

Hoping he'd put an end to the matter for the moment, Constantine moved to the sideboard, where a few silver chafing dishes ranged. He took a plate and lifted the cover of one dish. Porridge. Another. Coddled eggs. Another. A pudding so pale it seemed to have developed a consumptive habit.

His stomach growled, voicing its disappointment. Where was the bacon? The beefsteak and kippers, sausages and broiled ham? He'd anticipated a good, hearty, carnivorous English breakfast, the kind his mother served at Broadmere.

He'd woken with a bastard of a headache from his libations the previous evening and decided that the only way to drive away the devils was to take some punishing exercise in the fresh air. He'd come in, cold, wet and famished, only to be confronted by . . .

"Nursery food," he said blankly. "It's nursery food."

"Healthful and sustaining."

Slowly, he turned, to see Lady Roxdale regarding him as if *he* were the odd one. He feigned a start. "Good God, are you still here?"

She blinked, then ignored the question. "Try the porridge. It's particularly good today."

"I'd rather swallow my own tongue."

She took up a spoonful of the pap and slipped it into her mouth. He wrenched his gaze from the way her lips worked together as she chewed. Lord, hunger was deranging his senses! Surely a woman eating porridge must be the least erotic thing in the universe.

"I suppose you ordered all this just to spite me." He sounded petulant, but dammit all, he wasn't responsible for his actions when he was starving and the only sustenance within reach resembled the drivel they fed invalids and infants.

She raised her brows, seeming genuinely surprised. "Why should I? Frederick and I sat down to this breakfast every day. Ask Cook if you don't believe me."

She pressed a napkin to her lips and stood up, having eaten, he noticed, very little of her own meal. In that precise way of hers, she added, "Since you did not trouble to order what you liked, Cook served what she always serves."

He was supposed to order what he liked, was he? He'd simply assumed breakfast was normal here, the same as at every other gentleman's home in England.

His mistake. Nothing was normal at Lazenby Hall.

Suddenly, Constantine felt a deep sympathy for his predecessor. Poor Frederick. No wonder he'd stuck his spoon in the wall if he'd been obliged to choke down this mess every morning.

Lady Roxdale lifted her chin. "If you tell me what you require, I shall order it directly."

If he allowed her to maintain dominion over household duties, even temporarily, he'd never be rid of her. "Oh, no you don't."

He caught her elbow as she moved past him. Her bare arm was warm and soft, unlike her personality. The pliable feel of her flesh sent messages racing to the part of his anatomy he needed to keep under control around her. On pain of death, if Montford was to be believed.

She gasped and tugged against him. Her cheeks pinked. "You forget yourself, sir!"

No, I'm just remembering.

He stared down into her eyes, now stormy with alarm and confusion and something else that might be anticipation. The impulse to make those eyes flutter closed in sensual delight nearly overcame his good sense.

Surely he wasn't juvenile enough to want her simply because she'd been forbidden to him? Yet he burned to see if he could unsettle her as much as she unsettled him.

Well, why not? Last night, he'd looked past her icy surface, seen glimmers of passion beneath. Why *not* stoke those embers to a blaze?

"I'm moving to the master suite," he said, and noted the flare in her gaze, the ripple in her throat as she gave a hard swallow. "It must come to this sooner or later, you know."

He relaxed his grip, turning restraint into a gentle caress of trailing fingertips down her arm. That smooth, pliant skin nearly undid him. He wanted to touch more of it, kiss and taste it, make every inch of it flush with rapture.

Her eyelids sank, just a fraction, as if they might drift shut in silent enjoyment. Then, with a slight shake of the head, she recovered and seized the chance to slip free.

She stepped back, dragging in a breath that held a distinct—and satisfying—tremor. "It's your house. You must do whatever you wish."

He gave her a slow, carnal smile. "*Whatever* I wish?"

She glanced rather desperately at the sideboard, as if hoping the coddled eggs would leap up and ride to her rescue. "I apologize for breakfast. I ought to have anticipated . . ." The words seemed to stick in her throat.

So she'd decided to be conciliating, had she? What brought this on? He waited, not precisely enjoying her discomfiture, but curious as to what she'd say. How far would she humble herself to please him?

She tried again. This time, with a determined smile. "I shall speak with Cook and order a breakfast fit for a king for tomorrow. You'll see."

Her smile nearly vanquished him. Forced as it must have been, it lit her face, burnished her eyes to silver. Most especially, it drew his attention to the full lips that stretched and curved over her white teeth. Her lips were a rich, dull red that owed nothing to rouge. They looked full-bodied and delicious, like a fine burgundy.

Since when have you sighed like a mooncalf over a lady's smile?

Women, he reminded himself, smiled at him for one of two reasons—they wanted something, or he had just given it to them. Constantine Black knew the game, and the odds were just the way he liked them.

That softened expression was not at all guileless, was it? Even she, even his dead cousin's wife, smiled because she wanted something. His ring on her finger.

"Never mind," he muttered. "I'll speak to Cook myself."

His stomach cramping with hunger, he bowed and left her, striding off to the kitchens, which were placed as far as possible from the dining room and the breakfast parlor, too. An inconvenience he meant to remedy. Or he would, if he had a penny to bless himself with. Irritation whipped into anger at the thought.

In the hall, he encountered Montford and Beckenham, who looked like they'd just returned from their own ride.

As Montford handed his hat to the butler, his brows rose. "Ah, Roxdale. Well met."

Starvation lent savagery to Constantine's satisfaction. "If you are looking for a decent breakfast, you're doomed to disappointment, I'm afraid."

Beckenham shrugged out of his greatcoat, allowing it to fall into the waiting hands of the butler. "Oh, don't concern yourself, Roxdale. We breakfasted in the village."

"The village," Constantine repeated.

The duke smiled, slapping his gloves against his bare palm. "Yes. The King's Head lays on a bang-up breakfast, does it not, Beckenham? We never miss it when we come to stay."

"They do have a way with bacon there, don't they?" Beckenham agreed. "Something in the curing, I think. Quite splendid."

At the mention of bacon, saliva surged into Constantine's mouth. His stomach gave a growl so audible that the duke raised his quizzing glass and lowered his gaze to Constantine's midriff.

Without a word, Constantine swung on his heel and headed into the bowels of the house. Bloody know-it-all Westruthers! Obviously, they were wise to the ways of this household as Constantine was not.

If he married the Ice Maiden, he'd never be rid of the rest of her devilish family. They'd be crawling all over his house at will.

Constantine jogged down the narrow, winding staircase that led to the kitchens and catapulted back to his childhood.

Ah, this kitchen, with its chessboard floor and its big wooden table and the cooling bench by the window, where he'd swiped hot buns and ginger biscuits as a lad. The scent of baked bread and herbs and beeswax. And the warm, floury hugs of Marthe.

Would she still be here? His spirits rose at the thought, light and warm as one of Marthe's loaves.

Not a soul in the kitchen. Constantine heard the clink of cutlery on china and the murmur of voices from the servants' hall down the corridor. He'd intended to raid the larder, but that could wait. He had to see if Marthe was here.

When he appeared at the doorway of the dining hall, the chatter and movement ceased like a snapped thread. The servants rose as one, with scraping chairs and a clatter of forks that had paused, suspended in the air between plate and mouth, when he walked in.

He looked around. There were one or two familiar faces he couldn't quite place. But at the foot of the table, one face stood out like a beacon, round, rosy-cheeked, and wreathed in a smile.

He grinned. "Hallo, Marthe."

"Master Con!" His name, like a joyful prayer, galvanized him. He strode forward and plucked the middle-aged woman off her feet, swung her around.

For which he received a soft cuff over the ear. "*Tiens, milor'!* What'll you be at now, to come down here where you're not wanted?"

"Marthe, it does my heart good to see you." He glanced at the sideboard, which groaned with proper breakfast fare. He grinned. "It goes even better with my stomach. Mind if I help myself?"

Without waiting for an answer, he snatched up a plate and loaded it with large helpings of everything. Licking his thumb clean of bacon grease, he glanced around, to realize that his staff still stood to attention.

"Oh, do sit down." He hefted his plate. "I'll, um, take this to the kitchen."

Marthe seemed to regain her wits. "Get on with your breakfast, all of you. I'll see to his lordship."

She bustled out after him, alternately apologizing for the lack of decent victuals above stairs and chastising him for failing to visit her sooner.

"Ah, but *la pauvre petite*!" she continued. "The mistress, she has not two taste buds to rub together, that one." With a dramatic sigh, the cook turned down her wide mobile mouth and shook her head. "It is a travesty, but what can I do? I must follow orders and serve up this bland English mess." She threw up her hands. "Pudding! It is enough to make one weep."

"I'm surprised you're still here." Constantine's own taste buds exploded with pleasure as he savored a mouthful of fried mushrooms in a creamy sauce laced with herbs and brandy.

A Gallic shrug. "I am tied here by more than loyalty."

He winked. "Fell in love with the butler, did you? The old devil! Didn't know Feather had it in him."

Marthe drew herself up. "That cadaver! Is it likely that I would love such a one?"

"Who, then?"

A twinkle replaced the indignation. She fluttered an airy hand. "It matters not who."

Grinning, he recalled his own youthful *tendre* for a pretty little parlor maid. "Is Violet still here? Now she was a saucy piece."

"Ah, but she had ambition, that one," said Marthe. She shrugged. "Some visiting milady took a liking to her and lured her away to become her personal maid."

Constantine swallowed. "Good for Violet." He looked around the kitchen. "I'm amazed the fine milady didn't lure you as well."

Marthe shrugged. "Many have tried, but me, I am paid very well and I have been content. But *eh voilà*! Now that *you* are here, I can create!"

He grinned. "Excellent. Marthe, you shall create to your heart's content." He waved his fork in a shooing motion. "But I am keeping you from your meal. Go, I insist!"

"Yes, milord." With a chuckle, Marthe bobbed a curtsy and left.

Constantine devoted himself again to his plate, but the clatter of footsteps down the stairs disturbed his enjoyment. He looked up to see a dark-haired boy erupt into the kitchen, then stop short.

One glance told Constantine this was no kitchen boy. The cut of his nankeen jacket and the quality of its brass buttons proclaimed his status as a member of the family.

The boy seemed to collect himself. He made a quick, jerky bow and panted, "Lord Roxdale, sir."

Constantine smiled. "And you must be Luke."

"Yes, sir."

Rising, Constantine moved around the table and held out his hand to his ward.

Luke tilted his head a little, as if confounded by his guardian's offer to shake hands. Then he stretched out his own and gripped Constantine's with a slightly aggressive force.

Ah. So Lady Roxdale wasn't the only one who objected to his presence at Lazenby.

Lightly, Constantine said, "If you've come down here in search of a decent breakfast, let me recommend the bacon. It's excellent."

A furtive glance to the servants' hall betrayed the boy. His eyes grew round when his gaze alighted on Constantine's heaped plate.

"I won't tell if you don't," said Constantine.

Luke swallowed and sent another glance toward the kitchens. "It's just that I don't like to hurt Aunt Jane's feelings."

"I quite understand. But this sort of grub is more what a man needs for sustenance than that, er . . . *lighter* fare upstairs," said Constantine. "Load your plate and bring it back here, will you? You and I ought to become better acquainted."

The boy's highly expressive face reflected the war of conscience and desire that went on in his mind. Desire finally won, and he scampered off to collect his own meal.

Upon his return, he sat on a chair a little removed from Constantine's. Luke kept his eyes on his plate, shoveling Marthe's flavorsome food in his mouth, presumably so he didn't have to talk to his companion.

Undeterred, Constantine kept up an easy stream of reminiscences about his time at Lazenby. "When we were boys, Frederick and I would come down here and visit Marthe. We'd pack our saddlebags full of treats from the kitchen and ride all around the estate. We were knights, slaying dragons and rescuing fair maidens." He grinned. "I liked the rescuing part."

There was a touch of envy in Luke's gaze. "Aunt Jane says

I'm too young to ride my pony without a groom along. She rides with me sometimes, but . . ." He shrugged a shoulder.

Constantine frowned. "How old are you again?"

"Six and three quarters," said Luke, his voice tinged with indignation.

"Hmm." At that age, Constantine and Frederick had been up to all sorts of mischief, enjoying the freedom of boyhood to the full. He didn't blame Luke for the despondent tone to his voice. Taking along a groom was not conducive to high adventure.

Clearly, Cousin Jane restricted the boy to an unreasonable degree. Not out of malice. No, she wasn't a cruel woman, anyone could see that. Perhaps merely overprotective. Either way, it wasn't good for the boy to be coddled.

Constantine framed his response carefully. "You are fortunate that Lady Roxdale takes such a keen interest in your safety. However, there are some things ladies do not understand. I'll speak with her and see if we can come to a better arrangement."

Luke's face lit with hope. Almost immediately, though, his expression faltered. His eyes dimmed and lowered; his mouth turned down at the corners.

"Not that it'll do any good," he muttered. "You are sending us away."

Constantine reached out and tilted up Luke's chin so that he had to look him in the eye. "I am *not* sending you away. And that, my dear Luke, is a promise."

"You wished to see me, Your Grace?" Jane entered the drawing room at the appointed hour, braced for the coming discussion. She was armed to the teeth with arguments for her cause, regardless of her prospective groom's reluctance to tie the knot.

The duke must have surmised by now that she'd been avoiding him. Last night, she'd pleaded fatigue. This morning, she'd refused his invitation to go riding even though she longed for a good gallop and fresh country air. But she couldn't delay this interview any longer. The duke was leaving for Town shortly.

Montford looked up from a letter he'd been reading. "Yes, my dear. Shall we sit down?"

Jane glanced at the letter. For a missive to find the duke here, it must be important. "Not bad news, I hope?"

The duke raised his brows. Jane braced herself for a setdown in return for her curiosity.

But the duke merely folded the letter and slid it into his coat pocket. "Not at all. Some urgent business I must attend to. I regret I'm obliged to curtail my visit and leave immediately for London."

"So Rosamund told me. How tiresome. I'd thought you'd all stay the week, at least."

"Yes, I'd thought so, too." He paused. "You, however, would do well to remain here while the solicitors sort out the estate. Keep an eye on things."

"Yes," she agreed, a little surprised that Montford would not cavil at her remaining under the same roof as someone of Constantine Black's reputation. "I'm persuaded my departure at such a moment would create more confusion than there is already."

Jane sat on the sofa and the duke followed suit, choosing a spindle-legged chair. He looked elegant and at ease and Jane wished she'd learned the trick of concealing her own feelings so well. Ah, but perhaps it was not a trick. Perhaps what they said of him was true: the Duke of Montford had no feelings at all.

"Tell me, Your Grace, is the situation really as dire as Beckenham thinks?"

The duke sighed. "Constantine Black has been left with Lazenby Hall and its contents, and all of the surrounding land. The rest—investments, stocks, bonds, and so on—are held in trust for you."

"But I don't want it," Jane said.

"Nevertheless."

She licked her lips. "Is there no way I can give it all back?" In exchange for Luke, of course.

"That would be complicated. The trustees would be in breach of their duty to allow it." Montford spread his hands in an unaccustomed gesture of helplessness. "It is a great shame that Frederick sought to break up the inheritance in this manner, but there's not a great deal we can do about it now. Put it in the hands of lawyers and it could drag on into the next century. You know what they're like."

The duke steepled his fingertips together and pressed them to his lips. "You're an intelligent woman, Lady Roxdale. You must have realized by now that there is but one way to piece this jigsaw back together, and that's for you to marry the new baron."

She bowed her head. "Your Grace—"

The duke held up a hand. "I don't advise it, however. Were he a man of a different stamp . . ." He pressed his lips together, marking his disapproval. "But Constantine Black would make any lady miserable. His reputation is shocking. He is barely received in society."

Jane blinked. Had she heard correctly? Had the duke actually advised her to seek personal happiness above familial duty? But how inconvenient that his change of heart should occur now, when she would gladly make that sacrifice to keep Luke.

"What on earth did the wretch do?" She tried to make the inquiry sound offhand. "I seem to remember talk of some scandal, but Frederick would never speak of it."

"He seduced a young lady and abandoned her," said the duke, not mincing his words. "He'd earned the reputation of a hellion well before that, but that particular episode put him beyond the pale. The family tried to hush it up, of course, but these things will out."

A heavy sensation in her stomach felt like disappointment. She blinked in surprise. She'd known Constantine Black for a scoundrel, hadn't she? Why should she be disappointed?

"What happened to the young lady?" she asked.

The duke shrugged. "Oh, they married her off to some other fellow. A barrister, I think. Hardly comparable to what she might have become had Black done the decent thing by her."

Had Black done the decent thing, that unknown lady would supplant Jane as mistress at Lazenby Hall now . . . Oh, *oh*. What a horrible, selfish creature she was. That poor young lady, obliged to marry a barrister! There, that was the proper sentiment.

So much for Cecily's brilliant plan. Even if Jane succeeded in seducing Constantine Black, history showed he could not be shamed to the altar. Besides, she'd despise herself if she played such a low trick.

She could well understand the temptation Constantine Black must have presented to an unseasoned girl. She herself felt the immense power of his charm, and she was neither a silly young lady, nor did she have any romantic illusions about bed sport.

"How old was he at the time?" And why did she grasp at extenuating circumstances?

The duke shrugged. "Twenty? Twenty-one? Old enough to know better."

Young enough to make a mistake.

Jane shook herself. Defending him, now, was she? She'd no more sense than that poor, deluded young lady. An honorable man would never refuse to marry a gently born girl he'd ruined, no matter how young he was.

It seemed the duke would not assist her in her plans to marry the new Lord Roxdale. She would have to secure Constantine's agreement on her own.

If the duke's disclosure was anything to judge by, Constantine Black was ruthless when it came to avoiding the parson's mousetrap.

Reverting to their original topic of conversation, she said, "Whatever the case with the estate, I ought to remain here to ensure the reins of the household are handed over without too much disruption."

"Yes." The duke took out his watch and flicked open the lid, then returned it to his pocket. "I would caution you to have a care, however. Constantine Black is not to be trusted."

She thought of the previous evening in the chapel. How reckless she'd been! But he hadn't ravished her, for all that. Hadn't even stolen a kiss. He had merely . . .

Unbidden, a thrill shivered up her spine.

To cover her reaction, Jane smoothed her skirts over her lap. "You needn't be concerned, Your Grace," she said. "*I* am not a silly young girl. Indeed, I am perhaps the last woman on earth who would fall for the wiles of such a man."

The hooded eyes regarded her for a moment. "Hmm. Yes. Still, it is not desirable that you remain in the same house with him for too long. I wouldn't countenance it at all if it were not for the awkward way in which things have been left."

"Lady Endicott has promised to stay to lend me countenance," she reminded him.

Montford nodded. "To be sure. Where is the countess? I haven't seen her since the funeral."

"She took to her bed yesterday evening with a sick headache. Her maid told me the countess is usually well again after a day's rest."

He frowned. "It is to be hoped the lady doesn't remain indisposed. She is hardly an adequate chaperone if she never leaves her bedchamber."

Jane lifted her chin. "As I said, I'm not a silly young girl, Your Grace. Constantine Black is unlikely to trouble me." She regarded him steadily. "You do not think he would press his attentions on an unwilling woman, do you?"

"No. No, I expect he would draw the line at that," said Montford. "Still, it would be best if an alternative arrangement could be made, as Lady Endicott won't wish to remain here for long. I will think on it and advise you."

Should she mention Luke? Perhaps that wouldn't be wise. If Montford knew how much she wanted Luke with her, he might suspect her motives for remaining at Lazenby. He might step in to stop her courting Constantine Black.

A bustle outside brought the duke to his feet. Unhurriedly, he moved to glance out the window.

"Ah. It seems all is ready for our departure. I must take my leave." In his elegant, leisurely fashion, the duke drew on his gloves.

He looked down at her for a long moment. "Good-bye, Jane."

Her name. He'd used her name. She gazed back up at him in wonder. Did she merely imagine that his expression had softened? A trick of the light perhaps . . .

She made no response, but turned to accompany him down to the carriage.

CHAPTER SEVEN

The duke's entourage departed. Jane stood beneath the portico and waved until the carriages were blurry figures drawing out of sight. Though she knew why they went, she could not help but feel a touch abandoned.

However, there was no time for such maudlin thoughts. She needed to steel herself for her campaign to court Constantine Black.

She'd tried reason. She'd tried being pleasant—although that effort had not been entirely wholehearted, she'd admit. Cecily's suggestion that Jane should let Constantine compromise her to force him into marriage was rendered moot by Montford's revelations about the scandal concerning Miss Flockton. Clearly, the new baron did not care for anyone's good opinion. Even if Jane could bring herself to play temptress, it would be for naught if Constantine Black refused to marry her.

Perhaps Cecily's other suggestion was more likely to bear fruit. Jane needed to charm Constantine Black into marriage. He would never love her, but if he liked her well enough and found her moderately attractive, he might choose to wed her instead of pursuing other means of repairing his fortune.

So, it was up to Jane to captivate him. She sighed. Captivating gentlemen had never been her forte. Another reason she'd been glad to eschew a London debut and marry Frederick at seventeen.

Jane turned to go inside, to find Constantine standing at the top of the steps, watching her. She met his eyes, and that jolt of . . . *something* hot and vital surged within her.

She colored—stupid blushes!—and his expression warmed with appreciation. He descended the steps in a leisurely fashion, never taking his gaze from hers.

A silly, panicked fluttering struck up in her chest. She tried desperately to think of something pleasant to say to him, but his demeanor, redolent of male satisfaction, made her hackles rise. Her instinct was to deliver a frigid snub, but that would not help her.

Remember the plan. Remember Luke. Forget your pride.

Constantine tilted his head, as if to examine her more closely. "I think it must be the translucence of your skin that makes your blushes so delightfully ready. May I touch it?"

Her face reddened further. "No! You may not!" She darted a look around, but there was no one near them to hear this embarrassing exchange.

A glint of triumph lit Constantine's eyes. Clearly, he'd intended to fluster her and was pleased with the result.

Remembering her cousins' strictures, she bit back an acid retort. Her lips stiff, she said, "It is a fine day. Would you— would you like me to show you the gardens?"

He didn't dispute the patent untruth of her comment about the weather. Nor did he point out that he was already acquainted with the house and its gardens.

Instead, he gave a slight shrug of those broad shoulders. "Why not?"

Constantine made as if to take her arm but she swept past him and stepped briskly toward the path. "This way."

Jane led him to the parterre garden, a geometrically designed relic of a more formal age. She kept up an informative commentary as they moved along. All the while, she was aware that his gaze never left her, even as she pointed out several unusual species and points of interest.

She decided to take the bull by the horns. "You seem distracted, my lord."

He glanced into the distance, then transferred his gaze to her. "Might we put an end to this foolish and quite unnecessary formality? We are cousins by marriage, after all. *Jane*."

She'd always thought her name prosaic, but it sounded quite different when he said it. Warm and intimate, like a caress. The thrill that single syllable produced shocked her.

She ought not to allow the familiarity, not from a man of his reputation. In ordinary circumstances, she'd refuse him.

Yet, was it not her objective to promote goodwill between them? As long as that goodwill didn't extend too far . . .

She temporized. "I admit, it is a little confusing to call you Lord Roxdale, after Frederick. And we are related by marriage, as you said." She gave a crisp nod. "Very well, then."

He halted her by placing a hand on her arm. "And still, you have not said my name."

Of course, he wouldn't let her elude him so easily. Jane stared up at him for some moments. In a clear, deliberate voice stripped of emotion, she said, "Constantine."

She wondered if he experienced a thrill similar to hers. His darkened expression told her he had. Or perhaps that look signified satisfaction at so easily getting his own way. What did he want with her?

Suddenly, she felt as if the two of them were very much alone out here. Jane's blood rushed in tune with the fountains playing behind them. The breath hitched in her throat.

Before she knew it, he'd reached out and brushed a crooked finger down her burning cheek.

"You're doing it again," he said. "Regrettably, I have business to attend to this morning or I'd find a thousand more interesting ways to make you blush."

She couldn't mistake his meaning. A panicky wave of excitement washed through her. How on earth was she to captivate Constantine without finding herself thoroughly seduced? She could almost laugh at how naïvely she'd adopted this plan. Courting the new Lord Roxdale was like making overtures of friendship to a jungle cat. One was most likely to be devoured.

Then she registered what he'd said. "Business?" she repeated. "To do with the estate?"

"Yes." He leaned down to pluck a malingering daisy
from the lawn. "You needn't sound so incredulous," he murmured, presenting the cheerful bloom to her. "I'm not wholly
ignorant of the principles of estate management."

There was a touch of hauteur in his tone that struck her as
out of keeping with the care-for-nothing demeanor she'd
observed thus far. She was chastened by it.

After a slight hesitation, Jane accepted the daisy he proffered. She didn't object when he took her arm and altered
their course away from the fountains.

"I recall now," she said. "You own an estate in Derby-
shire, don't you?"

A frown entered his eyes. "That's right. Broadmere."

She wondered what made him look so grim. "Don't you
wish to live there?"

He shook his head. "I haven't set foot in the place since I
inherited it."

Jane stared at him. No wonder Frederick had railed about
Constantine being a neglectful landlord.

"At least it will be no penance to be indoors on such a
day." Constantine squinted up at the sky, which held yet
more rain over their heads like a threat. "Tedious work, no
doubt, but I need a more thorough understanding of the
way Frederick left things before I can decide how I should
proceed."

Did he mean before he decided whether to marry her?

She said, "You may choose not to believe me, but I truly
regret the way things have been left. It seems so irresponsible,
so unlike Frederick to land us in such a mess."

Constantine shrugged. "Perhaps he thought there was
time to fix things before he went." He was silent for a moment. "Perhaps he wanted to punish me. We parted bitterly
all those years ago."

"Oh?" Had they quarreled over that lady Constantine had
used and abandoned?

He inhaled deeply through his nostrils. "You want to know why."

"Only if you care to tell me," she lied.

He looked down at her a moment. "I'm not sure that I do."

As Jane stood, transfixed, those green eyes softened and deepened, full of shadows and mystery, like an enchanted forest. The emotion in them . . . She couldn't place it. Sorrow? Regret?

Had he felt anything toward the lady he'd disgraced? Did he ever think of her now? It was all so many years ago. He must have had dozens—hundreds—of women in his bed since then.

An image of strong limbs, gleaming olive skin, and tangled sheets flashed into her mind. She lowered her eyes, hoping they hadn't betrayed her.

His nearness affected her profoundly; the air thickened between them until she anticipated his next touch with every breath.

How on earth was she to court him and still fend off his immoral advances? Her sheltered existence had given her no experience of rakes' wiles. She'd never even been to London for the Season. She'd never encountered anyone like Constantine Black.

He used one gloveless fingertip beneath her chin to tilt her head upward. She saw that his mood had shifted. His expression grew intent.

Tightly, Jane said, "You take liberties where you have not earned the right, my lord."

His voice was husky. "Ah, but stolen pleasures taste twice as sweet. Don't you find?"

With a small choke of dismay, Jane shook her head and backed away from him.

He followed, until her back brushed a high hedge behind her. She realized they'd strayed into a secluded part of the garden, shielded from the house by a high yew hedge. How had she not noticed that? Her attention had been consumed by him.

He was too close; the heat of his body seemed to surround her. Humiliating to feel her own flesh blaze to life, her skin tighten in response.

"Yes," he murmured, as if he knew precisely what his nearness did to her. "You would have been wiser to have accompanied your cousins back to London, Lady Roxdale. I rarely resist temptation, you know."

"How good of you to warn me," she said waspishly. "Otherwise, I might have been *quite* taken in."

The purposeful look vanished. With a short laugh, he stepped back. "Viper! But come, now we understand one another." His regard slid over her, and she felt it like a hand brushing her skin in forbidden places. "It's not a crime, Lady Roxdale," he murmured. "What harm in us finding pleasure in our circumstances?"

"But I don't wish to pleasure you," said Jane. "I wish to *marry* you, my lord."

She had the dubious satisfaction of seeing his brows contract. But before she could enlarge on that statement, Constantine's attention switched to something beyond her.

His lips curved into a humorless smile, his eyes suddenly hard and bright with mockery. "Ah. Our upright neighbor, come to call. Excellent timing, as ever."

Jane turned her head to see her neighbor, Adam Trent, hat in hand, striding across the lawn toward them. "You know him?"

"I've had that misfortune since we were boys."

The same amused, faintly contemptuous expression he'd worn when the duke departed earlier settled over his sculpted features.

The object of his regard was a tall, athletic fellow dressed in a neat brown suit. He was said to be the handsomest man in the county—and Jane had thought so, too, until now. Beside Constantine Black's vivid dark beauty Mr. Trent reminded her a little of her morning porridge. Sandy hair, fair complexion. Eyes that could have been hazel, or green, or light brown.

Bland. Unexciting. And how ungenerous of her to call him so. He'd been Frederick's dearest friend.

"Good morning, Mr. Trent. How do you do?" Jane curtsied as he approached.

"Lady Roxdale." Trent took her hand and bowed over it. "I had scant opportunity to express my condolences yesterday, but please believe I am desolate for your loss."

"Thank you," she murmured. "I know you must feel Frederick's passing keenly on your own account, sir."

"Indeed. He was a good man. The best of fellows."

Jane turned to indicate Constantine's presence with a light gesture. "You are acquainted with Lord Roxdale, I believe."

Constantine nodded a greeting. "Trent."

There was a long, protracted pause against the steady rush of the fountain. A lone birdcall flooded the silence with sweet, piercing song. Adam Trent did nothing, made no reply. He simply stood there, his gaze fixed on Jane's face.

As if Constantine Black did not exist.

Indignation spurred hot blood to Jane's cheeks. She turned to Constantine, ready to smooth over the discourtesy, but she was too late to salvage the situation.

Gravel crunched as Constantine spun on his heel and walked away.

With a frown, Jane rounded on her neighbor, but caught herself before unleashing the scold that rose to her lips. Who was she to defend Constantine Black? And why should she wish to?

The gentleman gazed after Constantine's retreating form. With a grimace, he said, "I didn't know *he* was here."

"If you had, you would not have set foot on his lands, I daresay," said Jane. She despised sanctimony and disliked ill-bred behavior even more. One did not give the cut direct to a man in his own home, no matter what kind of scoundrel he was.

Trent didn't seem to notice the reproof. "Lady Roxdale, there is something . . ." He turned the brim of his hat in his hands, a frown wrinkling his brow. "Jane, I must speak with you. Caution you about that fellow."

She gave a light laugh. "Believe me, Mr. Trent, I am well aware of Constantine Black's reputation. If you are concerned for my honor, you need not be. I stand in no danger from him."

Oh, Jane, what an utter bouncer!

Trent narrowed his eyes, as if to observe her more closely. "Very well, then. I'll say no more on the subject. The tale's not fit for your ears, anyway."

Montford hadn't balked at telling her, had he? In spite of herself, Jane was intrigued. Montford had related the bare facts, but she wanted to know more about what led to Constantine's disgrace. Perhaps Trent knew. He'd been Frederick's closest friend, after all.

She bit her lip. Looking for extenuating circumstances, was she? For a breach of honor like that, there could be none.

Mentally, Jane shook herself. She shouldn't even consider listening to idle gossip about her husband's heir. She didn't need to hear whatever Trent had to say in disparagement of Constantine Black. It was none of her business, anyway.

"Well, I won't stay," said Trent, glancing at the house as if he'd rather like to stay, all the same. Surely he couldn't expect her to invite him in, after he'd behaved so rudely toward the new baron? "I merely came to inquire as to your health after yesterday."

"How kind," said Jane a little stiffly. "I am well, sir. As you see."

"Yes, I notice there is color in your cheeks today. That is excellent." He offered her his arm. "Would you care to walk back with me a little way?"

What could she do but acquiesce? She placed her hand on his arm and strolled with him. No pulse of awareness disturbed her when Trent was near. Not like it did with Constantine Black.

After a silence, he said, "What are your plans now, Lady Roxdale?"

She gave the answer she'd given Montford. "I shall stay here until I can hand the reins of the household over." *Until Constantine Black agrees to marry me,* she corrected silently.

He raised his brows. "Indeed? I assume you are well chaperoned."

"Lady Endicott. It's most obliging of her." The countess had not yet left her bedchamber after her hysterical episode last night, but Jane wouldn't mention that to Trent.

"What a pity you must leave Lazenby," he said. "You've done so much good here."

Yes, she would miss it, if she had to leave. With a deep breath of rain-scented air, Jane gazed around her at the wide terraces of fountains and gardens, at the lake and the romantic arch of the stone bridge, framed by weeping willows.

A gust of wind flurried her skirts, ruffling the lake's surface. The sun suddenly burst through the iron-gray clouds, dancing along the ripples like a shower of yellow diamonds. The deep green of the hills called to her in a whisper that scurried down the hedgerows.

Ah, she needed to ride. After a solid week of rain, it was time to clear her head and shake the dust of mourning from her feet.

"Is it only the estate you'll miss?" Trent's deep voice intruded on her thoughts. "You may be sure that *I* shall miss *you,* Jane."

Her gaze flew to his, but his expression was friendly, not amorous. She exhaled a relieved breath. "Of course. That goes without saying, I hope."

She put out her hand in kind but firm dismissal. "Thank you for the stroll, Mr. Trent. I have much to attend to this morning. I trust you'll excuse me."

He took her hand and held it warmly between his own. "Please believe . . . If there is anything you need, you have only to ask." His jaw hardened. "And if that blackguard offers you the least offense, you must tell me. I shall know how to deal with it."

Recovering her hand, Jane curtsied. "Thank you, Mr. Trent, but I'm sure there'll be no necessity."

When Jane reached the Hall, she found a great buzz of activity. Liveried footmen laden with baggage traipsed through the entrance hall and up the stairs in a seemingly endless stream of hunter's green velvet and silver lacing. Had the new baron begun inviting people here already?

"There you are, my dear!" A clear, crisp voice carried effortlessly through the cavernous space.

Oh, great heavens, what next? Slowly, Jane turned. "Lady Arden. How . . . unexpected."

Although she should have expected her, shouldn't she? Lady Arden was an inveterate matchmaker. If Jane wasn't mistaken, Frederick's relative had arrived to make sure Jane did her duty and married Constantine Black. That suited Jane very well, indeed. She needed all the help she could get.

The older woman rustled forward, arms outstretched, delicate drifts of lace dripping from her wrists like expensive cobwebs. No matter the circumstances, Lady Arden always appeared deliciously cool and elegant, not a wisp of her honey-brown hair out of place. Jane envied her poise to the bottom of her soul.

Instead of taking Jane's hands, Lady Arden enveloped her in a scented hug.

Drawing back, Lady Arden touched Jane's cheek. "You poor dear. How inconsiderate of Frederick to up and die in such a fashion." She swallowed and blinked hard. "The man had no sense of what is appropriate."

A small break in Lady Arden's voice robbed her words of callousness. Moisture glazed her eyes, and Jane realized she'd never seen the grande dame of the Black clan look so human.

"It was sudden," said Jane softly. "There was no time to prepare anyone, though we've known for the past year or so that it was only a matter of time."

Lady Arden nodded her understanding. "The funeral was yesterday, was it? Yes, I thought so."

"I'm sorry," Jane said. "I did write."

"Not your fault, dear. The letter didn't reach me in time. I was touring the Scottish holdings." Her ladyship stiffened her spine, as if determined to shake off her melancholy. "Shall we go somewhere we can be cozy? I would give my eyes for a cup of tea."

"My sitting room." Jane smiled, leading the way upstairs. She pulled the bell to order tea and invited Lady Arden to sit.

A smile playing about Lady Arden's mouth, she said, "I hear that rogue Constantine is here."

"Yes," said Jane. "I believe he's closeted with our estate agent and solicitor. Things have been left in rather an awful tangle."

"Really?" said Lady Arden. "How tiresome for him."

"Not only for him," Jane muttered.

"Oh, there is nothing so tedious as business. Let's not talk of dull matters." Lady Arden dismissed her relative's financial crisis with an elegant wave.

"So!" she continued, her eyes sparkling. "You've met the blackest of all the Blacks." Lady Arden propped her chin in her hand. "My dear Jane. Tell me all!"

CHAPTER EIGHT

Constantine glanced at the clock in the muniments room. Half an hour until the dinner gong.

He scanned the various maps, account books, legal documents, and other paraphernalia scattered over tables and stacked on chairs. They'd made good progress, considering. He had a much better picture now of exactly how his finances stood.

The time had sped by, which surprised him. Even more astonishing, he'd warmed to his task after a short while, assimilating information, drawing conclusions, issuing orders as if he'd been born to it.

Which of course, he had been, hadn't he? Broadmere was his birthright as the elder son and he'd been trained to manage it. Now, he found that habits ingrained young died the hardest deaths. Clearly, his schooling had not been in vain.

Papers crackled and fluttered as his cousin's land agent and solicitor pored over them. He'd worked them hard for more than six hours without a break. Time to let them go.

"We'll leave it there for today, gentlemen."

Murmuring assent, Mr. Greenslade and Mr. Larkin gathered up their papers.

"No, leave those," said Constantine. "I wish to go through them one more time."

The lawyer sent him a startled look. As if he'd suggested

he might fly to the moon rather than stick at this work until the wee hours, as he planned to do.

Constantine said gently, "Perhaps I'll find something you've missed."

He was clutching at straws, of course, trying to find some hidden value in the estate's account books. In fact, today's exercise had shown him more areas in which money needed to be spent.

To his credit, the solicitor merely blinked at the suggestion that such an infamous and indolent rogue could be more thorough than he. "Yes, my lord."

"Shall we say noon tomorrow?" said Constantine.

The lawyer bowed. "I am entirely at your disposal, my lord."

"For that, I thank you most heartily." He leaned one hip against the desk. "Where are you putting up?"

"At the King's Head."

"Yes?" Constantine raised one eyebrow. "I hear they serve an excellent breakfast there."

The solicitor permitted himself a smile. "Indeed, my lord."

Mr. Greenslade bowed himself out, but when the land agent made to do the same, Constantine said, "One moment, Larkin."

The man jumped and took on a hunted look, like a rabbit scenting a fox. The pale, carrot-topped fellow was far too thin for the prevailing fashion to do him any favors. He resembled nothing so much as a dandelion, with his stalky physique and puffball hair. The slightest breath of opposition and he'd blow away.

As far as Constantine could tell, the young man was conscientious but ineffectual. Had he been in Frederick's confidence? Unlikely. But then, one never knew.

"How long have you been employed here, Larkin?"

"Almost three years now, my lord."

"Would you say you were well acquainted with Lord Roxdale?"

Larkin's Adam's apple wobbled. "No, my lord. The former Lord Roxdale did not concern himself too closely with the day-to-day running of the estate."

"Left it all to you, did he?"

"N-not to me, my lord. To Mr. Jones. He was agent here until he . . . retired about a year ago."

"Ah. I remember Mr. Jones." He recalled all too vividly some scathing reprimands from the hardheaded steward, too. He'd most likely deserved them. As a boy, Constantine had always been up to mischief.

Jones still lived in a cottage on the estate. Constantine had seen his name in the account books. "I didn't realize he was so advanced in years. Had to be pensioned off, did he?"

But Larkin couldn't express an opinion on that. Or on anything else, for that matter. In the end, Constantine let him go and retreated to his own chamber to dress for dinner.

He pondered his estate agent. A well-meaning but diffident individual, if first impressions were anything to go by. Not at all what he required in a steward. He'd put the fellow to work in some other capacity. He needed a strong, shrewd character to manage the estate.

George sprang to mind as the perfect choice. But his brother had his own property to run. Constantine sighed. He must request his solicitor to draw up the necessary documents to transfer Broadmere into George's name. There was no doubt in his mind about that. Not even to escape marriage would he sell the family home out from under his brother.

His mind slid to the Ice Maiden. He'd told her the truth last night: he *hadn't* made up his mind whether to propose marriage to her. In light of his discoveries today, however, wedding her seemed the only option.

He needed to repay the debt on that mill or risk losing it altogether. One and a half months was too short a time to come up with that kind of money from thin air. He could carve up the estate and sell off some of the land, perhaps, but that would take time. Moreover, it went sorely against the grain. Tenants lived with the promise of eventually purchasing a long-term lease of the land they worked. It would go hard for morale if Constantine started selling that land out from under them.

And despite what *certain people* might think, he was fully cognizant of his duty to future generations. It was his obligation to preserve the estate, not sell bits of it off, willy-nilly. Wedding Lady Roxdale would be preferable to that.

Constantine's hands paused in the act of tying his cravat. The very notion of marriage curdled in his gut like sour milk. His utter refusal to wed when polite society dictated that he should had affected his life in disastrous ways. Ah, but he'd been raw, unsophisticated, passionate in his sense of betrayal. Everything had been black-and-white in those days.

He checked his reflection in the mirror, then allowed his valet to assist him with his coat. A deep, rich burgundy that hugged his shoulders like a besotted whore.

Constantine twitched a cuff into place. No, despite the grim picture he'd gained that day, he hadn't given up on finding a solution to his financial woes.

Tomorrow, he'd track down Frederick's old steward. What Jones didn't know about Lazenby wasn't worth knowing. If there was a way to save the mill, he'd wager Jones would hold the key.

By the end of the week, he should have a more accurate idea of the sum total of his assets. Aside from various investments in the funds, his personal fortune did not amount to much, for he didn't count Broadmere. A few prime-blooded horses, his carriages. His collection of curiosities might fetch something. He'd sent to town for an auctioneer who was versed in such matters.

Ah, hell, perhaps he'd sell off the family silver, as well.

Jane was not obliged to force a pleasant expression to her face when Constantine strolled into the drawing room that evening. Keeping company with two women of very strong and decided opinions like Lady Arden and Lady Endicott could be wearing on the nerves. Relief, as much as her determination to be charming, fueled her smile.

Nervous tension wound through her body. She'd donned the most becoming mourning gown she possessed, discarding the fichu she usually would have tucked into her neckline to cover her bosom. Her hair . . . She still wasn't sure about it. Her maid assured her this style was all the crack in London. It felt loose and pretty, almost decadent, as if it might tumble down around her shoulders at any moment. Jane resisted putting her hand up to make sure her curls were secure.

Constantine halted on the threshold, his eyebrows lifting in surprise.

He moved forward. "Good evening, Cousin Jane." Constantine bowed over her hand in the correct manner. He didn't press her fingers or seek to kiss them, but the fleeting contact was quite enough to make her senses spring to awareness.

She hoped she concealed her irrational and wholly inconvenient response, but his eyes glittered wickedly as they quizzed her.

"You looked genuinely happy to see me, just now," he murmured. "Are you feeling unwell?"

"There you are, Constantine!"

At the sound of that musical voice, Constantine's head jerked up. He looked beyond Jane, to the far side of the drawing room.

"Oh, hell," he muttered.

Jane stifled a spurt of laughter. Constantine covered his exclamation of dismay with a cough and moved forward to greet his relatives.

"Lady Arden." He bowed and raised her hand to his lips. "You grow lovelier every time I see you."

Eyes dancing, Lady Arden said, "Don't think you can turn me up sweet after all these years, you rogue. I'm immune to your charm."

Which was absolute rot, of course. Jane couldn't help but enjoy watching the unflappable Lady Arden flutter a little at Constantine's attentions.

He even managed to turn Lady Endicott up sweet, a feat Jane would never have thought possible. Jane had listened to the countess rant about Constantine's lack of manners, morals, and filial feeling for the last half hour. Yet, a few adroit compliments from Constantine and his aunt sang a sweeter tune.

At dinner, they sat informally, with Constantine at the head of the table, Jane at his right hand, Lady Arden and Lady Endicott at his left. Soon, the older ladies had put their heads together, catching up on family gossip, leaving Jane and Constantine to their own devices. Jane braced herself for flirtation, but Constantine offered her none, confining his conversation to neutral topics until dinner was served.

As the footmen trooped in with silver salvers and serving dishes, Jane relaxed a little. Perhaps, with his female relatives within earshot, Constantine would behave himself.

Constantine accepted service from a dish of buttered lobster. "I suppose you miss your cousins, now that they're gone."

If he implied she ought to follow their lead, Jane chose to seem oblivious to the hint. "Yes, they are very dear to me."

He tilted his head, as if considering her. "The duke is formidable. What was it like, growing up under his roof?"

"His Grace didn't have an awful lot to do with us when we were children," said Jane. "My cousins and I were left to our own devices for much of the time." She considered. "I suppose living at Harcourt was rather fun. The boys teased us mercilessly, of course. But we wreaked our revenge. Cecily was particularly ingenious at thinking up ways to make them pay for their crimes."

Constantine nodded to a footman, who poured claret. "I'd gathered Lady Cecily was rather a handful."

"Undoubtedly. But so charming and funny with it that no one can withstand her. She is not out yet, strictly speaking, but she has been betrothed to the Duke of Norland since the cradle, so there is no need for undue haste."

"And Lady Rosamund? I suppose her marriage is arranged also. Such a beauty would have been snapped up in her first Season, otherwise."

He could not fail to notice Rosamund's beauty, of course. That made Jane a little wistful. "She is remarkably lovely, isn't she? Lady Rosamund is to wed the Earl of Tregarth. Do you know him?"

"I think so. He's a deVere, isn't he?" He leaned over to murmur, "Don't mention that name in Lady Arden's hearing. The deVeres and the Blacks have been mortal enemies for centuries."

Constantine's warm breath tickled her ear, sending a shiver down her spine. To cover her reaction, she forced a smile. "No, really? I thought that sort of thing had died out in Elizabethan times. The Montagues and the Capulets and all that."

"Oh, not at all. The old rivalries are alive and well, even if they find expression in a less violent manner these days." His jaw hardened the slightest amount. "Most of the time."

Had Constantine ever fought a duel? Perhaps over that lady he'd loved and abandoned . . . ? No. She would not think about that lady tonight.

Jane accepted service from various dishes, scarcely noticing what they were. Regardless of the harmless nature of their conversation, she couldn't fail to be aware of Constantine's every movement and expression. Apprehension tied her stomach in knots. She couldn't eat a bite.

"Did none of you Westruther maidens pine for love?" asked Constantine. "Three fine, intelligent women must have found such gothic arrangements quite irksome, surely."

Irksome? He didn't know the half of it. She lifted one shoulder in a shrug. "A Westruther does not expect love in marriage. In fact, I—I believe it must be more comfortable for both parties that way."

Constantine regarded her for a moment as if he wanted to

make some remark. Then he seemed to change his mind and merely gestured with his fork. "You should try the veal fricassee. It's superb."

She glanced down at her plate, as yet untouched. Ordinarily, food held little interest for her. In fact, most often she had to be reminded to take sustenance.

"You sound just like my old nurse, urging me to eat," she said, taking up her cutlery. What an inappropriate comparison! Anyone less like plump, homely old Nurse than the wild, beautiful man next to her would be difficult to find.

"Eating well is one of life's great pleasures," said Constantine. "Unlike some other enjoyable vices, it has the added advantage of not hurting anyone." He shrugged. "Why not indulge?"

The slight rasp in his low voice played over her nerves like a bow on violin strings. She wondered if his invitation extended only to gastronomical delights. Then she noticed that his eyes gleamed with devilry and she became quite certain that it did not.

Jane surveyed her plate with a keener understanding of how Eve must have felt when confronted with an apple-wielding snake.

With a hint of defiance, she pressed the tines of her fork into a sliver of veal and raised the morsel to her mouth. She barely repressed a groan as the explosion of flavor thrilled her taste buds. It was almost too intense a sensation after the blandness of the fare she'd grown accustomed to.

"Well?" he demanded.

She swallowed, schooling her face to indifference.

"Perfectly adequate," she managed.

His brows drew together. *"Adequate?"*

Jane strove to preserve an innocent front. He must have read something of the truth in her expression, however, because a slow smile spread over Constantine's face. His gaze seemed to sharpen on her mouth. Did she have a spot of sauce there? Self-conscious, she licked her lips.

His eyes heated, but his voice remained nonchalant. "I

would berate you for stifling the talents of a true master, Lady Roxdale, but it's clear to me that you are more to be pitied." He shook his head. "*Adequate.* Do not pass on that sentiment to Cook. She'd give notice on the spot, and I'd be forced to follow."

Jane savored another mouthful, valiantly suppressing a sigh of appreciation. He was right; she'd not realized what she was missing. Frederick's doctor had forbidden him rich food years ago. It would have been a little unsporting to partake of subtle French delicacies while Frederick suffered through boiled mutton and peas.

"I believe Cook will have to content herself with your more fulsome praise, sir," she said, taking a sip of wine. She frowned in agreeable surprise. "Is this from our cellars?"

"I'd never insult Marthe's creations with inferior wine." He reached for his glass. "A good claret is meant to be enjoyed, not hoarded like miser's gold."

"You are a hedonist," she said, with a hint of reproof.

"A sensualist," he corrected. "I take pleasure where I find it."

Spoken in that husky tone of his, the words made heat curl inside her. She felt breathless, off balance, unsure. And more convinced than before that she'd acted wisely by refusing to admit how revelatory this meal had been.

The candlelight burnished Constantine's skin to bronze, highlighted the sculpted edges of his cheekbones, the strong lines of his jaw. She became fascinated with his fingers as they toyed with the stem of his wine glass. Long and tapering, with a subtle strength in the flex of them. The white ruffle of his cuff fell elegantly against his broad, tanned hand.

He raised the wine and drank deeply. Their gazes caught and held.

Lady Endicott's strident voice shattered this strange tension. "Constantine! Jane! Did you hear what I said?"

Annoyance flickered across Constantine's features. Jane was conscious of irritation herself, yet she ought to thank the countess for deliverance.

Without waiting for an answer, the countess barreled on. "Lady Arden has just given me the most alarming news from Town." She turned her glare upon the other lady. "Really, Emma, I don't know why you didn't think to mention it before. Dreadful harpy with her talons in my son," she muttered. "I will not have it! Jane," she added, "I must return to London. I am sorry if this leaves you in a difficult position, my dear, but this is important!"

Constantine blinked. "You are leaving us, Aunt?" He could scarcely believe his good fortune.

"At first light!" The lady threw down her napkin and a footman leaped to service as she rose from her chair. "I must see to packing."

Lady Arden airily waved a hand. "You must do as you see fit, Griselda. To be sure, we shall manage here without you."

Looking suspiciously innocent, Lady Arden raised her wine glass to her lips as the older woman bustled from the room.

Constantine regarded his redoubtable relative with his brows raised. She was up to something. She always was. An inveterate matchmaker, Lady Arden had, of course, fixed her sights on him and Jane.

A beatific smile was all the response Lady Arden gave his look of inquiry. "That's settled, then."

"But ma'am," said Jane, "if Lady Endicott leaves for London on the morrow, who will stay to lend me countenance? You'll agree it's improper for me to remain here alone with Constantine."

"As I said, it sounds like an excellent plan." Constantine grinned and received a cool gray glance. Damned if he hadn't thought she'd softened a little toward him this evening, but that look told him he had a long way to go yet.

Lady Arden threw up her hands. "Of course you will not stay here alone with this rogue, my dear! *I* shall remain at Lazenby for the present. I'm sure the duke would expect it."

"You?" said Constantine, an incredulous smile playing about his mouth. "Kick your dainty heels in the country for weeks on end in spring, of all seasons? I should like to see that."

"I was raised in Cambridgeshire, I'll have you know." Lady Arden sniffed. "A few pigs and horses won't scare me."

"Sheep." Jane brought her glass to her mouth to hide a smile. "We run sheep at Lazenby."

"Well, of course you do, dear. It's the Cotswolds, isn't it?" Lady Arden picked up her knife and fork. "I shall be charmed to reacquaint myself with the place."

Jane said, "Well, that's settled, then. My thanks, ma'am. I don't know what I should have done without you."

The two of them bent speculative gazes upon Constantine.

Well, of course. It didn't take a genius to guess they were in league against him. Clearly, if Lady Arden had her way—as she so often did—his days as a bachelor were numbered.

Still, he'd fought his way clear of matrimony against more numerous and determined opponents than his dinner companions. He wouldn't concede victory yet.

He offered them a bland smile in return.

As the ladies resumed their conversation, Constantine contemplated Jane. She'd done something different with her hair tonight. It was softer, more feminine. Deep swirls of auburn-tinted tresses, caught up almost casually, as if she'd just risen from her bed. The bare swells of her breasts rose and fell gently as she breathed. Around her throat, a set of jet beads gleamed, contrasting with the whiteness of her skin.

She'd surprised him tonight. He hadn't missed the fleeting expression of bliss on her face when she'd tasted Marthe's cooking. He burned to put that rapture there himself, in the most intimate of ways.

The memory of that look continued to tantalize him throughout the evening. He coveted it, wanted to steal it for his own.

It shocked him, the intensity of that craving. That so cool

a creature should inspire such a burning need in him. Oh, on the surface, Jane was all chilly aristocratic arrogance. He'd made a game of needling her, tapping tiny chinks in that icy façade. But tonight, he'd seen passionate depths to her that even he hadn't suspected.

He must take care he didn't drown in them.

Tonight.

Jane gripped her hands together, pacing the floor of her bedchamber in agitation.

Yes, it must be tonight. This very minute, in fact. If she didn't do it now, her courage would fail her utterly.

She was going to kiss Constantine Black. Or rather, she would let *him* kiss *her.*

Her heart pounded against her rib cage at the thought.

Why did the prospect of kissing Constantine Black terrify her? One meager kiss was not much to give in return for the chance to keep Luke. Yet, she had the stirring, uncomfortable suspicion there would be nothing at all meager about Constantine Black's kiss.

After failing at every attempt, Jane had been at a loss to know how to persuade Constantine to take her as a wife. How did ladies ordinarily entice gentlemen to offer for them? She didn't think he'd be swayed by her talent at needlework or her skill in managing the household accounts. The more pressing concerns of forfeiture and bankruptcy hadn't convinced him to wed her.

Seduce him, Cecily had said. Even if Jane hadn't been thoroughly opposed to the idea, seducing the new baron would be futile, given his scandalous past. Constantine Black did not marry his lovers, even to save them—and himself—from disgrace.

What, then, could she do to make Constantine *want* to marry her?

Only one answer presented itself. It shocked her that she would even consider it, much less take steps to implement such a stratagem. But Luke was worth any sacrifice, even the risk of ruining her reputation.

At dinner, Jane had noticed Constantine staring at her mouth, his eyes hot with desire. Stupid as she was at reading men, even she couldn't fail to see this as a sign. He wanted, quite desperately, to kiss her.

The most foreign and surprising thrill of power scintillated through her. She couldn't persuade Constantine into marriage by reasoned argument or shame him into wedding her, either.

Might she *tempt* him into it? Make him so wild for her that he would marry her simply to get into her bed?

It was a bold stratagem, one she was hopelessly unqualified to employ. It was underhanded, contemptible, even. But what other course was open to her at this point?

Jane hesitated, her hand closing on the doorknob. She took a deep, shaky breath. Before doubt could creep in and corrode her resolve, she wrenched open the door and went in search of Constantine.

She found him in the muniments room, of all places, writing what appeared to be a letter in a firm, bold hand. She saw a pile of correspondence addressed in that same hand stacked by his elbow.

So he'd been attending to business since he'd excused himself after dinner. She'd expected to discover him in the library, draining the brandy decanter and brandishing a cheroot.

Jane hovered on the threshold, reluctant to break his concentration. While she debated whether to wait or obey the most craven impulse to escape, Constantine signed the letter with a flourish and looked up.

"Jane." Slowly, he rose to his feet. "Come in."

She found herself watching *his* lips as they formed those few syllables. The husky timbre of his voice made his words of welcome sound like an invitation to sin. Or did she imagine that, given her own wicked intentions? Her nerves thrummed with fearful anticipation.

Courage, Jane. She must not forget that she did this for Luke.

With an effort, she lifted her chin and prepared to go ahead with her plan.

Suddenly, she realized she'd no earthly idea how to broach the subject with him. Should she try some sort of physical overture? That seemed far too bold. Perhaps she ought to wait for him to take the lead. But how would he know that she'd changed her mind? She'd spurned his advances in the garden in no uncertain terms.

His brows lifted a fraction. "Did you want something, perhaps?"

The perfect opening. She seized it. "Yes, I . . ." She gasped. "I want you to kiss me," she blurted out.

Heat surged upward, filling her cheeks, scalding her ears. Her heart was having palpitations. Could one die from sheer embarrassment?

For many moments, Constantine didn't answer. His fingertips drummed on the surface of his desk as he searched her face.

Miserably aware that she'd been as subtle as a brick, Jane choked out a hasty apology and turned to go.

"Wait."

Jane halted, her head bowed. She didn't dare to look at him. She waited, her chest rising and falling rapidly with each breath. Would he grant her request despite the inept way she'd phrased it?

She closed her eyes. *I am simply no good at this.*

When he spoke again, he stood directly behind her. "Don't run away." His tone swept over her skin like raw silk.

Jane swallowed hard, groping for her courage, but it slipped through her fingers and flitted away, eluding her grasp. She ought to have known she couldn't handle this, couldn't handle *him*.

The warmth of Constantine's breath stirred the curls at her nape. "Turn around and look at me," he commanded.

She obeyed him. Her eyelids seemed weighted. She

couldn't raise her gaze past his mouth. A mouth that had flattened to a hard, uncompromising line.

Shaken, she did look up then. His eyes no longer held an appreciative glow. They glittered, hard as emeralds. "This is a ploy, isn't it?" he said. "You've come here to offer your kisses like some sort of virgin sacrifice. Haven't you, Jane?"

Alarm rocketed through her. "No! Of course n—"

"Just how far would you go to get my ring on your finger?" His regard was direct and unfettered. It raked her body, lingering at her breasts.

Inwardly, she shuddered, but not with revulsion.

"Believe me," he said, "you won't succeed."

She knew Constantine Black was shameless. He was a scoundrel of the first order. He'd slaked his lust on an innocent girl, then refused to marry her. He would mete out the same treatment to her.

If she allowed it.

The thought made her spine stiffen. Who was he to judge her actions? At least *her* motives were pure.

And she couldn't afford to back down now.

Recalling how he'd reacted when she'd licked her lips at the dinner table, Jane quickly ran her tongue over them. She hoped she didn't look foolish.

His muttered obscenity should have shocked her, but triumph lifted her spirits. Men like Constantine were slaves to their passions, weren't they? All she needed to do was present him with temptation and his male urges would do the rest.

Her heart thumping in her throat, she closed the distance between them with one, deliberate step.

Quick as thought, he gripped her chin and tilted her head up so their gazes clashed.

"Don't try it." His thumb stroked along her lower lip, sending a dart of heat to quiver in her loins. "I won't stop at ravishing that pretty mouth of yours."

A challenge shimmered in the air between them.

Jane struggled to clear her brain. She knew he wouldn't

force himself on her. That being so, his threat was an empty one, wasn't it? He couldn't *make* her want more than kisses. She'd call a halt if he moved beyond the safety of a chaste embrace.

So what did she have to fear? His powers of persuasion? Or her own weakness?

As she stared up at him, not moving, Constantine's features darkened with intent. His perfectly sculpted lips parted. Curiosity, excitement, and strongest of all, fear, jangled inside as he bent toward her. He moved so slowly that she marked a dozen panicked heartbeats before she felt the whisper of his breath on her lips.

The heat of his body surrounded her; his presence bound her with a sensual spell. The only parts of him that touched her were his breath and the finger and thumb that tilted her chin. Yet, she felt panicky and trapped.

As his mouth crushed down on hers, the panic rose up to choke her. Fear shuddered through her body. She *couldn't*! Jerking her head away with a strangled cry, Jane whirled on her heel and fled.

Later, Constantine stood on the terrace outside the library, indulging in the vice that had so offended his hostess the first time they'd met.

The night was so dark as to be almost black. He could make out very little of the landscape through the persistent drizzle. A damp wind blew; the air was chill. He drew on his cigarillo. *Ah, the joys of spring.*

The London Season would soon be in full flight. Strange. He didn't miss Town with its variety and its diversions. His cronies would be trawling the seas of sharp-eyed ladies and accommodating courtesans about now, selecting this Season's mistress or that night's lover, or pursuing random, anonymous encounters in the Haymarket and Covent Garden.

No, he didn't miss all that. But he'd been celibate too

long for a man of his temperament. Which made his rejection of Jane's little gambit tonight distinctly unsettling. At another time, with another woman, he would have accepted what little she offered, murmured sweet reassurance as he beguiled her into giving him everything he desired. He would not—most definitely *not*—have warned her off.

He thought of Jane with her dangerous schemes and where they might lead and took a contemplative drag of smoke.

"Here you are, my dear." A low, feminine voice spoke behind him.

He turned to see Lady Arden step onto the terrace. Her bright eyes were alert, sparkling with determination. A lady on a mission.

Constantine sighed. He was in for it now.

Out of politeness, he indicated his cigarillo. "Do you mind?"

"Not at all," she replied, moving toward him. She hesitated. "I am glad to have the chance to speak with you alone."

He gave a grim smile. "I suppose I can guess the reason behind Lady Endicott's dismissal."

"I did *not* dismiss her."

"No, you simply told her some designing woman has her claws in that precious son of hers. Nothing more likely to send her hotfooting it to Town." He extended an arm beyond the balustrade and tapped ash over the side. "It must be obvious, even to Lady Roxdale, what you are about."

"She'd have to be a ninny not to guess," agreed Lady Arden. She glanced at him. "You are minded to be stubborn, aren't you?"

His shoulders shook. "Stubborn? I?"

Lady Arden's lips pressed together in impatience. "But you *must* marry her! Surely even you can see that. I hear there is a massive debt due on the mill and no funds to repay it."

"Yes, that's right." He'd done his utmost to find the necessary funds. So far, he'd failed.

There was always the stock exchange, of course, and he'd sent instructions to his broker that day. But counting on a large return on a few high-risk investments to save him would be almost as foolhardy as relying on the gaming tables. He needed a windfall, and soon.

"Jane seems to like you," said Lady Arden. "That, I had not expected."

His smile had a bitter edge. "Most women love a rake, I'm told."

"Not women like Jane," said Lady Arden seriously. "Still, I applaud her for having the sense not to cavil at doing what must be done. She is a good, dutiful girl. She will do what's right."

"And you're here to see to it that she has every opportunity to do so," he murmured.

"At the least, I shall not hinder the process, as Griselda would have done. What possessed you to ask her to stay?"

"What do you think I had to say in the matter?" He shook his head. "Besides, if I hadn't agreed to let Griselda remain, Cousin Jane might have left for Town with the duke. That would not have done."

"No." She eyed him for a moment in silence. Then she turned to gaze out at the night, tapping her fingertips on the balustrade.

He could almost see the cogs whirring in that intricate mind of hers. "Allow me to chart my own course, ma'am."

She hesitated, then turned to face him. "Very well. I shall . . . facilitate. But for the moment, I shall not interfere." *Let us see how well you do,* was her unspoken challenge.

"Be assured, I'm fully sensible of my obligations."

"I'm glad of it. And a touch surprised. I thought I had my work cut out for me with you." She regarded him narrowly. "You haven't developed a *tendre* for her, have you? That would never do."

His hesitation made her eyes widen a little. Then he said, "God forbid."

Lady Arden's brow furrowed. Perhaps she recalled the last time he'd dallied with a respectable lady who wanted marriage. "Take care what you are about, Constantine."

He took a long drag of smoke and blew it into the night. "Oh, yes," he said. "I will."

CHAPTER NINE

"J ones!" Constantine dismounted and held out his hand. "I'm obliged to you for meeting me."

The grumpy old fellow appeared reluctant to shake hands with Constantine, but after an internal struggle, he clasped it briefly. "I's put out ter grass two year ago, my lord."

Constantine recognized by the broadening of the man's accent that he was not minded to be cooperative. He couldn't blame Jones for being less than pleased to have him as landlord in these parts. As a boy, Constantine had given him no end of trouble with his pranks.

That aside, Constantine needed his help. And if he knew the former steward's interfering bent, it wouldn't be long before Jones would overcome his reluctance and start ordering him about like a schoolboy again.

"Jones, I need your advice."

The older man rubbed his craggy jaw with the side of his thumb. "Don't know what ye think I'm able to tell ye."

Constantine laughed. "Oh, don't give me that. I'll wager you've forgotten more than I'll learn in a lifetime about running this estate." He squinted upward. "I want to consult you about many things, but my primary concern at the moment is this mill." They both surveyed the imposing structure, nestled at the foot of the valley.

The building had once been the focus of a thriving industry. To Constantine's shock, Larkin had informed him that the mill stood empty now, disused. He'd not quite believed it until he'd ridden up here and found the place deserted. The stream that had powered the woolen mill had dried to a trickle. Was this why Frederick had so blithely mortgaged the place? Perhaps he hadn't cared if he forfeited it.

"Aye," said Jones, rubbing his cheek with the side of his thumb. "A great shame, that was. All the weavers out of work, and forced to beg for a place up at Bronson's. On a fraction of the pay, mind."

"You mean the mill on Adam Trent's land?"

"That's right. He don't run the mill himself, though. Leases it to a fellow called Bronson. Never seen about these parts, lets his foreman manage the place. But Bronson's a hard man. Took his chance to pay less and make more profit when the workers here were turned away." Jones shrugged. "Where else could they go?"

Constantine was surprised that other work couldn't be found for them on the estate, if the conditions at Bronson's were so intolerable. Why hadn't Frederick done something?

A trickle of water flowed through the streambed, a meager legacy from the recent downpour. Not nearly enough to power a mill. "I want to know what can be done to make this mill run again, Jones. Build a reservoir, divert another tributary. I don't know. Something."

Constantine pulled off his hat and shook droplets of water from its brim. "It never stops raining in this place. I can't believe there's no water to power my mill."

"As to that, my lord . . ." Jones hesitated, perhaps torn between his own desire to see the mill back in operation and his natural abhorrence of giving Constantine assistance.

"Come, Jones, I'm depending on you," said Constantine. "Young Larkin is a good fellow but hasn't an ounce of your judgment. If you want your old position back, it's yours. And if you know something, tell me."

Constantine saw at once that the older man was mollified by his promises. Perhaps his dismissal had wounded the man's pride.

Jones nodded. "Well, my lord, there's a trick these mill owners have of making sure the competition goes out of business. You see Bronson's mill?" He pointed to another stone building in the distance, farther up the valley. "They's upstream from this'n. So . . ." He spread his hands.

Constantine frowned, his jaw tightening. "Do you mean to tell me the blackguard has dammed this stream so our mill doesn't get any water?"

"Aye, that's about the size of it." He tapped the side of his nose. "Or at least, that's a way I know of making sure other mills suffer."

"Good God!" Fury possessed Constantine. Why had no one else thought of this? Why hadn't that idiot Frederick?

"Did you tell my cousin of your suspicions?" he demanded.

Jones regarded him with scorn. "'Course I did. He wouldn't listen. Didn't want to know." He shrugged a shoulder. "Master Frederick never did hold with the mill."

Constantine swore. That would be Frederick all over, refusing to take an interest in an enterprise that didn't fit with his notions of gentlemanly pursuits. One might collect rent from tenants but God forbid one pursued income from trade. His father hadn't been so high in the instep.

"Do you know this Bronson's direction?" said Constantine.

"That I don't. But Mr. Trent will."

Grim-faced, Constantine mounted his horse. "I'm going up the valley to see for myself. And then I'll hear what our neighbor has to say."

Constantine strode into Adam Trent's house, ignoring the bleating from his butler. "In the breakfast parlor, is he? Thank you, I'll find my own way."

He discovered Adam Trent in the south parlor discussing a breakfast of ham and eggs.

Constantine slammed his hand on the table, making the flatware jump. "I want a word with you!"

Trent looked up in astonishment, then fury dawned. "Good God, Black! What do you mean by bursting in on me like this? I ought to call you out!"

"It's Roxdale to you," growled Constantine. "And you'd be wise to keep your challenges to yourself until you hear what I have to say. I've just come from Bronson's mill."

Trent's eyes lost none of their righteous outrage. "And? Is that supposed to mean something to me?"

"It damned well will mean something to you! Your tenant, Bronson, has put countless Lazenby men out of work. He has dammed the stream that used to flow down to our mill, making it impossible to power it."

"I—I knew nothing of this," stammered Trent, rising. "It must be a mistake."

"No mistake. I saw it with my own eyes." Constantine paused, his chest rising and falling. "Well? What are you going to do about it?"

Trent blinked at him. "Why, I . . . What can I do?"

Constantine spoke through his teeth. "Order him to get rid of that dam so that my workers can come back and earn a decent livelihood! The thing's badly constructed and full to bursting with all the rain we've had. If you can't think of my people, think of your own. I wouldn't wager a groat against the whole structure collapsing with the next downpour."

"The mill is Bronson's responsibility. I—"

"And your tenants are yours!" said Constantine. "Order Bronson to come down here or take care of it yourself, I don't care. Have that dam dismantled within the week or I'll be up there to do it with my own hands. Good day to you!"

His mouth tightening, Trent threw down his napkin and shot to his feet. "If you set foot on my lands again, Black, I'll have you arrested for trespass. And don't think I won't do it! I'd like nothing better than to see you rot in jail."

The urge to smash his fist into Trent's self-righteous face nearly got the better of Constantine. But that had always been his problem, hadn't it, acting on impulse? Trent would point to the new Lord Roxdale's barbarous behavior and Trent's own culpability would be forgotten. With the utmost restraint, Constantine held back.

"I see I was right about you, Trent," he said. "You haven't changed a bit."

Constantine returned from his ride in a towering rage. He'd half a mind to take some men up to Bronson's mill now and tear down the dam himself. Certainly, Trent's parting shot might have been calculated to goad him into doing just that.

But Constantine was no longer a hotheaded, impetuous youth who could be manipulated into doing foolish things just to prove he had the courage. The mill—men and women's livelihoods—were more important than his pride.

Given the state of that dam, if it were not dismantled correctly, it might flood Bronson's mill and the settlement of cottages surrounding it. No, the matter needed to be approached with care. He'd send for an engineer from Bristol if he couldn't get satisfaction from Trent. In fact, he'd best summon one anyway, to ensure whatever work was carried out there was done properly.

He summoned Greenslade and instructed him accordingly. The solicitor bowed and was about to leave, when Constantine bethought himself of something.

"One moment, Mr. Greenslade. You have a copy of the mortgage over the mill, don't you?"

"Yes, my lord. Shall I fetch it?"

"No, that's not necessary. The mortgagee is a company called Bronson and Company, is it not?"

The solicitor pushed his spectacles up his nose. "Yes, I believe it is."

"Can you find out who the directors and shareholders are and whatever background detail you might glean about them? I wish to know exactly who I'm dealing with."

"Of course, my lord. I shall inquire."

Constantine dismissed him with thanks and went upstairs to change.

When Constantine reached the master suite, he found it buzzing with activity. His belongings had arrived by cart from London; it was time to do the thing properly and move in.

With great reluctance, he'd sent orders for the most valuable items in his collection to be sold. The prices they fetched weren't enough, but the proceeds would at least tide him over while he raised money to repay the loan. What remained were mere curiosities, but none the less valuable in his eyes.

The sight of so many treasured and familiar pieces lightened his mood somewhat. At least, it saved him from being obliged to hit someone.

He was a great believer in starting as one meant to go on, which encompassed both his role as lord of Lazenby Hall and his intention of enticing Lady Roxdale into his bed. He'd delay no further in taking over the suite of rooms traditionally occupied by the master of the house.

A pair of footmen grunted, heaving a great old trunk between them.

"Ah, good," said Constantine. "That will go here, in the antechamber."

The trunk contained curiosities and treasures he'd collected over the years. He liked to have them close, for what was the use of such things locked away in cabinets, gathering dust? He liked to handle them often and without ceremony. The antechamber to his bedroom, with its cozy atmosphere, seemed the perfect place to enjoy them.

Next came a suit of armor that went by the name of Oswald. He gave Oswald's helmet an affectionate pat and watched another three footmen totter along under the weight of a man-sized marble nose, allegedly broken from an ancient Greek statue.

"Hmm," said Constantine, as they struggled through the

door. "Perhaps you'd better take that along to the gallery and find a place for it. I'm not sure it helps achieve the right ambience here."

"Yes, my lord." With a concert of grunts, the footmen tottered away.

Constantine strode through the aperture to the bedchamber. This room pleased him exceedingly. He'd ordered the plain hangings and drapes removed and replaced them with his own lush silks, velvets, and brocades in hunter's green, black, and silver—the colors of the Blacks. The total effect was tastefully exotic, luxurious but by no means effeminate.

He took in the grand ancestral bed with its heavily carved mahogany posts and curled his lip. "That will have to go," he muttered. "But it's a start, at any rate."

He needed to unpack the awaiting trunk and find some of the pieces he wanted for the bedchamber. As he walked through to the antechamber, a voice hailed him from the doorway.

A movement caught his eye. Constantine turned to see Luke hovering on the threshold.

"Hello, there."

The boy hesitated, and Constantine saw that he held something gingerly in his cupped hands, as if it were delicate and precious.

Constantine smiled at him. "Come in, Luke. I won't bite. What have you there?"

"I found this downstairs." Luke showed him a small jade sphere.

His Chinese puzzle ball. How had that fallen free of its case? "Where was it?"

"On the drive. Next to the furniture cart."

"Thank you." Constantine took the jade and blew on it gently, ridding it of a wisp of straw and the small particles of seashells that clung to it from its ignominious roll on the drive outside. He smoothed his fingertips over the intricately carved surface, checking it for damage.

Discovering none, he said again, "My thanks. I should not have liked to lose this."

He set the jade curiosity on a lacquered side table pending a better arrangement.

Constantine saw Luke glance longingly over at the trunk that now stood open in the corner of the sitting room, displaying its treasures like pirate's booty.

He smiled. "Would you like to see what I have in there?"

Luke's face lit. "By Jupiter, wouldn't I just?" Then his smile faded. "Oh. But I'm due to take my lessons now." His shoulders slumped.

"Lessons?"

Luke nodded. "I don't mind history so much. It's the Latin," he said despondently. "And mathematics, too. Four hours every day. It's awfully hard on a fellow."

Constantine was inclined to agree. "Well, you can tell your tutor I gave you a holiday." He called to a maid who bustled past and instructed her to inform Luke's tutor that he wasn't needed.

"Come," he said to Luke. "You can help me unpack."

The boy gazed up at him with those big, dark eyes as if he'd handed him the moon. Then he darted a glance after the departing maid. "But . . . but you can't do that."

Constantine lifted his brows. "Oh? Who says I can't?"

"Aunt Jane—"

"You may leave Aunt Jane to me," said Constantine. He would speak to her about reducing this punishing academic schedule. Certainly, Luke ought to be prepared for the rigors of a public school education, but driving the boy too hard would surely give him a distaste for the business. Besides, there was more to learn about life than could be found in a Latin lexicon. As Constantine was about to demonstrate.

He kneeled in front of the trunk and reached in, handing various items to Luke, explaining them as he went. He never bought anything simply to own the object itself. Every piece had a rich history, spoke of exotic lands and strange customs.

And when he owned that piece, he owned a small slice of history, too.

Constantine didn't have much experience of boys Luke's age, but he seemed a curious, intelligent child. That Luke shared his own wonder in the collection pleased him. He'd expected the novelty to pall on such a small boy much sooner.

A maid interrupted them. "My lord, beggin' your pardon, but where to put the malachite table?"

"Ah." He rose to his feet. "Excuse me a moment." He indicated the trunk with a wave of his hand. "Have a rummage. See if anything else interests you."

He returned to find Luke examining a telescope-shaped object.

"Ah, you found the kaleidoscope, did you? Do you know how it works?"

Luke shook his head.

"Put this end up to your eye and close the other one. Like that, yes." He watched Luke squint into the lens. "Now, turn this bit, here." He reached out and gently twisted the end of the toy.

The boy crowed in delight as all those colorful fragments of glass fell into new patterns. He became absorbed in the kaleidoscope while Constantine sorted through the jumble left in the trunk.

Finally, he came up with what he'd been looking for. A toy from his own childhood, a reminder of happier days.

"Tell me, Luke," said Constantine. "Have you ever played fox and geese?"

Jane had searched high and low for Luke all over the house before concluding that the scamp had most likely taken off for the village or some more amusing pursuit than sitting with his tutor. The last place she'd expected to find him was in Frederick's sitting room.

Constantine's sitting room, she corrected herself, taking in the scene.

Constantine looked like a sultan or a pasha lying there on the carpet, completely at his ease. Exotic treasures lay scattered around him like the spoils of war or offerings from foreign princes eager to win his favor. In the midst of all this paraphernalia, he and Luke seemed to be engaged in some sort of game.

"There you are, Luke!" Jane said, putting her hands on her hips.

From his prone position on the floor, Constantine looked up through a lock of hair that had fallen over his brow. Then he smiled at her, a slow, inviting smile. A hot stab of excitement pierced her belly.

She'd managed to avoid being private with him since that horrifyingly embarrassing incident in the muniments room. At the time, she'd been furious with herself for failing to carry through her plan to kiss Constantine. Upon reflection, she'd realized he'd never intended to cede any power to her in their relationship. Her efforts had been for nothing.

He'd *meant* to frighten her away.

Constantine rose to his feet, running a hand through his hair to tame it. Once more the correct English gentleman— at least on the surface.

It took Jane a few moments to retrieve her exasperation. She turned to her charge. "Luke, have you any idea what time it is?"

Luke scrambled to his feet. "Sorry, Aunt Jane. Lord Roxdale was teaching me to play fox and geese." An impish smile flickered. "I beat him."

"Beginner's luck!" protested Constantine, ruffling the lad's hair.

How had Constantine built such easy rapport with Luke in so short a time? She'd predicted he'd have no facility with children, but clearly she'd been mistaken. That was a good thing, she told herself, smothering an ignoble spurt of fear.

"Luke, you were due to start your lessons an hour ago." She meant it as a gentle reproof but the rascal appeared far from chastened. His eyes shone as he looked up at Constantine. He must deem the results of his truancy worth her scolds.

She persisted. "Nurse says Mr. Potts went home but I've sent a message for him to return at once. Go to the schoolroom now, please, and wait for him there."

Luke scowled. "But Aunt—"

"You'd best do as Aunt Jane says," said Constantine. "Don't worry. I'll explain everything."

The boy looked as if he might argue, but with a note of finality to his voice, Constantine said, "Go now."

At Luke's crestfallen look, Constantine smiled. "You will allow me a rematch at fox and geese, won't you?"

Luke plucked up at that. He chuckled. "'Course, sir. I'll give you another thrashing."

The boy took himself off, leaving Constantine alone with Jane.

Eyes twinkling, Constantine watched him go. "A fine little fellow. You are to be complimented."

Her chest warmed with pride. "Yes. Yes, he is. I take no credit for it, though. He has been a delight to me from the first."

Constantine's regard turned curious. "Indeed?"

"Of course." A rush of emotion made Jane's eyes itch and burn. She blinked a few times and glanced toward the door. "I—I cannot think why Mr. Potts would have taken himself off without making the least attempt to find Luke."

"He went because I dismissed him," said Constantine.

Her lips parted in surprise. "What? You—"

He held up his hand to silence her. "And before you say I have no right to do so, I will remind you that as his guardian, I have every right, Jane. That lad is too young for such rigorous studies." Gently, he said, "Luke needs the freedom to be a boy."

She was so stunned by his criticism that she couldn't answer him. So this was how he saw her? As an overbearing, unfeeling disciplinarian? "What has Luke been saying to you?"

"Don't misunderstand me. Luke has not complained. He just seems . . . more restricted than many boys of his age." Constantine frowned. "If he's mollycoddled now, Luke will find it immensely difficult once he goes to school, you know. You did intend to send him to school in due course, didn't you?"

"It was out of the question when Frederick was alive," she murmured, forcing down the hurt. Perhaps she had been too protective, but she'd meant it for the best.

She drew a deep breath. "Frederick was rather high in the instep, you know. He would not have hired a tutor at all for Luke, much less send him to school. He only allowed me to employ Mr. Potts on condition that Luke passed regular examinations. I suppose that's why I became so strict about his lessons. I didn't want him to fail."

But she could relax that punishing schedule now, couldn't she? Constantine was right

Constantine tilted his head. "High in the instep? Frederick? What do you mean?"

She tried not to show her bitterness. "Oh, Frederick wouldn't lower himself to consider the welfare of a poor relation. I daresay if it had been up to him, Luke would never have come to live here. He acted as if he resented Luke's presence."

"But you never saw Luke as a poor relation, did you?" said Constantine softly. "You love him."

She pressed her lips together. Her eyes grew moist. "He is a son to me. I—I beg that you will not force me to part with him."

He didn't answer her immediately. Desperation shifted its stranglehold from her chest to her throat. She could not speak, but what good would her words do, anyway? He knew what she wanted. Why couldn't he accept the solution to both their troubles and make her his wife?

"You have given me food for thought," he said, after a long silence. "I had not realized . . . Forgive me if I seemed harsh. I see now that I judged the situation without knowing all the circumstances."

He picked up a sphere of carved jade from the sideboard and stared down at it, turning it over in his hands.

The breath caught in her throat. Did that mean he was reconsidering whether to wed her? It was too much to hope for, and yet . . .

She waited, every faculty suspended in anticipation of his next words.

But he said no more, seemingly lost in contemplation of the jade curiosity. On a shaky sigh, she turned and left him to his thoughts.

The correspondence that awaited Constantine at the breakfast table the next morning consisted largely of sundry missives of condolence and thinly veiled congratulation. Amusing, the people who now claimed him as an acquaintance or friend who would have crossed the street to avoid him a fortnight ago.

The mail never brought good news. Yesterday, he'd received a letter from his broker, outlining the losses he'd sustained upon selling up his long-term investments.

Constantine had sent instructions to reinvest those proceeds in certain short-term, high-risk ventures. He could have waited until his more prudent investments matured but that would be too late to save the mill. As it was, he needed to gamble on windfalls from several short-term trades.

As a last hope, it wasn't a solid one.

He'd spent the previous evening tallying his assets against the debt he owed Bronson. He'd concluded that he must, indeed, marry Jane. Unless his share-trading brought spectacular profits, there was no other way he could save the mill.

But the most persuasive factor was the clear evidence of

Jane's love for Luke that he'd witnessed in his antechamber. He would be cruel to part them.

That day had been full of surprises, in fact. He'd discovered in himself a latent desire to step into the role of protector and guide to the engaging little boy. A laughable proposition, given Constantine's past, but no less powerful for that. Frederick had scorned to fill the role of preceptor, deeming Luke beneath his notice. The boy had been starved of male influence, but that was about to change.

So. Constantine would save the mill and do what was best for Luke in the process.

He would marry Jane.

He was wise enough about women not to present the matter to her as a fait accompli, however. He still had time to court her, woo and seduce her. He felt a driving need to make her want him for himself, not for what he could give her.

Constantine's lips twisted in a cynical smile at his arrogance. Was it merely pride that spurred him to such tactics? Or the instinctive desire to be the hunter, not the trapped?

No matter. He had a month to repay the debt to Bronson. That was time enough.

As he sorted through his correspondence, an official-looking letter caught his attention. He ripped it open, and swore.

It was a demand from Bronson. Constantine scanned the short letter, which informed him of his obligation to repay the mortgage within thirty days. As if he didn't know it! Further, Bronson made it clear he had every intention of foreclosing if the debt and interest wasn't repaid to the penny by the due date.

Bronson also stated he was sending an agent to value the mill property in anticipation of foreclosure.

A musical voice interrupted his string of oaths. "Oh, good gracious! The air is turning quite blue in here."

Constantine glared at his irritating relative. There was a teasing laugh in her tone, but he was in no mood for levity. Rising at the lady's approach, he said, "I beg your pardon."

Lady Arden waved a hand. "Do sit down."

She turned to help herself from the chafing dishes set out on the sideboard. When she'd placed a sparse selection of morsels on her plate, she came to the table. "What has made you so ill-tempered, pray, Constantine? Is it bad news?"

His brows twitched together. "No." He sought to change the subject. "Did you know I've inherited a ward along with this house?"

"Inherited a ward?" Lady Arden said. "I've never heard of such a thing."

"Not an inheritance, as such," he amended. "Frederick named me guardian to Lucas Black."

"The delightful dark-haired imp I've seen about the place?" said Lady Arden.

Constantine nodded. "That's him. Son of Mary and Ernest Black, I believe. Or at least that's what Greenslade told me. I've never heard of them, have you? Apparently, they died of a fever when he was still in leading strings."

Lady Arden blinked. "But how old is the boy? Not more than seven, surely."

"Six," said Constantine. "Why?"

"My dear Constantine, if he was the child of that pair, it must have been a miracle birth. Why, Mary would have been at least five-and-fifty when she bore him."

He frowned. "Perhaps I have it wrong, or Greenslade did. At all events, I am now responsible for the boy."

A home, a child, and possibly a wife. Wouldn't his London cronies split their sides laughing? He felt a sudden, strong desire for escape.

He touched a napkin to his lips. In fact, escape was precisely what he'd do, if only for a morning. Leaving half his breakfast untouched, he rang for his phaeton to be brought around.

Lady Arden observed him keenly. "What a splendid idea. I always find driving calms the nerves. Why don't you ask Jane to accompany you? I'm sure the poor creature hasn't been out of the house for days."

"I don't wish—" He broke off at Lady Arden's minatory look. Sighing, he said, "Yes, I'll ask her. Although Cousin Jane does tend to be a high stickler. She might well object to driving out alone with me."

Lady Arden shrugged. "In an open carriage with your groom in attendance, there can be no objection."

Lazily, he smiled. "What a poor opinion you have of my ingenuity, Lady Arden."

Her bright eyes flew to his, brimful of warning. "Tread carefully, Constantine. I might allow you a certain amount of license, but you must remember that your behavior reflects on me. I won't have Jane's honor besmirched."

He raised his eyebrows. "In other words, hands off?"

She gave him a long, cool look. "In other words, Constantine, *be discreet.*"

CHAPTER TEN

With a subtle jerk of his chin, Constantine signaled to his groom that he wasn't needed. Kiever stepped away from the horses' heads and they moved off with a swift, smooth forward action.

If Jane objected that he had not brought Kiever with them, she didn't say so. Perhaps she was as glad as Constantine to escape the Hall for a time.

Well, what better way to court a lady than to take her driving in the sunshine?

"They're fresh this morning," he commented, nodding toward the gleaming chestnut horses that snorted and strained against the resistance of their harnesses. "This should take the edge off." He dropped his hands and they shot through the leafy tunnel of the oak grove.

Jane clapped a hand to her bonnet and laughed a little at the speed. Her laughter held a silvery quality, like water flowing in a brook.

He'd never seen her so animated. Despite the unrelieved black of her costume, her eyes sparkled, her skin glowed with dewy softness, and those delectable lips parted in a joyous smile.

He wanted to feel those lips beneath his once more. He'd find a way to do it, too, before this drive was over. A sweet, tantalizing kiss that would pave the way for more.

"Luke will be envious," Jane said. "He would say these beautiful creatures are *something like!*"

"Aren't they just? Softest mouths in England. My one true extravagance."

"Fine horseflesh is no extravagance," she commented. "I suppose you don't let anyone but your groom drive them."

"You'd suppose correctly." He glanced down at her with a glint of humor. "Why? Do you covet my chestnuts, Jane?"

"I'm positively eaten up with jealousy," she admitted, making him laugh.

She sighed. "Frederick was no judge of horseflesh. Unfortunately, he could not be brought to acknowledge the fact."

"You're a rich, independent woman. You may purchase your own cattle now."

She grimaced. "Not independent enough to visit Tattersall's."

"I'll nose around and see who might be selling privately. Then you could judge for yourself."

That suggestion seemed to act like magic. "I could? Oh, that would be marvelous, indeed. Not that I don't trust your judgment, of course."

"I quite understand," he assured her. "It's a very personal thing."

She seemed pleased at his comprehension. "Yes, it is, isn't it? Frederick always thought he knew best."

"Don't I know it?" murmured Constantine. "Did he ever tell you about the time—" He broke off. "Well, I suppose one shouldn't abuse the fellow now that he's dead."

"You may abuse him to me with a clear conscience," said Jane. "I'm livid with him over that will. Besides, I don't see that death changes anything about who a person might have been when he lived."

His feelings were so much in accord with hers that he was startled into silence.

After a moment, she said quietly, "I must seem heartless to you."

He blew out a breath. "Not at all. In fact, in all honesty, I'm relieved to hear you say it." He didn't fancy marrying a woman who still pined for his cousin.

Turning the subject, he said, "When I die, I'd like my friends and family to raise a toast, tell a few jokes at my expense, and send me on my way."

"I shall endeavor to remember it," she said demurely.

Now, this was promising. His raised an eyebrow, quizzing her. "You are so confident I'll predecease you?"

She flicked a hand. "It is the usual way of things with men and women. And you are *years* older than I am, after all."

He laughed, thinking that a sense of humor was definitely a point in her favor. She hadn't displayed much tendency to joke in the short time he'd known her. Of course, he'd been too busy provoking her to laugh with her before.

The proximity of her slender body was making itself felt in all kinds of small, tantalizing ways. The intermittent press of her thigh to his, her hand clutching his arm as they featheredged a corner, her shoulder brushing his when he swerved to avoid a stray sheep that chose that moment to wander onto the road.

"What a pleasant day," remarked Lady Roxdale, a trifle breathlessly.

His voice scraped a little. "Yes, isn't it?"

A strong wind had blown the clouds away, and the sun shone brightly. He'd almost forgotten the impulse to let the chestnuts have their heads and carry him straight back to London.

No, there was no escape from any of the responsibilities Frederick had flung in his lap, and he didn't wish to, not really. Strange. After the painful excision of his youthful self from Broadmere, he hadn't expected to fall back in love with his second home, Lazenby, so quickly.

The narrow country lanes were badly rutted due to the prolonged rain. Their repair would have to wait until he came to an understanding with Jane.

Though Frederick had been a good landlord in many

ways, repairs and maintenance were always required on an estate of this size. The church, the vicar told him, needed a new roof.

But his primary concern was the mill. Freeing the property of that monstrous debt, getting rid of the dam that stopped the flow of water to power the machinery inside it, luring his workers back and making the whole thing profitable again. He would not succeed as landlord of this estate unless he could accomplish all those things. It was time to put pride aside and accept Jane's help.

He took a circuitous route, following the road that ran along the high limestone cliffs. To their left, down the valley, the woolen mills stood, hunkering along the wide stream. Despite their practical purpose, they were grand buildings, made of Cotswold stone, nestled snugly into the valley as if they'd grown there.

He frowned. "Tell me, what do you know of that fellow Bronson, who leases the mill on Trent's lands?"

Jane shook her head. "Nothing at all. He doesn't visit here. I think the neighborhood must be grateful to him, though. When the water supply dried up, I was relieved our weavers had somewhere to go."

Yes, they had somewhere to go, all right. A mill where they were paid a pittance and worked harder than ever before. Lady Roxdale wasn't to know that, however.

Constantine narrowed his eyes. "The man is not such a hero as you think. It appears Bronson has found a way to stop the water flowing downstream to our mill at Lazenby, and *that* is why the stream dried up. There was no longer power to run the mill, and therefore, no work for the weavers."

She gasped. "That is monstrous! Why didn't Frederick do something about this?"

"I don't know. Jones tried to tell him."

"I see." Jane hesitated. "What are we going to do?"

It was a small thing, really. One trivial two-lettered pronoun. But it made a vast difference to him.

For the first time, Jane ranged herself on his side.

It took him a moment to respond. "I'm going to get that dam torn down. With or without Trent's permission."

"Do you think he even knows about the problem? I understand he allows Bronson free rein to run the mill."

"He knows now," said Constantine grimly. "And if he doesn't do something about it within the week, I'll destroy the benighted thing myself."

Suddenly, the crenellated bell tower of St. Edmund's broke above the line of trees, always the first sign of the village. The chestnuts swept around a corner and Constantine slowed them to trot past the King's Head, purveyor of superior breakfasts.

The sight reminded Constantine of Montford.

If he wanted to marry Jane, he would have to find a way to persuade the duke to withdraw his objections. Constantine was not in awe of Montford, not at all, but he'd be a fool to ignore His Grace's omnipotent reputation. That, and his very real power over his former ward.

As they climbed the hill toward the church, a small figure darted in front of them, seemingly from nowhere. Constantine drew hard on the ribbons. "Whoa, there!"

The child hesitated, long enough for Constantine to see his dirty, tear-streaked face, then he turned and pelted up the street, toward the church.

"That's Luke!" Jane clutched Constantine's arm. "What on earth—"

Constantine had seen enough to know that the boy had been in some sort of fight. Received the worst end of it, too, by all appearances. A quick glance in the direction from which the boy had come revealed half a dozen boys in homespuns, the obvious culprits.

When they saw him looking, their faces whitened and the boys scattered like spillikins. No matter. He'd let them go.

"Oh, stop!" cried Jane. "Let me down. I must help him."

"No, I'll do it." He pulled up and handed her the reins. "Keep them moving, will you? I won't be long." He slanted a glance at her and one corner of his mouth twitched. "They're a little fatigued, so you should be able to control them now."

Her indignant snort made him grin. Before she realized he'd provoked her on purpose to take her mind off going after Luke, Constantine jumped down from the phaeton and followed in the direction the boy had taken.

His presence caused a stir among the villagers, but he didn't take much notice, beyond politely tipping his hat and dispersing sundry greetings. They'd react in the same way if a two-headed cow was led through the high street. He was still Lord Roxdale of Lazenby Hall, even if mothers of nubile daughters crossed themselves as he went past.

The boy had disappeared in the general vicinity of the village green, so Constantine stepped onto the verdant sward that unfurled like a rug spread between the church and the market square.

An enormous horse-chestnut tree stood in the center of the green, perfect for climbing. He walked over to it and looked up. "Luke, you can come down now. You're not in trouble, and I won't embarrass you by seeking to punish those young ruffians. I just want to talk with you."

No answer, save a small scuffle as the boy moved higher among the branches.

"Come down, will you? There's a good chap," said Constantine. "I'm getting a crick in my neck standing like this. Besides, any number of the good people of Lazenby are staring at me at this moment, wondering if I'm having a conversation with a magpie. They'll dub me the mad Lord Roxdale if you don't show yourself. *Not* an auspicious start."

There was a snort, a kind of smothered chuckle. After a pause, Luke said, "Oh, all right, then."

The boy came slithering down the branches, nimble as a monkey. But as he jumped to the ground, a loud rip rent the air. He held his arms wide and looked over his shoulder at his ripped jacket. He muttered a ripe curse. "Aunt Jane will skin me."

Constantine took note of other rips and grass stains over

his clothing. The boy didn't seem hurt, just badly mussed. "Looks like someone's already taken care of dusting your breeches for you. Who were they?"

The boy's mouth turned mulish. "No one, sir."

Constantine waited for a moment, but the boy wasn't going to cry rope on anyone. "I see."

Clearly, those bullies had given Luke a rough time of it, but the boy wasn't a sneak. Constantine respected him for it and decided not to press him.

It occurred to him that he now stood in loco parentis to Luke and he ought to offer some sort of worldly advice on the subject of avoiding getting one's nose bloodied. Or at least on the subject of giving a good account of oneself in the process.

"Come," said Constantine. "Lady Roxdale is with me. We'll drive you back to the Hall."

Luke's eyes shifted in the direction from which he'd run. "No, thank you, sir."

Constantine raised his brows. "Thirsty for some more of the home-brewed, are you?"

"I don't want you to drive me," he muttered. "It'll only make things worse."

"I see." What those "things" were, exactly, he couldn't guess. But he had a notion Luke was correct; that his interests wouldn't be served by the lord of the manor taking a hand in the matter. Constantine wouldn't always be there to protect him. His interference might draw more of these boys' taunts.

Still, he was reluctant to leave the lad. Clearly, the numbers hadn't been even in that recent scuffle, and that jarred with Constantine's innate sense of fairness.

He smiled, deliberately charming. "I think you've had enough punishment for today, don't you? You're full of pluck, but the odds weren't in your favor. If you stay, I'm afraid I'll have to answer to Lady Roxdale for the condition you return in. She'd have my hide if you are set upon again, and she'd be right."

The boy remained obstinately silent. Well, why should he care if Constantine's credit suffered with Jane, after all?

Constantine sighed. Jane *would* have his head for this, but it couldn't be helped. Some matters were simply beyond the female ken. He set his palm against the tree. "Tell me, do you know how to get to the crossroads without going back along the high street?"

"'Course I do," said the boy, a flicker of a proud smile lighting his woebegone face.

"Take that way, then. And mind you go straight home."

Luke thought about this and gave a short nod.

Rueful, Constantine squeezed the boy's shoulder. "Off with you, now. Don't dawdle."

Constantine turned back and looked across the green to the high street, where Jane sat minding his horses and watching. Hell. He was going to catch it when she heard about this.

Jane certainly had her hands full while Constantine dealt with Luke; she'd underestimated the strength of his horses. As Constantine walked toward her with no Luke in sight, she blew out an exasperated breath. She'd love nothing more than to drive off and leave him stranded, but she wasn't at all sure she could manage the beasts.

Fatigued, indeed! They were likely to rip her arms out of their sockets.

"Where's Luke?" she demanded as Constantine swung himself back into the phaeton.

He took the reins and said, "He's going home his own way."

Jane buffeted his big shoulder with her gloved hand. It was like hitting rock. "You left him *alone*? Go back and get him!"

He turned to her and his green eyes were sympathetic. "I'm not going to do that. We came to an understanding. He'll make his own way back to the Hall."

"Make his own way?" she repeated. "He shouldn't be

here without his nurse in the first place. He must have given her the slip."

"He'll be perfectly fine," said Constantine.

"You are an unfeeling brute! He was hurt and scared. *I* saw the look on his face."

"Not so hurt he couldn't scramble up and down that tree like a cat." Constantine gave his horses the office and drove up the high street. "Trust me, it's better this way."

Jane all but bounced in her seat. "Trust you! Who do you think you are? You've been the boy's guardian for all of five minutes and now you are an expert?"

"You would have marched in there and given those boys a scold, I suppose." Constantine shook his head.

"You could at least have brought him back to the carriage. He's just a little boy."

He slanted a glance at her. "It may interest you to know that I've had some experience as a male of the species—and surprisingly enough, I was once a six-year-old boy. That does make me more qualified than you to judge the situation. And yes, dear Jane. In this case you are wrong." He smiled at her. "And I am right."

"Insufferable!" Jane angrily tugged at the ribbons of her bonnet, intending to retie them. She was all fingers and thumbs. Not least because when he smiled at her like that, her insides turned to mush.

He laughed. "Allow me."

Before she could protest, he removed her hands from the black satin ribbon that knotted at her chin and pressed the reins into her grasp. Automatically, her hands closed over the leather straps. Her arms tensed for battle, but the chestnuts remained quiescent, perhaps aware their master was near.

She watched Constantine unbutton his driving gloves and strip them from his hands. Large hands they were, with long, capable-looking fingers.

He turned to her. "Now, let me see what we have here."

His fingertips brushed the underside of her chin as he

gathered the tangled ribbons of her hat. Tingling warmth radiated from that spot, like ripples in a pond.

She didn't know why she'd allowed him to take over this task; it brought his compelling features in disconcerting proximity to hers.

Black brows drawn into a slight frown, Constantine worked at the stubborn knot. He was so close, Jane felt the warmth of his breath feathering over her lips. His irises were not pure emerald, as she'd thought, but a slightly lighter hue, flecked with black.

As he wrestled with the recalcitrant knot, Constantine muttered something under his breath, drawing her gaze to his mouth. The upper lip was chiseled and firm, the lower slightly fuller. As well defined as the mouth on a Greek statue—sensual, yet utterly masculine. She thought of those lips crushing hers in the muniments room that night. Her breathing hitched; her own lips parted in longing.

His gaze flickered up to her face. She blushed to have been caught staring at his mouth. Something dangerous burned in his eyes, but he only allowed her a glimpse before lowering them again to his work.

"There," he said softly, letting the ribbons fall. She looked down to see that he'd retied them in an elegant bow.

Her lungs seemed to have seized in the moment his eyes had met hers. Jane managed to dredge up the breath to thank him. Her heart pounding, she waited until he'd put his gloves back on to hand him back the reins.

It took many moments to drag her mind back to the point she'd been making before that disturbing interlude. Luke. Had Constantine thought to distract her with all this tying of bonnet strings?

Embarrassment at his success lent an edge to her words. "Would you care to explain to me why, in all your mighty wisdom, *O masculine one,* you left a small boy to walk home by himself when he has been set upon by bullies, perhaps to face more of the same before he gets there?"

"I thought you'd never ask," said Constantine. He was

positively enjoying this; she could see it in the slight smile playing over his mouth.

He sobered. "Luke is being bullied for a reason. Perhaps it's because he is small and an easy target; perhaps because he gets to live at the Hall and wear fine clothes. There could be any number of reasons that would seem trivial to you and me."

"But—"

Constantine held up a hand. "So for us to come in like lord and lady high-and-mighty to rescue him would increase their resentment. And as I don't intend to imprison the boy in the house, I expect he will come to the village again. And when he does, he'll receive a worse drubbing than he got today."

He found a place wide enough to turn the phaeton. While he was occupied with the maneuver, Jane thought about what he'd said.

Reluctantly, she had to agree that it made sense. And it reinforced a notion she'd had for some time: Luke needed a man in his life to deal with such things. Her love for him was not quite enough.

She sighed. "I suppose you are right. Though it kills me to say so."

Constantine didn't evince any sign of triumph at her admission. "Luke is not badly hurt, or I would have insisted on conveying him back to the Hall. He knows how to avoid the high street on his return. I don't think there's cause to worry that he'll be set upon again today."

Transferring the reins into one hand, he found hers with the other. He'd intended the gesture to comfort her, no doubt, but his touch shot through her body like a burning arrow, setting it aflame. With a gasp, she slid her hand away.

They were in the high street, for goodness' sake!

CHAPTER ELEVEN

So much for his wicked intentions toward Lady Roxdale. Constantine grimaced. One couldn't make love to a lady suffused with righteous anger over the bullying of her beloved boy.

He'd resigned himself that there would be no kissing those pretty lips on this particular outing. When she'd looked at him with such longing in those clear gray eyes as he tied her bonnet strings, he'd come dangerously close to ravishing her mouth and damning the consequences. Thank God he'd managed to restrain himself. That would not have ended well.

Disconcerting to find that brief interlude on the high street had affected him so powerfully. It was the kind of ploy he'd often used to get close to a woman, but never had such an innocent flirtation stirred such strong desires in him before.

He wanted, quite desperately, to make *her* want *him*. Not only as a solution to her problems, but as a husband, lord, and lover, too.

Unfortunately, the power of that desire made him clay in her hands. By the time they reached the Hall, he'd committed to doing a number of things in furtherance of Luke's interests that he would never have done except to please her. He liked the lad, and he would certainly deal with the bullying in his own way. But the rest . . . He sighed. He was turning into a sad case.

When Constantine caught up with him later, Luke was unexpectedly recalcitrant. He stonewalled any discussion of the incident in the village no matter how casually Constantine approached the subject. Constantine tried, and so did Jane, but to no avail.

For the moment, there was nothing much Constantine could do besides give the boy some strategies to get out of fights altogether, and if pressed, with which to defend himself.

He'd imagined Jane would scarcely condone such violent measures and was surprised at her quick nod of acceptance when she saw what he was about. Winning her approval gave him the strangest feeling of warmth in the region of his chest.

The better he got to know Jane, the more significance this marriage business seemed to assume.

But he'd need to put the question soon, so they could work on gaining Montford's approval and making the arrangements to repay the debt on the mill.

Lady Arden would be instrumental in talking Montford around. The two of them were as thick as thieves, after all.

He discovered his relative busily arranging flowers in a vase in the drawing room the following day.

"There you are, Constantine." Lady Arden finished her work and swiveled the vase so that her arrangement appeared to best advantage.

"Making yourself at home, I see." He quirked an eyebrow. "Tell me, does Montford know you're here?"

Despite her assurance, he could tell he'd hit a sore point by the slight quivering of her aristocratic nostrils. She picked up a deadly-looking pair of shears and replaced them in her sewing basket. "No, why should he?"

"Why, indeed? Don't tell me he'd approve of your meddling, for that I won't believe."

She turned her sparkling dark eyes upon him. "Let's leave the duke out of this discussion. You must—absolutely *must*—marry Jane." She threw up her hands. "Why isn't she in love with you already, for heaven's sake?"

That startled him. "What an odd thing to say."

He eyed his relative warily. Lady Arden most often achieved her ends when she set her Machiavellian mind to it. He wanted Jane's desire and her respect. But love? The last thing he needed was for Jane to think herself in the throes of some grand, enduring passion.

He grinned. Actually, he'd pay good money to see Her Iciness in the throes of passion of a lustful nature. But infatuated women were irrational and a nuisance and downright embarrassing. He didn't wish for such a lopsided marriage.

He picked up a stem of greenery and twirled it idly between finger and thumb. "When I ask Lady Roxdale to marry me, it will be a purely commercial transaction. Being a Westruther, I'm sure she knows how these alliances work."

Lady Arden nodded. "Oh, undoubtedly. There was no love between her and Frederick but they dealt admirably together."

He doubted it, but didn't argue the point. "Then there'll be no more talk of love. It will be a business arrangement, no more."

Just then, the lady herself walked into the room and smiled at him. This time there was no gentle malice or stiff politeness in her expression. She appeared delighted to see him. Her eyes glowed, her cheeks displayed a pretty pink blush.

Constantine sucked in a breath. He felt like he'd been hit in the solar plexus. The greenery fell, unheeded, to the floor.

"You were saying?" Lady Arden murmured.

He didn't answer.

As he watched Jane walk toward him, he made the most minute and significant discoveries about her. That her eyebrows were not quite evenly arched: one was slightly more peaked than the other, giving her that disconcertingly skeptical mien. That her lips were even fuller and darker than he remembered; that her lashes were black, despite the lighter tone of her hair. And as she drew nearer, he looked into her eyes and realized they were not clear gray, but made like a mosaic from flecks of granite and smoke and flint and silver, a kaleidoscope of precious metal and stone.

Like a fool, he stared down into her eyes without speaking, and that enchanting blossom of color swept along her cheeks.

"I'll leave you to conduct your, er, *business,* then, my dear." With a soft laugh, Lady Arden rustled away.

Constantine forgot to breathe. He was sharply aware of every line and curve of Lady Roxdale's body, every texture that he longed to stroke and savor, every mystery he intended to explore. In his brain, a door snapped closed, or opened, he didn't know which, but he knew what it portended.

Come hell or high water, he would make this woman his, in every sense of the word.

Someone cleared their throat. "Your bonnet, ma'am." It was moments before either Constantine or Lady Roxdale realized that the butler stood a respectful distance away, bearing another of those ridiculously ugly hats.

The lady started as if someone had fired a gunshot.

"Thank you, Feather." Recovering enough to accept the bonnet, she set it on her head, tying the ribbons beneath her chin.

Constantine drew a deep breath that was a little ragged at the edges.

What had just happened to him? To them both?

Unwilling to examine the answer too closely, he cleared his throat. "It's a fine day."

"Yes," she said, breathless. "I was just about to . . ."

He held out his arm. "Shall we?"

The moment had spooled between them, then snapped like a severed thread. Jane felt off balance, disoriented.

She blinked. "I beg your pardon?"

"Shall we walk, Lady Roxdale?" He was smiling now, yet oddly distant.

After a slight hesitation, she took his proffered arm, catching her breath a little at the hard strength beneath his finely tailored green coat.

Her skirts brushed his long legs as they walked. Unless she held herself away from him in an absurdly awkward fashion, she could not prevent it. Ordinarily, such impersonal contact wouldn't signify, but with Constantine, she noticed everything. Every gesture of his hands, every turn of his head, every touch, however impersonal.

"Are you happy at Lazenby, Jane?" said Constantine.

Startled, her gaze met his. Then she glanced away. "You have enough worries. You need not concern yourself about me."

"Oh, but I do concern myself about you," he said. "In fact, you occupy my thoughts almost exclusively."

"Really?" She tried for a tone that was dryly skeptical. It came out as more of a breathless squeak.

"Yes. I'm afraid . . ." He sighed. "I'm afraid I shall be obliged to ask you to marry me, after all."

Abruptly, her face drained of warmth, and there came that dizzy, disorienting feeling again. She stopped dead, disengaging herself. "Because of the estate."

He gazed down at her, and his eyes burned with some emotion she couldn't name. He looked away. The rasp in his voice turned harsh. "Yes. Of course. Because of that."

She couldn't seem to swallow past the hard lump in her throat. Marriage to Constantine Black. It was what she'd longed for, wasn't it? It was the only way to keep Luke.

The reality of it suddenly terrified her.

"I cannot be like Frederick," began Constantine, squinting into the distance, toward the westering sun.

A glimmer of humor stirred in her. "No. That *is* rather obvious," she murmured.

Vividly, painfully so.

He continued, as if he hadn't heard the ironic comment. "I can never be what Frederick was to you. I would not even try."

She glanced at him curiously. Surely he didn't suppose a great love or even a great romance had existed between her and his predecessor?

What had there been? she wondered now. Familial duty and obligation. Liking that had mushroomed (on her side) into infatuation at about the time of her sixteenth birthday. Later, distance. Yes, oceans of it, and resentment, too. But always a civilized veneer.

Jane had learned the art of maintaining appearances only too well.

But she'd failed in part of her obligation, hadn't she? She hadn't given Frederick that highly desirable heir. She hadn't shared his bed after those first few painful, humiliating occasions.

How many hours had she spent castigating herself for that? Had Frederick's heart been engaged at all in the business? Could she have won him if she'd fought hard enough?

Ah, what did it matter? What had it ever mattered? Frederick had made his choices without any regard to her. One didn't compete for a lover's heart as if it were a Derby cup.

A short silence passed before Constantine halted them and turned to face her. "My father once told me that marriage between persons of rank is a commercial transaction and has nothing to do with love. I don't wish to flummery you, Jane. Obviously, neither of us has had time to form a lasting attachment of that nature. I wouldn't insult you by pretending I had."

He smiled down at her, and if he only knew what that smile did to her, he would not feel so noble; he would know the advantage was all his.

"What do you say, Jane? Shall we join together what Frederick has torn asunder?"

This was what she'd wanted, wasn't it? She knew it in her

head, but her heart rang out a warning as clear as clarion bells.

This man was dangerous. Not because of his wicked past, but because of what she saw—or thought she saw—beyond the rakish façade.

Despite everything she'd heard about Constantine Black's reprehensible reputation, something about him called to her. Perhaps it was the way his spirit seemed so solitary even while he charmed everyone around him. She knew what it was to feel alone in the midst of a crowd.

Or was she merely beguiled by a spectacular form of male beauty, imagining depths in him that were not there?

No, it was more than his looks that drew her. Constantine Black was no hero from a fairy tale. But he was not the villain he was painted, either. She felt it in her bones.

The thought flashed through her mind that he was a man in pain. What had it been like for him to become a pariah at such an early age? A harsh sentence to bear, no matter how richly deserved that ostracism had been.

She could not find it in herself to hold his past against him as she should. She was beginning to like him too well for his own sake.

But that did not mean he was trustworthy or a safe receptacle for her love. No, she would not fall into *that* trap again. She would not bestow her heart where it wasn't wanted.

Resolutely, she met that brilliant green gaze. "I appreciate that you do not seek to cozen me with falsehoods about romantic attachment and . . . and so on." She gripped her hands together. "I am grateful for your proposals and I honor you for them."

A particularly bloodless response, if she did say so herself. A dire contrast to the turmoil inside her.

"And your answer?" he asked. How like him to behave as if he were unsure of her reply, as if she'd never made that improper proposal in the chapel only days before.

She bit her lip. "Yes. The answer is yes."

Her lack of enthusiasm did not seem to distress him. Maybe he hadn't noticed or it was just that he was a very good actor. Or perhaps he simply did not care very much.

"Thank you. You do me a great honor." He took her hand and bent to kiss her fingers. The light, hot brush of his lips over her knuckles sent tingles racing up her spine. *Oh, Lord! This would not do at all.*

Constantine paused, still bent over her hand, and looked up. Caught the flush in her cheeks and the dismay in her eyes. He smiled, as if he sensed how her stupid heart beat harder at his touch.

She thought he might kiss her then, and her courage failed her. She rushed into speech. "I would ask one boon, however. Might we keep our betrothal secret until I can speak with the duke?"

"He is not your guardian any longer," Constantine pointed out. "You no longer need his permission to wed."

"That is true. But to smooth our path, we would do better to seek his approval. It would be churlish of me to do otherwise, I believe."

His mouth tightened. "Very well." He paused. "I daresay Montford will advise you against the match."

"He already has," she said.

"Oh? Did he give reason?"

Her glance flicked to him and away. "I suppose you can guess. Your reputation."

A breath hissed between his teeth. They walked on, retracing their steps toward the gravel path. It was so long before he spoke again that she didn't think he would answer her at all.

"Montford ought to know better than to warn you against me. In my experience, nothing makes a man so interesting to the fair sex as a wicked past."

"I do find your wicked past . . . intriguing, I admit."

He shook his head. "*Intriguing?* My dear Jane, it is quite the reverse. I have done nothing to merit your curiosity."

"I am sure you would not say so if I were a man," she retorted.

"Oh, you wish to hear *those* stories." His lips twitched in amusement. "And here I'd thought you were so straitlaced."

"Yes, I suppose I am, compared to the hussies you normally consort with," she snapped. The twitch of his lips goaded her into adding, "However, my natural repugnance for your past actions does not outweigh the sense of duty I feel toward the estate."

"Ah. So this marriage will be in the nature of a sacrifice?"

She looked sharply at him. He still smiled, but anger simmered in his eyes. "I should not like to put it that way." After a pause, she added, "I am sure you will be a satisfactory husband . . . according to your lights."

Jane watched with interest as a muscle jumped in that firm, decided jaw.

He bowed. "I'm flattered by your confidence, ma'am."

Tilting his head, he studied her form, running his gaze over her body with a lingering insolence she knew was meant to provoke her.

"And you, Jane?" he said, his voice low and rough as the gravel beneath their feet. "Will you be a satisfactory wife?"

Resolutely, she ignored the heat spreading low in her belly and made herself give a careless shrug. "I shall be precisely the sort of wife you deserve, Constantine."

The dangerous look vanished and he laughed. "The Lord have mercy on my soul."

CHAPTER TWELVE

Y ou're taking Luke fishing?" Jane stared at Constantine, then looked out the window. "But it's going to rain again."

Constantine clapped his curly-brimmed beaver hat on his head at a rakish angle. One side of his mouth quirked up. "We shan't melt."

A cook maid bustled in with a hamper stocked from the kitchen. She bobbed a curtsy. "Cook says there's pork pie and ale, and jam tarts for sweet, just as you ordered, m'lud."

"Excellent! Thank you." He took the basket from her with a smile, sending the maid away all aflutter.

Jane rolled her eyes. She'd been obliged to speak rather sternly with the housemaids about the way they giggled and tittered over their handsome master. Constantine appeared oblivious to their reaction; he never took much notice of the female members of staff beyond their function in the household. However, unlike Frederick, who had rapped out orders like an army sergeant, Constantine was kind and courteous to his staff. It didn't take much more than a smile from him to encourage the silly girls.

Indeed, a smile from Constantine was quite enough to encourage any poor female to fall into daydreams. Jane supposed she could not entirely blame them.

After checking the contents of the hamper, he resumed

their conversation. "What's a little rain? You wanted me to get to know the boy better."

"I wanted you to have a serious talk with him about our marriage and your guardianship, not take him fishing in the wet."

"Ah, but then you don't know the male of the species well, do you, Jane? They don't sit around and *talk* to each other. They *do*. Any conversation is purely incidental. Why do you think I've gone to the trouble of arranging a fishing jaunt? The boy's more likely to let down his guard and confide in me if he's actively occupied with something. He told me fishing is his favorite activity."

"Outside of drawing."

"Well, yes, but unless I commission him to take my portrait, sketching is a solitary sort of thing." He appeared struck. "Do you think I *ought* to have my portrait painted? Lend the long gallery a bit of cachet?"

He was laughing at himself. Privately, Jane thought a portrait of Constantine would cast every one of his ancestors' likenesses in the shade. "You should commission one," she said lightly. "They're often allegorical, aren't they? Perhaps, since we're in the Cotswolds, you could pose with a sheep."

"A *black* sheep," murmured Constantine, his eyes dancing.

She laughed. "Precisely."

"I'm ready!" Luke tramped in, carrying rods under one arm, his sketchbook under the other, his tackle box and his tin of charcoals.

"Here. Let me help you." Constantine took the rods with a quirk of his brow. "A sketchbook?"

Laughing, Jane ruffled the boy's hair. "He never goes anywhere without it, do you, Luke?"

Luke shrugged. "You never know what might need drawing." He slanted a glance at Constantine. "Lord Roxdale here might catch a big 'un, and I should need to capture *that* for pos . . . pos*terity*."

"Ho, now I'm on my mettle," said Constantine.

Chuckling, Jane glanced outside. Though overcast, the rain seemed to be holding off for the moment. She was supposed to meet with Cook this morning but . . .

Impulsively, she said, "May I come with you?"

"Yes!" Luke cried. "My lord, wouldn't that be splendid?"

She glanced an inquiry at Constantine. He tilted his head, and there was an appreciative smile in his eyes. "Indeed. I'm sure there are more than enough jam tarts for everyone."

As Constantine had predicted, the fishing expedition was a success. Luke accepted the news of Constantine's guardianship with a thoughtful nod that made all Jane's worry on the subject seem as if it had been for naught. To Luke, it mattered little who was legally responsible for him, as long as his day-to-day existence wouldn't change.

Now that the question of their marriage was settled, Jane was able to reassure him that it would not. Having a man in his life who spent time with him doing masculine things seemed to be benefiting Luke. He'd never had that sort of relationship with Frederick, much as Jane had tried to promote amity between them.

She hadn't been able to coax Luke to tell her more about the bullies in the village, however. While there didn't appear to have been any repeat of that behavior, the incident still concerned her.

She was sitting in the drawing room, embroidering a cushion cover and worrying, when Adam Trent strode in.

"Jane!"

Startled, she jumped and stabbed her finger with a needle. With a cry of annoyance, Jane put the embroidery aside and stood to face him, sucking the blood that bloomed on her fingertip.

Oblivious, Trent rapped out, "I heard you drove with that fellow to the village. Alone! Without even a groom to lend you countenance!"

Icily, she said, "I *beg* your pardon?" What did he mean, storming in here to lecture her?

He threw up his hands. "It was all over the village. Probably all over the county by now."

"Mr. Trent! Whom I choose to drive out with is not your concern. What's more, *that fellow* happens to be the master of this house, and I'd thank you to remember it."

He also happened to have secured her hand in marriage, but she wouldn't tell Trent that. The betrothal still didn't feel real to her. She suspected she would not trust in it until she had Montford's approval.

For a moment, Trent looked taken aback. Then he gave his urbane smile. "Ah! You don't understand, Jane. But how could you? You've lived so sheltered, you have no notion what men like Constantine Black are."

The soothing, patronizing tone irked her. No matter how Constantine might provoke her, he never treated her like an infant who was unfit to tie her own bootlaces.

She raised her brows. "Did it never occur to you, Mr. Trent, that I have family and protectors enough who have already warned me against Lord Roxdale? Your interference is superfluous, and yes, officious, too."

"They don't know him the way I do," he muttered.

Hoping to steer the conversation to less personal matters, she replied, "Ah, yes. You were acquainted as boys, weren't you?"

Trent's eyes narrowed, as if to bring the past into perspective. "Black was always wild to a fault. Always getting into trouble. Forever charming his way out of it, too."

Trent's upper lip curled. "Turned my stomach the way they all fawned over him, even old Lord Roxdale. Frederick thought the sun shone out of him until he saw his true colors, at last. At least there's that satisfaction." Trent seemed to speak to himself. "Now, everyone knows Constantine Black for the scoundrel he is."

He fixed his gaze on her. "Except you, Jane. Why do *you* insist on remaining blind?"

It was exactly the question she'd avoided asking herself. Touched on the raw, Jane's fury erupted. "For heaven's sake! It was a drive to the village, Mr. Trent, not a midnight jaunt to St. James's!"

The sharp breath Trent inhaled through his nostrils told her he was grievously shocked by her outburst. Ladies like Jane should know nothing of the nocturnal activities in the region of London's gentlemen's clubs.

Trent shook his head, as if to clear it. "Obviously, your nerves are still overset by Frederick's death." Jane wondered if he realized how pompous he sounded and decided he hadn't the faintest clue.

"I came to see *you,* not wishing to speak of him," Trent added. "But . . . Well, I must warn you to be on your guard."

"Against what, pray?"

Her neighbor's mouth took on a curiously constipated look. As if he burned to unleash a torrent of words but he simply couldn't bring himself to force them out.

She guessed the reason. Trent dearly wished to regale her with some horrid tale of Constantine's debauchery expressly designed to shock and disgust her. However, her neighbor's priggish nature forbade him to utter such an anecdote to a gently bred lady.

Thank heaven for small mercies. The faint tug of curiosity she felt was one she could easily ignore. Such curiosity was prurient and unworthy of her; she did not wish to receive such tawdry confidences from Mr. Trent.

He darted a glance at her. "Jane, I—"

Jane tilted her head. "Do you know, I believe you are right, sir. I find my nerves *are* overset, what with recent events, not to mention your unmannerly interruption just now. In fact, I should very much like to get back to my needlework, if it's all the same to you."

"But—"

She rose, putting an end to conversation. "Thank you for calling, Mr. Trent. Good day."

With a high choler and a hardened jaw, Mr. Trent bowed and took his leave.

Dear Lady Arden,

No doubt you have received Lord deVere's urgent summons to a meeting of the Ministry of Marriage in order to discuss Lady Roxdale's future. I have managed to delay the proceedings somewhat, but you know how deVere is; I cannot stave him off forever.

Discreet inquiry has revealed that you are—shall we say—taking the bull by the horns. It will not do, madam. DeVere has his own candidate to put forward— a good one. You'd best make haste to Town for the meeting, or you will have no opportunity to argue your case. I cannot answer for the consequences if you fail to appear.

Yours, etc.

Montford

Constantine didn't finish in the muniments room until well after midnight. He'd pored over ledgers and documents for so many hours that his eyes were starting to feel the strain and his joints ached like an old man's.

A good bout of physical activity would sort him out, but the only kind of nocturnal exercise he craved wasn't available to him at Lazenby Hall.

Yet.

She'd been skittish ever since they'd agreed to wed. Uncharacteristically, he'd resolved to behave himself. Though he burned to take every advantage of his new status as her betrothed, some niggling apprehension held him back.

Their wedding couldn't come soon enough now, as far as he was concerned.

Pending that auspicious occasion, he tantalized himself

with heated imaginings. His mind slid into a fantasy of soft white skin and wine-red lips . . .

Constantine woke to find himself in near darkness, a single, guttering candle throwing a sporadic glow over his desk. He rubbed his hands over his face and stretched his legs, feeling oddly alert.

Ordinarily, he'd be three sheets to the wind by now, but lately he'd made a habit of falling into bed alarmingly sober. And it wasn't brandy he craved at this moment, he realized, but some more of Marthe's excellent cooking.

The house was silent as he made his way down to the kitchens, a warm feeling of anticipation in his chest. Raiding the larder was something he hadn't done since his boyhood. He found a good portion of roast lamb, mint jelly, and potatoes with butter and some herb or other that lent a piquant flavor to the dish. He loaded a tray with these as well as brandied apricots and a pot of cream.

Something sleek and sinuous wove through his legs, startling him. An imperious *miaow* told him he was in the company of the kitchen cat. He looked down to see a pair of luminous green eyes staring back unblinkingly from the darkness.

"I suppose you wish to join me," said Constantine. "Come along, then."

Discriminating creatures, cats. They didn't make friends with just anything on two legs. On the whole, cats liked him. Generally, he left them alone, but when they came to him, he knew exactly how to appreciate them.

Constantine hacked off a couple of hunks of bread and carved a few slices of lamb, feeding tidbits to the big tabby as he went along. "I know I shouldn't, for you won't bother catching mice if I feed you, but I don't suppose it matters just this once."

Delicately the cat accepted another succulent morsel of lamb. "Genteel manners for a kitchen cat," commented Constantine. "I wonder where you learned them."

A snicker from the stairs caught his attention. He raised his candle, but the light didn't reach that far.

"Who's there?"

"Only me," said a low voice. A furtive figure in a long white nightdress flitted down the stairs.

"Jane." His chair scraped a discordant note on the tiled floor as he rose.

"Hush! Do you wish to wake the household?"

He feared she'd retreat, but she didn't. She tilted her head to listen. After a frozen second or two she drifted forward, gathering her shawl tighter around her.

"Are you cold? Here." He shrugged out of his dressing gown and moved forward to put it around her shoulders. Her long, unbound hair was trapped beneath the gown. Without thinking, he threaded his fingers through the curly mass and lifted it free.

Soft . . . His hand wanted to stroke through those heavy tresses until she purred like the kitchen cat. The scent of lilies filled his head. He had to force himself to stop there, to step back.

"What were you doing down here?" she asked.

"What? Oh." He indicated the tray he'd been preparing. "A midnight feast."

She took in his attire, and he was reminded that he still wore his evening kit, minus his coat. That his cravat must be disordered, his shirt points limp. "Have you been up all night?"

He nodded. "Wrestling with the accounts."

"Oh." She made a face. "Dull work."

"Strangely, I find it's not so tedious, after all," he said, leaning against the table. With a gleam of humor, he added, "But don't tell anyone I said that, will you? My credit would never survive."

It was a good thing his mouth operated independently of his brain. He couldn't seem to clear his senses. He still felt the soft brush of her curls against his fingertips, the delicate turn of her nape under his hand. The scent of lilies lingered in the mists of his brain.

Jane looked tousled and heavy-lidded, as if she'd risen from a troubled sleep. Outrageously feminine, a contrast with the mannish tailoring of his dressing gown.

"It suits you," he said.

"Thank you." Unconsciously, she lifted a hand to touch the silk, tracing her fingertip along the gold embroidery.

Constantine swallowed hard. For some reason, he felt her gesture on his own skin.

"You should keep it," he said.

The candlelight was too dim for him to see her blush but he was certain she did. "Oh, no!" She laughed, gathering up all the excess folds of silk. "What would I do with it?"

Come to my bed in it, he thought. *In that and nothing else.*

Perhaps his thoughts showed in his face, for she stammered a little. "I c-came down for some warm milk." She gave a hospitable wave of her hand. "Won't you sit and continue with your meal?"

His voice rasped. "I find I'm . . . not hungry anymore."

"Oh," she said again. Her eyes widened. Her lips parted. Desire slammed into him with the force of a stampede. He had to clench his fists at his sides to stop himself reaching for her.

There was a quiet thump on the table. He looked down to see the cat poised above his plate, about to help herself to his meal. Laughing, he scooped up the feline and set her down on the floor. "Not so well-mannered, after all."

Remembering his own manners, he indicated the tray. "Would you like some? Or shall we find you some milk?"

Slowly, she shook her head. "I'm not hungry, either. And I don't want milk."

Their gazes locked. His heartbeat seemed to throb in his brain, reverberate through his body, pound in his cock. She moistened her lips—out of nervousness, he supposed—and his member gave a decided twitch.

She took a small step toward him, but in one last attempt

at nobility, he held up a hand. "Restraint has never been my strong point, Jane. Go back to your bedchamber. Now."

He heard the soft gasp she gave, watched her throat ripple as she swallowed. Slowly, she put up her hands to remove his dressing gown, presumably to give it back to him. But before the garment left her shoulders he was there, catching the warm, slippery silk, bunching it in his hands, pulling her toward him.

She made no resistance. As the heat of his body mingled with hers, she put her hand on his shoulder and that hand did not push him away.

Hungrily, he sought her mouth, and the sensation of her lips beneath his was beyond everything he'd dreamed, like a ribbon of warm satin, like cream. She tasted of tooth powder and innocence, her kisses shallow and fluttering, like butterflies' wings. She responded as if she'd never been kissed by a man before.

Hot blood roared through him, and it took all of his will to deny his own needs while he explored and discovered hers.

He still held the dressing gown, not her, and their bodies never touched; he sensed he might frighten her if she knew the full power of his desire. Illogical, yes, given her widowhood, but his instincts overbore logic. He didn't want to ruin it all by rushing this. When she was his wife, they'd have all the time in the world.

So he didn't deepen the kiss, but instead let his lips drift along her cheek, whispered hot praise of her beauty into her ear that made her shiver and throw her head back. He kissed her throat where the pulse beat beneath his mouth and heard her wordless cry. He brushed that sensitive zone over and over, resisting the urge to mark the spot with his teeth.

Her hand moved restlessly along his shoulder to settle against his nape and press him closer. Her quiet, pleasured moans told him she was ready for more.

The silk dressing gown slipped from his grasp and hushed to the floor. One hand found her waist; the other drove through her hair to cradle her delicate skull. With his lips and tongue, he coaxed her mouth open and licked inside.

She stiffened for a moment, but he continued regardless, until she sighed and relaxed into it, tentatively stroking his tongue with hers.

That fleeting, hesitant touch set him ablaze. His arms tightened around her until her every curve molded to his, his burgeoning erection hard against her softness. Dimly, he realized his body was taking over from his brain, that in no time he'd have her flat on her back on the kitchen table, but he couldn't seem to remember why he ought to stop.

Until Jane gave a choked, panicked cry. Her body twisted and strained; two small hands flattened against his chest, pushing him away.

Constantine let her go as if she'd burned him. He was breathing heavily, disoriented, aching, suddenly furious. He'd lost control when he'd been determined to keep it. He'd sensed the depth of Jane's uncertainty, her physical reticence. He'd planned to seduce her in a slow, tantalizing slide into sin. Yet he'd mauled her like a goddamned animal.

He heard a sob and the skitter of slippers on the tile as she fled.

CHAPTER THIRTEEN

J ane didn't stop running until she flung herself onto her bed. She wanted to cry. She wanted to scream. She wanted to hit something. She bunched her sheets in her hands and growled all her confusion and anguish into her pillow.

How could she have *done* that?

She'd offered herself to him, encouraged him. A rake like Constantine wouldn't stop at kisses! She'd been stupid not to expect he'd take matters to their logical conclusion. And yet, the strength of his arms around her, the sensual mastery in his kiss—all of that led her to the point where she hadn't been thinking anymore.

But she'd woken from that pleasure-ridden haze the instant he'd pressed himself against her. She remembered with vivid, horrible clarity the pain and humiliation that went along with an aroused male organ.

When she married him, she'd have to suffer that, wouldn't she? Regardless of his need for an heir, Constantine Black was not the kind of man to accept a frigid wife with complacence. Even now, the heat and power of his sensuality made her body tremble with pleasured recollection. Why did all that lovely kissing have to culminate in such a disgusting, painful way?

Nights of clumsy fumblings in the dark flooded back, cramping her stomach. Frederick had been hasty, vigorous, and not at all gentle. Her first time had been so excruciating, she'd begged him to stop, the tears streaming down her face. He hadn't even heard her; he'd simply kept pumping away until it was over, then left immediately afterward, oblivious to her devastation.

He could never understand why she'd still suffered pain after that first occasion. Though he'd never said it in so many words, she'd sensed he'd wished she'd simply cease complaining. *Lie back and think of something else,* he'd said.

Frederick had offered no solution to this awful problem. The only women Jane might have felt comfortable asking were all maidens. She tried her best to relax, as Frederick told her to do, but every time he paid her a conjugal visit, her insides went rigid with the fear of pain she knew would come.

When, finally, she'd barred Frederick from her bedchamber, Frederick had called a doctor to examine her. The experience had been mortifying, but she'd been willing to suffer it if some remedy could be found. No such happy event occurred, however. The doctor gave his opinion that her body simply wasn't made the right way to endure Frederick's attentions. Frederick had never visited her bedchamber again.

But he'd visited many, many other bedchambers, hadn't he?

She buried her face in her pillow. The few moments when Constantine had pressed against her told her he was even larger than Frederick in that department. She shuddered at the thought of *that* impaling her on their wedding night.

But this time, she would simply have to suffer bedding without complaint. She owed that much to Constantine, after all.

Jane rode out alone the next morning, determined to put as much distance as she could between herself and the humiliation of last night. The sun shone, fighting to convey its warmth through a chill, persistent wind.

Of course, there was no escape from the painful thoughts that chased one another around her head.

She hadn't slept for thinking of Constantine. It had seemed as if three nights passed before the dawn finally arrived. With a click of her tongue, she spurred the mare forward, riding hard to block out the images that rose to her mind.

She was panting and more than a little thirsty by the time she reached sight of the stream beyond a high hedge that bordered the field.

"I suppose you'd like a drink, too, old girl?" She patted Sirralee's neck, intending to dismount and find a way to push through the hedge.

Startled bleats of sheep rang out behind her. At the sound of hoofbeats, she turned her head to see a large white stallion with a dark figure astride it. Unreasoning panic rippled through her. She spurred Sirralee forward.

Stealing a glance over her shoulder, Jane saw Constantine was gaining faster than she'd have thought possible. Knowing what a risk she took, she urged her mount on, slowing to a steady pace toward the hedge. She held her breath and silently sent up a prayer as the mare gathered herself and launched them over the timber barrier, landing soundly on the other side. Miraculously, Jane kept her seat.

Laughing with relief, she hunched low over the saddle, like a jockey, and let Sirralee fly. In her bones, she knew this flight was hopeless, but the sick feeling of humiliation made her desperate to get away.

The white horse drew abreast of her before she even reached the stream.

"Draw rein!" She'd never heard such a note of command in Constantine's voice before. A glance at his face told her he'd grown pale under his tan and his features were hard with fury.

Still, she rode on, wondering if Sirralee had it in her to clear the stream, but it was too foolhardy to attempt. She wheeled away from Constantine, urging her mount to run along the stream's edge. In no time, with scarce a check, the big white stallion ranged between her and the water, herding her away from the slippery bank.

She couldn't outrun or outsmart him. It was undignified to try. Panting, Jane threw Constantine a fulminating look and slowed her horse, then reined in.

She sat rigid in the saddle, feeling foolish and angry at herself.

Before she'd retrieved her dignity, he was at her side, reaching up. Large hands spanned her waist, lifting her down as if she weighed no more than a rag doll. His strength, the sheer size of him, made it even more imperative to get away.

"What the *hell* did you think you were doing?" he demanded, now gripping her shoulders and bending so he could glare into her face. His green eyes had lost every vestige of his usual cynical amusement. They drilled into hers.

"Well?" Constantine never wanted to relive those heart-stopping moments when Jane had sailed over that hedge and he'd lost sight of her. The barrier had been too high for that mare to jump; Jane was certain to break her neck.

That she would risk such danger to get away from him horrified him. Later, when he'd realized she was well and unharmed, it had angered him, too. Granted, he'd crossed the line last night, but that didn't make him a monster. Didn't she know that?

He ought not to have given chase when he saw her riding away from him. He'd endangered her by doing so. After the miracle of seeing her alive on the other side of that towering hedge, he ought to have let her go.

The notion made him even more furious—at himself.

He gave her a small shake. "Answer me, damn you!"

He couldn't even summon the patience to temper his words to her, despite the fact she trembled, her gray eyes wide. Her body was so slender, so fragile. He could break her in two. Yet, she rode with the courage of an Amazon and the skill of a born huntress. Latent pride in her warmed his chest, even as his brain seethed with anger.

With a gasp, she wrenched from his hold and stepped

back. "Isn't it obvious what I was doing? I came out here to be alone!"

"And instead, you nearly got yourself killed. Don't *ever* do that again!"

Her sleek brows snapped together. "You are not my husband yet, Lord Roxdale. Don't presume to lecture me."

"You may thank the fact that I am not your husband for my restraint! Have you no consideration for your horse, if not for yourself?"

She opened her mouth to argue, then shut it. Her lips pressed together; her nostrils flared.

"You are right," she admitted. "*Confound* it! I knew it as soon as it was done, but I—" She passed a shaking hand over her eyes.

Jane's frank acknowledgment that she was in the wrong disarmed him.

"Why?" he said huskily. "Why would you do such a thing?"

Her struggle was almost painful to witness, but he didn't break the fraught silence that ensued. He sensed that whatever the problem was, it loomed very large for her. At this moment, her defenses were down. He'd have no better chance of finding out than now. Thank God she wasn't a weeper; he could never resist feminine tears and would have let her off the hook without another word.

"Come," he said gently, taking her hand in a light clasp. "Our horses are refreshing themselves. I've no doubt you are parched, too."

She went with him willingly. She bent over the clear, cool stream, where he made a cup for her with his hands. She held his wrist to steady it. He tried to keep his mind off her lips as they inadvertently brushed his palms.

She murmured her thanks, dabbing at her damp mouth with her fingertips, then waited while he satisfied his own thirst. He gestured to a nearby tree and assisted her to sit in the shade.

No sooner had he made himself comfortable beside her than she sprang up and began to pace. With an inward sigh, he made as if to rise also, but she waved at him in a gesture that he took to mean he should remain where he was.

One hand clenched into a fist, Jane bit the tip of her thumb through her glove. Then she turned to face him, the skirts of her black riding habit swishing about her boots.

"Do you still wish to marry me after . . . after last night?"

Constantine well knew that the man who hesitates over that kind of question is lost.

"Yes," he said.

"Oh." Apparently, that came as some surprise to her. Her gaze was so pointed in its concentration, she seemed to be trying to read his mind.

He smiled. "In fact, at this moment, I can't think of anything I would rather do."

Startled gray eyes flew to his. "Really?"

"Really."

"Even though—even though I ran from you?"

"You were naturally unprepared for such a display of, er . . . passion," he reasoned. "It is I who bear the blame. I have no excuse, except that I lost my head over you."

And was likely to do so again, because she colored so charmingly at the oblique compliment. Her black beaver hat set off her auburn curls to perfection and all that pent-up emotion had made her eyes sparkle with cool fire. Her lips, perhaps chapped by the wind, were cherry red. Made for kissing. It was as if a cruel god heard Constantine's resolve to behave himself and flung it in his face.

But despite the temptation, he *would* behave himself. He wanted more from this woman than a quick tumble in the grass. Marriage was a serious business, which was why he'd so assiduously avoided it in the past. And clearly, seducing Jane required more patience, subtlety, and self-control than even he had guessed.

"Last night was . . . disconcerting," he added, in a flash of honesty.

Unimpressed by a disclosure that had, in fact, cost him something, she shook her head.

"You don't understand." She made as if to clasp her hands together, and ended by rubbing them over her face. "You don't understand, and I can't begin to tell you."

"Am I so forbidding, then?" He said it lightly to cover his real concern.

She made no reply, though her agitation seemed to vibrate from her in waves.

After a moment, he added, "You know, I always thought that confessions ought rather to be made to sinners than to saints. Sinners have so much more compassion." He thought about that. "Well, they don't often sit in judgment, anyway."

She seemed struck by his words, fallible though the logic might be. For some moments, she chewed on her lip before she turned to face him. Unsmiling, he gazed back at her, willed her to unburden herself of this terrible secret.

Her lips parted; her eyes softened. One strand of that glorious hair rippled across her face . . .

Then she looked away, blowing out a long, unsteady breath, her confidences borne off by the wind.

An ache formed in his chest that had no business being there. Why the hell should she confide in him? What would he do with her troubles anyway?

Make them ten times worse, his father would have said.

"I have to get back." Disappointment roughened his tone. Foolish and unreasonable of him, but he wanted her to trust him.

He rose, putting on his hat.

She nodded, still refusing to look at him. For a moment, he watched the gauzy black scarf that trailed from her hat flirt between her shoulder blades. He wanted to shrug off the unsettling, unnamed emotion that made him linger without an agenda or a plan, or even a clue, if it came down to it.

The silence seemed to stretch forever between them.

Finally, he cleared his throat. "Jane. Grant me a favor?" He tugged on his gloves.

She stiffened. "What is it?"

He glanced back at the hedge, and then at her mount. "Please. Take the long way home."

CHAPTER FOURTEEN

Extraordinary Meeting of the Ministry of Marriage

Agenda (*notes by Oliver, Lord deVere*)

Attendance, apologies	*Where is that blasted Arden? Lazenby?!*
Minutes from last meeting	*Mr. Wicks verbose as ever. Get on with it, you old woman!*
Candidates:	
Lady Amelia Black	*Awful mother. Excellent dowry. Bad teeth.*
Miss Melanie Pitt	*Pretty enough. Don't like stable. M can have her.*
Lady Emma Howling	*Ape leader. Ugly as sin. They'll never fire her off unless they whack another £10,000 on the dowry. And even then . . .*
Lady Jacqueline deVere	*!!!*

Lord Maccles	*Genteel fortune. Political ambitions. No chin.*
Sir Stanley Westruther	*Rich as Croesus, bit of a pill. Might do for K.*
Mr. Thomas Black	*Bounder. Owes me a monkey.*
Other business: Jane, Lady Roxdale	*I'll have Arden's pretty hide for this!*
Buns or scones with tea?	*What idiot put that on the agenda? Bloody Wicks.*
Adjourn	*Thank God! Load of upper-crust inbreeds!*

The Duke of Montford sat in a deep leather armchair at White's club in St. James Street, London, drinking good brandy and amicably trading barbs with Oliver, Lord deVere.

Their rivalry had lost much of its former heat. As the years rolled by, Montford found himself with increasingly more in common with the head of a rival house. Not that either of them would ever admit it aloud, least of all to one another.

"Think you're vastly clever, don't you?" DeVere's voice was a deep aristocratic rumble. "Think I don't know the pair of you are in league together."

Eyes half closed, deVere slumped in his chair, swirling his brandy. The man was in his forties, drank deeply, yet maintained a fit and muscular physique. Montford often wondered how he managed it.

The duke didn't trouble to answer the charge deVere laid at his door. Even if he denied it, the man wouldn't believe him.

The hastily convened meeting of the Ministry of Marriage had unfolded exactly as Montford had foreseen. He'd heard the cases put forward for each candidate and the proposed matches. He'd taken due note of every point for and against, smoothing over the arguments that naturally erupted between proud and volatile personalities with so much wealth and position at stake.

He'd adjourned the matter of Lady Roxdale until he'd had time to consider further. Given the way Frederick had left his fortune, it was clear that not just any candidate would do.

"Lady Arden was conspicuous by her absence today," commented deVere.

"Yes." Montford sipped his brandy. "One would assume she'd be eager to put Constantine Black's case, wouldn't one?"

With a brooding glare, deVere tossed off the rest of his brandy and slammed the glass down on the table. "Damn it, she's making fools of us all! What would you wager she's not down there interfering? Meddling and matchmaking, trying to get the drop on the rest of us."

When Montford didn't reply, deVere scoffed, "You wouldn't wager a groat. She's at Lazenby Hall this very minute, and you know it."

Mildly, Montford replied, "There is no reason Lady Arden cannot visit Constantine Black if she chooses. If she contravenes the rules, she will be disciplined."

"*I'd* like to discipline her," said deVere, his eyes kindling. "Damned fine figure of a woman. Pity she's such a termagant." He cocked an eyebrow. "You have an interest there?"

Montford suppressed the urge to lie. "No."

Not at present. When this particular business is over, then perhaps . . .

But it was never over, was it? And in the end, he was simply making excuses.

"Hmph. You're a wily cove, Montford. I don't trust you, but at least with you, I know where I stand. Or don't, as the case may be." With a slightly owlish cast to his eyes, deVere raised his glass as if in a toast. "More than that, I cannot say about any man I know."

The convoluted logic of this statement very nearly eluded Montford, but he believed it was meant as a compliment and he took it as such. A rare gift from deVere.

The big man rose. "Think I'll travel down to Gloucestershire to stay with my nephew for a few days. Give him a nudge along. Do some meddling on my own account."

He drew out his quizzing glass and swung it to and fro. "About that other girl of yours. The beauty. Rose . . . Rosemary . . . *Rosamund,* that's it. Ready to set a date yet? Only, my boy's champing at the bit, d'ye see?"

With a slight, incredulous smile, Montford rose also. He doubted that the Earl of Tregarth champed at the bit to be leg-shackled to Rosamund. He'd made no attempt to pursue his interest with her since they were formally betrothed. More likely, it was Lord deVere himself who was impatient to see the alliance between his kinsman and a Westruther heiress signed, sealed, and delivered.

He clapped his companion on the shoulder. "Patience, Oliver. At present, the issue is a trifle . . . fraught. You would not wish to trammel the lady's delicate sensibilities. Let us speak of it again in the new year."

As they parted on the stairs, Montford considered Lady Rosamund Westruther. How much simpler it would be if young people could see their little infatuations and flirtations through the wiser eyes of their elders. As a man of considerable experience, Montford knew the concept of enduring romantic love was a fable.

Infatuation, desire, passion—all of them existed, of course. But a deep, *lasting* passionate love between a man and a woman—in that, he did not believe. Affection, liking, respect, yes. But from what he'd seen, those things most often sprang from marriages where the parties did not consider themselves in love in the first place.

He'd observed so-called love matches. Time and again, the parties to them turned bitter or bored or elsewhere for affection once the flame of infatuation had burned out.

Some called him cynical, mercenary, power-hungry at

the expense of his young relatives' happiness. He shrugged that off, for he knew the truth: the most contented marriages were based on strategic alliances, not on love.

He would not give Rosamund his blessing to run off with her dashing cavalry officer. Nor would he allow Jane to hide herself away at Harcourt, where, despite her wealth, she would dwindle into some form of appendage or other: companion, chaperone, honorary aunt. She needed a family and a home of her own.

Jane would thank him one day for what she'd call his cold-blooded interference.

In spite of himself, he was counting on that.

Jane rambled through the wilderness on the other side of the lake. She'd told herself she'd come out here to enjoy the rare fine weather, but in her heart, she knew the real reason. She was avoiding Constantine Black.

She didn't know what to do. If she jilted Constantine, she'd do it at the expense of the Lazenby estate and she might lose Luke in the bargain. But if she went ahead with the wedding, she'd be obliged to tell him the truth about herself. Either that, or risk his anger when he discovered it.

A heavy step on the path nearby made her freeze. "Jane?" Constantine's voice. Had he seen her come this way?

Screened by shrubbery, she ducked low to avoid being seen. Without considering what she did, Jane turned and plunged farther into the wilderness.

Like everything else that comprised the Lazenby landscape, this garden had been carefully constructed to present an artless, tangled appearance. Even its waterfall was manmade, cleverly making use of local, rough-hewn stone, natural springs, and gravity to create an artless effect.

In the center of this cultivated overgrowth was a grotto, a picturesque ruin that seemed to grow out of the hillside.

Jane stole inside the grotto to hide. Gasping for breath, she pressed her palm to the cold, hard wall and leaned on it.

With the other hand, she tugged the ribbons of her straw bonnet loose and ripped it from her head, then pressed her forehead to the coolness of the grotto wall.

"What's the matter?" Constantine's voice, coming from behind her, sent a shock down her spine. "Jane, why are you avoiding me?"

Oh, God. What a ninny she must seem to him. Moments passed before she shook her head. "I'm not avoiding you."

"But you are." He took her hand and gently turned her so she faced him. The warm intensity was back in those green eyes. How could she resist him when he looked at her like that?

"Jane," he murmured, "you are going to be my wife."

Her gaze fluttered downward. Her heart gave a sharp pound. Of course he wanted her to . . . to respond to him physically. It was only reasonable. She'd accepted his hand in marriage, after all.

Could she grow to love Constantine, regardless of his past? She rather feared the answer to that question was yes. She liked, even esteemed, the man Constantine Black had become. Should a mistake he'd made in his salad days be held against him for the rest of his life? Foolish, perhaps, but she had a strong feeling that if only he'd explain his side of the story, her fears on that head would be allayed.

The more pressing question was whether she ought to give him the truth about herself. Surely, in other circumstances, she'd think herself bound to mention it. With Constantine, she simply didn't know. Would it make a difference to him, anyway? He needed her money.

And she needed Luke.

His fingertips under her chin coaxed her to look up.

"I'm sorry," he said softly. "I didn't realize our kiss that night in the kitchen would distress you so."

"It wasn't the kiss," she said. "The kiss was lovely, but I . . ." She trailed off, powerless to form coherent sentences when he looked at her like that. His closeness deranged what few wits she had left.

"How glad I am to hear you say that," he said. "Will you tell me what has upset you, then? Come here."

The concern in his gaze made her insides soften and heat. She made no protest when he drew her into his arms and closed them around her.

In spite of her doubts, she felt safe and warm in his arms. Constantine's embrace was unlike any she'd received from a man. Comforting and strong . . . and thoroughly arousing.

The thought startled her. She gripped the lapel of his coat and turned her face into his chest. Through layers of linen and broadcloth, she heard his heart beating a steady rhythm. She smelled him, a delightful mix of masculine scents, linen starch, and something faintly astringent, like lemon.

His palm skimmed over her shoulder and down her arm. He found her hand and clasped it in his. "What troubles you so?" he murmured.

She shuddered and shook her head. "It's too complicated."

"I have all day to listen. And all night, too, if you will it." He waited but she couldn't trust herself to speak.

He sighed. "You don't have to explain if you don't want to. Look at me, Jane."

Taking a deep breath, she raised her face, with the certain knowledge that when she did, he'd kiss her. Everything inside her yearned for that kiss, aye, and feared it, too.

She thought back to the last time, when they'd shared that stirring, breathtaking embrace in the kitchen. Perhaps . . . perhaps with him it might be different. Maybe she would not need to tell him her difficulties at all.

"Jane." His voice was a husky whisper. His fingers threaded between hers in a more intimate clasp.

In the dim light, his eyes glittered. He raised a hand to cup her cheek and she marveled that a man so magnificent could look at her as if *she* were precious and rare. She was so ordinary. *Plain Jane*. Yet, this beautiful man made her feel beautiful, too.

This was it. This moment. She should tell him the truth.

But his face swam in her vision, and his lips met hers in a

kiss that was light yet burning hot. With a soft moan, she returned the pressure of his lips. Truth slid from her grasp. Every rational thought flew away.

Her fingers flexed between his and he tightened his grip. Her mouth opened to him and he swiftly accepted that mute invitation, tangling his tongue with hers.

He broke the kiss to skim his lips down, past her ear, to her throat. Fiery tingles chased through her body. She gasped. He was breathing heavily; they both were.

"I want you," he murmured against her skin. "I've never wanted a woman more."

She didn't believe it, but that didn't signify at this moment. *She'd* never wanted a man more than she wanted him, and that was what mattered now.

His fingers slid beneath her fichu, a filmy white scarf she'd tucked into the bodice of her gown. Slowly, he drew it out, and the soft linen slid from her neck with a shushing sound, baring her décolletage to the cool air.

She shivered. "Oh, what are you doing to me?" This must be a rake's arts; Frederick had never done anything remotely like this.

Constantine trailed his fingertips over her bare flesh, making her shudder again. Uncharacteristically solemn, he said, "I am kissing you.

"Here . . ." He bent his head to brush her collarbone with his mouth. "Here . . ." He kissed the top of one breast. "And here." His lips pressed the swell of her other breast.

"So beautiful," he murmured. "I need to taste you."

Barely able to draw breath, she watched his dark head as he bent to her again. Her breasts were pushed together by her corset. He licked into the crease between them.

The sensation was hot and wet and leisurely. Sinful. Her knees nearly buckled, but his strong arm came around her waist, supporting her. His other hand pressed against her stomach, then skimmed upward, to cup beneath her breast.

The heat of him, the forbidden decadence of his touch, nearly overwhelmed her. But there was something more she wanted. Her nipples were hard and aching beneath the layers of gown and shift and corset. She wanted . . . oh, she wanted . . .

His hand moved upward, and the instant his fingertips touched her nipple, her body flamed with pleasure. He kneaded and stroked and she couldn't stop the shudders that took her.

"Yes, that's it, that's it," he murmured against her shoulder, kissing it softly. "Let go, Jane. Let go."

But it wasn't enough. All those layers of clothing . . . She'd never felt this hunger before. She'd never wanted so much to have a man's hands on her skin.

Through the haze of frantic delight, she registered Constantine's hand gathering her gown, his palm skating up, past her garter, past her bare thigh.

Instinct made her panic, begin to pull away, but he said, "Jane, let me touch you. Please."

She couldn't respond to that, but she held still while his clever fingers brushed over her inner thigh. She gasped. A great throb set up between her legs and she realized with dismay that she'd grown moist there.

She clamped her legs together. "No, I—I can't."

Denied its destination, his hand moved to her flank, then to shape one cheek of her bottom, caressing languidly. "Open your legs for me, sweetheart." He breathed the words against her neck. "I want to touch all that lovely soft heat."

The words would have melted her if she hadn't been suffused with shame. Frantic now, she pushed at him, struck at his chest. "No! Don't!"

He froze. Then his embrace abruptly fell away, casting her off balance. She stumbled past him and ran out of the grotto. She had no destination in mind, just the need to get away.

"Jane! Come back. Jane!"

Before she reached the path, he'd caught up with her, his hand gripping her elbow. "What happened back there?" he demanded.

She halted. She owed him an explanation. She knew it. She ought not to blow hot and cold on him like this. Besides, she'd accepted his proposal of marriage. He had a right to know the truth about her.

"Why, Jane?" His voice was husky. "Do you find me so repugnant?"

Her courage faltered a little at that. "That's not it at all. I find you . . . quite the reverse of repugnant."

"Quite. Well, that's something, I suppose," he said in a flat tone.

She stared stonily above his head at the tree behind him while she spoke. "I fear it is only fair to tell you . . . It will seem to you as if I have been dishonest. I *thought* perhaps I could, but I can't."

She took her underlip between her teeth and looked upward, blinking hard to hold the tears at bay. "Constantine, I cannot be a proper wife to you. I—it is not *you;* it is the conjugal act that is repugnant to me."

CHAPTER FIFTEEN

This was indeed a shock. Constantine stood silent a moment, taking it in.

"Oh? What do you find particularly objectionable about it?" he asked conversationally.

What on earth had that dunderhead cousin of his done to the poor girl?

Then he blocked that image, because thinking about Jane in Frederick's bed was not conducive to keeping a clear head.

Perhaps reassured by his unemotional reaction, she said more calmly, "It is painful for me. The doctor said I am not made the right way. My shape . . . it is impossible for me to have relations of an intimate nature without pain."

He frowned. "The doctor said this?" He had no great opinion of doctors, as a breed. At best, they knew their limitations. At worst, they killed more patients than they cured.

She nodded, blinking hard. Poor darling; she was trying desperately not to weep.

He didn't know what made him do it. "That is a very serious problem, of course."

Her brow puckered. "I know. I shall never give you an heir, so you see—"

"But it so happens," he interrupted, "that you have come to the right place."

She stared at him then, openmouthed with astonishment.

He waved a hand. "Yes. You see, I am something of an expert on the subject . . ."

Her eyes narrowed.

Grinning, he ignored her forbidding expression. ". . . and I cannot believe that what that idiot of a doctor said was true."

"*Not true?* But every time we . . ." She faltered, scarlet painting her cheeks. "Oh, this is ridiculous! I might have guessed you'd turn this into a joke. I can't believe I'm even discussing it with you."

At that, he crossed the space between them and took her hand in his. "It is not a jest. I pledge you my word it is not a jest." He cupped her jaw in his hand. "Ah, Jane, I can give you pleasure beyond your wildest dreams, if only you'll let me."

Her breathing altered. Her eyelashes fluttered down. "But what if you can't?" she said sadly. "After we're married, it would be too late for you to turn back."

After they were married . . . "Why not before?"

The more he considered it, the more it made sense to him. "Yes, why not before we get married? We cannot wed until we obtain Montford's blessing. What if we do our best to, er, get you accustomed to the idea in the meantime? If you still find the notion abhorrent, you can cry off."

His mouth took on a cynical twist. "Everyone will say you're well rid of me, so you don't need to fear damage to your reputation over that."

She gazed at him in wonder. "You would agree to such a thing?"

"Sweet Jane." He laughed a little. "Believe me, I'd be getting the better end of the bargain."

Of course, he didn't consider himself so damned irresistible that a woman with serious problems would be miraculously cured by his attentions. But he'd never heard of a woman who simply wasn't made for bed sport.

Jane had been given a rotten time of it by that oaf Frederick, no doubt, and he'd made matters worse by heaping blame on her head instead of accepting it himself.

How long had she and Frederick been married?

"You poor love," he said softly. "What agonies you must have suffered through."

He drew her into his arms and kissed her gently. Feeling her tense with apprehension, he said, "No, I'm not going to begin now. But if you have any pity in you at all, princess, don't keep me in suspense any longer. Will you, Jane, do me the great honor of becoming my wife?"

She squeezed her eyes shut, took a deep breath, then exhaled. "Yes, Constantine. I will." She opened her eyes and looked up at him, very grave. "I shall be your betrothed, at any rate."

Again, that ache in his chest. He released her and took her hand, placing it on his arm as they turned back toward the house.

He spoke carefully. "In a perfect world, you would preserve the correct period of mourning for Frederick before we became engaged. However, I believe we must announce our betrothal soon, so that settlements may be agreed upon and the debt on the mill repaid."

"I expect you're right," she said. A small sigh escaped her, as if she didn't relish the prospect.

He paused. "I trust you won't find too much embarrassment in your situation. People will talk, of course, but once it is widely known how the estate was left, they'll applaud you for doing your duty." He glanced down at her. *However distasteful that might be.*

She blinked at him in surprise. "But I don't give a fig for what people think."

Ah, of course. He'd forgotten, for the moment, that she was a Westruther. "Then what troubles you?"

Her gaze lowered. "I must admit, I dread telling the Duke of Montford. He was against our alliance from the outset."

He frowned. "You are not afraid of him?"

"No! No, it's not easy to explain." She spread her hands. "He is the most redoubtable gentleman. If he sets out to achieve something, he always does. I've never known him at a stand over even the smallest thing." She brought her thumb to her lips and worried at the side of it with her teeth. "I fear that if he wants to stop us marrying, he'll do it."

Surely her worry was needless. "What can Montford do? He has no control over you."

"Oh, I don't know! Even though I'm a grown woman now, with Montford I still feel like a lost little girl." Her gaze flicked to Constantine. "Did Lady Arden tell you much about my history?"

He shook his head.

She drew a deep breath. "I was eight years old when the Duke of Montford found me."

They reached the stone bridge that arched romantically over the lake. Jane picked up her skirts to begin the climb to its apex. "My mother ran away from home soon after I was born, taking me with her. I don't remember her at all. They told me that within a short time of arriving in London, she died."

"They?" he repeated.

"The couple at the boardinghouse who took me in." Her lips quivered; her eyes darkened, as if at a frightening memory. "They were . . . not kind people. I was luckier than many children in that part of London, however. While they hadn't been able to discover my identity, my keepers deduced that I belonged to the Quality. They could have appropriated the money my mother left and thrown me into a foundling hospital, but instead, they fed, housed, and clothed me. You see, they gambled that one day, someone from my family would come in search of me and repay them handsomely for their care."

Constantine listened to this tale, appalled. His delicate Jane, in the hands of such monsters? He couldn't imagine what she'd suffered. No wonder she found it so difficult to give anyone her trust.

"And that's what happened." His voice sounded rusty to his ears. "Montford found you."

"Yes. The duke. They pawned my mother's belongings and somehow Montford got wind of it and found them. He came down on that awful pair like the wrath of God." She lifted one shoulder. "I still don't know exactly what happened to them. His Grace simply told me he'd taken care of it and I wasn't to trouble my head about them ever again. For the first time in my life I felt safe."

They'd reached the top of the bridge's gentle curve. Constantine took her hand and held it. He hated to think of her so fearful and alone. "I'm glad a man of Montford's steel dealt with them. I don't think I'd be content with anything less." He hoped the duke had wrung their bloody necks and thrown them into the Thames.

He hesitated. "Your father?"

"Oh . . ." She looked away, out over the lake. "I wasn't the boy—the heir—he wanted, apparently. He didn't trouble to look for me. I never knew him, but I'm told he was not a nice man. When he died, the duke was appointed my guardian. I was quite an heiress as the only child of a wealthy earl. That's why the duke searched for me so diligently."

For a few moments, Jane gazed out over the blue brilliance of the lake. Then she took Constantine's arm again, and they descended to the other side.

"So you see," she finished, as they stepped off the bridge, "Montford has always loomed large in my life. If he could search England and find a small girl . . . Well, stopping our marriage would be child's play." She shook her head. "It sounds foolish to you, I daresay."

"No, not foolish. It is natural for you to feel that way. We would do well to enlist Lady Arden's aid in securing Montford's agreement." He took her hand in his. "But let me assure you that I have not the slightest urge to bend to Montford's will. Whatever pressure he might place on you, *my* determination to marry you will not change."

She seemed to consider that. "May I ask you a question, Constantine?"

"Of course."

"Why do you wish to marry me?"

He didn't allow his easy amble to falter. She had

disconcerted him, however. The longer he hesitated, the more apparent that became.

In an attempt at recovery, he gave her a glinting smile. "For your money, my dear. I thought you knew that."

A small frown puckered the space between those sleek eyebrows.

Before she could puzzle out the truth, he drew her into the concealing shade of a tree and took her into his arms. "However," he added, "there are definite side benefits."

Constantine's mouth found Jane's before she could voice a protest. He swept her up into his embrace, trusting that the heat of his lips and tongue on hers would melt her objections, that she'd lose herself in passion.

When he raised his head at last, he felt as dizzy as a boy stealing his first kiss.

"Midnight," he whispered against her lips. "I'll come to you tonight."

"Yes." She shivered in his arms, whether in fear or excitement, he wasn't sure.

When he would have drawn back, she followed him into the kiss and prolonged it, moving restlessly against him, dancing her tongue over his, running her palms along his shoulders. With questing forays of her mouth and hands, she questioned him. And, God help him, he answered, told her all she wanted to know.

He emerged much later with the disorienting feeling that Jane had turned the tables on him, though he didn't quite know how. But as they finally recollected themselves and strolled back to the house, it struck him that she was now well informed of the truth of his intentions, even if he'd meant to keep her ignorant. Perhaps better informed than he was, and that didn't suit him at all.

"Oh, my dears! That is wonderful news. How thrilling! I had not the least notion of it when I saw you this morning." Lady Arden's expressive features lit with delight.

"Disingenuous, ma'am," said Constantine, stealing an arm around Lady Arden's waist and kissing her cheek. "You've been angling for this outcome from the first."

"Only because I'm persuaded it's what's best for you both," she asserted.

Her ladyship sank onto a couch in a cloud of muslin. "Do sit down and tell me all about it."

When Constantine made as if to join them, she flicked her hand in a dismissive gesture. "No, not you, Constantine! Men are shockingly in the way when it comes to discussing proposals and bridals. Jane, dear. Come and take some tea."

With a comical look of dismay, Constantine turned to take Jane's hand in a warm clasp.

This time, he did not merely bow, but raised her hand to kiss it. The action made a caress of the courtesy. Gentlemen did not kiss ladies' hands anymore, or at least not in public.

The brush of his lips across her knuckles sent heat scintillating through her body. She gasped and felt her cheeks redden. When Constantine looked up, there was a world of sensual promise in his eyes. The look was swift, but none the less powerful for that. Before Jane had quite recovered from this interlude, he was gone.

She turned, to find Lady Arden busy with the tea things, turning the tap on the silver urn to let hot water rush into a delicate china cup. Thank goodness she had not observed that exchange.

Jane's cheeks were feverishly hot, her body jittery. She made herself draw a deep, calming breath before she sat opposite Lady Arden over the tea urn.

When she'd finished her preparations, Lady Arden handed Jane her cup.

She observed Jane with an air of satisfaction. "You are just the woman I would have chosen for Constantine! I prophesy you'll deal extremely together."

She'd said exactly the same about Frederick, as Jane recalled, so it was difficult to take comfort from the assurance. Of course, Lady Arden hadn't an inkling about the true nature of Jane's marriage. In their youth, Jane and Frederick had been friends. Lady Arden could be excused for predicting their union would be a happy one.

"Tell me, Jane," said the lady, picking up her own cup and gazing at her over its brim. "Is this a love match?"

Jane thought of Constantine's answer to a similar question. Controlling her voice, she said, "Good God, no! It's for the estate."

Of all people, Lady Arden would understand that motive. She would be less inclined to credit Jane's other reason.

Luke. Constantine was going to be an excellent father, even if he didn't know it yet.

Lady Arden nodded. "Very wise. Well, I am vastly pleased that you are both being so practical, at last. I'd be even better satisfied if you hadn't developed a *tendre* for one another."

Jane jumped and a little tea spilled in her saucer. "Oh, drat!"

"Never mind, dear. I daresay you'll both deny it, so I'll hold my peace." She selected a biscuit. "Nothing wrong with having a *tendre* for the man you are to wed, of course, but beware, won't you? Men like Constantine might appear besotted in the first flush of courtship, but once they get what they want from you, their ardor often dies."

The brilliance in Lady Arden's eyes dimmed a little. She set down the biscuit, uneaten, on her plate. "You will be financially secure, of course. Montford will make sure the settlements are generous in your favor. I'm sure Constantine wouldn't have it any other way."

"As to that, ma'am," Jane said, "I fear we shall meet with opposition from the duke. He warned me not to consider marrying Constantine."

"Oh, don't worry about His Grace. I shall handle him." Lady Arden hesitated. "I did not like to raise the matter before, but now that there is an understanding between you, I feel it incumbent on me to mention it."

Jane froze. Lady Arden was going to rake up the past, just when Jane had made her peace with Constantine's part in that long-ago scandal. "Constantine's history is none of my concern. Truly, there's no need—"

"But there is, dear." Lady Arden smoothed her skirts a little, then folded her hands in her lap. With the air of one who was undertaking an unpleasant task, she said, "As his wife, you'll be affected by Constantine's standing in society in all manner of ways."

"I don't care for society, so that makes no odds," said Jane.

One of the reasons she'd agreed so readily to marry Frederick at seventeen was to avoid making her come-out in London. That, and the fact she'd been wholly infatuated with the man.

"Not care for society!" Lady Arden took out her handkerchief and fanned herself a little. "Oh, my dear. You *must,* for Constantine's sake, overcome your reluctance for polite company."

"For Constantine's sake?"

"Well, of course, dear. He would never admit it, but for a social creature like Constantine, being cast out the way he was . . . It wasn't easy for him."

"Perhaps he ought to have considered that before he seduced and abandoned an innocent girl," said Jane tartly.

Lady Arden raised her brows. "If that's what you think, I am surprised you countenanced his suit."

A very good point, and one Jane still wrestled with. She pursed her lips. "And *I* am surprised, my lady, that *you* have not already helped reestablish Constantine's character in the *ton.*"

Perhaps, before he became Roxdale, reestablishing him had not been such a matter of concern to Lady Arden. Now, *that* was a cynical thought! But it behooved Jane to remember that Lady Arden and the Duke of Montford were birds of a feather when it came to furthering the interests of their respective houses. One could never be too cynical in judging their motives.

"You are right. I failed," Lady Arden said, surprising her.

"Ordinarily, I do not admit defeat, but in this case . . ." She shrugged unhappily. "I could not help Constantine because he didn't wish to be helped. He went straight to the Devil and there was little I could do."

"His family?"

Lady Arden shook her head. "His father cast him off completely, and of course his mother and sisters were too timid to flout his authority. Constantine's brother George was the only one who stood by him, but George is a country gentleman, and a younger son at that. His stamp of approval counted for little among the beau monde."

Jane shifted uncomfortably. "I beg your pardon, ma'am, but I feel disloyal, talking about Constantine this way."

"My dear, it is not disloyal to discuss what we might do for him. We both have his best interests at heart. And the Lord knows he will never tell you this himself. The fact that he can still show his face at all in society is partly due to my intervention. I must say, it wasn't easy, especially when Constantine was so determined to shoot himself in the foot over the business."

She paused. "You say you do not care for society. You might think that is so, until an old friend cuts you in the street, or your children are ostracized by their peers. Scandal can taint your extended family, too, you know. How would you manage if your own cousins were prohibited from receiving you at Harcourt?"

"I'm persuaded that would never happen."

Lady Arden spread her hands. "Perhaps not. But it is what would occur in many cases. Constantine's papa barred him from his own home, you know. The poor boy didn't see his father again before he died. It is no easy thing to live with one foot in and one foot out of our world. You've never known what it is to be cast out, Jane, and I hope you never will."

Jane frowned over these words. "Are you saying I shouldn't marry him, ma'am?"

"I'm saying you need to help him. You are a Westruther,

an intimate connection of the Duke of Montford. The simple act of Constantine's marrying you goes a long way to reestablish him, but it will not be quite enough. You need to show the world that he has your full support, and that of your family."

The prospect gave Jane a panicky feeling in her chest. She'd rather have a tooth drawn than go to balls and parties in Town. But she couldn't ignore Lady Arden's plea.

A little shyly, she said, "You have an affection for him, don't you, my lady?"

"Oh, yes indeed! He was such an impetuous, wild youth, but always with a good, kind heart." She shook her head, her dark eyes sad. "I never understood why he didn't do the decent thing by Miss Flockton. Anyone could see he was mad for the girl. We all thought it only a matter of time before they tied the knot. And then that horrid scandal."

Lady Arden sipped her tea. "He and Miss Flockton were found together in his bedchamber at a house party, can you believe it? How *could* Constantine have been so indiscreet? Why couldn't he have waited till the wedding night, I ask you? Men! Sometimes they do not think with their brains, if you take my meaning."

Jane couldn't mistake the innuendo. Her cheeks heated. She tried not to think of this unknown Miss Flockton in Constantine's bed.

"The duke told me Miss Flockton married a barrister," she managed.

"Yes, well, what could the poor girl do when her idiot brother had the bad taste to challenge Constantine to a duel over her, and the parents wailed about her shame all over town? Trying to force Constantine's hand over it, I daresay. They were minor gentry, but ambitious. The girl hadn't a penny, but she was very beautiful, of course."

Oh, of course, thought Jane bitterly. Any girl Constantine ruined would be beautiful.

"Constantine came out of the duel unscathed but the brother did not," said Lady Arden. "The least Constantine

could have done was deloped—fired in the air, you know—
but not he! The ball lodged in the brother's shoulder and he
nearly died of a fever, poor fellow. It looked for a time that
Constantine would have to fly the country, but thank goodness, the brother rallied. And still Constantine wouldn't
marry the girl! She had no choice but to wed a nobody and
thank heaven she didn't suffer a worse fate."

Jane shook her head over it. She couldn't quite reconcile
this story with what she knew, or thought she knew, of Constantine. One thing it did teach her, however, was not to place
too much faith in his apparent affections. He must be a fickle
creature to have deserted a lady so in need of his help. A
lady, moreover, whom he'd made the object of his attentions.

Tentatively, Jane said, "Constantine and Frederick had a
falling-out, but I had the impression that it was not to do with
Miss Flockton." She hesitated. "I had heard Constantine lost
his fortune at cards."

"Nonsense! Broadmere is a prosperous estate and the
family is perfectly well-to-do. Where had you heard that?"

Jane frowned. "Do you know, I'm not sure. It must have
been from Frederick, I think."

Why would Frederick have said such things if they weren't
true? Perhaps he genuinely believed them. Or perhaps he'd
been so prejudiced against his cousin that he heaped every
kind of ill on his head.

Setting down her teacup, Lady Arden shrugged. "Oh, I
daresay Constantine plays—we all do—but he never lost
any large sums at the tables or you may be sure I'd have heard
of it."

Her brow puckered, Jane said, "I might have misunder-
stood, or perhaps Frederick did. I am pleased to know that it
is not the case. I should hate to see this estate laid to waste
from such a cause as gaming."

"You may rest easy on that score," said Lady Arden. She
leaned forward, fixing her brilliant dark eyes on Jane. "Will
you help him?"

Given her bargain with Constantine, she wasn't in a position to promise any such thing. If she needed to break their betrothal, she would only do Constantine's reputation more harm.

"I'll try," she said.

The afternoon had been unseasonably sultry, uneasy and tense, as if the atmosphere held its breath. With nightfall came the deluge, and a strong wind that swept up showers of rain and flung them against the windowpanes.

Jane shivered, only partly with cold. Despite the clouds finding release in this downpour, her nerves felt thoroughly on edge. Constantine had not come down to dinner, calling for a tray in the muniments room as he labored on.

She'd tried to calm her nerves by every means known to her. Warm milk that she left untouched, a novel that could not engage her, needlework that sat in her lap unheeded while her needle remained poised in midair.

When all was quiet in the house, she rose and went to the communicating door between her bedchamber and Constantine's. She pressed her ear to the panel but heard nothing within.

Midnight, he'd said.

Slowly, her fingers closed around the ornate key that held the door fast against his intrusion. With painstaking care, she eased the key around, and heard the tumblers unlock with a small click.

Her heart gave a great thump at the sound. She glanced around her chamber. There was too much light. Snatching up the snuffer from the mantelpiece, she doused all of the candles but one. Sitting down at her dressing table, she set the lone candle upon it.

A long look in the mirror told her she looked pale, her eyes hollow with apprehension; that her abundant, thick hair needed taming. She covered her face with shaking hands. Oh, God, how would she manage this? How could she have said yes to him?

How could she have said no?

Constantine Black compelled her, utterly. Even while she knew the risk she took, she still longed to go through with their midnight tryst. She thought of his hand on her thigh; his lips on the swell of her breast. She'd never felt so vital, so lacking in control of her body and her emotions as she had with him. Just thinking of it made her body thrum with excitement.

And soon, very soon, he would be here.

Now, Jane fully understood why that Miss Flockton had opened her bedchamber door to him, inviting her own ruin, all those years ago.

Really, how laughable! She'd thought herself superior to that silly, innocent chit; too wise, too cynical about the ways of men, *too cold-natured* to be taken in.

Yet, she was just as silly and malleable and hot-blooded as any other woman when it came to Constantine Black.

Sillier. She stood in grave danger of losing her heart to him.

A clap of lightning illuminated the room. For an instant, Jane saw the horror on her face reflected starkly in the mirror. Thunder rolled ominously above.

For a few shocked moments, Jane couldn't seem to draw a breath. She clutched the edge of her dressing table, and the ruched satin edging pressed into her palms.

No. Denial crowded her mind, beat in her chest. She couldn't possibly be so stupid as to fall in love with a handsome face.

But it wasn't just his magnificent form and features that held her captive, was it?

He was charismatic, magnetic; he drew people to him, then set them firmly at a distance without them even knowing it. Some instinct within her wanted—needed—to bridge that gap, to annihilate it. Sometimes, she thought she had, and then he threw up some other defense, or distracted her by saying something obnoxious.

She sensed that the more tightly their lives entwined together, the more he would fortify his defenses against her.

Well, if Constantine could show her pleasure in the marriage bed, it would be a gift, indeed. Perhaps she ought not to ask for more. Supplication was not in her nature; if he did not want to let her get close to him, she would not beg. Begging, she suspected, would be the surest way to make him turn from her, in any case.

The noise of a door opening and closing in Constantine's bedchamber put an end to her reflections. Low, masculine voices reached her ear—Constantine and his valet.

As she stared at her face in the looking glass, it occurred to her that she looked tragic, her eyes apprehensive, her mouth turned down a little at the edges. Not the most alluring prospect.

Jane pinched her cheeks and bit her lips to lend them color. She instructed her facial muscles to smile, but they did a poor job of obeying her command.

Apprehension tied knots in her stomach. The need to see Constantine warred with a plethora of fears. Fear of him, and of the act she was about to commit. But more than that, she feared herself, that if she gave herself to him, it would leave her weak. Defenseless as she hadn't been since she was a little girl.

She heard Constantine's bedchamber door close a second time. His valet must have left. Her heart leaped into her throat. Now, he would come.

Slowly, she picked up her silver-backed hairbrush and set it to her unbound locks with a hand that shook slightly. One hundred strokes, morning and night, her nurse had always said.

She was up to twenty when the light tap at the door came. She jumped, and the shawl slipped from her shoulders. Without waiting for her answer, the communicating door opened and there he stood.

CHAPTER SIXTEEN

J ane set down the brush and made as if to rise, but he
said, "No, stay where you are." She sank down again,
unable to take her eyes from him.

She'd expected he'd wear the same flamboyant dressing
gown she'd already seen him in twice, but other than removing his coat and cravat, he hadn't undressed.

She wasn't sure if she was reassured by that.

He held a bottle of red wine in one hand and a glass in
another. "I'm afraid we'll have to share the glass," he said,
moving toward her. "I couldn't think of a good reason to
give for needing two."

A reminder that what they did now was illicit, forbidden;
that he would be discreet.

He paused at a small occasional table by the fireplace and
set the wine and the glass down. Crouching before the
hearth, he looked back at her over his shoulder. "I'll build up
the fire, shall I?"

Her lips parted, but she couldn't find her voice to answer.
The need for more heat made her think of cool air on naked
skin. A thrill shivered down her spine.

Under his attentions, the dying fire flared to life, throwing
a golden, flickering light around the chamber. She watched
the broad lines of his back and the trim taper of his waist as
he took a long paper spill from a china jar on the mantelpiece and touched it to the flame.

Then he moved around the room, systematically lighting each and every candle that she'd so purposefully doused before he'd arrived.

Again, she tried to speak, but what would she say?

I don't want you to see me.

But Constantine Black had an intent look about him tonight. He wanted to set the stage for this seduction, and his demeanor made it clear to her that he would not be gainsaid.

When he'd finished, he tossed the spill into the fire. He took the open bottle of wine and poured a glass. He'd rolled his sleeves up to tend the fire, and she admired the tensile strength in his forearm as he held the bottle, gave it an artful twist to avoid spilling a drop.

He set the bottle down. Then he turned, held out his hand to her, and smiled.

Jane made no move to join him. She felt as if she'd been cemented in place.

One black eyebrow lifted. "Second thoughts?"

Slowly, she shook her head.

Again, he held out his hand. "Come, then. Sit here with me."

She forced herself to rise and go to him. Her legs were unsteady, her breathing erratic. She wished she could regain mastery over her body, but it was falling under his magician's spell.

On either side of the fireplace stood a wing-backed chair, with a deep-piled hearth rug spread between them. She moved to the chair opposite to where Constantine stood, but he caught her hand. "No, not there. With me."

He drew her down with him as he sat. On the chair he'd chosen, there was no room to do anything but sit on his lap. Stiffly, Jane obeyed, perching on him with a prim awkwardness that made him chuckle a little. She felt his muscled thighs beneath her, his heat surrounding her body. Her heart drummed in her chest.

Disconcerted by his closeness, she kept her gaze fixed on the fire. She didn't have the courage to look him in the face.

"Jane." His voice was huskier than usual. With his finger-tips beneath her chin, he tilted her face upward and took her mouth.

His kisses were slow and deep and intoxicating. Despite her nervousness, she gave herself up to him, helpless in the face of his skilled caresses, overpowered by her own long-ing. Gently, he touched her cheek and a rush of emotion rose up within her. She wanted this kiss to mean as much to him as it did to her, but the futility of that hope made her want to weep.

She gave a sobbing gasp, and he stopped immediately, raising his head, then pressing his forehead to hers. "Forgive me, I'd meant to take things slowly tonight. Stop me if I go too fast."

He was breathing hard, his big chest rising and falling against her shoulder. She rejoiced to know that he was af-fected as much as she was, at least in the physical sense.

The kiss had relaxed her body so that she now draped comfortably against him. She could feel the hard evidence of his arousal against her thigh but she was not panicked by it as she had been earlier that day.

He would not force himself on her; of that, she was cer-tain. However he might wound her heart, Constantine would never harm her body.

He shifted beneath her to reach for the wine glass. "Here." He lifted the glass until the rim touched her lower lip, his gaze intent on her face. Obediently, she sipped, let-ting the rich, smooth claret fill her mouth.

Constantine drank deeply, then set the glass down. His firm lips glistened with ruby wetness, and she experienced the strangest and most pressing urge to taste that wine on her tongue. Instead, she licked her own lips.

He tensed, the muscles in his thighs turning rock hard beneath her. "Jane." His voice became husky. "Tell me about Harcourt."

"Harcourt?" she breathed. "Whatever for?"

He pressed the corner of her mouth with one fingertip. "I thought it might be nice to get to know each other better."

He drew back and waited, his hand playing idly with her hair.

"I . . ." She sighed as his knuckle brushed the sensitive skin at the side of her throat. *I don't remember. What was the question?*

"Harcourt," he prompted. "You have happy memories of living there."

His hand skimmed down her side, settled at her waist. She laid her head against his shoulder and again stared into the fire. Her body's arousal hadn't abated, but with it grew a steady warmth. This must be what it was like to have a loving husband, this feeling of excitement, security, and contentment all bound up together. How wonderful.

Resolutely, she banished the thought.

"Harcourt . . . ?" she said vaguely. *I cannot think, much less talk, when you are touching me like this.*

With a soft laugh, he splayed his hand across her abdomen. There were no stays to impede his progress tonight. His hand moved a little higher, and her nipples hardened in anticipation, straining for his attention. How would it feel to be rid of all these clothes, touching him, skin to skin?

She'd never experienced that kind of sensual longing before, didn't know what to do with it.

His thumb and forefinger moved up her torso to frame the underside of her breast. Again, as before, he stopped short of the place she needed him the most. She moved restlessly, making a dissatisfied sound at the back of her throat.

"Tell me what you want," whispered Constantine, his hot breath caressing her ear. "I'll do anything. All you have to do is ask."

"You know what I want. Don't . . . don't make me say it." She squirmed, desperate enough to beg, but she couldn't formulate the words.

His hand left her breast and settled in the deep V of her neckline, a brand against her bare skin.

She longed for his hand to delve deeper, to give her more of that exquisite handling he'd given her in the grotto. She writhed in his arms, willing him to understand.

As if in answer, his fingertips moved beneath her night rail, smoothing the lawn down, over her shoulder, baring one breast.

He stilled. She opened her eyes to see him looking down at her with the expression of blatant hunger. She made a move to pull the night rail back into place, but his hand clasped her wrist.

"No. No, you must not hide yourself. My God, Jane, you are exquisite."

Without taking his eyes from her, he moved from beneath her to kneel at her feet.

Reverently, he peeled the other shoulder of her night rail down, to expose both breasts. She felt his gaze on her, as palpable as a caress. Liquid warmth pooled between her thighs.

Then he put up his hands to touch her, circling the nipples slowly with fingertips slightly roughened from what labor she knew not. Her eyes wanted to close, but she kept them open, too fascinated by him and by his absorption to look away.

Having stared his fill, he bent to her and fastened his lips on one nipple. The sensation was consuming; Jane moaned and threw her head back, gripping the arms of her chair. Ah, yes. Yes, this was what she'd wanted this afternoon. Instinctively, she'd known *this* would be sublime.

She set her hand to the back of his head as he laved at her with the flat of his tongue, lapped and sucked with finely judged force. He made a meal of one breast while he fondled the other with his fingertips and palm. The sensation of heat and fullness in her breasts was unlike anything she'd experienced, and a strange ache settled low in her belly. At that moment, she would have done anything he asked of her, as long as he didn't stop.

She gasped his name, and that seemed to spur him to greater exertion. He moved his hands up and down her torso, making her night rail gather around her waist. Straightening, he shoved his hands through her hair to cradle her head while he kissed her mouth.

She edged closer, desperate to kiss him back with all the passion he had stirred inside her. The smooth silk of his waistcoat rubbed against her nipples. She nearly slid from the edge of the chair in her eagerness to return his embrace.

His hands at her waist steadied her. Then he bunched the bottom edge of her night rail in his hands, moving it upward as if to bare all.

Alarm rocketed through her. He'd made her feel so beautiful, so sinfully desirable, but if he saw her uncovered he'd know how ugly she was. How wrong.

She pushed at his hands. "No, don't! Don't . . ." she said desperately. "Don't spoil it. I don't want you to see me."

He froze, his large hands gripping her thighs. His gaze, stormy with passion, took a few moments to focus. Then he sat back on his heels and lifted his hand to cup her jaw.

"You are beautiful," he murmured, and despite her panic, she thrilled at the wonder in his voice. "Beautiful, amazingly responsive. But I desire you for what is in here"—he kissed her forehead—"and in here." Bending to her, he lightly brushed his lips over the place above her heart. "That won't change."

No, no, he didn't really mean that. Everyone knew men prized beauty in a woman above all else. A rake like Constantine could have any woman he wanted.

Mutely, she shook her head.

"Jane," he whispered. "Our bodies . . . all this, it's just trappings. It's nice to look at, but so is a piece of art, and a man doesn't want to make love to a statue. What fires the soul and stirs the passions is something that comes from within."

Fine words, but she might suppose he said such things to

all his conquests. He must be a master at persuading women out of their clothes.

"I . . . It is difficult for me," she said. "Impossible. I'm sorry." She plucked at her night rail in an effort to find the edge of her bodice and pull it back into place.

Lightly, he gripped her wrists. "Don't. Come. See for yourself."

Sliding his hand to hers, he drew her to her feet and led her to the cheval glass in the corner.

As they moved away from the fire, she shivered, but when he placed her before the looking glass, he stood so close behind her that his body warmed her again. She still clutched the night rail at her waist like a petticoat, but her breasts were scandalously bare.

She rarely looked at her naked body in the mirror and she'd never before seen it as an object of desire. The intensity of Constantine's regard left her in no doubt of that.

Helpless, she watched their reflection as his dark head bent to her. He lifted her hair away from her nape and kissed the point where her neck met her shoulder, sending darts of pleasure to quiver in her loins. His lips drifted over the sensitive skin there, pressed against her pulse. Holding her gaze in the mirror, he touched his tongue to her earlobe, then gripped it lightly with his teeth.

The sight of him doing these things to her sent her arousal to a higher pitch.

She swayed, and he steadied her, his hands closing over her breasts. "Watch us, Jane," he whispered into her ear. "Look how beautiful you are."

She gained an impression of the darker skin on the backs of his hands as they moved against the whiteness of her breasts, then her gaze took in her own flushed face, the glazed, drugged look in her eyes.

"Look at me now, Jane," he whispered. "Look how I worship you."

He *was* a wizard, after all, for his gaze captured her and she couldn't look away, barely registered what he did when he tugged her night rail free of her grasp and let it fall at her feet.

"Look at yourself, princess," he breathed. "Think how desirable you are to me, how much I'd give to be inside you, right now."

He skimmed his lips down her jawline, while rubbing and tweaking gently at her nipples. "Are you wet for me, Jane?"

The shock of his words made heat flare and race through her body. She sighed, but she couldn't have answered him if her life depended on it. The confusion of emotion nearly sent her mad. She wanted him, she *was* wet for him—embarrassingly so—yet, still she couldn't relax her guard. He'd called her beautiful; she'd hate it if he turned away in disgust.

"You're hot and slick between your legs, aren't you, Jane?" he murmured. "That's how I want you. That's how I know you're ready for me."

His touch slid lower, but she clamped her hand on his wrist to stop him. She couldn't help it.

"No?" he said, kissing her collarbone. "Then you'll have to touch yourself for me. Just to see if I'm right."

Somehow, his hand slid from her grasp and wrapped around hers, guiding it down her body. Down, over her stomach, through the hair between her legs to a place that was wet and hot and slick—all those things he'd said.

That husky voice in her ear. "Did Frederick make you wet like this?"

She gasped.

"Did he?"

She shook her head. "No. Never." There'd been no preliminaries with Frederick, no kissing, no touching. Just dryness and force and pain.

"Have you ever touched yourself there before, Jane?"

She swallowed, and shook her head. On some level, she was horrified to be doing such a thing in front of him, but heat and longing and curiosity won out over reluctance. This must be the secret, the mysterious pleasure that caused otherwise sensible women to ruin themselves for love. He was teaching her, and God help her, she wanted to learn. If she could.

Constantine had been fighting the demands of his body since he'd walked into Jane's bedchamber. The sight of her long, slim fingers delving into her intimate flesh nearly made him crazed with lust. He wanted nothing more than to take over her task, set his mouth between her legs and make her scream with delight.

There was nothing wrong with her that he could see, and absolutely everything right. Damn Frederick's boorishness! No wonder she'd been so terrified of having a man inside her if he'd never bothered to prepare her properly.

He whispered reassurances and instructions to her, forced himself to watch her pleasure herself, receiving tantalizing glimpses of pink, moist flesh as her hand moved and her fingers circled. His own desire heightened to the point of insanity.

Her skin was every bit as soft and silken as he'd dreamed, her body supple and delicately rounded. He wanted her with a passion so fierce it was a wrestle to keep himself in check. He'd promised himself he would not bed her tonight.

Instead, he watched her keenly in the looking glass, gauging her response, noting what pleased her and what didn't with the eye of a practiced rake.

Yes, he was practiced, and the experience stood him in good stead tonight. But this night was unlike any other; this woman was unique among his vast array of lovers. He'd never met with such innocence and responsiveness in one woman. Even if he had, it would not be the same, for that woman would not have been Jane.

His Jane.

Her panting breaths came closer together now; he sensed she was near to breaking point. Soon, she would understand a little, but she would have only the slightest inkling of how it might be between them.

He whispered in her ear. "Let go now, Jane. You must let go."

"Can't . . ." The faint moan she gave set him on fire. How long would he have to wait before he could take her and show her how they could be together? How long before he could truly make her his?

Mine.

Sheer animal lust overtook him. He cupped her breasts, pulling her hard against him, and sank his teeth into the side of her neck.

Then she broke. She gave a sharp gasp and threw her head back, shuddering in his arms. Her body slid down, as if her legs had given way.

He caught her and turned her, lifting her off her feet. Crushing her against his chest, he kissed her roughly, passionately, unleashing the full force of his pent-up desire. She flung her arms around his neck and kissed him back, the first wholehearted kiss she had given him—messy and wet and full of tongue and enthusiasm.

"That was the most beautiful thing I've ever seen," he said against her lips. Skimming down to the tender skin of her throat, he added, "But next time, I'm going to be the one who makes you shudder like that. And I promise you, it will be infinitely better."

He was prepared to exercise this superhuman restraint only once. It would kill him to go through all this a second time and not have her.

Before instinct overcame his better judgment, he carried her to the bed. Gently, he laid her on the mattress. Her eyes flared with apprehension.

He smile was strained. "Don't worry, princess. I'm not going to join you tonight."

He found her night rail and tossed it to her, watching the faint, delicious bounce of her breasts as she struggled into it and smoothed it down over her hips.

Then he pushed her so that she lay back against the pillows. Looming over her, he planted a hand either side of her on the bed. Constantine watched her for a moment, so gorgeous and tempting in her rumpled satiety.

He smiled down into her eyes. "Tomorrow."

With a kiss on the tip of her patrician nose, he left.

Constantine slept fitfully that night and woke before dawn. If there'd been a moon to light the way, he would have ridden out, but the clouds blotted any light from the heavens. Rain fell in a steady rush, like distant applause.

He rose and padded to the side table to get himself a drink. Then he clicked his fingers. God, he'd almost forgotten! The wine.

Pulling on a pair of breeches, he eased open the communicating door to Jane's bedchamber. He paused on the threshold and listened for her breathing. He didn't want to wake her. She needed her sleep.

Certainly, she required rest for what he'd planned for tomorrow night.

He moved silently into the room, toward the fireplace where he'd left the bottle and glass. He needed to get in and out quickly, before the skivvy arrived to sweep the hearth.

A sound from the bed halted him.

It was a sigh, a soft exhalation she made in her sleep, but it drew him to her. He moved to the bed and looked down.

She rested exactly where he'd placed her, on top of the sheet. Despite the night's chill, she hadn't drawn the coverlet over her or closed the curtains that surrounded the tent bed. It was as if she'd dropped into slumber as soon as he'd kissed her good night.

Sleeping Beauty.

She lay, curiously abandoned and defenseless, one hand under her cheek, rosy lips softly pouting, quivering with every breath.

Her body, her breasts, were a standing temptation; her

long, slim legs extended, bare, beyond the hem of her plain night rail. The skin there was so white and soft and perfect, the turn of her ankle elegantly enticing. A small mole nestled next to her anklebone. He wanted to kiss it, then kiss his way up . . .

His loins stirred with acute interest. His body ached. *Patience,* he reminded himself. *Not now.*

With a sigh that sounded harsh in his ears, he pulled the coverlet over her and went to retrieve the evidence of their evening together.

The room was cold. He ought to have built up the fire before he'd left her last night.

Jane woke to the sound of metal clinking near the fireplace. She opened her eyes, at first disoriented and alarmed to see the figure of a man returning a fire iron to its stand. Comprehension followed swiftly, however, as he bent to pick up a wine bottle and glass from the table beside the fire.

Constantine.

Her senses sprang to life, awakened, stimulated by the mere sight of him.

He wasn't wearing a shirt, and Jane's lips parted in wonder at the sight of his unclad back, the shift in muscles and ribs as he leaned down. The way his skin appeared gilded by the firelight—golden and smooth and irresistible. If she hadn't been so afraid of where it might lead, she'd go to him now, run her hands over his shoulder blades, down his spine to that tapering waist.

Speculation gnawed at her. He'd seen her completely nude, but she had yet to see him.

He turned, then, and her eyes feasted on his chest and stomach, the firm strength of him, the lack of any softness whatsoever. How strange that she, a soft, pliant female, should relish all that hardness, want it for her very own.

Her gaze traveled down, and she realized that though he had pulled on breeches, he hadn't buttoned them fully.

"So you are awake," he murmured, a laugh in his voice.

With a gasp, she snatched her gaze from that intriguing line of investigation and transferred it to the bedpost. She made a noncommittal noise in her throat.

"Hmm." He reached down to toy with the waistband of his breeches, drawing back her gaze. "See anything you like?"

She bit her lip against a scandalized laugh. The unabashed arrogance of him! He was not the slightest bit embarrassed that she'd been covertly admiring his form. Well, why should he be embarrassed? He'd put any number of Greek statues to shame.

She ventured to meet his gaze. He was smiling at her in a way that made her heart pound and her mouth go dry.

Well, it wasn't in her nature to simper. Boldly, she lifted her chin. "Quite a lot, actually."

He laughed, a deep, full-throated chuckle.

She glanced at the door. "Hush! Do you want someone to hear?"

Still smiling, he said, "No, I don't want that. I was not here to show off my manly physique, either. I merely came to retrieve the evidence." He held up the wine and the glass.

He paused. "I suppose I'll be going now."

Not even a good-morning kiss? She folded her arms. "Yes, you do that," she said grumpily.

He gestured down at himself. "It wouldn't do for me to get caught in here like this, now, would it?"

Mutely, she shook her head. But she couldn't take her eyes from him. She'd never realized men looked like *that* underneath their shirts. Frederick had always worn a nightshirt on the few occasions he'd visited her bed. And she was most . . . intrigued by the way Constantine's hip bones curved downward, disappearing into his breeches, as if pointing the way . . .

She twisted a curl around her finger. "May I have some wine before you go?"

He raised an eyebrow.

Eyes wide, she said, "I'm thirsty."

"All right." He sloshed a few mouthfuls into the glass and approached the bed. He held the glass out to her, and their fingers brushed as she took the wine from him.

"Drink up," he said. "I need to get this out of here."

He stood at the edge of her bed. She could reach out and touch him if she only had the courage. Or he could touch her.

Her nipples pricked in anticipation. That lovely, hot, liquid sensation gathered between her legs.

Holding his gaze, she raised the glass to her lips. Then she drained the wine in one long swallow and handed it back to him.

She couldn't help herself. She put out a hand and pressed her palm to his midriff. He felt smooth and hard. His skin was cool to the touch.

His hand caught hers and removed it from his stomach. "Believe me, princess, there's nothing I'd rather do, but if you don't want to create a scandal, we must stop now. The dawn is already here."

He was right. The risk was too great. She bit her lip, a little startled that a notorious rake had been obliged to remind *her* of the proprieties. He'd turned her into a wanton overnight.

A quirk of his lips told her he'd had a similar thought. "Believe me, the anticipation will make what comes next all the sweeter." He took her hand and bowed over it, meeting her gaze with those somnolent, wicked green eyes. "I assure you."

She fell back against the pillows, all jittery and breathless. "I shall never sleep now."

His smile grew. "Make ready to ride with me, then. I'm going up to Bronson's mill to check that work is progressing there."

The idea struck her favorably. Physical exercise was exactly what she needed. "There won't be any trouble, will there?"

He shrugged. "Not in your presence. If we're early enough we won't be spotted."

*   *   *

Later, as they walked down to the stables, Jane inhaled deeply of the cool, crisp air. The ground was sodden beneath her boots. She was obliged to lift the skirts of her habit to save them from the mire.

Mist hovered over the dewed grass like a ghostly blanket. The landscape was quiet, though the distant crow of a cockerel marked the new day.

It marked a new era for Jane. A sense of wonder and deep well-being built up in her this morning. She'd thought Wilson must have noticed the change in her when she'd helped her dress. Everyone must see it. Surely Constantine's deliciously sinful touch must be branded on her skin.

She found herself shy of looking at him. Yet, her awareness of his body, and the confident way he moved at her side, was greater than ever before. A hunger gathered inside her. For the first time since the early weeks of her marriage, she craved a deeper physical connection.

Hope unfurled in her heart. A tiny, precious bud of it.

The stable block was a handsome stone building, large and well appointed, though not as fully stocked with prime cattle as Jane would have liked. As they neared the entrance, they heard masculine laughter. The laughter held a jeering edge that made Jane halt in surprise.

Jane glanced at Constantine, who frowned.

"Stay here," he said.

She ignored the order, following him into the stable yard. She pulled up short, a cry escaping her lips.

There, surrounded by three stable boys, was Luke.

He was covered in muck, as if he'd fallen into a steaming pile of manure nearby. They were pushing him between them, jeering, their eyes alight with malicious glee. The boys were not much older than Luke himself, but he had no hope against three of them.

"Dunk him!" With a glance at the horse trough, one boy reached for Luke.

"Let him go." The hard, menacing voice in which Constantine gave the order was one Jane scarcely recognized.

She didn't blame the boys for their slack-mouthed obedience. They unhanded Luke instantly.

Luke tottered, unsteady on his feet, tears streaking down the grime on his face.

Jane's heart gave a sickened lurch. She rushed forward to help Luke, but Constantine put out a hand to stop her. "I told you to stay outside."

Disregarding the admonishment, she stepped around him, hastening to the boy's side. "Luke!"

Kneeling on the cobblestones, she reached out and pulled him into her arms, regardless of the stench and muck that covered him. "Oh, darling, what have they done to you? We must get you back to the house."

She sent a dagger look over her shoulder at the culprits. The largest boy stared sullenly back at her. The others bowed their heads and wouldn't meet her eye.

"Shame on you all!" She rose to her feet. "You'll be sorry for this."

"My sketchbook," gasped Luke.

Jane glanced around. Luke's precious drawings had been flung atop the heap of horse manure.

Taking hold of one, unsullied corner, Constantine fished the sketchbook out of the mire and handed it carefully to Luke.

"Perhaps some pages can be saved," Jane said. She put her arm around Luke and glared at the stable boys. "And as for you three—"

Evenly, Constantine said, "Lady Roxdale, go with Luke up to the house. I'll handle this."

"But—"

"Thank you, my lady." With his most charming smile, Constantine bowed, dismissing her. There was nothing for her to do but leave.

While a bath was drawn for Luke, Jane ordered some hot water to be brought to her sitting room so that she could help him wash the worst of the grime away.

When he was relatively clean and she was somewhat calmer, she rang for tea and some lemonade and a currant bun for Luke. He took a tiny sip of lemonade. The bun went untouched.

If she'd needed any proof of the depth of his pain and humiliation, she had it in his loss of appetite. She'd never seen him so uninterested in food before.

"Come. Sit with me." She drew him to her and cuddled him close.

"I am so sorry, darling." She shook her head. "That such a thing should happen here, at our stables! I wouldn't have credited it if I hadn't seen it with my own eyes."

"I did all the things you and Lord Roxdale said. I told them to leave me alone in a big strong voice. But then they picked me up . . ." His mouth contorted in an effort to hold back his sobs.

"Oh, darling, I know. I know you did your best. Sometimes there's nothing you can do. But you may be sure that Lord Roxdale is dealing with those boys in a way they won't like." She'd never considered herself a violent woman, but she burned to box those bullies' ears for them. She must trust in Constantine to punish them fittingly.

She waited a while before she asked, "Why did they treat you that way?"

Luke flushed and bit his lip. He shook his head. "Don't know."

"But you do know, don't you, Luke?" She hesitated, not quite knowing how to phrase her concern. "Did you, perhaps, do something to those boys?"

"Nothing! I've done nothing at all." His lip quivered. He was trying his best not to weep.

Jane's heart twisted. "I am sorry, darling. I didn't mean to suggest it was your fault. Well, what is it, then? Can't you tell me why they were teasing you?"

Her gentle questioning seemed to upset him all the more. She would not hurt him for the world, but she had to know why this kept happening so she could try to put a stop to it.

"Won't you tell me, Luke? You can say anything. I won't be shocked or disappointed. But I want to know."

He kicked the leg of his chair with his heel. "It's *nothing,* Aunt Jane. Really, it isn't. I—I made some rude sketches of them, that's all."

Somehow, she didn't think impudent cartoons were responsible for such widespread animosity. "Oh? And did you make sketches like that of the boys in the village, too?"

He hunched a shoulder and didn't reply.

"Luke?" She felt so helpless; she was on the verge of tears herself, but that would never do. "Darling, I can't bear to see this happening to you. You must tell me or Lord Roxdale, so that we can do something about it."

"You can't!" He was on his feet, shouting at her. "You can't do *anything* about it, all right?"

Tears streamed down his cheeks. Jane went to her knees on the floor and wrapped her arms around him to hold him tightly. Murmuring endearments and reassurance, she stroked a hand through his hair. His small body shook; then he buried his face in her shoulder and broke into sobs, ugly, wrenching sobs that seemed to rip from his chest.

"They say I'm a bastard. That my mother was a . . . a—"

"Yes, I can imagine what they call her," she interrupted, to save him the embarrassment of using such language to her.

What on earth? "But it's not true, darling. Your parents were most certainly married and your birth is as respectable as mine."

Jane's heart wrung with pity for him. If she could have taken his pain into herself to spare him, she would have done it.

He raised his face. "Why would they say such things if they weren't true?"

Jane shook her head, soothing his hair from his brow with one fingertip. "I don't know, my dear. Sometimes children say hurtful things with no regard at all to the truth."

She drew back, searching his woebegone little face. "I

want you to know that whatever happens, I will always love you and take care of you, and so will Lord Roxdale. We'll find a way to stop this. You'll see."

She heard a step outside and turned her head to see Constantine standing in the doorway.

"What happened?"

He came in, moving toward Luke with a frown in his eyes.

Reaching to tip up the boy's chin, he held his face to the light. "Full of pluck, aren't you, son?" He lifted a brow at Jane. "Bruises? Bones broken?"

She shook her head. "He is very shaken, though. And upset. And the stable boys?" asked Jane. "What did you do about them?"

There was a grim set to Constantine's mouth. He rested a hand on Luke's head. "I dismissed them. I can't have lads like that on the estate."

Luke's head jerked up in surprise. His gaze fixed with almost worshipful intensity on Constantine's face.

Jane frowned, unsure whether she approved. "I think they'd have preferred a horsewhip."

"Possibly," said Constantine. "But I don't hold with corporal punishment. I gave them the choice of various highly unpleasant duties or leaving my employ. They chose the latter." He sighed. "It goes against the grain with me to rob lads of their livelihoods, but they are young and strong. They'll find work elsewhere. And their dismissal will serve as a warning to others that Luke is under my protection." He paused. "We can't have the poor lad terrorized in his own home, can we?"

Luke had finally stopped trembling. Something like hope shone in his eyes.

"Let's hope that's an end to it," said Jane. "If anything like this happens again, you must run and tell us straightaway." She hugged Luke to her and kissed the crown of his head, then released him. "Now, up to the nursery with you. Your bath should be ready by now. We must get you all lovely and clean."

"And afterward," said Constantine, "how about another game of fox and geese?"

That night, Jane went up to the nursery to fulfill her promise to read Luke three entire episodes of Sir Ninian's adventures. She didn't even get through the first story before Luke slipped into dreams.

For a long time, she sat watching him in the quiet.

She loathed what had happened to him that morning. She ached for his pain, would have done anything to take it away. A hard lesson to learn that she couldn't. He must bear it, and she must simply help him do that. Constantine had said something to her that resonated: Luke would be stronger for having survived this day.

Constantine had spent hours with Luke today, joking and playing games, letting the boy forget about the horror of the morning. By suppertime, Luke had regained his usual buoyancy. Constantine had been wonderful, truly. She doubted any father could have bettered his performance.

She anticipated that the awful incident would resurface in Luke's mind often in the coming days and weeks. But she hoped the sting of it would lessen after today.

Jane wiped her eyes with her knuckle and rose to look out of the window. Twilight lay soft in the air outside. The days were lengthening, and so was this magical time when the world hung between daytime and night.

She took a deep breath and exhaled it shakily. Then she went down to her bedchamber to fetch a shawl and left the house.

Constantine had been at work in the grotto's innermost chamber for the past two hours or more. He was pardonably pleased with the result.

A multitude of silk cushions and pillows covered the floor, while embroidered hangings draped over its walls, softening the cavernous space. A bottle of champagne nestled snugly in its silver bucket. Beside that, he'd set two crystal flutes and a selection of viands delectable enough to tempt the most jaded palate. Wisps of incense smoke wafted from a miniature Oriental burner, scenting the air with a subtle hint of the exotic.

He'd just lit the last candle when a movement behind him made him turn around.

Jane stood at the chamber entrance, clutching the edges of her shawl together at her breast. She still wore her day gown but her hair was unbound, tumbling in glorious auburn waves around her shoulders. His fingers tingled with the need to sift through that soft, flowing mass.

So elegant and slender, Jane appeared almost ethereal in the mysterious shadows of the grotto. Too pure and delicate for the profanity of his touch.

His heart kicked into a hard gallop. He'd anticipated a moment like this for a very long time, perhaps since that first glimpse he'd caught of Jane staring down at him from her window. Only now did it occur to him that he'd never felt so . . . *anxious* about bedding a woman before.

Everything hinged on this night. Their future together depended on his making the next few hours the most pleasurable of Jane's life. What was more, she trusted him to accomplish that feat, despite the horror she'd suffered through with Frederick. It was enough to daunt the most hardened rake into nonperformance.

But his apprehension didn't stop his cock straining against his breeches at the sight of her. The primal, animal part of him roared in triumph. Finally, he would have this woman, possess her body, claim her in a thousand intimate ways.

He waited for her to glance away from him and become aware of her surroundings. He'd taken some trouble to set the scene for this momentous occasion.

She didn't notice any of it, but walked straight into his arms.

Then she said his name in her soft, clipped voice, took his face between her palms and kissed him with those warm, satiny lips. Something inside him flipped over. Constantine Black, celebrated rake, flung all his practiced maneuvers to the winds and wrapped himself in Jane.

He splayed his fingers and plunged them through her hair, devouring her mouth with deep, long kisses, over and over again.

He ran his hands over her, caressing the small of her back, pushing the shawl from her shoulders, touching, stroking, impatient for more. Clothing became an irritation, thwarting his progress. With a muttered oath, he turned her to face away from him. Fumbling a little, his fingers worked at removing her gown.

Various aids to seduction that he'd arranged on the shelf remained where they were, all but forgotten. His plans for slowly stripping her in a long, drawn-out seduction unraveled faster than the damnably complex lacings on her corset.

As her stays finally came undone and her petticoats fell away, he swept her hair aside to press kisses at her nape, resting his lips at the vulnerable place where her neck and shoulder joined. Gently, he bit down.

She moaned his name, sagging a little in his arms.

"Yes, you like that," he murmured, pleased. He let his mouth linger, tracing the delicate blue shadow of a vein with his tongue, tasting the salty tang of her skin.

When Jane shuddered, he bit down harder, then sucked her flesh to soothe it. Her knees buckled but he held her up, one arm around her waist, one hand sliding under the neckline of her chemise to fondle the soft, firm flesh of her breast.

The sudden press of her bottom against his groin made him gasp into her shoulder blade. He turned her and slid the sleeves of her chemise from her shoulders, baring her lovely breasts, letting the soft undergarment whisper to the ground.

Jane surprised him then, reaching out to bunch her hands in his shirt to tug it free of his breeches. She gathered the linen in her hands, lifting it up. Obediently, he raised his arms over his head and helped her remove it.

The appreciative light in her gaze as it wandered over his bare torso made his balls tighten painfully. She did that to him with just a look. What could she do with her hands, her mouth?

To distract himself, he reached out and palmed her breast, curled his fingers underneath it, weighed it in his hand. With deliberate precision, he flicked one tight nipple with his thumb. Her eyelids fluttered closed as she gave a small, pleasured moan.

Encouraged, he played there for a while, touching her with light, tantalizing strokes until she begged for relief. "Constantine. Oh, please."

He swept her up in his arms and carried her to the mountain of cushions. He laid her down, then stretched out beside her, marveling at the pleasurable anticipation in her gaze. This time, she didn't seek to cover herself or shy away.

The trust in her silvery eyes humbled him. He would make everything perfect for her or die in the attempt.

Jane put out her hand to caress his chest, running her fingertips lightly through the hair there. She flattened her palm and trailed it down the bumps of his rib cage and across his abdomen, making his stomach muscles jump. His skin burned where she touched it; he couldn't stand too much of this.

Capturing her wrist, he pinned it lightly back against the cushions beside her and bent to kiss each breast in turn. He teased her with light sweeps of his tongue around each heavenly aureole, made her writhe as he lightly kissed the hardened tips.

He sensed the restlessness in her body, the yearning for more. While he drew out her need with gentle kisses and licks, he released her wrist and trailed his palm down her side to the crease where her hip joined her stomach.

Her belly tightened at his touch; she froze.

Constantine clamped his lips over her nipple and drew on it firmly, flicking the peak with his tongue.

Jane cried out, her back arching with tortured pleasure. He took his chance and stroked between her legs to the hot, moist flesh, never relenting in his torment of her breast.

She let him caress her freely this time, and the feel of her was miraculous. She was searing hot and abundantly wet. He longed to put his mouth on her, but Jane wasn't ready for that yet.

He found the small knot of sensitive flesh and rubbed gently with his thumb. She gasped out a plea, lifting her hips. He obliged with a firmer touch.

Her breath came in sobs. She was close to her crisis; he sensed it waiting for her like an approaching storm. Without breaking his thumb's circular rhythm, he eased one finger inside her. She whimpered, perhaps in alarm, but she didn't push him away. Her internal muscles clamped down as if they resented the intrusion, but he introduced a second finger after the first and pushed them in further, seeking the perfect, blissful spot in that tight, wet sheath.

By now, his body was as primed and ready to explode as hers was. His cock throbbed painfully against the falls of his breeches. His teeth ground together with the effort of holding back his own climax.

Jane's whimpering cries escalated and he knew it was time. He pressed with his fingers and stroked with his thumb and sucked at her breast, and she came in great pulsing waves that convulsed her body and made her shriek out his name.

With one last, voluptuous lick of her distended nipple, Constantine lifted his head to watch Jane ride the crest of her pleasure, sightless and scarlet-cheeked and gasping for air. He reveled in her sensual abandon, scarcely believing he'd once dubbed her the Ice Maiden. Tonight, she was pure fire.

Before she could regain her senses, he pulled his member

free of his breeches and settled between her legs. He reached down to moisten the head of his penis in her juices, deliberately rubbing against her sensitive bud, making her body quiver again and again.

Hot pleasure surged through him in a dizzying rush. Gasping with the effort of holding his climax at bay, he pushed into her entrance the smallest way.

At once, her body stilled; he thought her breathing suspended. She wasn't nearly as abandoned to passion as he'd wanted her to be.

His jaw ached from clenching it; his entire body was strung tight with need. Instinct urged him to thrust into her, hard and fast, but that was the opposite of what he must do.

"All right?" he gritted out. Oh, hell, he hoped so.

"Yes." The word was what he wanted to hear, but it came out as a fearful squeak.

Jane didn't push him away. She didn't clamp her legs together as she had last night, but she didn't crave him inside her, either. She *braced* herself for him.

Constantine hesitated, poised above her, his muscles straining, his cock pounding, begging for release. He wasn't fully master of himself, he admitted that. If he wrecked this for her, he wouldn't get a second chance. Jane trusted him, but oh, *Christ,* he didn't trust himself to be as gentle and patient as he needed to be.

He tried to tell himself that this was just another woman, that he could last all night with others, that he'd never, ever lost command over his body. Not since he was a randy youth.

It didn't work. He made the decision and rolled away from her, wrapping his hand around his turgid cock. After a couple of quick pulls, he came hard, his seed spurting in hot jets over the cushions.

He was aching and far from sated and utterly, comprehensively furious with himself. What a hellish, unmitigated disaster.

After a few moments of fulminating silence, he made

himself turn back to face Jane. He must try to salvage something from the wreck he'd made of this night.

He drew her into his arms, and when he kissed her cheek, he tasted tears. He squeezed his eyes shut, cursing himself for a brute and a fool.

"Jane, Jane, I'm sorry—" But she pressed her fingertips to his lips, halting his apology.

"No, no," she said. "I want to thank you." Raising herself on her elbow, she smiled down at him.

"What?" Why the devil would she *thank* him? He'd failed her. Constantine searched her face but found no hint of irony in her expression.

"You might not think it, but you have given me a great gift tonight."

She must have read bafflement in his eyes, for she smiled again. Leaning over, she brushed her lips against his in a soft, tender kiss. "Constantine, don't you see? You have given me hope."

In the end, Montford elected to accompany deVere to the Cotswolds. He'd been toying with the idea, but the letter from Jane requesting his presence decided the matter. Better to be on hand to direct matters—subtly, of course—than to be obliged to mediate a raging battle of wills later.

Lady Arden was not the type of woman to cower at a display of deVere's temper. The Blacks and the deVeres could never deal well together; his lordship was spoiling for a fight, and Lady Arden would be all too willing to give him one.

Montford certainly hadn't undertaken the journey out of a desire to rush to Lady Arden's rescue.

Nor was it to ensure deVere did not take advantage of the lady in an amorous sense. No, Lady Arden could take care of herself. It was one of the things he admired in her the most.

He'd elected to ride, because hours on end shut up with deVere in a carriage was more than he could stomach.

Besides, the baron was a little like a child: exercise him well, and you took the edge off his tantrums.

Instead of going directly to Lazenby Hall, Montford decided to put up at deVere's nephew's house. He could keep an eye on things well enough from there.

Montford had some acquaintance with the nephew, Adam Trent. He was a presentable young fellow, and from all appearances, as good a candidate as any for Lady Roxdale's hand. Trent had the added advantage that Jane knew and liked the man. Then, too, if she lived at Trent Manor, she'd see young Lucas Black as often as she wished.

An alliance to further strengthen the ties between the deVeres and the Westruthers was also an excellent piece of strategy. Particularly if Rosamund balked at the final hurdle and refused to marry Griffin deVere, Earl of Tregarth.

Montford and Lord deVere had put off their traveling clothes and adjourned, at Trent's suggestion, to the billiards room, a well-appointed apartment on the ground floor.

Montford surveyed his host as Trent racked up the billiard balls on the table. One point further in Trent's favor—no one had heard anything ill of the man's morals. His honor, unlike Constantine Black's, was entirely intact. He was also a most talented swordsman, as Montford had discovered on previous visits to Lazenby.

A vast pity the gentleman was such an ass.

"Your Grace, you do me great, great honor by visiting me here. I trust you will let me know if there's any way I might serve you."

Make that a sycophantic ass.

"Not at all," the duke replied. "I trust my intrusion won't cause you any undue inconvenience."

He interrupted Trent's assurance that he was delighted, honored, more than happy . . . "To be sure." Montford smiled. "The sooner we get the matter of Lady Roxdale's marriage settled, the sooner I may be on my way."

With a grunt, deVere made his shot, scattering balls over the baize-covered slate. "Ha!" He prowled around the table, and sank two more balls before he missed one and gave up his place.

Montford took his cue and leaned over the table, lining up his shot. He paused. "DeVere tells me you have an interest in the lady, Trent."

Trent looked from deVere to Montford and back again. "Well, I . . ."

"Aye, he has an interest," growled deVere. "I'll not let That Woman get the drop on me again."

Montford potted his ball with an elegant carom off the side of the table, then looked up. "And what does Mr. Trent say to that?"

Trent reddened. "As to that, Your Grace, my interest was fixed well before my lord deVere had anything to say in the matter."

"Ah, so yours is a long-standing regard?"

Trent turned white, clearly realizing the trap into which he'd fallen. "No!" He licked his lips. "Well, of course, Frederick was my greatest friend. I wouldn't have dreamed . . . I mean, I've always held Lady Roxdale in high esteem. Of course!"

"Oh, of course." Montford raised his brows. "You have no need to explain yourself. I understand you quite well, you know."

DeVere was impatient. "What the hell does it matter, all this talk of regard? Trent will marry her because he's my candidate and because I say so, and there's an end to it!"

A frown creased Trent's noble brow.

Montford said gently, "You don't think it will be that simple, do you, deVere?"

DeVere stabbed a finger in Montford's direction. "It *will* be that simple because *you* will make it so! And you!" He turned on his hapless nephew. "What have you been doing to fix your interest with her, hmm? Bit of slap and tickle never goes astray in a case like this."

In freezing accents, Montford said, "Might I remind you, you are speaking of a lady?"

"I haven't even seen her, much less touched her," muttered Trent. Explosively, he said, "That blackguard Roxdale has her bewitched! I tried to tell her what he was like but she wouldn't listen. She won't even see me."

Startled, Montford repeated, "Bewitched?" *Jane?*

DeVere grounded the end of his cue stick and regarded his nephew in disgust. "Turned tattletale, did you, you spineless whelp! I'm not surprised she has nothing to say to you.

"Women," deVere growled, "like a man who shows her he'll brook none of her nonsense. A man who takes just a bit more than she's willing to give."

Trent looked uncertain, then glanced at Montford, but the duke merely shrugged. Let Trent dig his own grave, and deVere hand him the shovel. He didn't believe ham-handed tactics would work with Lady Roxdale, but it was early days. Perhaps Jane needed to be shaken out of her cool complacency.

Somehow, he doubted that Trent was the man to do it.

However, they would see.

CHAPTER SEVENTEEN

Lady Arden fingered the curtain of Jane's sitting room aside. "I hear Montford has arrived at Trent Manor," she said. The words were idle, uncaring, but tension showed in the lady's slim shoulders.

Jane stared at her, disconcerted. The duke? Why hadn't he written to warn her? When she and Constantine had become engaged, she'd written and asked him to come so that she could break the news of her betrothal in person, yet she felt totally unprepared to deal with him now.

Lady Arden turned. "My dear, is something the matter? I trust you're not fretting over whether Montford will approve the match. I daresay he might not have chosen Constantine for you, but he will soon be obliged to admit himself in the wrong. From what I've seen, Constantine is taking his new duties very seriously. He told me he will take his seat in Parliament when all is settled here."

"Parliament," murmured Jane. That meant London. A wave of apprehension swept over her.

"Ah. Here they are." Unhurriedly, Lady Arden moved away from the window. "The drawing room, I think. Come along, my dear."

What Jane really wanted to do was hide under the covers in her bedchamber like a child and wait for the storm to pass.

She wished Constantine were here. Or no, perhaps she

didn't wish it. He and Montford were sure to lock horns over her.

In the drawing room, she and Lady Arden sat pretending to embroider while they waited for the gentlemen to be announced.

"My dear, it will be best if you allow me to raise the subject of your betrothal," said Lady Arden, setting her work aside. "There will be a to-do, I don't deny it; certainly now that Lord deVere has seen fit to meddle, there is likely to be a little heat in our exchange." The lady's eyes kindled. "But you must not concern yourself. *I* shall prevail."

"Indeed, ma'am." A craven impulse made her blurt out, "Perhaps it might be best to say nothing about the betrothal at this juncture."

"Say nothing? No, no, that would never do. Leave it to me, my dear."

With a growing tightness in her chest, Jane waited. Finally, Feather appeared, announcing their guests. Not only Montford, but Lord deVere and Mr. Trent, too.

The gentlemen bowed; the ladies sank into curtsies. The duke came forward and took Jane's hands in his. "My dear Lady Roxdale, how do you do? I must apologize. My business kept me in Town longer than I anticipated when I left you."

Jane murmured some platitude and the duke turned to Lady Arden. He gave a slight smile. "I might have guessed."

She raised her brows. "Indeed, you might." She fluttered an elegant hand. "Do sit down."

Lady Arden engaged in lighthearted small talk with Montford and Trent, ignoring Lord deVere completely. The baron sprawled in a chair that looked far too delicate for his huge frame, his gaze fixed on Lady Arden's face. He seemed unconcerned by her ladyship's coldness toward him and disinclined to enter into the conversation.

Finally, deVere reached out a boot and kicked Mr. Trent, who shot out of his seat. Clearing his throat, Trent turned to Jane. "I'd hoped to ask for your company on one of our old rambles, Jane, but the weather grows ever more inclement. Would you like to take a turn with me in the gallery?"

Jane glanced at Lady Arden. "What a good idea," said the lady. "You young people go and enjoy yourselves. The gentlemen and I have dreary business matters to discuss."

Eager to escape, Jane rose and curtsied, placing her fingertips lightly on Mr. Trent's arm.

Trent didn't speak until they reached the long, rectangular room where the Blacks of generations past glowered down at them from their gilt frames.

"Lady Arden is making her home at Lazenby Hall, I see," he said in a tone of marked disapproval.

"For the moment, yes," said Jane. "I am obliged to her ladyship for her company. Circumstances have led me to remain at Lazenby Hall longer than I'd planned."

It was on the tip of her tongue to inform Trent of her betrothal, but she'd agreed to let Lady Arden break the news, hadn't she? And in truth, Jane was glad to postpone the inevitable explosion when Trent found out.

He frowned. "I heard about the particulars of your inheritance from Montford today. A damnable position to place you in, if you'll forgive me."

She was saved from answering him, for Trent stopped short, understandably astonished at the sight of a six-foothigh nose standing in one corner of the room.

"Good God, what the . . ." His voice petered out as he examined the new addition.

"Yes, it does take some getting used to," agreed Jane. "Lord Roxdale brought it. The provenance is unknown, but he thinks it quite possibly part of an ancient Greek statue. I believe he said he bought it from a smuggler in Rye."

Oh, Lord, she was babbling. Anything to keep Trent's mind from whatever purpose he had in bringing her here.

"Good God," he said again. Then he shook his head. "An abomination. I don't know how he can . . . But never mind that. Shall we?"

He indicated a striped satin couch that stood against the

wall. Strategically placed, no doubt, so that the person sitting there could admire the portrait of the fourth baron. This particular ancestor had rather the look of Charles II: all rolling black curls and heavy-lidded eyes. In fact, the portrait could have depicted Constantine, if the nose hadn't been so large and the mouth a little less on the cruel side.

"My dear Jane." Trent regarded her gravely. "I beg your pardon for approaching the matter so suddenly. I'd intended to wait until after you'd preserved a decent period of mourning—"

Her eyes widened. Was this a declaration? "Dear sir, no! I beg of you—"

"But I must!" Suddenly fierce, he leaned toward her and gripped her hands. With a wordless cry of protest, she tugged at them to free herself but he didn't release her.

"Listen to me!" he said, gripping her hands tighter. "For God's sake, just listen!" In a low, urgent tone, he said, "Roxdale is a blackguard, but he's so deuced handsome and charming, none of you can see it! Lady Roxdale—Jane—I care for you for your own sake as well as for Frederick's. I must speak!"

"*What* is this?"

The words sliced through the air, as cold and sharp as a whip. Jane's head snapped around. Constantine stood only a few yards away, glowering as fiercely as the first baron in that portrait.

Never in her life had she been so lost for words. Good God, she surely appeared as flushed and guilty as if she'd been caught with her garters showing. What must he think of her, alone with Mr. Trent, her hands in his? Surreptitiously, she tugged at them once more. Trent's grip tightened, making it impossible to pull away.

Head tilted, Constantine studied her for a long, silent moment. Then his regard switched to his neighbor. "I think the lady wants her hands back, my friend."

"I'm no friend of yours!" spat Trent, but his grip relaxed as he stood to face Constantine.

With a wary eye on her furious betrothed, Jane stepped between the two men, a hand slightly outstretched in either direction, as if to keep each of them at bay.

Not a vestige of his customary smile lurked in Constantine Black's eyes. The lazy grace that ordinarily characterized his movements had wholly deserted him. His face was hard as Carrara marble, his stance alert and aggressive, with that obstinate chin leading, as if begging to be hit.

Oh, he was spoiling for a fight. She trusted Trent would not give him one.

A glance at their neighbor told her his blood ran equally hot. Oh, no! In her experience, once the male of the species began hitting one another, they didn't stop for anything. The situation called for swift, preventive action.

"Mr. Trent was just leaving, *were you not, sir*?" She threw as much haughty command into her voice as she could, which was a considerable amount. She was a Westruther, after all.

Holding their neighbor's gaze, Constantine opened his arms wide and stepped clear of the doorway.

But either Trent had greater confidence in his pugilistic talents than Jane did or he was laboring under a terrific sense of injustice.

"Lady Roxdale! Are you going to let a shameless libertine dictate to you in this fashion? He is obviously afraid of what I might tell you about him."

"Is that so?" Constantine's eyebrows climbed. "*I* thought I was afraid you had your dirty great hands on my lady and she didn't seem to be relishing it above half."

His gaze flickered to Jane. "Or have I that wrong?" he said, softly dangerous. "Perhaps it is I who should leave."

Her temper flared. "Don't be ridiculous!"

Trent pointed a finger at Constantine. "You might have cozened her, Black, but you don't fool me, d'you hear?"

"I'm sure you can find your way out," replied Constantine. "Let me know if you require assistance, however." He smiled, showing his teeth.

Disregarding the implied threat, Trent lingered. His hazel eyes gazed steadily into Jane's, as if he could communicate all his knowledge to her through the space between them.

Slowly, she shook her head. She was willing to believe he had her interests at heart because he'd been Frederick's greatest friend. But in this, he was misguided. She would not listen to gossip about Constantine from him.

Jane lifted her chin. "Please go, Mr. Trent. Whatever you have to say, I do not wish to hear it."

Trent threw out a hand toward Constantine. "Ask *him,* then! Make him tell you why he was forbidden this house! Then see if you think he is worthy of you!"

With a last, venomous glance at Constantine, Trent strode from the room.

Constantine watched him depart. "The sad thing is, he was born like that," he commented. "A self-righteous, sneaking prig. Hard to believe his mother's a deVere."

"He meant well."

Constantine's nostrils flared. "Don't be so bloody naïve."

"Sir! I'll thank you to watch your language."

Green eyes blazed down at her. "Why do you think he was holding your hands like that? He wants you."

"He was holding my hands because he was trying to make me listen to him and I would not!" Jane couldn't contain a spurt of incredulous laughter. "The notion he wants me in *that* way—why, it's ludicrous! He was Frederick's dearest friend."

Constantine muttered something under his breath about silly little innocents. Then he poked his index finger at her. "Don't entertain him alone again."

"But I—"

"Did you tell him?" he demanded abruptly.

"Tell him what?" Her lips parted in bewilderment at this change of subject.

"That we're betrothed, of course! Did you tell him?"

Heat rushed to her cheeks. "I—there was no opportunity . . ."

Again, the ice. "I see."

There was a long, tense pause. Constantine was pale, breathing hard. He seemed to read all manner of negative things into her omission, but it hadn't been like that. She hadn't yet grown accustomed to the idea of . . . They'd decided to wait until Montford had been informed to make the news public . . . She'd promised Lady Arden . . . Any number of excuses came to mind.

But none of them quite approached the truth.

His jaw tightened. "I may not be your husband yet, my lady, but I am your betrothed and your protector under this roof. And if that weasel tries again to touch so much as a hair on that pretty head of yours, I'll rip his damned hands off. Do I make myself clear?"

Jane stared up at him, bewildered at such heat. Could this be jealousy? Certainly, his fury smacked of a possessiveness that had nothing to do with a gentleman's duty to protect his betrothed. "I can handle Mr. Trent."

He curled his lip. "Looked to me like *he* was handling *you.*"

Jane opened her mouth, then shut it again. She pulled her upper lip between her teeth and released it with an exasperated sigh. "I see there's no reasoning with you. I concede you are at liberty to bar whomever you wish from this house, but you have no right to censure my conduct or dictate to me about whom I may and may not see."

"Stay away from him, or you won't like the consequences."

She said nothing, merely studied the angry lines of his face, a hundred questions running through her mind. Paramount among them was: why did she want so much to believe there was good in this man, the blackest of the Blacks?

Montford had laid bare the facts of Constantine's disgrace. No one—not even Lady Arden—disputed what had happened. Yet, why didn't Constantine's reprehensible past fill her with disgust?

Somehow, she knew that whatever Trent meant to tell her, that wouldn't matter, either. Oh, she was a hopeless case.

Constantine looked down at her in silence for some moments. His face slowly lost its tightness. The dangerous light died in his eyes and that wry twist to his mouth reappeared.

He set his shoulder against the wall. "Go on, then. Ask. I'll tell you whatever you wish to know."

She did not like the way this concession had been forced from him. She didn't want to be his interrogator, with the threat of Mr. Trent's revelations hanging over his head.

But the truth was, Constantine owed her an explanation if he expected her to share in his fall from grace. She'd been wandering in a dreamland not to demand one from him before.

"Very well, then. What *did* you do that led my father-in-law to bar you from this house?"

He stared straight ahead, avoiding her gaze. "I seduced a young lady of gentle birth. When we were discovered, I refused to marry her. And then I nearly killed her brother in a duel over it."

It was the same story she'd heard already, yet his cold recitation stung Jane like a slap in the face.

That was all? At the very least, she'd expected him to produce extenuating circumstances. Perhaps he disdained to do so. Or perhaps he was a scoundrel in truth. Perhaps she was, yet again, grasping at straws because she wanted so very much to believe in his decency.

Jane sucked in a breath. "Yes, I've heard that version. Now I wish to hear yours."

His jaw tightened. "There *is* no other version. I did the deed. I pay the price."

She stared at him, and after a moment, she realized she was shaking her head, over and over, in denial.

A jeering laugh broke from him. "Did you expect I'd been wronged by my family, by society? No such luck, my sweet innocent. There's no way to whitewash my sins. If you marry me, you will have to take me as I am, not with a spun-sugar coating you've woven around me."

Jane flinched at his tone. This hard, sneering devil was not the Constantine Black she'd grown to care for. Others had called him scoundrel, but it was a long time since she'd truly thought of him that way. Now, he looked more than ready to play the part.

A burning sensation sprang up behind her eyes. His words, his mocking tone, made her ashamed of overlooking his crowning sin so blithely. It was, indeed, a heinous one.

He'd ruined a young lady's life. Yet, if he'd offered any kind of justification, however spurious, Jane would have clung to it gladly. She'd already woven various self-serving scenarios in her head. Fantasies that painted Constantine as the wronged hero and not the villain of that particular melodrama.

How pathetic she was.

In truth, she was not so naïve as to believe a man could change his character. Yet, she'd wagered her happiness on just such a miracle occurring, hadn't she? Not only by agreeing to marry the Bad Baron, but by growing to care for him, too.

"You're right," she whispered. "You're absolutely right. I don't know you at all, do I, Constantine?" She put her fingertips to her temple, feeling lost, like a tiny cork floating in a vast sea. "I'm afraid I can't . . ."

Like a sleepwalker, blindly, she turned and left him alone.

Though she wished for nothing more than solitude and a good bout of weeping, Jane returned to the drawing room, determined to give the best performance of her life. She needed Montford to believe she was content in this marriage, when in fact, she viewed it with something very near despair.

When had Constantine become more to her than a means to secure a future with Luke?

The gentlemen rose at her entrance. "Where's my nephew?" demanded deVere.

"Oh. Is he not here?" said Jane vaguely. "Mr. Trent and Lord Roxdale had, ah, words up in the gallery. I believe Mr. Trent must have gone home."

Montford's lips twitched. Lady Arden gave a small choke, as if she stifled a laugh.

"Gone home?" DeVere erupted, launching out of his chair. "Be damned to him!"

Without taking his leave, deVere strode off, leaving Lady Arden shaking with mirth. "Oh, I ought not to laugh, but he entertains me vastly." She fluttered her hands, gesturing for Jane to be seated. "Now, at last we can get to business. Montford, I have happy news. Jane and Constantine are to wed."

There was a pause. Softly, Montford said, "Then it appears I must congratulate you, Lady Roxdale."

Jane rushed into speech. "I know it is against your wish, Your Grace, but I believe this alliance is best for everyone and vital for the estate."

The duke watched her with a meditative air, the kind of contemplation that had made her squirm and babble all her secrets as a child. Indeed, even now, the effect of that mild, inquiring stare was much the same.

"Eminently sensible, my dear!" chimed in Lady Arden, saving her from speaking. "Don't, I beg you, allow Montford to put you off. We've agreed, have we not, to a short engagement? Your Grace, I believe that by the time those months pass your fears will be allayed. In fact," she added with a glinting smile, "*I* prophesy that you shall eat your words about Constantine."

The supreme confidence with which her ladyship spoke only made Jane's heart sink lower. She excused herself as soon as she could.

As she left the drawing room, she heard Lady Arden invite Montford to stay for dinner.

Wonderful! What an interminable ordeal that was going to be.

* * *

Jane didn't find the solitude she craved in her bedchamber. Luke lay in wait for her in her sitting room, an accusing look darkening his features.

Not now, she thought. *Please. Not now.*

"You forgot our picnic," Luke said without preamble. "And now it's coming on to storm!"

"Picnic?" Jane pinched the bridge of her nose. "I don't recall planning a picnic."

He regarded her with the pitiless eyes of a child denied a promised treat. "On the next fine day, you said. And Lord Roxdale was to come, too. *He* said he'd ask Marthe to pack a hamper 'specially and we were going to visit some ruins. And now it's too late to go, besides the fact it's *wizzling* down outside. And I wanted to see those ruins something awful, Aunt Jane, and now it'll rain for weeks and weeks and I'll *never* go!"

Ordinarily, Jane would tease him out of a mood like this, but the torrent of childish recriminations filled her cup to the brim.

Quickly, she turned her back on Luke, biting her lip in the struggle to stop herself bursting into tears. She couldn't let him see her weep.

She drew air into her lungs in great, shuddery gulps and waited until she had command over herself. Then she turned back to answer him.

"Luke," she managed in a low, calm voice, "it is a pity that you fixed your sights on today but didn't inform either me or Lord Roxdale of the fact. You should have reminded me sooner and then perhaps we could have gone."

She wished Luke *had* reminded her. She wished the three of them had tripped off merrily on an expedition with no thought in their heads beyond pleasure. She might then have been spared a vast deal of pain.

But no. She'd been overdue for a rude awakening, hadn't

she? An excursion today would merely have postponed the inevitable.

Luke looked far from mollified. Patience was almost beyond her at the moment, but she did her best.

In a rallying tone, she said, "Come here, you silly sausage." She draped an arm around him and gave him a hug. "There's no need for you to be so cross. We'll go another day."

"It won't be the same." He shrugged out of her hold and folded his arms across his skinny chest, glowering at her from beneath lowered brows like a malignant pixie.

Exasperation warred with the strong urge to laugh. She knew he'd only get madder if she gave way to hilarity, so she bit her lip again to stifle the threatening guffaw.

Why was she the only one to receive the brunt of Luke's displeasure? Constantine should be here to get a taste of it, too.

"Where is Lord Roxdale?" she asked.

"He's ridden off somewhere without me," muttered Luke.

Ah. So that's what this was about. Constantine had taken to letting Luke accompany him on his hacks around the estate. Luke had come to depend on those jaunts with his idol.

Heroically sacrificing herself in return for some peace, she said, "I'm sure Lord Roxdale wanted more than anything for you to go with him, but I daresay he knew I'd skin him alive if he kept you out in a storm."

Luke's brow cleared a little. Then he rolled his eyes. "I won't *melt,* you know, Aunt Jane."

And he sounded so much like his guardian that Jane's laugh had a catch in it. She ruffled Luke's hair and sent him off to wash his hands for supper.

She turned to gaze out the window. To the west, the sky looked blacker than the pits of hell. She hoped Constantine would find shelter when the storm hit.

Constantine was soaking wet when he returned home that night. He'd gone up to Bronson's dam to check the water level again, or that's what he'd told himself. In truth, he was spoiling for a fight and hoped Trent or one of his henchmen would give him one.

But the guards Trent had posted must have deserted their posts in the worsening weather. In the teeming rain, there was no one to be found.

The dam looked dangerously high. Clearly, Trent meant to do nothing to stop it flooding the surrounding area.

Some rebellious impulse urged Constantine to forget the whole business. What did it matter to him if Bronson's mill flooded, or if Trent's tenants suffered in the deluge? It wasn't his mill. They weren't his people. Once the dam broke, *his* mill would be back in business. Why couldn't he let sleeping dogs lie?

But even as the thought occurred to him, he knew he would have that engineer there tomorrow, that he would fight tooth and nail to do the work that must be done. He hoped to God it could wait that long.

He rode. He knew not how many miles he covered before the storm hit with a vengeance, forcing him to turn back. As the lightning flashed around him, he galloped across country until it grew too dark to see. Fool that he was, he'd been obliged to dismount and lead his horse, trudge all the weary way home.

Penance, was it? What was he punishing himself for? He could only hope the long, sodden walk had done his threadbare soul some good.

He'd known what Jane wanted when she'd asked him for an explanation of that long-ago scandal. She wanted a surety, something to bank against her trust. Well, it was a bit late for all that. He'd never bleated excuses or justifications for his conduct at the time of Amanda's disgrace and he wouldn't begin now.

He and Jane had been going on so well together. Couldn't she see *that* was what mattered, not a folly that had occurred years ago? The present was sweet; the future was theirs for the taking. Why stir all the murky waters of the past?

But he'd railed at fate too often to revisit those tired old arguments. In the end, one needed to stop complaining about the injustice of life and get on with living. Jane would learn to trust him, or she wouldn't, and there wasn't a damned thing he could do about that. After all these years of silence on the subject, he refused to start sniveling into her sleeve now.

The dinner hour was long past when Constantine reached Lazenby Hall. He ate a large, hasty meal, dripping on the kitchen floor, while hot water was drawn for his bath.

He took the stairs two at a time, stripping as he went. The bath that awaited him stung his extremities as they thawed, but it was a good pain, a satisfying one. He laid his head against the high back of the tub and closed his eyes.

Jane. He'd failed to thrust her from his mind during that long, idiotic ride in the storm. Now she was on the other side of the communicating door, perhaps undressing, preparing for bed. A shudder of visceral longing shot through him. God, how he wanted her.

His body had been weary when he'd lowered himself into the bath. Now, all his senses were alert, his cock standing to attention.

Down, boy, he ordered wryly. After the upheaval of today, there was no way Jane would take him into her bed.

He picked up the soap and rubbed it over his chest.

She'd been living in a lovely little soap sud, weaving dreams around him that did not fit with harsh reality. He'd disabused her; pricked that iridescent bubble. And now, he paid the price.

Perhaps he should have acted the sly rogue and embroidered a tale of his own to win back into her good graces. If he had, she would have clung to it. All she'd been looking for was a secure peg upon which to hang her faith in him.

Yet, she hadn't broken the engagement, for all that he'd disappointed her, spoken too harshly. She was a sensible, dutiful woman, Jane. And she'd never pretended to care for him, had she? This marriage was all about keeping Luke.

He rubbed his hands over his face and the rough stubble along his jaw scraped his palms. The thought of a shave made him give a snort of derision. Ah, the grandiose plans he'd made for tonight. All for naught.

Yet . . . it was a serious tactical error to leave Jane to her own devices for too long. If he abstained from visiting her chamber now, he'd only find it more difficult to breach her defenses the next time. That overactive brain of hers would start working again when he needed her to simply let her will slip free of its moorings and trust him to guide her where she needed to go. If he delayed, he'd have to begin this lengthy process of seduction all over again. He didn't think he could survive another night like the previous one.

Constantine squeezed the excess moisture out of his sponge and set it aside. Then he rose and stepped out of the bath, reaching for a towel.

He'd already dismissed Priddle, but the valet had thoughtfully laid out his dressing gown on the bed before he went. Having dried himself with a few swipes of the towel, Constantine shrugged into the silken garment.

He moved to the communicating door, anticipation heightening with every step.

Softly, he knocked on the panel, then turned the handle.

CHAPTER EIGHTEEN

Jane's door was locked.

The plummet of his spirits made him bow his head and rest it against the panels. Again, that stupid, irrational optimism! He ought not to have hoped. What woman would open her door to him after the events of the day?

Why did he expect differently of Jane?

Footsteps approached in the corridor. With some presence of mind, he pushed away from the connecting door.

"My lord!" Feather hurried through the antechamber and stood in the doorway. "You must come. Come quickly! Bronson's dam has burst!"

Constantine swore. "Call for my horse! Not Caesar, another one. Kiever will know. Send the other grooms to round up all the men they can. Tell Mrs. Higgins we'll need linen and blankets and medical supplies and anything else she can think of. Get Cook and the women to gather provisions and tell Joseph to ready the cart."

Cold fear gripped Constantine as he yanked on his clothes. If the dam had burst, there was no time to waste. What if he was already too late?

A hundred other directions tripped off his tongue. Larkin arrived, looking as if he'd just scrambled out of bed, and Constantine sent him to inform Trent of the state of affairs. "Tell him to get his men up there as soon as he can and don't brook any argument!"

Larkin's eyes popped in alarm and Constantine knew a qualm at sending such a diffident fellow. Constantine ought to sort out Trent himself but there was no time.

After making all the necessary preparations, he ran down the stairs, out into the rain, and vaulted onto the chestnut stallion that a groom held waiting for him.

"If she wakes, tell her ladyship not to come out in this. She's to sit tight until she hears from me. Understood?"

"Yes, m'lud!"

With a kick to the horse's flanks, Constantine rode into the night.

Jane opened her door to see a maid running down the corridor toward her. The whole house bustled with noise and raised voices. She grabbed the maid's arm. "Betsy! What's the to-do?"

"Oh, ma'am, Bronson's dam's burst and the master's gone up there."

"And no one informed me of it?" She pulled Betsy into her bedchamber. "You must help me dress. Quickly, girl! Put down those linens and help!"

In no time, Jane was garbed in her riding habit, her hair shoved into a severe knot.

"His lordship has already gone, you say?"

She'd heard the commotion from Constantine's bedchamber. Why hadn't he told her the news?

"Yes, ma'am." Betsy's hands twisted and she moved from one foot to the other. "My sister lives up there by the mill and I'm that worried about her, ma'am. She has three children."

Jane paused and gripped Betsy's shoulder. "Then we must trust in the master to save them. And pray."

In the meantime, there was much to be done. "Tell Mrs. Higgins I want to see her. And Cook, too."

These redoubtable women had all in hand on Constantine's orders, so Jane assisted in wrapping the provisions, blankets, and supplies in brown paper. A poor protection from the wet, but they'd throw a tarpaulin over the lot when it was stowed.

Lady Arden, who had rushed downstairs shortly after Jane, rolled up her sleeves and helped.

"How could Trent let this happen?" she said.

"Sheer pigheadedness," said Jane. She looked up as Larkin burst into the room.

"My lady, it's no good! Mr. Trent says he'll not send anyone to help in this weather. They'll see what's to do in the morning."

"The morning will be too late! Send Mr. Trent my compliments and tell him if he doesn't get his men up there, I shall make him wish he was never born."

Larkin goggled at her.

"Well? What are you waiting for? Go!" She watched Larkin hightail it, then muttered, "Not that it will do any good."

"This is the last bundle that will fit in the cart, my lady," said the footman, hefting another package.

"Right." Stripping off her apron, Jane ripped off her scarf and tied it over her head like a peasant woman.

"What are you doing?" said Lady Arden.

"I'm riding up there with the cart."

"But Roxdale gave orders that you were to stay here. Can't Mrs. Higgins go?"

"I need to be there," said Jane. "There's nothing more for me to do here." She gave Lady Arden a long, compelling look. "You would do the same in my shoes."

Lady Arden hesitated. Then she said, "Yes, I suppose I would."

Jane gave her a grateful smile. "Please, will you direct things while I'm gone?"

"I'll do that. And tell Constantine . . ." Lady Arden's smile went awry. "No, never mind. I shall see him soon enough."

The devastation was worse than Jane had feared. The mill itself was under three feet of water, but no one had been inside the building when the flooding occurred. The surrounding cottages had borne the brunt, as Constantine had predicted they would.

People were everywhere, running, milling, wading in to salvage belongings from the flood. Jane directed the groom to pull up and called down to one man, "Have you seen Lord Roxdale?"

"He were over yonder, my lady," the man said, indicating the opposite bank of the stream. "But the bridge is out, swept away. Ye'll never get 'cross there with that cart."

Jane saw immediately that it was hopeless. A horseman might wade his horse across, but the cart would never survive.

"We'll set up on this side, then. Will you direct me to a barn, or some other large building? Somewhere dry?"

They found an outbuilding that looked like some kind of storage shed. Mercifully, it was on higher ground and had escaped the flooding. Jane delegated duties to the women who were able to help her, and soon the injured and the suffering streamed in.

She did not see Constantine for many hours, though she heard people speak of him with awe in their voices. Jane's throat tightened as she listened. Tonight, he'd become a hero to them.

She wondered where he was now, and if he was safe. She hadn't heard anything to the contrary, so she remained collected, despite her anxiety. She longed to go and try to commandeer a horse to find him, but she would only get in his way. Here, she could be useful.

Resolutely, she labored on.

Mr. Larkin arrived, bearing another load of blankets. Jane dispatched a few of the women to help him unload the cart.

"Mr. Larkin, have you news of Mr. Trent?"

"No, ma'am, but Lord deVere and His Grace are up at the mill and Lord Roxdale says you are to go home. It's not a fit place for you."

Jane put her hands on her hips. "Then you go and tell Lord Roxdale from me that I'm not leaving until he comes to fetch me." She had no intention of abandoning her post, but at least if he came she could get some food into him and check whether he had any injuries that needed attention.

With a visible gulp, Larkin bowed and took himself off.

But her ploy didn't work. It was more than an hour before Constantine came, and when he did, it was not for her.

A sudden silence fell over the gathering. Jane looked up to see Constantine standing in the doorway, bearing a woman in his arms.

Water ran in rivulets from his hair, dripping into his face. His features were gray, taut with exhaustion and, she thought, despair. He was coatless, hatless; his white linen shirt was plastered to his body, ripped in some places.

"Constantine!" Jane ran forward. "Quick! One of you make a pallet with these blankets here, on the floor. We must try to get her warm."

"Too late. She's dead." Constantine's voice cracked. He laid his burden gently on the makeshift bed. "I'm sorry."

A wail went up from one of the women. Jane was thrust aside as the dead woman's family and friends gathered around her.

"What happened?" she asked Constantine.

Constantine rubbed a hand over his face. "As far as I can gather, she must have slipped and fallen down the stream bank, hit her head on something as she went in."

Bleakly, Constantine watched the outpourings of grief.

Jane took his hand—it was gloveless and freezing—and led him away.

She moved to get him a blanket. "No," he said, "I have to get back."

"You need to rest," Jane insisted. "There are others to do this work."

Anger blazed like lightning across his face. "Do you think I could? Do you think I could rest when there are still more people out there?" He shook his head. "Jane," he said huskily. "You don't know me at all."

Panic threatened to choke her. She'd missed something. Something vital. She felt as if she'd lost something important and would never get it back.

She swallowed down her fear. Shakily, she said, "You expected *me* to go. You told Larkin to order me home."

For a long moment, Constantine stared at her. "That was different."

Unable to bear his intensity, the pain she saw plainly in his eyes, she lowered her gaze. "How is that different? Because I'm a female?"

"No." He reached out and traced her jaw with the back of his finger. "Because I never expected you would obey me and go."

Constantine didn't allow himself to rest until well into the next afternoon. By midday, he'd assured himself that everyone in the district was safe and accommodated, at least temporarily, billeted at nearby cottages, in the church hall, or at the King's Head.

His own tenants had risen to the occasion, bringing meals and taking in those who couldn't get shelter closer to home. It would have been far more convenient to have put them all up at Lazenby Hall, but these folk were proud and understandably nervous about bedding down at the local baron's house. They were better off, so Jones had assured him, with their own kind.

Jones fixed him with a long, hard stare. "I'm coming back."

Constantine was so tired, he almost missed the fellow's meaning. Then it dawned on him that Jones had offered to resume his former position as steward of the estate. Constantine's smile felt like it would crack his face.

"Good man!" he said, putting out a hand for Jones to shake. Jones hesitated for only an instant before gripping

Constantine's hand. Larkin would be demoted but the boy needed more experience, and would doubtless be glad of Jones's guidance for a few years yet.

Glad that at least one good thing had come out of last night's devastation, Constantine devoured a sandwich and a tankard of ale at the King's Head and then set off again to confer with the engineer who'd arrived from Bristol. Lord deVere and Montford had both returned from the manor, having eaten and changed their raiment. Of Trent, there was no sign.

"I can start work as soon as may be, but I need permission from the owner of the land," said Mr. Granger.

"You have permission," growled deVere. He fixed Constantine with a basilisk stare. "I'll take care of it."

Constantine nodded. "Do the work."

Granger shouted to his men and Constantine turned to Montford and deVere. "I'm obliged to you both."

Wordlessly, deVere clapped him on the shoulder and left.

"Go home, Roxdale," said Montford. "You're no use here, dead on your feet."

Constantine bowed his head, unwilling to accept dismissal. He knew, however, that Montford was right. He ought to go. And he would, too, if he could manage to move one foot in front of the other.

Montford lingered, to what purpose Constantine didn't know. He was too exhausted to fathom the duke's intentions.

The rumble of carriage wheels grew louder. Constantine turned his head to look.

"Ah," said Montford. "Perfect timing."

Constantine stared at the carriage as if he'd never seen one before. "My horse," he said vaguely.

"My groom will see to him. Go home, Roxdale. I'll send word if you're needed."

Getting into the carriage was the last thing Constantine remembered before he woke in his own bed. Sunlight streamed through the window, slathering the walls with a buttery glow. Had he slept all afternoon? All night as well?

He flung an arm across his eyes as the anguish of last night came flooding back. He cursed the sunshine. If only it had come sooner. If only he'd swallowed his pride and used persuasion to secure Trent's cooperation instead of insult. If only he'd ridden roughshod over Trent and taken it upon himself to dismantle that dam days ago.

All the *if only*s. If any one of those things had happened, that poor woman would not have had to die.

Hester. That was her name. He'd heard a woman keening it as he'd walked out again, into the storm.

Shuddering, he sat up and buried his head in his hands. It was as if that sobbing, communal grief crowded the bedchamber. He could hear it, feel it inside him.

Those sounds . . . they came from him, he realized. Dry, racking sobs that seemed to lodge and burrow deep in his chest.

Too late. His pride and Trent's stubbornness. Between them, they'd killed an innocent woman.

A breath of air stirred at his nape. Two slender arms came around him and a tender kiss was pressed to his shoulder. A soft voice whispered, "No man could have done more."

He exhaled a long breath. "Don't."

Jane crawled around to face him. Those clear gray eyes were so fierce, they seemed to grip his so he couldn't look away. "Constantine, you must not blame yourself. It is *not* your fault."

He didn't answer her. He couldn't.

She put her hands on his shoulders. "The responsibility was and is Trent's. He's a coward and a fool, Constantine, and his tenants know it." Leaning forward, she stroked his jaw with a gentle hand. "You should have heard the things they said of you last night," she whispered. "You are a hero to them. I was . . . very proud."

At her touch, so welcome, the tightness in his chest eased, just a little. He closed his eyes and pressed a kiss to her palm.

When he opened his eyes again, her face was close to his. Her gaze lowered to his mouth and went back to his eyes, then lowered again. Planting one hand on the bed next to him, she leaned in to brush her lips over his.

Jane was unbearably aroused by that simple, soft kiss. She'd waited for Constantine to wake up for so long she thought she'd go mad with impatience. Earlier, she'd given orders that neither of them were to be disturbed on pain of dismissal. She'd unlocked the communicating door and crept into his bedchamber to watch him sleep.

He was shirtless, but he'd been put to bed in his breeches, barely able to stand when he'd arrived home the previous afternoon.

Now, she waited for him to take her, but Constantine sat curiously still, his features hard and drawn. More than anything, she wanted to hold him, to tell him all would be well. She slid her arms around his torso, but it was like embracing a statue. He didn't yield to her, didn't return her embrace.

Hurt, she sat back, her brows knitted in confusion.

Suddenly, with a muttered curse, he caught her face between his hands, kissing her desperately, driving his fingers through her hair. Then he hauled her into his arms and buried his face in the crook of her neck.

His breathing was harsh in her ear. "Oh, God, Jane. I need you. I need you and I can't—"

"Hush, it's all right." She wanted to give herself to him. Wanted it more than anything, more than her next breath. She no longer cared whether she could accommodate him comfortably or not. She would suffer pain if that was what it took to give him some measure of release. He was torturing himself with needless guilt and it killed her to see it.

His fingers were already fumbling at the ribbons of her bodice. "But I can't be . . . I can't go slowly, make it perfect for you. Not this time."

"It *will* be perfect," she said, smiling a little. "It will be perfect because it's you."

He found her breasts then, gathered them in his hands, and the power of speech abruptly deserted her. He lavished attention on first one breast, then the other, and when she gasped with delight, his fingers found her sex, delving into the wet folds, touching her as he'd instructed her to do that first night.

No longer did such liberties feel wrong, or a violation or a precursor to pain. She moaned with pleasure as he pushed one finger inside her, then two. She let her legs fall open, giving everything to him, letting him in.

This time, she suffered no embarrassment. It felt right—utterly perfect—when he covered her body with his. The heavy flesh of his penis came to rest against her thigh. Instead of fear, a wave of longing swept over her. She needed this as much as he did. She ached for him, deep inside.

Jane opened her eyes and looked up at Constantine as he reached down between them. Her heart was so full of love for him that fear became a state beyond her comprehension.

She loved him! And the joy and terror of it were beyond anything she'd ever imagined.

Jane slid her hands up his braced arms to his shoulders, glorying in his muscular beauty.

She knew she had to tell him what she wanted, so that even if he did cause her pain at the crucial moment, he would know how much she'd craved him.

"I need you inside me," she said. "Constantine, please."

His shoulders tensed beneath her hands. The head of his erection nudged forward, and with one great thrust, he was sheathed inside her.

And it felt . . . a little strange . . . but mostly . . . *wonderful*.

Constantine groaned, the tendons standing out in his neck. "Did I hurt you?" he gasped.

"No." She threw back her head and laughed, wrapping her legs around his waist.

"Oh, thank God," he managed. "I'd die if I had to stop now."

That struck her as so amusing, he had to kiss her to muffle her relieved, delighted laughter.

She gloried in their closeness, in the way their bodies fit together. He began to move inside her and she stopped laughing and moved with him, chasing after a prize that she hadn't even dared to dream about for so long.

She loved the feel of him, so warm and hard, yet with skin so smooth beneath her touch; she loved watching sunlight define the musculature of his shoulders and gleam in his thick dark hair. She loved the scent of him, earthy and masculine. She loved the husky timbre of his voice when he whispered her name.

I love you, she wanted to tell him, but she didn't know if she deserved to say it yet. She'd misjudged him and she had yet to pay the price.

He changed the angle of his thrusts and she lost that thread of thought altogether, became a mindless collection of pleasured nerve endings and sighs and building heat.

"Ah, Jane. I can't hold on much longer."

He reached down and pressed the flesh above where they fitted together. A sudden burst of light scattered across her eyelids as all the heat inside her gathered and exploded, sending waves of pleasure through her body.

She clung on, coasting the waves as his thrusts increased in power and speed. His breathing grew more labored until his entire body jolted and he pulled out of her with a hoarse cry. Shuddering, he collapsed on the mattress beside her, one arm lying heavily across her breasts.

Jane lay beside him, entranced by the echoes of delicious sensations that still played like ripples of music through her body. She was sore in places she'd never known existed, yet she'd never felt so alive, so full of joy, so connected to another human being. How could she have survived without this for so long?

Constantine turned on his side and gathered her to him, so that his front curved around her back.

His hand closed possessively over her breast. His lips skimmed behind her ear. "I lost my sanity back there." He hesitated. With a soft laugh, he said, "I never thought I'd need to ask this question, but tell me how it was for you."

With a sigh, Jane snuggled back against his chest.

"Perfect," she said. "It was perfect. As I knew it would be."

He captured her hand and held it pressed against the valley between her breasts. The gesture was so intimate, so tender, that she had to blink back a tear.

They lay there for a long time without speaking, until soon, Constantine's deep breathing told Jane he'd fallen asleep. She ought to leave and seek her own bed, but he held her fast, his long, muscled legs entangled with hers. She wouldn't wish to wake him by moving, so she let him be, and allowed her eyelids to drift shut.

When Jane woke again, it was dark, but candles lit the room and a fire crackled and snapped in the grate. She turned her head to see Constantine staring at her with that intensity back in his gaze.

He smiled. "I've never seen someone so dead to the world as you were just now."

"You've been watching me sleep?" She wasn't sure if she liked the idea.

He leaned over to kiss her. "Sleeping Beauty. You enchant me."

She frowned. "I don't recall Sleeping Beauty having any magical powers. Didn't she just doze through the entire book?"

He grinned. "You have a very literal mind, my dear." He sat up. "Are you hungry? I'm sure you must be. I'll go down to the larder and see what I can find for us."

"That would be most appreciated." She threw her arms over her head. "Ah, I could live in this bed forever, but there's so much work yet to be done."

He smiled and reached for his shirt. "Yes, but the work must wait until daylight, so we still have tonight."

While he was gone, Jane donned her wrapper and got back under the covers. Her body was alive with sensation, her mind alert. She could scarcely believe that after all the agony of self-doubt she'd suffered since her wedding night, Constantine had so quickly and easily made her feel like a full-blooded, passionate woman, a sensual, healthy whole.

The revelation was stunning in its simplicity. She was a normal woman, after all.

She was tender and achy in some intimate parts of her, but it was a good and satisfying ache. A delicious thrill scintillated through her. They would have all night.

When Constantine returned bearing a tray stocked with a feast fit for two kings, they both fell upon it and ate with gusto.

"Mmm." Jane closed her eyes in delight. "This tart is pure heaven. We must increase Cook's wages immediately." She wiggled her fingertips, which were covered in fruity goo.

"It seems I forgot napkins," said Constantine. With a wicked glint in his eye, he reached for her hand. "Allow me."

Jane gasped as he bent and closed his lips over one fingertip. The moist, warm flesh of his mouth made a languorous pleasure steal over her body. His gaze never left her face and that gaze was hot with desire.

When he'd finished making a meal of her fingers, he turned her hand and pressed a kiss to her palm, then moved up to her wrist. Her pulse quickened under his lips, leaped at the touch of his tongue.

"Oh, you are a wicked, wicked man," she breathed.

"I can be far more wicked than that." He drew her toward him for a kiss, this time so suggestive and lascivious that he might have been making love to her mouth. Her body melted; her mind grew dazed.

He drew back. "Jane, we have to talk."

CHAPTER NINETEEN

After that kiss, Jane took many moments to regain her focus.

"Talk?" she said vaguely. *Talk?* When she had years of experience in the bedchamber to catch up on?

"Yes. I need to tell you about what happened all those years ago."

He picked up the tray and set it down on the table by the window. Then he shucked his breeches and crawled back into bed with her.

She tried to keep her eyes off certain intriguing parts of him. It was rude to stare. And of course, he pulled the covers to their waists so she didn't have the opportunity to investigate further. Jane sighed. So much to learn.

A quirk of his lips told him he guessed the reason for her sigh, and she blushed.

"You wanted to tell me . . ." she prompted, gathering her tattered dignity around her.

He looked a little grim at that. "Yes, I must." He paused. "You asked me to explain about my disgrace. Well, I suppose you might say it's a little like the boy who cried wolf."

Perplexed, she shifted against the pillows. "How do you mean?"

Constantine lay back against the banked pillows, one bent arm behind his head, one arm around Jane.

He exhaled a long breath through his nostrils. "Oh, I was

a wild child as a youth, there's no doubt. I was bored and rich and reckless and I discovered early on that I loved women. I was nearly sent down from Eton for various transgressions and my father refused to send me to Oxford because of it. He said I'd waste my time there, just as I had at school.

"Certainly, my pranks weren't at all to my credit, but there was no great harm in them. I grew out of it, but my father was a stern, righteous man, and he didn't understand that. He thought my character fixed at the age of seventeen."

"That does seem severe," Jane said. "My cousins cut all kinds of larks through school and university. I don't think it did them any harm."

"Ah. But then came Amanda." He gave a dry, sardonic laugh. "Lord, she was the answer to a man's prayers, the beauty of the Season. Her parents weren't wealthy or titled, but they invested all they had into giving their exquisite daughter a chance at a great marriage. They were determined to make a large return on their investment."

Ordinarily, Jane might have been jealous at his praise of this young lady, but his biting sarcasm made it clear he harbored no residual feelings for her.

"What happened?"

"I fell head over heels in love with her, of course," said Constantine. "I wasn't quite the glittering prize her parents wanted, but in the months they'd been in Town they must have realized that without a large dowry or grand connections, Amanda was not destined for a coronet. The Blacks are an old family and the property at Broadmere that I stood to inherit, while not as grand as Lazenby Hall, was large and prosperous. They must have thought I was the best prospect she had."

Jane had a feeling she knew what was coming.

His mouth curved in derision. "It was so ludicrous, so *unnecessary*. I fully intended to offer for her once I'd secured my father's blessing. He was being difficult about it. I thought at the time, as young men do, that he was determined to thwart me whatever I did. Looking back, I believe he suspected Amanda's parents were the grasping, mercenary kind. I knew that—Amanda had confided some of her woes to me—and I didn't care. I wanted to be her knight in shining armor." His mouth twisted. "But the truth was, she was no princess."

He reached for his wine glass on the bedside table and offered it to Jane, but she shook her head. He took a deep, contemplative sip. "No doubt you've heard I compromised Amanda at a house party. The truth is—and this is for your ears only—she compromised me."

He set down the glass with a snort of derision. "So wet behind the ears as I was at—what?—twenty? I had no more notion of trying to seduce a gently bred lady than I had of flying to the moon. Yes, I was a wild 'un, but I wasn't a fool. I knew compromising a lady went beyond the pale. I couldn't believe it when she appeared in my bedchamber in the dead of night like that."

"You were discovered," Jane said, taking his hand.

"Oh, yes." He stroked her palm with his thumb. "By design, of course. Nothing had transpired between us, but the mere fact of her being there . . . And the most amusing part—really hilarious—is that I would not have twigged to the scheme if Amanda hadn't shown me her triumph. She told me, you see. She'd never cared for me. She was as ambitious as her parents and twice as clever, for she'd never let down her guard, as they had."

His mouth turned down in disgust. "Oh, I was so full of violent passions and idealistic fervor. I truly thought I loved her. I was prepared to suffer estrangement from my family if that was what it took to make her my wife. And . . . she laughed at me."

Jane ached for that wild, passionate young man. Fury filled her, thinking of the woman whose greed had destroyed his good name. Her hand clenched his.

He glanced at her, then looked down at their joined hands. "I was full of pain and wounded pride. I knew Amanda was ruined in the eyes of the world but I couldn't bring myself to marry her after that."

"They all talked at you, I suppose," said Jane.

"Oh, yes, there were many stern lectures, ranting and raving. People—dear friends, even—cut me in the street. I pretended not to care. I fell in with a crowd who didn't give a fig what my morals were, but I never felt a part of it."

"And your father?"

His jaw tightened. "Looking back, I think that at first, he tried to understand. In between the rants, he demanded an explanation. I gave him none. To have revealed Amanda's scheme would have damned her completely. But it was more than that. It hurt that my father would so far misjudge me as to believe I would have taken Amanda to my bedchamber and treated her with dishonor, when he *knew* I wanted to make her my wife. I thought he was better acquainted with me than that. Yet, he didn't draw a distinction between my past exploits and the present crisis."

"The boy who cried wolf."

"Yes. They believed the worst because of what they already knew. So, I became an outcast, a libertine whose name was only whispered in connection with some scandal or other. I had to resign from my clubs. Any place low enough to have me was somewhere I usually didn't care to go. Only George stood by me. Only my brother George."

"What of your other family?"

He sighed. "My sisters, believing their marital prospects ruined, shunned me. Mama . . ." Jane ached for the pain that crossed his features. "Well, she'd never stood up to my father before. I haven't laid eyes on her since. My father disowned me, you see. Banished me from the family home. In fact, he was in the process of cutting me out of his will when he died."

"Constantine, I'm so sorry," she whispered. "So that's why you never went back."

He shrugged. "George was meant to have Broadmere. As far as I'm concerned, the place is his. For the last twelve years, I've only drawn the younger son's allowance. Perhaps I shouldn't have taken a penny, as was my father's intention, but George refused to accept the property if I didn't. Now that I've inherited Lazenby Hall, I'm trying to persuade George to formally take title to Broadmere, once and for all."

No wonder Frederick had assumed Constantine was an absentee landlord. Now, it all made sense. "So you've existed all this time on a younger son's allowance."

"Augmented by profits made on the Royal Exchange, yes."

She stared at him. "Not from the gaming tables, then."

He laughed. "I may be a fool, but I'm not stupid. When I play, I make sure I don't bet beyond my means. Why, I'd have been rolled up within the month, otherwise."

She nodded, deep in thought. "Did you ever regret not marrying her?"

He shook his head. "At the time, I certainly regretted all that I'd lost. But . . . no, I didn't regret refusing to wed Amanda. And she ought to be glad of it, too. I would have made her a devil of a husband, hating her as I did. Sometimes . . . Well, sometimes I did wonder whether I should have just married her and lived apart from her, as so many men do." He turned his head and raised her hand to his lips. "But now I'm glad I didn't. Because of you."

Joy bubbled up inside, burst from her in a brilliant smile.

His eyes burned into hers. "My God, Jane, when you smile at me like that I can't breathe for wanting you."

She took his face between her hands. "I love you, Constantine. Make love to me."

She kissed him before he could say a word in response, too scared that he might repulse her love or try to give some kind but inadequate answer. The only reply that would satisfy her was those three words.

How terrifying a realization that was.

When he'd taken her earlier it had felt like he must love her, but she knew she could easily be deceived on that score. Part of a rake's charm must be that he could make a woman believe he adored her.

Constantine pushed aside her wrapper and kissed his way down her body, lingering long at her breasts, then pausing to swirl his tongue around her navel. A sensual haze took over her brain, until all her worries melted away.

"Ohh," she gasped. "That's *wicked*."

His warm breath tickled her stomach as he laughed. "My innocent." Then he trailed his lips to her hip, pressing kisses along her thigh.

She moved restlessly, her sex throbbing for his touch. The brush of his tongue on her inner thigh sent heat curling through her. His unshaven jaw was scratchy with the beginnings of a beard, but in a pleasant way, one that made her skin tingle to a heightened awareness.

She needed him; she was ready; he was taking too long. She put a fluttering hand on his head, trying to urge him up so they could get to the best part, but he chuckled and remained where he was.

"I want you . . ." She gasped and writhed with need, until his hands gripped her inner thighs and gently pushed them apart.

His breath was hot on her sex as he parted her folds and— her eyes snapped open—oh, good Lord!

"What are you *doing*?" She shot up the bed, scrambling to get away from his questing tongue.

Constantine returned her horrified gaze with a wicked glint in his eye, resting his chin in his hand. "You'll love it. I promise."

"N-no, I won't. You . . . you can't just . . ."

He raised his brows.

"It's indecent!"

"Decency has no place in a bedchamber. Not in our bedchamber, anyway." He gripped her ankle and began pulling her toward him, but she clung to the headboard, determined not to let him do such a scandalous, embarrassing thing.

His eyes narrowed with amusement, but she knew by the angle of that stubborn chin that he wasn't going to let her get away. He raised himself and crawled toward her like a green-eyed predator. Her eyes widened; a delicious panic fluttered in her chest. Clearly, Constantine was not minded to play the gentleman and concede to the wishes of a lady.

He leaned in to kiss her cheek, then he gave her earlobe a playful lick. With his lips against her ear, he whispered, "You wanted me to teach you pleasure, Jane. There's so very much I can teach you."

He kissed her neck, then gently took her skin between his teeth.

Jane gasped.

"You like that?"

She nodded.

He drifted down. "And this?" He closed his mouth over her nipple and sucked, until pleasure raced from that sensitive flesh to her loins in a fiery current.

"Ah!" She writhed beneath him.

He reached down to cup her sex with his hand, used the flat of his fingertip to circle gently, building the tension inside her.

His lips moved against the slope of her breast. "Is this right?"

Her head tipped back, "Oh. Yes."

"Imagine what it would be like for me to kiss you down there."

She couldn't breathe. She couldn't speak.

"If this were my tongue and lips on you, how would it feel? I want to taste you, Jane. I'm dying to cover you with my mouth."

A whimper of helpless longing escaped her. She didn't know how to answer him, but when he touched her like that, and said those sinful things . . . she felt her reluctance slipping away.

He pressed gentle kisses to her stomach while he pleasured her with his hand.

"Jane, do you trust me?"

She was too far gone to answer. It was easier not to.

That husky voice came at her again, commanding this time. "Do you trust me, Jane?"

"Yes. Yes."

"Then let me."

"Yes."

He settled between her legs again and she felt his tongue take over the work of his fingers, swirling and flicking, testing, exploring. He set her on fire with his tongue and lips, and the last vestige of her shame burned away in the conflagration.

When he found one trick that made her moan his name, he used it unrelentingly until she knew she would perish from the pleasure, burn and burn until nothing was left of her but ash.

Fleetingly, she touched his hair, then her hand dropped to the side as the pleasure exploded, racking her body, obliterating her mind.

And then he was inside her, stoking the flame, riding her with deep, slow thrusts, pushing her to the limit, until she cried out a second time. The world went black, and she lost any sense of what came next in the storm of her release.

Jane smiled as he collapsed beside her. She'd lost part of herself to him, and she didn't ever want it back.

In the days that followed, Jane only grew to love Constantine more. The way he'd taken charge of the situation at Bronson's mill commanded even Montford's respect; certainly, the duke said no more about Constantine's lack of suitability before he left Lazenby Hall.

Daylight hours were filled with hard, rewarding work, overseeing the repair and rebuilding of cottages, since Mr. Trent had abandoned his estate for the time being, apparently called on urgent business to Town.

Constantine had obtained finance on the strength of his and Jane's betrothal, and preparations were under way to ready their own mill for production. All of the Lazenby weavers who'd been forced to seek positions at Bronson's were eager to begin work. Under the threat of mass desertion from his own weavers, Bronson had been forced to raise his wages to match those Constantine had set.

Even in the midst of all this labor, Constantine never forgot the one casualty of the flood, the one woman he couldn't save. He ordered a special memorial service to be held in the village church and laid flowers at Hester Martin's grave.

At night, Constantine became Jane's dark, sinful lover. He coaxed her to do things she would never have dreamed she'd do, let alone enjoy. Her narrow world expanded to a universe of pleasure, beyond anything she'd hoped for when she'd agreed to submit to his instruction.

Yet, love had made her greedy. She wanted more.

He'd never said the words, never referred even obliquely to her impulsive declaration. He behaved as though he thought only of her, as if her happiness were vital to him. But until he said the words . . .

"What are you thinking about?"

She looked up to see Constantine smiling at her across the dinner table.

"Oh, I'm terribly sorry I was in a brown study. Forgive me." She took up her spoon and dipped it in her soup. She had no intention of revealing the tenor of her thoughts.

With a glance at Lady Arden, Constantine let the matter drop. He sipped his wine. "I want to take you to London next week, Jane. Would you like that?"

"London?" Her eyes widened in alarm. "Whatever for?"

"I have business there. And I wish to track down Trent and bring him to a sense of his responsibilities. His tenants need him."

"So . . ." She hesitated. "No balls, or . . . or parties."

"There's Montford's ball, remember?" he said. "I believe we are to be the guests of honor."

She'd forgotten all about it.

Lady Arden cut in. "You are still in mourning so you

cannot dance, but you need not forgo *every* pleasure, my dear. Perhaps it is a trifle unusual for you to appear at a ball so soon after Frederick's death, but when your betrothal is announced, people will understand. As Constantine's affianced bride, you are needed at his side."

The lady cast her a meaning look, and Jane recalled their conversation about reestablishing Constantine in society. Her heart sank. She must go, of course, for his sake.

Ah, but she'd always loathed social occasions. Her manner was too direct to appeal to members of either sex and her tongue tied when she attempted light conversation. While Cecily was known for her eccentricity, people loved her for it, too. Jane's oddness was less endearing. It was merely . . . odd.

But there was another reason for Jane's reluctance. She gazed at Constantine, with all his magnificence and virility, and realized she'd been living in a cocoon with him these past weeks. Wrapped up in him, with the world far away, she'd grown confident of his attentions. She'd felt safe.

In Town, with so many more interesting diversions to draw him, whatever charm Jane possessed would quickly pale.

There would be other ladies, too. More sophisticated, more beautiful, more experienced. How could she hope to compete with them?

The prospect cast a harsh, unforgiving light on her interactions with Constantine in the past weeks. He'd used many warm, caressing words, but none of those words had been the ones she most dearly wished to hear.

All of a sudden, reality slammed into her. For many moments, she couldn't breathe. Why did she continually delude herself about him? Why did she insist on living in some fantasy land when a cold, hard examination of the facts would lead any sensible person to conclude the truth?

Constantine had never said he loved her. He'd never promised to be faithful, either. He was an unrepentant womanizer, and though she was certain he'd not had another woman while at Lazenby, it might simply be lack of opportunity rather than steadfastness that had prevented him.

From the start, Constantine had proposed a business arrangement between them. He'd never flummeried her on that score. Oh, certainly he had affection for her. She knew he cared. But Frederick had seemed to care for her at the outset of their marriage, yet it had not stopped him keeping a succession of mistresses throughout. That was the way things were in their circle. Wives were expected to turn a blind eye to their husbands' philandering, and to take their own lovers after they'd produced one or two sons of the marriage.

Was that the kind of arrangement she'd have with Constantine? Pain cramped her stomach at the thought.

Suddenly, she felt adrift, even more vulnerable than she'd been as an unhappy seventeen-year-old. Jane longed to believe in Constantine's love and in his fidelity. But without his reassurance on those points, she couldn't face the trip to Town with anything but dread.

CHAPTER TWENTY

As soon as Constantine opened the door to her late that night, Jane fell upon him with frenzied kisses, her hands ripping at the fastenings on his dressing gown.

The feel of her fingertips on his bare skin made him catch his breath, but he sensed a desperate edge to her lovemaking tonight. It unsettled him.

He put his hands on Jane's shoulders to hold her still. "Whoa, there," he said softly. "What's the hurry, princess?"

Without a word, the vixen slipped from his grasp and slid down his body. Caressing his hips with her hands, she pressed gentle, openmouthed kisses to his chest, flicking his nipple with her tongue. His member hardened instantly, but he was determined not to let her take his mind off what he wanted to know.

"Jane . . ."

She moved farther south, giving his stomach playful licks that felt like tongues of flame. *No, no.* Before he lost his mind completely, he needed to know why she was behaving like this.

He touched the back of her head, trying to recall her attention. In a strained voice, he said, "Not that I don't appreciate the . . ." He broke off with a long moan as she took him in her mouth, scattering his thoughts to oblivion.

Something about this picture was wrong, but Constantine

was damned if he could puzzle it out while her tongue fondled his cock with the skill of an experienced courtesan. The notion of Jane being the one to do this to him made the blood roar through his body in a dizzying rush.

Shuddering, he threaded his fingers through her hair, his buttocks tensing as she took all of him. He'd taught her the basics, but in the past weeks, she seemed to have perfected the art.

He held on for as long as he could, which, it turned out, was no time at all. Too soon, his mind blanked, and with a guttural cry, he came so hard his head swam.

And they hadn't even made it to the bed.

When he'd regained his senses, he pulled her up for a long, drugging kiss, then guided her to the bed with a firm hand on the curve of her delectable bottom. She wasn't wearing a stitch of clothing—another novelty—and though he appreciated the view he was getting, her nakedness plucked another string of unease.

His chest was still heaving when he settled back on the pillows, pulling her down to him. "I'm going to need a minute before I reciprocate."

She lay in the circle of his arm, biting the edge of her thumb in that way she had. He'd learned the gesture meant she was agitated about something.

So. His instincts at the start of this torrid encounter had been correct.

"Jane, what's wrong?"

"Wrong?" She looked up at him through the wild tangle of her hair. "Why should you say that? I . . . you enjoyed that, didn't you?"

God, had he enjoyed it? "Of course I did. But you don't have to do that if you don't want to, you know. It's not mandatory."

"I like doing it. I like . . ." Her lips curved in a secretive smile. "I *love* having you at my mercy."

He laughed, and kissed her temple. His voice grew husky. "I'm your slave, princess. You know that."

She fell silent.

And there it was again, that tension. He could feel it in her, even as she snuggled close.

This was the moment in most of his dealings with women where he'd get the hell out of there. He'd leave, or he'd commit some unforgivable sin, and when they tossed him out of their beds he'd heave a sigh of relief and move on.

Now, it was not so simple. Jane wasn't one of those women. He cared for her. He was going to marry her. He couldn't leave, even if he wanted to. And he *didn't* want to.

She'd told him she loved him, but she hadn't repeated the sentiment, and he'd learned better than to believe a woman knew her own heart in the afterglow of sexual release. Even if she truly believed she loved him, it might all be an illusion. He'd been her first real lover, after all. Sometimes women liked to fool themselves that they slept with a man for more altruistic reasons than the sinful pursuit of pleasure.

But he was uneasily aware that if he made a wrong step now, he might well lose everything they had together. And what they had was new to him, precious. He hadn't allowed himself to care for a woman since Amanda. He'd deliberately chosen lovers as hard-hearted and sophisticated as he was. If they ever developed more tender feelings toward him, he simply left. No danger there.

Gently, he kissed the top of Jane's head, stroking her bare, lovely arm with his fingertips.

The words "I love you," which she'd bestowed on him so effortlessly, were not so simple for him to say. An ache built in his throat as he tried desperately to think of a phrase that told her how important she was to him, how uniquely dear. A sentiment that would not seem like a sop to her feelings, a second-best to love.

He couldn't. And in the end, he reached for her and pulled her on top of him and dispensed with speech altogether.

*   *   *

As soon as he heard of Trent's return from Town, Constantine was on the man's doorstep. This time, instead of barging into Trent's breakfast room, Constantine most correctly sent up his card. After a lengthy wait, he was shown into the library.

Promising. Trent had not barred him from the house, at least. Perhaps he would have, if the notion had occurred to him.

When Trent came in, Constantine walked forward, holding out his hand. Trent ignored it.

"You wished to see me?" The tone was cool, but Constantine sensed the resentment seething underneath.

"Yes, I wished to see you. And I'll tell you now, I have not come to pick a fight." He looked around. "Do you mind if we sit down?"

"You won't be here long enough," said Trent. "State your business and go."

Constantine regarded Trent with a small measure of sympathy. Perhaps he ought to let the man vent his spleen. "DeVere gave you a dressing-down, did he? I am sorry for it."

"He held *you* up as an example. To *me*!" Trent's square jaw hardened.

"He must be in his dotage," said Constantine lightly.

"That's what I thought! There's madness in the deVeres and his lordship has it in spades." With a start, Trent seemed to catch himself, perhaps remembering that he was (a) himself a deVere on the distaff side, and (b) speaking to a Black, the natural enemy of the deVere clan.

Trent cleared his throat. "Never mind that. What are you doing here?"

"I came to inform you of the work that is going on up at your mill."

"I know what's going on!" Trent snapped. "I've got eyes, haven't I? Rode past there this morning." He gave a short laugh. "If you're stupid enough to foot the bill for improvements on my land, then more fool you. *I* shan't stop you."

"No, I'm not fool enough to do that," said Constantine. "Lord deVere is footing the bill."

He paused, relishing the astonished consternation on his neighbor's face. Trent might wriggle out of repaying Constantine, but he didn't have the guts to deny his formidable uncle the funds he'd expended on Trent's land.

Recovering, Trent blustered, "At all events, Bronson holds the lease on the mill. It's no concern of mine what he does with the place."

His temper rising, Constantine said, "But your tenants are your concern, Trent. And you have a duty to them not to abdicate responsibility to a man like Bronson. A man who has been conspicuously absent in these parts."

Constantine's eyes narrowed. "Did you know those weavers' wages were barely enough to keep them alive? Do you know what hours those men and women and children were expected to work? Do you even care?"

Trent sent him a contemptuous look. "Don't come over all high-and-mighty with me. I'll not take lessons in my duty from a blackguard like you!"

The fury that exploded inside Constantine needed an outlet, but he'd promised himself he would not lose his temper today. Panting with the effort of holding back, he shook his head.

"No," he managed. "That, at least, is clear. You'll *never* learn, will you, Trent?" He narrowed his eyes. "I always knew you for a golden-haired hypocrite, Trent. But I never dreamed you would stoop to fraud."

A flash of emotion crossed Trent's features before his face shuttered. "What?" he said coldly.

"Mr. Greenslade did a little digging for me," said Constantine. "And do you know what he discovered? That you, Trent, are a director and principal shareholder of Bronson and Company. There is no Bronson. You made him up."

Trent's hands were balled into fists. His knuckles were white. His face betrayed nothing at all. "Why the hell would I do something like that?"

"I don't know," said Constantine. He pulled up a chair and sat down. "Shall I hazard a guess? You persuaded Frederick to run his mill as you run yours—like a business. In your capacity as Bronson and Company, you lent Frederick the funds to buy the very latest expensive machinery for the mill, then you made sure the mill foundered, by damming the stream that powered it. What was the plan then, Trent? The interest on that loan was crippling. Did you intend to bleed Frederick dry?"

Trent curled his lip. "What a nice little fairy tale you've concocted, Constantine. I hardly think—"

"When you dammed that stream, you lost this estate three seasons' worth of earnings. We had to pay *your* mill to weave *our* wool. And not only that, but our weavers had no choice but to accept work from you under harsher conditions and for fewer wages than they'd ever known."

"This is pure fabrication!" said Trent, but sweat beaded his upper lip.

Constantine leaned forward, planting his palms on the desk. He spoke softly. "And do you know what the worst part of this whole business is, Trent? You didn't even have the *guts* to perpetrate this villainy in your own name."

Constantine drew a paper from his waistcoat and threw it down. "Here is what I calculate you owe me in damages and lost earnings. You can instruct your solicitor to communicate with mine."

Trent barely glanced at the sheet of foolscap. "I admit nothing! None of this is true. But whatever I did, Constantine, you owe Bronson and Company a damn sight more money than this! You have one week to find those funds or you can say good-bye to your mill." He sneered. "You won't be such a hero to your people then, will you, Lord Roxdale?"

Smiling grimly, Constantine said, "Oh, don't worry, I won't be saying any farewells any time soon."

Trent's face whitened. "How? How could you possibly find the money? Frederick left you with nothing but land."

"That's right. He did." Constantine gave him a feral smile. "But Lady Roxdale has done me the honor of accepting my hand in marriage. Didn't you know?"

* * *

"Aunt Jane, Aunt Jane!"

Jane expelled a breath in a quiet *oof* as Luke cannoned into her. He wrapped his skinny arms around her and squeezed her tight. Then he released her to caper about the room. "Guess where we're going?"

She pretended to think. "To . . . the moon?"

He gave a gurgle of laughter. "No, silly! Guess again."

"Hmm . . . I know! Timbuktu."

"Timbuktu?" He hooted in derision. "What would we go there for? No, better than that."

She tapped her chin. "No, I'm afraid I simply can't guess. Why don't you tell me?"

"London!" Luke took her hands and swung them to and fro. "Can you believe it? Lord Roxdale says he'll take me to Astley's to see the performing horses, and Tattersall's, too. And to the print shops, so I can see all the latest cartoons. And Somerset House, and oh, all manner of places."

"Did he? That's wonderful," said Jane, perhaps a little too heartily.

Oblivious to her disquiet, Luke chatted away about London and its attractions, peppering his conversation with the phrase "Lord Roxdale says."

"That all sounds marvelous," said Jane when he at last drew breath.

"And best of all," added Luke, "Lord Roxdale says I can have a holiday from Mr. Potts!"

"Poor Mr. Potts," said Jane, laughing. But she raised no objection. She and Constantine had reached a compromise over Luke's lessons. In fact, they'd managed to merge their philosophies on rearing children fairly harmoniously. Constantine was learning that he had someone else besides himself to think of now; Jane did her best to curb her tendency to shelter Luke from every chill wind.

She'd never expected to view Constantine's guardianship as a boon. Yet, his presence had done Luke a great deal of good. Jane thought of Montford, and the good he'd done as her guardian. It was no small thing to be responsible for every aspect of a child's well-being. Negotiating with Constantine over their respective roles in Luke's life had given her a fresh perspective on her dealings with the duke.

Now, she said, "You like having Lord Roxdale as your guardian, don't you, darling?"

Luke nodded. "He's a prime gun!" His gaze lowered. "Aunt Jane? Lord Roxdale says I'm a son to him now. So . . . when you marry him, does that mean you'll be my mama?"

The hope in those soft brown eyes made her heart turn over. Happiness broke over her like a sunburst. "Oh, yes, Luke. Yes! I would love you to be my son. More than I can say."

She hugged him to her almost fiercely. He flung his arms around her neck and he hugged her back, making tears start to her eyes.

"I love you more than life." She whispered it into his dark curls, then kissed both his cheeks. How much longer would he want her cuddles? He was growing up so fast.

Suddenly, the ormolu clock on the mantelpiece chimed the hour.

"Must go," said Luke, wriggling out of her embrace. "I'm meeting Jimmy down by the lake. We're going fishing."

"Are you just?" Jane wiped away a tear, laughing a little at herself, and at the resilience of youth. "Catch a big 'un and I'll ask Cook to fry it up for your dinner."

"Huzzah!" said Luke, and with a cheeky grin that squeezed her heart, he ran off.

CHAPTER TWENTY-ONE

If solitude were to be found anywhere at Lazenby, the garden was the most likely place for it. Jane lifted her face to the sun, feeling the spring air shiver and hum around her, the sunlight dance on her skin.

Pleasantly heated, she moved into the cool of the wilderness, with its carefully tended disarray, and gave a luxurious stretch. She was a little sore from the marathon session of lovemaking last night. It was as if Constantine had heard her unspoken plea for reassurance and done his best to show her how he felt. Over and over and over again.

I'm your slave. When he made love to her so tenderly, passionately, when he teased and cajoled her into wickedness, when he spent time simply gazing at her as she slept, it was hard to believe Constantine *didn't* want her and her alone in his bed. Perhaps he did love her. Perhaps he simply didn't know it yet.

Courage, Jane. Fatal to corner him on the subject. If he wasn't ready to examine his feelings, she wouldn't try to force him. Nothing was more certain to make him set her at a distance than an impassioned appeal for his love.

In London, she would not sit back and let those other women stake their claim. She was a Westruther and Constantine's future bride. That ought to be enough to stiffen her spine. She would fight for him if she had to.

"Jane. I guessed I'd find you here."

She jumped. "Oh, Mr. Trent! You startled me."

Anxiously, she glanced around. Constantine would have Trent's head if he saw them together in the shrubbery, screened as they were from view of the house. While she still disputed Constantine's right to order whom she might entertain as a visitor, she didn't wish for another confrontation between the two men. Besides, Trent was scarcely good company these days.

"You shouldn't be here," she said quickly, trying to move past him so at least they were out of the shrubbery, in the open air.

He gripped her arm, not roughly, but firmly enough to hold her in place. "I know, but I heard . . . Dear God, Jane, I heard you are to *marry* him! How you could—" He broke off, shaking his head as if in disbelief.

When he spoke again, it was in a low, throbbing tone. "I have avoided sullying your ears with this tale for too long, it seems. DeVere warned me not to speak to you of this, and God knows I wouldn't if it weren't necessary, for it's sure to set you against me, so besotted as you are—"

"*Sir!* Not another word." Furious, she tugged at his strengthened grasp. "Let go of me! Mr. Trent, you will leave these premises immediately!"

Jane tried to pull away but he gripped her upper arms and yanked her back to face him. He was so close, she could see the perspiration that beaded his upper lip, pick out the pores in his ruddily fair skin.

His voice rasped, "At least hear what I have to say."

"Remove your hands, sir!" she said between her teeth, while her heart pounded in her chest. If he molested her here, no one would come to her rescue.

Instead of releasing her, he gave her a shake. "*I* had meant to court you with respect, to be patient, but that blackguard has not waited, has he? He has beguiled you with his handsome face and his rakish manners! *You,* Lady Roxdale! The most sensible, levelheaded female of my acquaintance. Yet even you cannot see him for what he is."

"That is enough! Let go of me. You make yourself foolish—"

He wasn't listening to her. Suddenly, his mouth firmed with determination. "Well, let *me* show you something."

Ignoring her struggles, Trent yanked her into his embrace. She fought like a termagant, but she was no match for his strength. "Don't! No! I don't want—"

His mouth crushed hers in a violent, inept kiss that made her feel bruised and helpless—and not in a pleasurable way. His breath came in heavy pants, laced with brandy and something sour that made her want to retch. His tongue thrust into her mouth and waves of revulsion tumbled through her body. This horrid assault was not at all like kissing Constantine Black.

With the heels of her hands, she thrust hard at Trent's shoulders, hoping to surprise him into letting go.

The miracle was that it worked. One second, Trent's body was pressed against her in a menacingly amorous manner; the next, it was as if he'd leaped away from her.

Then she saw Constantine free his hand from Trent's collar. That same hand clenched and hauled back. She cried out, but not before Constantine's big fist connected solidly with Trent's jaw.

The blow lifted Trent off his feet and sent him sprawling into the bushes.

For a moment, Constantine waited, his hands fisted loosely by his sides, but Trent didn't get up. Then Constantine turned his furious gaze on her.

"Thank you," she managed. She looked over at Trent, who hadn't moved. "Oh, but did you have to hit him so hard?"

"Yes." The statement was bald and flat. He pointed an accusing finger at her. "But I wouldn't have had to hit him at all if *you'd* stayed away from him, as I told you to do. I was right, wasn't I? I knew he wanted you."

"He proposed to me," she blurted out.

"Hardly a surprise. He wants your money, my dear."

She lifted her chin and looked him in the eye. "Well, then. That makes two of you, doesn't it?"

For a moment, he appeared thunderstruck. Then his eyes blazed into hers; his nostrils flared. He gave a humorless smile and shook his head, whether in denial or disbelief, she wasn't sure.

"In fact," she persisted, "there is no difference between you."

The anger that thinned Constantine's lips and hardened his jaw ought to have frightened her. She didn't know what had gotten into her. She was quite blatantly goading him. Into what, pray? Into admitting he loved her? She might as well tilt at the moon.

"Oh, there's a difference, all right," he ground out. "For all my sins, I have yet to press my attentions on an unwilling woman! What the hell did you mean by coming out here alone with him?"

On the defensive, she retorted, "He found me here! How was I to know he'd make a passionate declaration like that? I thought he was a respectable gentleman, and if my widow's status isn't adequate protection —"

"Well, of course it isn't adequate, you silly innocent! And as for Trent being a gentleman, haven't you learned anything since you emerged from the schoolroom? Men, my dear, are all the same under the skin."

She eyed him doubtfully. "All of them?"

"Yes, all of them. They only want one thing from a beautiful woman; it's simply that some of them hide it better than others."

He'd called her beautiful!

Oh, he'd praised her beauty in her bedchamber every night, but somehow, this offhand reference to it was more believable. Silly man. She was no beauty. She knew it, having stood in Rosamund's shade for more than half her life.

"In fact," he went on, his face softening as he drew her into his arms, "I can tell you firsthand that *I* want you right now. This very moment. And every other moment of the day." He ran his lips along her hairline, then kissed her temple.

Constantine's fingertips brushed her chin, then tilted her head up. He bent his head toward her. "Each moment we're apart, I ache for you, and I cannot wait to have you in my arms again."

He kissed her, softly, deeply, and long. She lost all sense of herself in that slow exploration. Her will deserted her entirely. She was his. If he wanted to take her, right there in the shrubbery, she would not have raised a protest.

"Want you for your money, do I?" he murmured, his lips drifting over her cheek. He laughed gently, a warm breath against her ear. "Oh, Jane."

He found her mouth once more and Jane gave a small moan as she moved against him. Her body seemed to remember the pleasure of last night, and the yearning inside her grew.

It was Constantine who finally ended the kiss, pressing his forehead to hers. He let out a long exhale. "I was forgetting we have company."

A loud groan came from the bushes. Constantine turned and they watched Trent stagger to his feet.

"You'll meet me for this, Black!"

Constantine flicked a piece of lint from his sleeve. "I don't think so."

"Am I to call you a coward?"

Jane felt Constantine's arm tense to rock hardness. "Listen here, Trent. You don't have a leg to stand on, you know. I'm betrothed to the lady and I found her struggling in your rather inept embrace. If bloodying your nose satisfies my sense of injured honor, you've no business pressing a duel on me."

Trent tugged on his cravat. "Montford will forbid you the match! The duke will never stand for this!"

Constantine showed his teeth in an unpleasant grin. "I believe I've already given you your cue to exit, Trent. But by all means, stay if you wish. Beating the tripe out of you would afford me immense satisfaction."

"Constantine!" said Jane.

"Oh, 'Constantine,' is it?" Humiliation appeared to lend a nasty edge to Trent's anger. "I suppose you've let *him* kiss you! Well, you may not know the character of the man you're dealing with, but I do. He fathered a babe on a maid in this house and then abandoned them both. Yes! Your precious Luke, my lady, is Constantine Black's son."

Trent's pronouncement had all the effect he might have desired. Jane gasped. Her gaze flew to Constantine, who had turned almost as white as his cravat.

"That is a lie!" she cried. "Tell him, Constantine!"

When Constantine maintained his stunned silence, she said, a little less certainly, "It's not true. Is it, Constantine?"

Her tone didn't carry enough conviction. The look Constantine gave her was one of undisguised pain.

"Which maid?" he asked, holding himself very still. He turned his gaze on Trent. "Was it Violet?"

Shock broke over Jane like a cold wave. A strangled cry ripped from deep inside her.

"My God!" said Trent, in accents of disgust. "How many maids did you tumble in your illustrious career? Of course it was Violet! They hushed it up, sent her packing as soon as she discovered she was increasing. No doubt they paid her handsomely to keep her mouth shut. But when the poor girl died, her family brought the babe back here." Trent's lip curled in a sneer. "Your uncle always was a soft touch, wasn't he? He took Luke in, claimed he was a distant relative."

This sounded more and more plausible. Desperately, Jane said, "It's not true! It *isn't* true, is it, Constantine?"

He'd told her he'd been a wild youth, that he'd discovered he liked women early. But he'd dismissed his peccadilloes as harmless pranks. Could he seriously suppose seducing a maid in his uncle's house counted as a harmless prank?

Constantine didn't answer her, didn't look at her. He stood staring, grim-faced, into the distance as if replaying history in his mind. She saw the strong column of his throat convulse as he swallowed hard.

Sickened, drowning in the horror of it, Jane fought back tears. "*Constantine!* Say something! Why don't you defend yourself, for God's sake?"

He watched Trent for many moments before he finally spoke. "Defend myself?" he said slowly. "What on earth would be the point of that?"

Without another glance in Jane's direction, Constantine turned on his heel and strode away.

Jane felt as if she were falling from a cliff. The world spun ever faster out of control. She simply stood there, reeling, one palm pressed to her stomach. It took some moments to catch her breath.

She rounded on Trent. "It's not true," she said in a low, trembling voice. "I won't believe it."

Trent tenderly touched his streaming nose, but the light of triumph was in his eye. "Believe it. Frederick told me of it himself. Black as good as admitted it! Didn't you hear the cur?"

Yes, she'd heard him. Oh, he hadn't admitted it, not in so many words. But his manner, the things he *had* said, betrayed him.

Even so, for some idiotic reason, she still hoped there was some explanation.

Perhaps she might even forgive him if he showed he understood now how wrong his behavior had been. But he didn't, did he? How could she love a man whose moral compass was so out of kilter with her own?

"No," she whispered. "It *can't* be true."

She turned to go after Constantine.

"Believe it, Jane," Trent called after her. "Don't throw yourself away on him!"

Sobs built in Jane's chest. Feverishly, she shook her head. She would *not* cry. There was no time for tears. If she wept, she couldn't keep a clear head for the coming confrontation.

She would make Constantine give her an explanation. He might not love her, but he owed her that, at least.

CHAPTER TWENTY-TWO

The walk back to the house seemed endless. Several times, Jane had to stop to close her eyes and take deep breaths to prevent the nightmarish horror from overwhelming her.

Constantine, Luke's father? She didn't want to believe it. But he'd as good as admitted it, hadn't he? And, much as her heart rebelled against the notion, it made an awful kind of sense.

Her father-in-law must have known Constantine was Luke's father. That was why he'd kept the boy, surely. A compassionate man he may have been, but even the old Lord Roxdale's beneficence would not have extended to welcoming Luke into his household if someone close to him hadn't been involved.

Her father-in-law *must* have known of Luke's parentage. Frederick knew it, too! *That* was why both of them had barred Constantine from the house and sought to disinherit him, not merely because of his indiscretion with Miss Flockton.

But they hadn't told Constantine he had a son. That might go some way to excusing his neglect of Luke in the intervening years. Yet . . . had he ever made an attempt to discover whether his activities with Violet had borne fruit?

And then there was the act itself. How could Constantine, a gentleman, have committed such a heinous crime as to seduce a servant girl, one whose will was compromised by her employment?

Jane's heart rebelled against accepting the notion. Such callous, sneaking behavior did not tally with the Constantine she knew.

Her stomach churned as her mind clamored with conjecture. If only Constantine would tell her it was all a lie.

She'd believe him. She would try.

At the library door, she hesitated. She pressed her fingertips to the oak panels as if to draw strength from the centuries-old wood. Then she squared her shoulders, lifted her chin, and went in.

She found him standing at the long window where they'd first met.

He squinted up at the sky. "Clouds are racing in. The sun never seems to shine for long in this place."

He spoke without emotion, but a muscle ticked beside his mouth. He widened his stance, as if bracing himself for a blow he was determined to meet squarely.

With his green eyes dark and steady on hers, the silence grew. She didn't want to question him about what they'd just heard. She wanted to run to him and hurl herself into his arms and passionately declare she didn't believe a word Trent said.

Use your wits, Jane. No other explanation made sense. And there was a look about Luke sometimes . . .

We were childhood cronies, Frederick and I. But I haven't laid eyes on him in, oh, seven years.

Seven years. Luke's six and three quarters plus nine months . . . Yes, it could have been Constantine.

The anguish in her heart was so great, it made her body weak. She gripped the edge of the desk that stood between them to steady herself.

She swallowed, gathering her courage. Then she lifted her chin and looked him in the eye.

"Is it true?" she said. "Are you Luke's father?"

His eyes burned into hers. Deliberately, he answered, "What do you think?"

"No!" She rounded the desk to him. "That is not good enough, Constantine!"

"I'm afraid it will have to be. I cannot . . . I find I've no other answer to give you now."

Did that mean he didn't know if Luke was his or not? In that case, he must have committed the sin of which he stood accused. He must have bedded a maid in this house.

Oh, God, she couldn't breathe. Tears sprang to her eyes. Despite her determination to stare the truth in the face, she'd longed for him to tell her it was all malicious falsehood.

She bit her lip. "Deny it and I will believe you. Deny it and we'll forget this ever happened!"

That stubborn chin jutted out. "I will not deny it."

"Oh, will you not?" Fury at his obstinacy lashed her. "Then I shall take it as confirmed."

"That would be one choice open to you," he said evenly.

"How can you be so unemotional about this?" she cried. "Luke has grown up not knowing you. He has suffered vicious taunts on your account. They called him a bastard, Constantine. They *knew*."

Did the entire estate know of this startling piece of information, then? Was she the last to remain ignorant?

Jane fell to pacing about the room. Hurt, confusion, and fury all welled up and clashed inside her. How could he be so utterly horrid? Just when she thought she'd found . . .

What? What had she found? When had Constantine ever made promises to her? She'd not even demanded his fidelity when she'd consented to be his wife, much less demanded his loyalty or his heart. She'd learned to expect very little from a husband.

She'd thought him unemotional, but when he did speak, each word seemed to cost him dearly. "I'd thank you not to say anything about this to Luke until I've . . . until I've managed to sort a few things out."

She narrowed her eyes. "No, as his *father*, I'm sure you have the right to tell him whenever you choose."

What a noble papa you have, Luke! How blind she'd been not to see it, not to guess. She kept moving, moving. If she didn't move, she'd disintegrate into tiny pieces.

His voice interrupted her thoughts. "Stimulating as it is to watch you storming about the room like this, I beg you will not keep me in suspense."

She jerked to a halt. "Suspense?"

His gaze flicked upward. The strong column of his throat convulsed as he swallowed.

"Our betrothal. I assume you wish to end it."

Jane laughed rather wildly. "Why should I do that? I knew you for a scoundrel when I agreed to the match."

"So you did." That fierce look was back in his eyes. "How . . . *reassuring* to know you haven't allowed any romantical notions to fill that elegant head of yours. Particularly after all the nights you've spent in my bed."

Her face flamed at the reference. For a few heated moments, she was back in his bedchamber again, trembling in his arms. A sense of loss welled up inside her. Not for the pleasure he gave her, but for the precious intimacy of those moments they'd shared.

Grief threatened to overcome her ire, but she thrust it away. Her dark prince had vanished, but the fairy tale had always been an illusion, hadn't it? She ought not to repine. Montford had warned her from the start what sort of man Constantine was.

She began to pace again. "Everyone cautioned me against you, but they all agreed on one thing—given that will, the most logical course is for me to wed you. Duty demands it, in fact."

"And you are, of course, a most dutiful lady."

"You're *damned* right I am!"

Constantine blinked. "Did you just swear?"

"Yes!" And Lord, it had felt *marvelous*.

She took another turn around the room, gripping her hands together, trying desperately to dredge up some semblance of calm.

Yes, she was sensible of her duty, but even so, she might well have fled the house then and there, were it not for Luke. She needed to help him grow accustomed to the shocking news of his parentage. She needed him to know she'd be there for him through thick and thin, even if his care-for-nothing father had not.

Finally, when she thought she'd managed a little control, she stopped to face Constantine. In a trembling voice, she said, "Our betrothal will go ahead."

She shivered, thinking of that poor maid, cast out of her workplace, heavy with Constantine's child. She did *not* want him in her bed tonight. Or ever again.

"But I'm not forgiven," he said.

Anger and sorrow flared within her. Was he truly so oblivious to the real victim in all this? Didn't he understand at all?

"It is not my place to forgive you," she said quietly. "It is Luke's."

Regret ripped at his insides as Constantine watched Jane leave him, her head held high as a queen's. The urge to go after her, to tell her everything, made him take several strides toward the door. Then he stopped, changed direction, and headed for the drinks tray.

Brandy scalded its way down his throat but did nothing to dull the pain.

Viciously, he swore.

Snagging the brandy decanter by the neck, he moved to an armchair and sat down to think. He sloshed more drink in his glass and set the decanter down on the table beside him. His hands were shaking.

Damn it to hell! He ought to have known this feeling of contentment would be short-lived. Happiness had always presaged disaster for him.

He slammed down the glass and put his head in his hands.

So many incomprehensible pieces of his life made sense to him now. Part of his frustration had been a failure to understand the reasons behind all that had happened those years ago.

Now, with this latest revelation, it was as if past events fell into place. Like that kaleidoscope he'd shown Luke, just one small twist and the same fragments changed shape, revealed a new pattern.

And the truth, when he saw it at last, slammed into him like a fist.

Constantine surged to his feet. His uncle, his cousin, his father, his sisters, all of them had believed this of him, while he'd remained ignorant that the accusation had been made . . .

And now, Jane.

For that, he had himself to blame. If only he'd had the presence of mind to deny Trent's accusation at once. He need never have seen the condemnation in Jane's eyes.

Rage rose within him, tearing at his brain, seething in his chest. He picked up his glass and hurled it into the fireplace. It exploded into glittering shards, drenching the air with the scent of smuggled cognac.

But there was no satisfaction from smashing expensive crystal. No way he could turn back the years and make it all right.

Three men had gone to their graves believing the worst of him. He'd never asked their forgiveness. Too late to seek it now.

But how could he live without Jane's good opinion? How could he marry a woman who thought so little of him?

Ah, Christ, why did *she* have the power to suck all those feelings to the surface? He'd existed for so long in this state of numbed denial. Nothing could hurt him because he wouldn't let it. And now she came along, and his defenses crumbled at her touch.

What the hell was he going to tell Luke? He knew Jane well enough to realize she would do it for him if he didn't make the decision soon.

Time. He needed time to think and plan what to do for the best. He couldn't allow Luke to be hurt by all this.

Constantine drove his fingers through his hair. The pain of it was almost more than he could bear. But he needed a clear head to resolve this mess. He wouldn't achieve that if he stayed here. He needed to get away from her. He needed to get out of this house.

CHAPTER TWENTY-THREE

W hat are you doing?" Jane stood at the doorway of Constantine's bedchamber, watching him pack his bags.

He barely spared a glance for her. "Exactly what it looks like. I'm packing for London."

"But we don't go until tomorrow."

When he didn't answer her, she addressed the servants who bustled about the chamber. "Leave us, please."

They bowed and curtsied and left the room. Jane shut the door. For a moment, she leaned back against the panels, watching Constantine. He had not ceased packing various curiosities into a large trunk.

"What is all this?" she asked quietly.

He straightened, then turned to face her. "It's as I said. I'm going to Town."

"Running away."

His eyes flared, but he merely shrugged. "If you wish to put it that way. I have some inquiries to make about Luke that cannot wait."

Something in the manner his gaze cut away made cold fingers wrap around her heart.

She whispered, "You're leaving me, aren't you?"

He blew out a long breath.

"You are." Her lips worked without making a sound. "But I—"

His head tipped in an ironic bow, but she couldn't miss the banked fury in his eyes. "Yes, you issued your royal decree, princess. You ordered that the betrothal continue, despite the opinion you obviously hold of me. Yet, I dare commit the treason of choosing for myself in the matter."

Blood drummed in her ears so loudly, she could barely take in his words.

Instinctively, she moved toward him. "But Constantine—"

He held up a hand. "Pride. I know, it's my besetting sin." He sighed. "I have tried to conquer it. Thought I had, but Jane . . . Was it too much to expect that you'd have faith in me, despite appearances? Just this once?"

The truth dawned on her then. "Oh, God!" she whispered. What had she done? "You are not Luke's father."

Slowly, he shook his head. "I can swear on anything you care to name that I did not—and never have—rogered any poor housemaid and gotten a brat on her."

His words crushed her righteous anger as a lion might crush a worm. She stammered, "But I . . . but you said Violet—"

"She was the most likely candidate," he said impatiently, "that's all."

"But why?" Her voice scraped over the hard lump in her throat. "Why did you let me believe the worst, Constantine? You could so easily have told me the truth."

"Yes, and I'd fully intended to do so, until I saw the condemnation in those fine eyes of yours." He blew out a long breath. "I'm a fool, aren't I? What a stupid impulse, letting you show what you truly thought of me. I wish to God I hadn't seen that. But I can't ignore what you revealed to me in the library just now. With the grave misgivings you obviously harbor about my character, it's clear to me our marriage would be a very great mistake."

Remorse flooded Jane's chest in a sickening wave. Why *had* she been so quick to doubt him? Constantine had shown her over and over that he was a good man. His attitude toward his tenants and his servants was exemplary. He'd never so much as flirted with any of the housemaids while he'd been at Lazenby. He'd even refrained from whipping those bullying stable boys, as most men of his station would have done.

And yet, she'd believed him capable of seducing and abandoning a housemaid in his uncle's employ.

Tears blurred her eyes at how grievously she'd misjudged him. Oh, his stubborn refusal to explain hadn't helped matters, but he was right. She'd convicted him before he'd had the chance to defend himself. She'd summed up the evidence like a judge passing sentence, not like a woman who loved a man.

So determined not to be taken for a fool a second time.

Jane stared into Constantine's face and the agony in his expression told her the truth. Even if he hadn't said it aloud, he loved her.

She'd betrayed him, refused to place her faith in his decency, just as the rest of his family had done.

And now she'd lost him.

She moved toward Constantine, intending to put her hand on his arm. Palpably, he braced himself, as if for a blow. With a pain that tore at her heart, she let her hand fall.

"Don't go," she whispered. "*Please*. I made a mistake. A huge one. But—"

His face seemed to shut, locking the pain away. "No, Jane, it's too late. It is finished between us. You will inform the duke that you have decided he's right. That you ought not to marry a—what was that expression you used? *Lout?*— like me." His jaw set. "And never fear, in London I'll give them all ample evidence of my depravity. No one will blame you for playing the jilt."

No, no, this was all wrong. All of it. Her brain screamed at her to take action, to stop him. "I can't break the engagement! Constantine, what will people say?"

He looked down at her for a moment. "Since when does a Westruther care what people say?"

"I *don't*! Not for myself, but . . . I cannot bear to cast yet another undeserved slur on your name."

He gave a humorless laugh. "Oh, I'll survive. I'm quite accustomed to it, in fact. Don't worry your head about me."

The thought of him going to the devil just to show everyone they were right about him made her furious at the waste. Courage flowed back into her, like blood through her veins. "I won't do it."

His dark brows snapped together. "What?"

"I won't release you." She stuck out her chin, scarcely conscious of mimicking his own obstinate expression. "You *will* marry me, Constantine. I'm not going to let you go."

"Still determined to sacrifice your happiness on the altar of duty, are you?" He favored her with a cynical smile. "Or perhaps it's Luke you would miss." He shrugged. "I'm sure I can send him to visit you on an agreed schedule. You needn't fear you'd be barred from all contact."

"This isn't about any of that!" Jane longed to reach out to him. She sensed his hurt underneath all that biting irony. "I love you, Constantine. In time, I hope you'll forgive me."

Closing his eyes, he shook his head. "Jane, Jane, it won't work. Let me go now. For your own sake, for your dignity, release me."

Ah, if only she'd learned the arts so many ladies employed to bring a man to his knees, she could use a few of them now. Desperate, Jane clung to his arm. "Constantine, you don't understand!"

He was tense as a bowstring beneath her hand. "I fear I understand too well, Jane. But then, I judge people by their actions, not by the pretty things they say. You have shown me your qualms, most plainly." He looked down at her. "What happens next time some scurrilous gossip is raised against me? Will you believe that, too? In your heart, won't you always have doubts?"

In a low, trembling voice, she said, "My *heart* told me to trust you. But I've been frightened, uncertain of the depth of your feelings for me. Uncertain about so many things . . ."

She licked her lips. "Constantine, do you know how Frederick died? He suffered an apoplexy while entertaining one of his whores. In those last weeks, he was confined to his bedchamber, but that didn't stop him bringing women into his room. I used to hear them . . ." She squeezed her eyes shut.

She took a shaky breath, and opened her eyes. "That night, a girl bashed on my door in a terrible state, babbling that Frederick was dead. I was obliged to smuggle her out of the house and pretend, for form's sake, that *I'd* been with him when he'd expired."

Constantine's green eyes had flared at her disclosure but his face remained hard as granite. "I am . . . appalled and more sorry than I can say that Frederick treated you that way. But not all men are the same, Jane."

It wasn't the understanding and forgiveness she'd hoped for. She'd hurt him too deeply. "I know it is not an excuse for thinking the worst of *you*. But can't you see how difficult it is for me to trust a husband after that?"

He took her hand from where it gripped his forearm and studied it. She felt the warmth of his fingertips—his hands were always warm. She ran her gaze over him, trying to imprint every beloved detail on her memory. Her heart was breaking; she could almost hear the crack as the fissure snaked through it.

At seventeen, she'd thought Frederick had broken her heart, but that had been a pinprick compared with the agony of this moment.

Still, she clung on. If she didn't let him go, they could eventually move past this awful moment, couldn't they? She could make him stay until he forgave her.

She choked on a sob. "I can't live without you, Constantine."

Gently, he said, "Perhaps you think that now. But in time, you'll realize it's for the best."

Hurt made her hit out. "The best for whom? I made a mistake, one I bitterly regret, but the mistake had to do with my own fears, not with you. Life has not taught me to trust people easily."

She softened. "Life has taught you to leave before someone can betray you. I understand that. And I wish I could go back and change it all, but I can't."

"You want to change what's past. What about the future?" He shook his head. "When I told you about Amanda, I thought you understood me. I thought you *knew*."

He gripped her upper arms. She almost flinched from the intensity in his face. "Everything I've done since I came to this place has been in your service. I wanted to show you . . ." He exhaled a sharp breath, and it occurred to her how unutterably weary he looked. "I wanted to show *myself* I wasn't the man the world thought I was. It seems I've failed."

Desperate for purchase, she clawed to fight her way back. "And now you're going to prove the world correct? Well, I'm not going to let you. You *love* me, Constantine. You're terrified of being hurt and you're wishing for an easy way out. I'm *not* going to give it to you."

Anger blazed across his face. "You'll give it to me if you want to keep your proud reputation, Lady Roxdale. Break the engagement. The news can't have spread far yet. Even if it has, you'll be congratulated on your lucky escape."

"My reputation?" She snapped her fingers. "What do I care for that? For me, there is no escape from my love for you, no matter where you are or what you do."

She took a deep breath. "If you want to end the engagement, Constantine, you'll have to act the scoundrel, indeed. You will have to break it yourself."

He'd looked pale before, but the last vestige of color now drained from his face.

She'd hit him with everything she had. She *knew* they could move past this hurdle if only he would give her time. Time to show him how vital he was to her, how much she loved him. How sincerely she believed in his innate decency.

The struggle to rise above her own pain seemed to wrench at her insides. "Constantine, you are the most courageous, honorable man I know," she said. "Think hard about what you do now. If not for my sake, for your own. You've held on to your honor all this time, through some of the worst tests a gentleman can endure. Since you've been at Lazenby you've earned the respect of more people than you can possibly know. Please, my love. Don't throw it all away."

A scratch on the door interrupted them. It was Feather. "Carriage is ready, my lord."

"Constantine!" Jane pleaded, careless of how she might appear.

His gaze was distant now, as if he'd already left. "I'll stay away for the Season. That should give you enough time to strip the place of what belongs to you." Without even meeting her eyes, he made a curt bow and walked toward the door, apparently forgetting that his trunk still lay open in the middle of the room.

The pain nearly overwhelmed her. Jane barely mustered the strength to call after him. "I'm *not* going to release you, Constantine!"

He stopped and turned back. There was grim acceptance in his face.

"You won't have to."

And then he was gone.

The silence was so profound that it buzzed in her ears. Jane put her hand to her mouth, fighting the harsh sobs that threatened to rip from her. She'd lost the battle. He meant to jilt her. Ordinarily, a gentleman could not, in honor, break a betrothal because that would damage the lady's reputation beyond repair.

But here, the circumstances were different. Constantine had already transgressed once. By jilting a lady of Jane's breeding and reputation, he would not injure her; he would brand himself a thorough scoundrel, so far beyond the pale that she dreaded to think of the treatment he would suffer at the hands of his peers.

Refuse to marry a country nobody who'd been found in his bedchamber—that was one thing. Break an engagement to a Westruther and he would be shunned the length and breadth of England. The Duke of Montford would come after him like an avenging angel, show him no mercy. Not to mention Beckenham and Andrew, and Xavier, too. Her cousins would tear him to pieces.

Constantine meant to destroy himself.

She couldn't let that happen. If she had to do the unthinkable and release him from his promises, she would not let him sink that far.

There was no time to waste. Even as a wrenching sob broke from her chest, Jane flew back to her bedchamber. She yanked the bell pull, mentally calculating all she'd need for the journey to London.

Jane glanced out the window, where clouds gathered once again, disavowing the bright promise of the morning. Spots of drizzle appeared on the windowpane.

She couldn't go anywhere tonight. There were a hundred matters to see to before she left. She'd have to break the news of their altered plans to Luke, as well. She didn't want to alarm him with a precipitate journey through the night.

The sense of loss, the despair, threatened to overtake her if she didn't keep moving, doing. She would not rest until she got him back. She'd wield every ounce of the power she held over him to bring him to his senses. She would make him see . . .

They belonged together. She couldn't countenance an existence without Constantine Black in it.

The sick feeling in the pit of Constantine's stomach grew as he issued last-minute orders to his staff. As he put on his hat, he realized he'd forgotten his collection of curiosities, and swore under his breath. He didn't want to go back there, and he didn't ever let anyone else handle them. He'd have to leave them behind.

"Feather, try if you can find Luke, please. I want to see him before I go."

He'd debated taking Luke with him, but he'd be damnably poor company for the lad. Then, too, he could not take Luke away from Jane, no matter what she'd done.

He looked forward with a grim sense of hopelessness. The trip to London would hardly be the sojourn he'd planned. He squeezed his eyes shut, trying in vain to block out the pain. The town house would ache with emptiness without her. Images flooded his mind, vignettes of everything he'd leave behind. All of them featured Jane.

"Where're you going, sir?"

Constantine looked down to see the face of his ward etched with concern.

Constantine attempted a reassuring smile, but his facial muscles cramped, refusing to oblige him. "There's been a slight change of plans. I must leave immediately for London. An urgent piece of business has arisen and I must deal with it."

"You're not waiting until tomorrow, to come with us?"

"No." He hesitated. He ought to inform Luke of the imminent change in circumstances. Jane would soon be gone from Lazenby Hall.

"Luke, I . . ." The words jarred painfully in his throat.

He put his hand on the lad's shoulder. "I need to go away now, but I'll be back for you soon. Whatever happens, I will come back."

His guts twisted at the way Luke screwed up his mouth to keep from showing his disappointment. God, why was this so hard? Before he came to Lazenby Hall, he hadn't needed to consider anyone else's feelings.

He bent to give the boy a manly hug, then drew back. "Will you do something for me, Luke?"

The boy's eyes widened. "Yes, sir."

"You're the man of the house now. Will you take care of Lady Roxdale while I'm gone?"

Luke's chest puffed out a little. " 'Course I will." He tilted his head to one side. Those hungry dark eyes seemed to swallow Constantine whole. "When will you be back?"

Someone besides himself to think of now. Someone to answer to. Someone who cared how long he was gone.

"I don't know, Luke. Soon, I hope. I will see you soon."

With a sense of ripping out some vital piece of himself, he set his jaw and climbed into the waiting carriage.

CHAPTER TWENTY-FOUR

L uke sat cross-legged on the window seat while he watched Jane order the packing. It was such a comfort to have him there, like an elf overseeing his workers. She'd sensed a new air of protectiveness about him. Had he guessed the reason for Constantine's early departure?

Perhaps Luke was like most children; he simply *knew* when things went awry.

"Lady Arden has agreed, we'll leave at first light," Jane said briskly. "I want to get to London as quickly as we can, but we'll be obliged to stop somewhere along the way. I've told Higgins to pack for you, but why don't you see if there are any special books or games you'd like to bring?"

He hesitated, as if reluctant to leave her, but she smiled reassuringly. "Go on, dear. I'm nearly finished here."

She stood by the window and looked out over the long, straight drive. In her mind's eye, she saw Constantine again, galloping up like a prince to rescue his fair maiden from the tower. A dark prince, she'd thought.

How wrong, how deluded, how prejudiced she'd been.

Far from wrecking the estate, he'd made it thrive. His people loved him. He'd met the crisis at the mill with a cool head and a strong, compassionate heart.

He was a hero to his tenants.

He was her hero, too.

Mine. Pride and possessiveness swelled in her chest until

she could barely breathe, until she thought she might burst like ripe fruit.

She'd let him go. Driven him away. She'd not been able to bring herself to trust him, but wasn't the ability to trust someone implicitly the foundation of love?

Fierce denial rose up within her. It wasn't too late. She would chase him down and make him see . . .

And she knew exactly where to go for help.

"Oh, my God, *no!*" Constantine glared at his brother, then sank his head in his hands.

George grimaced. "I tried to fob them off, but they demand to see you. Lady Arden looks like Athena, about to ride into battle."

"And Montford?"

"How can one tell?" George spread his hands. "The man's an icicle."

Constantine groaned.

"I told them you were indisposed," said George. He threw himself in a chair opposite Constantine. His eyes crinkled at the corners as he mimicked the west country accent, "But I be jest a simple coun'ry squire, at that. They won't pay no mind ter me."

Constantine ought to smile, but his mouth seemed weighted down at the corners. Thank God for George. Despite their argument after Frederick's funeral, he'd rallied around as soon as Constantine had sent word he needed him.

Constantine laid his head back against his chair and ground the heels of his hands into his eyes. Once again, he'd fallen asleep at his desk. His neck and back ached and the roof of his mouth felt like the devil's shoe leather, though he'd scarcely touched a drop last night. He'd arrived in London the day before and spent all his time wrangling with ways and means to make back the fortune he'd lost by breaking his engagement to Jane.

When the news came out—as it would, since he'd sent

the tidings to both the Duke of Montford and Lady Arden—
he would be a pariah. All the prestige of the Roxdale title
wouldn't save him. The only women of means who might
possibly be brought to marry him under those circumstances
were wealthy merchants' daughters on the hunt for a title,
any title.

And even then, they would only choose him as a last
resort.

He ran his hand over his jawline, feeling the stubble that
had grown overnight rough beneath his fingertips. He ought
to shave and wash and dress. But he couldn't seem to summon the will to move.

His weaker self screamed at him to go back to Jane on
bended knee. He needed her. What kind of master, what kind
of man could he be without Jane at his side? When she'd
looked up at him, so trusting and confident, he'd felt like a
god, not the lout she'd once called him.

Ah, but she didn't trust him, did she? Her admiration was
for his looks and his skilled caresses, not for his character.
Her love had been a lie.

And now he needed, more than anything, to show himself he could survive without her. The first step was to prove
he didn't need her money.

There was one way. But George, George . . . How could
he do it to his brother? He couldn't sell Broadmere from
under George's feet.

"Whatever you need to do," said George quietly, clapping
a hand on Constantine's shoulder, "I'm with you."

Constantine bowed his head. His brother's steadfastness
never failed to amaze and humble him. "Thank you."

"You know, I've often thought of moving to Gloucestershire," began George.

"Don't. George, you will *not* lose Broadmere. I have . . .
a number of irons in the fire. All will be well."

"Don't tell me you're speculating again! Constantine,
that's almost as bad as turning to the gaming tables to win
your fortune!"

He didn't need to hear these doubts. He had enough of his own. "Only if you don't know what you're doing."

What Constantine didn't tell George was that he'd borrowed against his expectations while still betrothed to Lady Roxdale. His bankers had been all too willing to accommodate him. No one had mentioned his forthcoming nuptials, but of course that had been the reason for the loan, granted on such generous terms.

He'd managed to double the money since then, but a large part of those funds had gone in the service of the estate.

Once news spread about his breaking the engagement, the bankers would call in the loan, and he'd be left with nothing. He had to do something, and quickly.

But first, he must face the unpleasantness downstairs.

"My dear Lady Arden," said Montford. "Calm yourself. All this agitated pacing is most wearying to watch."

She rounded on him. "I don't know how you can be so cool! He has *jilted* her, Julian!"

"Yes. If this gets out, you'll never show your face at the Ministry again."

"What do you think I care about that? Constantine has ruined himself. I had such hopes for him, and now . . ." Lady Arden turned her back, one hand clenched at her side, the other gripping the mantelpiece.

Montford felt in his pocket for his handkerchief. Moving to stand next to her, he proffered it, but she waved it away. Her eyes, when she turned her head to look at him, were bright with unshed tears, but she seemed mistress of herself again.

Her face took on a look of determination he knew from old. "We must do something."

"We will. When we find out how matters stand."

Truthfully, he was not so calm as he appeared. He wanted to rip Constantine Black limb from limb with his teeth, but if he showed that murderous impulse to Lady Arden, she'd fly to Constantine's defense. He didn't want that. When Arden set her mind to something, she usually got her way. She wasn't above exploiting her feminine appeal to do it, either.

It was one of the reasons he found her so . . . stimulating . . . as an opponent.

This time, however, the stakes were too high for such games.

"They are in love," he said.

"Yes."

"That was something I'd never bargained for."

She raised her brows. "If you had, you wouldn't have lent your support to the match, I suppose."

"Of course not." One side of his mouth raised in a cynical smile. "Nothing good ever comes of excessive passions. This fiasco proves it."

She swallowed and looked away. "I warned them. Constantine told me it was a business arrangement, but I knew otherwise."

"And what has their so-called love brought them?" he replied. "Scandal and disgrace."

"Not yet, it hasn't!" Her ladyship's delicate jaw firmed. "I won't let it." She whirled away from the mantel to take up her pacing again. "Where is the stupid boy? Making his toilet? Anyone would think he's one of the dandy set!"

"Heaven forbid!"

The rasping voice came from the doorway, where Roxdale himself stood.

Montford studied the man carefully. He appeared much as he had that day after the flood: pale, drawn, unutterably weary. His mouth turned down slightly at the corners. There was suffering in those heavy-lidded eyes.

"You look burned to a socket," said Montford. "Been dipping deep, have you?"

Constantine stared at him with a touch of hauteur. "I'm not answerable to you, Your Grace."

"You damned well are, and you know it." The words were

spoken without heat, but Constantine took a hasty step toward him.

"Give over, both of you." Lady Arden rushed to take Constantine's hands in hers. "*Why,* Constantine? How could you *do* such a thing?"

The hard, drawn features softened a little as Constantine gazed down into Lady Arden's face. "You know I can't answer that."

Between his teeth, Montford said, "Then let me inform you, sir, that I do not take kindly to your besmirching Lady Roxdale's name. Her cousins are baying for your blood, but I have reserved to myself the satisfaction of spilling it."

A gasp came from Lady Arden. "Julian, don't!"

"I regret your presence, my dear," he said gently. "Perhaps it's time for you to leave."

"I'm not going anywhere, and you're not going to fight. That won't solve anything!"

"He is a blight on his family's name," bit out Montford. "My lady, you ought to thank me for removing this thorn in your side."

"I'm not going to fight you," said Constantine, folding his arms. "It's no use trying to provoke me."

The duke raised his brows. "You think the difference in our ages sets me at a disadvantage? Let me assure you otherwise. Besides, I believe you said you were not a swordsman."

"What I said was I don't fence."

"No, and you shall not do so today!" Lady Arden rounded on Montford. "How can you be such a . . . such a *man,* Montford? I expected better of you!"

With grim humor, Montford said, "And how am I supposed to take that?"

"You may take it that I thought at least you would show some sense! If news of a fight between you gets out it will pile scandal upon scandal. We came here to contain the damage, not provide more fodder for gossip!"

Some part of Montford's brain knew she was right, but his bloodlust, that ancient, primal part of him that had been passed down through generations of Westruther warriors, beat strongly within him.

He wanted to carve Constantine up and throw him to the dogs for daring to expose Jane to the world's scorn. "We'll do it here, now, without seconds. No one will find out."

"Julian! Julian, this will not help her!" She took his face in her hands, gazing steadily into his eyes until they focused on her. "I know you love Jane like a daughter, but you must use your head now. Think, or you will lose her forever."

The words penetrated the red mist in his brain. He had already lost Jane once. She believed she loved this blackguard, or she would not have forced him to beg off the betrothal.

That gave Montford pause. The smallest reflection showed him Lady Arden was right. It was not something he enjoyed admitting.

With a disgusted snort, he turned his back on Constantine and stared out the window.

Behind him, Lady Arden took up her pacing. "The betrothal has already been announced, or we could pretend it had never taken place. Constantine, you have not made your decision public?"

"No."

There was a strained pause that caught Montford's attention. He turned to see Constantine's mouth twist. "I've had other things to think of."

Lady Arden set her hands on Constantine's shoulders. "Is there no possibility of a reconciliation? Constantine, consider carefully before you do this. If not for your own sake and Jane's but for the sake of your people!"

At her urging, Constantine turned white. If ever Montford had seen a man ready to crack, it was Roxdale.

Montford's anger lost some of its heat. Whatever reasons Constantine had for breaking that betrothal, he was suffering for it. Perhaps more than Jane herself. At least Jane had hope, reckless and foolish though that hope might be.

"Ma'am." Constantine removed her hands from his

shoulders and held them between his own. "My lady, believe me, I—" He broke off, his voice suspended by an emotion that seemed to cause him physical pain. He dropped her hands. "I must ask you both to leave this house. I am not fit for company."

Lady Arden's face took on an aspect of grim determination. "This is not finished, Constantine. We have only just announced your betrothal. I refuse to announce its end!"

He pinched the bridge of his nose between thumb and forefinger. "Do what you wish, ma'am. Announce it, or don't. You won't change the facts."

"I'd thought better of you, Lord Roxdale," said Lady Arden, her voice aching with sadness. "It seems I was wrong." With a last, despairing look back at Montford, she left.

Montford stood his ground. "Lady Arden's right. We won't announce this for the moment. You may yet come to your senses."

"I *have* come to my senses, believe me."

The duke sighed. "This is why I prefer dealing with young people whose affections aren't engaged in the process. It makes things so much simpler." He looked about him. "Shall we sit down?"

"No. I believe you were just leaving."

"Ah, but I have something to say to you about your finances that you will wish to hear."

CHAPTER TWENTY-FIVE

Constantine returned the duke's gaze steadily. Nothing the duke said could possibly change his mind. Nothing. But if it was a questions of finances, he ought to listen to what Montford had to say.

He indicated a chair with a wave of his hand and they both took their seats.

The duke settled back, crossing one leg over the other in a relaxed pose. "I saw Frederick, oh, about a month or so before he died. He knew the end was near, had been expecting it for some time."

That caught Constantine's interest. He said nothing, however, but waited for Montford to continue.

"Frederick was agitated, knowing the estate would go to you."

"If he was so concerned, why didn't he secure the succession?" Constantine ground out. "I never expected to inherit."

"Whatever the case, there was no child of the marriage." If the duke suspected the reason for that, he gave no sign.

"It was my notion to carve up the estate," Montford continued.

Shock slammed into Constantine like a fist. *"What?"* He could barely catch his breath. "You did this?"

Montford spread his hands. "Jane is an intelligent woman with great force of character. Frederick agreed with me that if anyone could ensure you didn't lay waste to Lazenby, she could. Our design was, of course, that the two of you would wed."

"My God," whispered Constantine. "This beggars belief!"

The duke continued as if he hadn't spoken. "However, in case you did not agree to marry, Frederick appointed me to see how you fared in your new role. If I judged you deserving, I was instructed to release the funds held in trust to you. If, after six months in the role, you did not prove yourself worthy, you would forfeit the entire fortune to Lady Roxdale."

Constantine couldn't get past the first part of the duke's disclosure. "But you forbade me to even think of marrying her!"

Montford inclined his head. "You are such a headstrong young firebrand, Roxdale, I would have been stupid to do otherwise. And at the time, I meant what I said. As you appeared to me then, I couldn't possibly countenance your marriage to Jane. Now . . ."

He shrugged. "I saw you in action during that flood, you will remember. I spoke with your steward and with your tenants. Despite your recent behavior toward Lady Roxdale, I thought—and still think—Frederick misjudged your integrity and your ability to run the estate. That being the case, I'm prepared to recommend to the trustees that they release the funds and the property to you. Lady Roxdale will have her jointure and she will be satisfied with that."

Constantine knew he ought to feel triumphant. The estate was saved. He'd be able to repay the loan and secure the mill property.

He was free.

Yet, it didn't feel like freedom. It felt more like a life sentence.

He eyed the duke. "You didn't do all this out of altruism."

Montford raised his brows. "Of course not. Why would I? Frederick's family was happy enough to accept Jane's inheritance when it suited them; the least they could do was uphold their end of the bargain and offer a substitute when Frederick died. Frederick himself was not under any illusion that I acted out of pure motives. But he was in a bind. He believed strongly that you were entitled to the estate, but he wanted some sort of assurance you'd take your responsibilities seriously. The solution I proposed suited him, too."

"You were manipulating me—us—the entire time!"

"Set you to dancing like marionettes, yes," murmured the duke with a cynical twist to his mouth. "I goaded you into running after Lady Roxdale and then left you to it, knowing Lady Arden would soon be there to move matters along." He raised his brows. "Clever of me, was it not? But you've had the last laugh, haven't you, Roxdale? I never bargained for Jane falling in love with you."

The tightness in Constantine's chest threatened to crush his lungs. Harshly, he said, "She hasn't."

"That's not what she says. And it's not what I've observed, either." Montford rose to his feet. "I tell you now, I do not want this for her, all this upheaval, this confusion. She was ever an anxious child. She needs peace and stability and she won't get that from you with your wild passions and your overweening pride. I will convince her to release you from your betrothal and we will say nothing more about your attempt to jilt her."

His Grace spread his hands. "So. I give you your precious freedom. You don't need Jane anymore."

The glaring, painful untruth of that statement screamed in Constantine's brain, squeezed his heart and turned his guts into a roiling mess. He put his head in his hands, so full of conflicting emotions, he was near crazed.

The duke's voice sounded far away. "I'll make the arrangements. You may leave everything to me. You're an exceedingly wealthy man, Roxdale. I wish you joy of it."

"*Joy.*" His voice cracked. He wanted to laugh like a maniac at the mere notion, but he couldn't seem to make another sound.

"In the meantime," said Montford, "I have two requests. You have a card for the ball at Montford House tomorrow night. Use it. And . . . find a lady friend for the evening."

Oh, God, no! There could only be one reason for this suggestion. Constantine looked up. "She's here? In London? She's going to the ball?"

Montford nodded. "You will not speak to her. You will not look at her. You will make it clear to her and to everyone else that you have no intention of resuming that unfortunate betrothal. And then you will leave and you will never see her again."

The duke paused. "From my observation, these wounds heal much faster when there's a clean break. Give her a reason to hate you and she'll get over you soon enough."

He ought to be in full agreement with Montford about this, yet everything inside him rebelled against it. He'd be damned if he'd attend that ball, torture himself, use some woman to make Jane jealous . . . and all to make the break easier for her.

He *wanted* her to suffer, didn't he? Too soon, she would forget him and marry some other prime candidate, some protégé of Montford's. Someone suitable.

He struggled against it, but the words slipped out anyway. "I suppose you'll marry her off to Trent in the end."

"No, I won't do that," said Montford. "I like Trent even less than I like you."

Constantine gave a humorless laugh. "And the second request?"

"Give up custody of the boy to me."

"No." Out of the question. Luke needed him, depended on him. God knew what the duke would do to the lad.

The duke's brows climbed. "Oh, come now, Roxdale. You cannot possibly wish to be saddled with a six-year-old child."

"No, I said! I told Lady Roxdale he will visit her often, but Luke belongs at Lazenby Hall. He belongs with me."

"If you think to use him as some sort of bargaining chip—"

"Do not judge me by your standards, Your Grace," said Constantine harshly. "We can agree on a schedule of visits here and now, if you like. I won't need to communicate with Jane at all."

Another twist of the knife in his chest. He'd thought himself scarred forever by Amanda's betrayal. The weak inclination he'd felt for her had been as a candle to the sun when compared with his love for Jane.

Love.

Oh, God. It was as if admitting it in his head opened the floodgates to agony greater than any he'd known.

The duke was saying something. He forced himself to listen.

"Did you ever discover who Luke's father was?"

"No, but I have my suspicions." He shifted a little. "I suppose, being your omniscient self, you must have heard the rumors that he was mine."

"I did hear something of that nature, yes. It seemed to explain why your uncle took the boy in."

"Well, he's not my son. Though you're probably right about my uncle. I realize now that he thought Luke was mine and that's why he provided for him as he did." The impotent fury threatened to overtake him again. His uncle had gone to his grave believing the worst. There was nothing he could do to change that.

The duke leaned forward. "Ah. Well, now, that is interesting. One wonders whose he is, then?"

Montford accepted his word, just like that? Constantine fought to check a sharp rush of emotion, intense and double-edged. He did not wish to harbor any gratitude toward this man.

He licked his lips. He couldn't voice the suspicion in his mind. In the end, he had no proof, and he'd achieve nothing by voicing his fears. "I've no idea." He shrugged. "It could easily have been Trent. He was nearby, had ample opportunity, and—"

"He is exactly the sort of fellow who would take advantage of a maid in a gentleman's house," added Montford, his up-cut nostrils flaring in disgust.

A novel experience, to have someone take his part over the seemingly angelic Adam Trent.

"I've no proof and he would never admit it, so let's leave it at that."

"Yes, I think that's best." The duke paused, regarding Constantine with a kinder eye than he'd shown him yet. "I see you feel strongly about the boy. But I'm afraid this point is not negotiable. Lady Roxdale wants him. And I think he needs her, too. It would be selfish of you to part them."

Constantine ran a hand through his hair. Jane would care for Luke, had loved him for years. He himself was a newcomer who might more easily pass from Luke's life. Montford was right, it would be less wrenching for the lad if he stayed with Jane. But Luke must know he was wanted. That Constantine had not abandoned him, that he had not broken his promise.

At last, he exhaled a long breath. "You're right. She can take him. But I'll remain his guardian—nothing can change that. And he will spend every second summer at Lazenby Hall." He fixed his gaze on Montford's. "And *that's* not negotiable."

More of a wrench than he'd thought possible to let the boy go. His growing affection for Luke notwithstanding, it felt like the last link between Constantine and Jane had just been efficiently and cleanly severed. That was Montford's intention, of course.

The duke considered. "That seems reasonable. As long as you agree to have no further contact with Lady Roxdale, I think I can persuade her. Any communication will be made through me, not to Jane."

Jane. Every time the duke mentioned her name, it was as if giant hands wrung one more drop of pain from Constantine's soul. Constantine lowered his gaze rather than show Montford his agony.

"Oh, I almost forgot." The duke drew out a sealed letter

and handed it to him. "Frederick wrote to you, explaining all I've just told you."

Automatically, Constantine took the proffered note, running his thumb over the impression of a seal that now belonged to him. Without caring whether Montford went or stayed, Constantine broke the seal and spread the letter open.

The contents blurred before his eyes. God, he was so very, very tired.

But as his vision gained focus, he suddenly felt very alert indeed. This was not just an explanation; it was an admission, of the most serious offense.

> *I know it was a despicable thing that I did, allowing my father to believe the babe was yours, Constantine. But you were in disgrace already over Amanda. One more mark against you made no difference, whereas I was doomed to a dog's life at Lazenby if the truth got out.*
>
> *I convinced myself it was justified, that it might as well have been you as me. But living under the shadow of death as I have these past months, I've faced the matter squarely. The responsibility is mine. I should have been man enough to accept it at the time.*

Deep inside, he'd known, hadn't he? Not Trent. Frederick had betrayed him, almost to the very end.

The sheer, bloody effrontery of what his cousin had done took Constantine's breath away, seemed to sap the very last ounce of his strength.

Silently, he handed Montford the letter. At length, the duke said, "Ah. We have our answer. Well, at least now we've no need to fear that Trent will try to claim the child."

He placed the letter on the table. "I'd keep that somewhere safe, if I were you. You never know when you might need it."

Constantine barely heard him. He was numb, stricken. Stunned didn't even begin to describe it. He'd realized that his uncle and perhaps even the rest of his family had believed him guilty of an unforgivable sin. But that Frederick *himself* had perpetrated such a fraud on them all . . .

The weight of grief and disillusionment seemed to press down on Constantine's shoulders until he could barely remain upright. First Jane and now this. His uncle had gone to his grave believing him capable of taking gross advantage of a maid in his house. Had his father heard of it, too? His mother, his sisters, did they all believe this of him? Why shouldn't they? He'd never tried to right himself in their eyes.

Constantine's life, which had seemed rich and full of burgeoning promise only a week before, now resembled a vast and cold wasteland.

"I'll take my leave," said the duke quietly. "Until tomorrow evening, then."

Constantine didn't look up.

There was a long pause. Then Montford said, "I recommend you return to Lazenby on a repairing lease when all this is over. If you don't mind my saying so, Roxdale, you look like utter hell."

"I *must* win him back." Jane turned to her cousins. "Rosamund, Cecily, I need your help."

Jane and Luke had parted from Lady Arden at her door and reached Montford House the previous evening, fatigued and dusty from the road. They'd arrived amid a whirl of preparations for the duke's annual ball.

Jane had slept little, but a restorative bath and sheer nerves kept her alert, her head seething with conjecture and plans.

Rosamund and Cecily exchanged glances. It was Rosamund who spoke. "Darling, we would help you, you know we would, but . . ." She bit her lip. "He is making you so unhappy. Perhaps it's best if you let him go."

Jane shook her head. "You don't understand! I love him. I must make him see we belong together."

Rosamund's jaw dropped a little. Cecily blinked. "This is unexpected, to say the least."

Jane had no time for doubts. "I know. I know what you must think, but it isn't like that. He loves me, too, I'm sure of it!" She struck her hands together. "I need to make him understand . . ."

But the more she considered it, the more hopeless her quest seemed. Was Constantine even now drowning his sorrows in debauchery? She closed her eyes as a sickening wave of pain hit low in her belly.

With an effort, she lifted her chin. "I need you to help me get ready for the ball tomorrow night."

"You? Go to a ball?" Cecily glanced at Rosamund. "She *is* in love!"

"Yes, and I'm going to wear the most daring gown I can find!"

Rosamund's brow was still puckered. "But you're in mourning."

Jane set her jaw. "I told Constantine if he was determined to go to the devil, I'd go along with him. We accepted the duke's invitation weeks ago, so he'll be here at the ball tomorrow night. But he won't expect me."

"I doubt he'll come, after all that has happened," said Rosamund. "The duke was furious with him. Lady Arden told me he challenged Constantine to a duel."

"What?" Jane turned a shocked gaze on Rosamund.

"Nothing came of it. I believe Constantine refused, and Lady Arden made Montford withdraw the challenge. A fight like that would only add fuel to the scandal." Rosamund seemed to choose her words carefully. "Her ladyship made a remark that took me aback, Jane. She said that for once, His Grace lost his cool demeanor. Why do you think that was?"

Impatient, Jane shook her head. "I have no idea. Perhaps Constantine provoked him. He can be infuriating sometimes."

"Perhaps," conceded Rosamund.

Jane paused. "You think he lost his sangfroid out of concern for me?"

Could it possibly be true? That argued a deeper feeling on Montford's part than Jane had thought possible.

"We'll help you, won't we, Rosamund?" Cecily jumped up. "Let's get our bonnets. We'll go to Bond Street. There's not a moment to delay. I'm perfectly ready to assist in outrageous behavior." She winked at Jane. "Not least because it distracts everyone from what I might get up to."

That caught Jane's attention. "You're not out yet. What can you get up to at a ball?"

Cecily fluttered her thick lashes. "My dear, sweet, innocent Jane. You'd be surprised."

"Abominable girl!" But Jane smiled, appreciating her cousin's efforts to entertain her. "You go and make yourselves ready. I must have a word with His Grace."

Montford stood by the window of his library, wondering why he felt so ill at ease over the entire business of Constantine Black.

He was right; he knew he was right. Jane was better off without all that suffering and turmoil. And yet . . .

Ah, he was getting soft in his middle years, was he not? A hardened cynic like him, wishing for a fairy-tale ending? What nonsense.

Still, he couldn't shake the feeling. He'd watched Constantine Black carefully while he'd told him of his newfound wealth. And he'd detected neither jubilation nor relief, but abject disappointment. Despair.

Of course, there was still the matter of Lucas Black. Montford hadn't been able to get sense out of Jane on the subject; she maintained that it wouldn't matter who took the boy because she and Constantine would be together again soon.

Montford sighed. When young people fancied themselves

in love, they became unpredictable, illogical, and headstrong. Jane had always been so biddable in her youth, it was a novel experience to be obliged to deal with her while she was in the throes of love.

A scratch on the door made him turn to see the object of his thoughts on the threshold. "Jane," he said. "Come in, come in."

He led her to a comfortable chair by the fireplace, then took his own seat on the couch. "I have spoken with Roxdale."

"Yes, I heard," murmured Jane. "Forgive me, Your Grace, but what possessed you to challenge him to a duel? I would not have credited it!"

What *had* possessed him? he wondered. Unusually, he found himself without an answer.

"That is none of your concern."

At seventeen, Jane would have accepted that.

"But it is my concern," she insisted. "Is it because . . . is it because you think he has hurt me? My feelings, I mean?"

"This is a most improper conversation. I merely did what any man in my position would do."

She raised a skeptical eyebrow, but said no more on the subject.

"Your Grace, I wanted to tell you . . ." Rising, she came to sit on the sofa beside him. To his surprise, she even took his hand. "I wanted to thank you for your care of me, over the years. I've been ungrateful."

Where on earth had this come from? "Not at all."

"You don't know. I *have* been ungrateful, in my heart. Things . . ." She heaved a sigh. "Things did not go very well between me and Frederick. I blamed you for it. But you couldn't have known. The fault was his. And mine, for not taking steps to remedy the situation myself."

The old feeling of helplessness caught him unawares. Not an emotion he dealt with well. He studied their hands. "I sensed you were unhappy, but you would never be brought to speak of it, so I let the matter rest. Good rarely comes of meddling between man and wife."

"No, there was nothing you could have done," said Jane. "And I've realized . . . Since undertaking the responsibility of Luke, I've realized how difficult it is to know what to do for the best on a child's behalf. You had six of us to think of, and you were a young man, too, weren't you, when we came? You've always seemed so for—" She broke off in a little confusion.

"Forbidding?"

She smiled. "I was going to say 'formidable.'" Her gaze softened. "But you have always done what you thought right. If you had not found me in that horrible place . . ." She shivered. "Goodness knows what would have become of me."

A tightness in his throat made it difficult to speak. "I wanted to fight Roxdale because I hate to see the trouble he has brought you. Though I must say," he added, looking her over critically, "Roxdale looks in a much worse state than you do at this moment."

Her eyes lit with hope and he cursed himself for the slip. What was happening to him? His calculating mind seemed to be unraveling a little lately.

Then she frowned. "He needs someone to take care of him." She raised her eyes to Montford's face. "Did he speak of me?"

"Tangentially. We discussed business and we also talked of Luke. It seems . . ." Yes, Jane had a right to this information. "It seems we were all under a misapprehension about Luke's parentage."

Her cool gray gaze flew to his. "Why? Do you know who Luke's father is?"

He nodded. "It was Frederick. He left a letter, explaining his motives." The image of Roxdale receiving that news haunted Montford. He'd never seen a man look so utterly defeated. "Roxdale had begun to suspect Trent. At least we don't have that contingency to deal with."

"But *Frederick*! Why, of all the cowardly, selfish blackguards!" She gripped Montford's hand with both of hers.

"Oh, Your Grace, don't you see, I must go to Constantine. He will be suffering so greatly . . ."

Montford felt obliged to say it. "He doesn't want you, Jane. Let him be."

He cleared his throat, determined to finish his task. "Roxdale is prepared to let Luke live with us on the condition that he spends alternate summers at Lazenby Hall."

Her lips trembled. "I see." Blindly, she gazed into the fireplace. "Yes, I see."

Unease struck Montford again. It was a tension in his shoulders, in his chest. With a little difficulty, he continued. "I've managed to persuade him to let us handle the official announcement that your betrothal is at an end."

"I will not release him," Jane said quietly.

"It's either that, or letting him suffer the disgrace of jilting you," said Montford. "If you truly love him, you wouldn't want that."

She didn't answer, but he felt her body slump a little.

Then she looked at him. "Will Constantine be at the ball tomorrow night?"

"I believe so."

Tears clung to her lashes. "Give me just one night, then. The night of the ball. Please, Your Grace. Before you announce the engagement is broken. Give me one more night."

How to resist that pleading look? When had she asked anything of him, anything at all? "Jane, Jane, he is not good for you. Look what he's done to you."

She shook her head. "No. It's me. It was all my fault. *I'm* the one who wronged *him.* Don't you see? I hurt him! So badly, so inexcusably . . . *I'm* the one who is not good enough."

"But surely he's the last man on earth who'd make you happy—"

Fierce now, she said, "Constantine has made me feel so much joy I cannot possibly express it to you. It's as if I've been dead all these years and he has made me feel alive as

I've *never* felt before! And he needs me. To take care of him, to believe in him. I must make him see—"

She broke off, and he wondered if she regretted saying so much.

In spite of himself, he was moved by her speech. Always self-contained, quiet, sometimes displaying a dry humor, Jane had never exhibited this kind of animation—this kind of passion—before. He was forced to conclude her experience with Black had done her some good, after all.

He hesitated. It would be nothing short of a miracle if she could bring Roxdale to heel in one night, given the man's demeanor that day. And if she could, well then, Montford might be obliged to let her have her way. She was her own woman now, independent of him. There was only so much he could do to hold her back if she insisted on following her heart.

Lady Arden was right. He didn't want to lose Jane again.

"Very well," he said finally. "I'll give you one night."

She flung her arms around his neck and kissed his cheek, her eyes shining like stars. He gazed down at her, and was plunged back to a time when she'd always looked at him like that. Her prince, she'd called him, when he'd rescued her from that sordid boardinghouse in the slums.

But she'd never embraced him so warmly before. He'd been scrupulous about keeping his distance, hadn't he? He'd never wanted to be accused of impropriety where his wards were concerned. For the first time, Montford abandoned caution. He closed his arms around her and hugged her close.

And it came to him that Roxdale was a lucky man to receive this young woman's unstinting devotion. Roxdale was her prince now, and that was as it should be.

But if her prince wouldn't fight for her, he didn't deserve such a woman as this. If he *did* fight, well, perhaps Montford might reconsider his objections . . . For the good of the family, of course. Lazenby was still a rich and desirable prize no matter who was its lord.

Whatever the case, Montford rejoiced for the moment in having his little girl back. He would not willingly do anything to jeopardize this fragile rapprochement.

Giving in to impulse, he kissed the top of Jane's head and murmured, "All will be well in the end, little one. You'll see."

CHAPTER TWENTY-SIX

O n the evening of the ball, Jane's fingers trembled so much, she couldn't trust herself to attempt even a flick of the powdery haresfoot over her nose.

"Here, I'll do it." Rosamund took the instrument from her fingers and gently dusted a little powder here and there.

Then Rosamund stood back to examine her. "Your color is deliciously high, so we don't need rouge. Perhaps a touch on your lips, though . . . There. That is beautiful. Look."

Jane turned to stare at her reflection in the mirror. With her hair piled on her head in elaborate swirls, it looked darker, only a hint of auburn showing through. Her eyes were bright; her cheeks displayed a becoming blush. Her lips looked soft and plump and red.

"Ready for the gown, my lady?" Wilson's tone vibrated with disapproval. Ignoring her maid's displeasure, Jane nodded.

"This is going to be the fun part!" Cecily practically bounced up and down, heedless of crushing her sprigged muslin gown. She, too, had dressed for the ball, which ought to have concerned Jane, since Cecily was not supposed to be attending it. But Jane's head had little room in it for anything but Constantine tonight.

Wilson brought forward the gown, a glorious swirl of crimson, cut low across the bosom. Jane had never worn such a daring garment in her life, but it matched her mood tonight. The color made her think of fire, of passion, of the way Constantine made her blood pound and sing.

Wilson threw the gown over Jane's head. It whispered and hushed around her, the silk smooth and decadent against her skin. She held her breath as her maid set to work on the row of buttons down the back.

When Wilson was finished, Jane turned to look in the cheval glass. After weeks of unrelieved black, the flamboyant color made her spirits soar.

Rosamund beamed at her. "Oh, Jane, you are a goddess! I've never seen you look so radiant."

"That color is *perfect* on you. Didn't I tell you it would be?" Cecily clapped her hands and went to rummage in Jane's jewel box. "I cannot wait to see Montford's face!"

"I cannot wait to see *Roxdale's* face," murmured Rosamund. "Do you think he'll dine with us this evening?"

Jane's heart knocked against her ribs. "Let's hope so. I want him to be there when I make my announcement."

"Announcement?" Cecily's head shot up. "What announcement?" She fell to rummaging again. "Ah. Here we are." Carefully, she lifted a heavy necklace from the velvet-lined drawer. It scintillated madly in the candlelight.

"I cannot tell you," said Jane. "It's a surprise."

"Well, that's too bad of you, goosey. I won't get to hear it because I won't be at the dinner." Cecily tapped her lips with her fingertip. "Unless I borrow Diccon's livery and pretend to be a footman."

Rosamund shuddered. "You say that as if you've done it before. No." She held up her hand. "Don't tell me the details. I don't wish to know."

Shaking her head, Rosamund added, "Thank goodness Tibby comes to us next week to act as chaperone. I shall relinquish that responsibility gladly."

"*You* are *my* chaperone?" Cecily frowned. "I thought I was chaperoning you!"

"Oh, is that so? Pray, in what civilization would anyone think you an adequate duenna, Cecily?"

Jane smiled, letting her mind drift away from her cousins' amiable squabbling. As the dinner hour came upon them, so did her nervousness ratchet up a notch.

Deep breaths. Deep breaths. She needed to calm herself. If she appeared hesitant or frightened in the next few hours, her entire purpose would be thwarted.

Constantine needed her to reestablish him in society. That's what she'd do tonight.

The secret to carrying off anything extraordinary among the beau monde was to behave with utter unconcern at the sensation one created. Westruthers never bothered themselves with the opinions of others. She'd learned that from Montford, and from her cousins, too.

She'd need all her courage to make this grand gesture tonight, and all her poise to carry it off without a falter. For Constantine's sake, she prayed she'd succeed.

The first guests Constantine saw upon his arrival at Montford House were Lady Arden and Lord deVere.

He bowed, unable to dredge up much by way of greeting. His heart was pounding and his guts were as tight as a drum. He didn't even know why he was here. Perhaps some misplaced sense of obligation toward Montford? Certainly, it was not to see Jane.

"Constantine." Lady Arden spoke in a low voice, taking him by the elbow and drawing him aside. "I trust your presence tonight means you've thought better of playing the jilt."

"I wouldn't say I'd thought better of it," he murmured, looking about him. "Montford undertook to secure my release. Good of him, wasn't it?"

He looked down at her. Worry and frustration shadowed her dark eyes. He regretted she'd been dragged through this mire.

In a softened tone, he said, "It will all be very civilized. You needn't worry. I'll behave."

Constantine hoped he'd not be obliged to behave himself for long.

If only his brother hadn't begged off the ball, he'd have an ally, but George loathed society affairs. Besides, George hadn't expected to be in London at the time. He was only here now, Constantine suspected, to stop his elder brother doing something rash.

With a minatory glance at Constantine, Lady Arden allowed deVere to escort her to the drawing room. Constantine lingered in the hall. He wished he hadn't accepted the invitation to dinner as well as to the ball. In a ballroom, it was easy to pass unnoticed, simple to escape whomever one wished to avoid.

But he couldn't very well go to the ball without attending the preceding dinner, too. Originally, Montford had planned to celebrate Jane and Constantine's betrothal.

Constantine sighed. There'd be Westruthers and Blacks aplenty here tonight.

"Constantine, my dear!"

He turned. "Mama! You're here?" He moved forward to kiss her cheek. "But . . ." He stopped short when he saw his sister, Lavinia. "A family gathering, I see," he said coolly, nodding to her.

"Constantine." Lavinia accorded him an equally frigid bow. Well, at least she hadn't cut him this time. A marked improvement, some would say.

He looked at his mother, wondering what on earth he ought to say to her after all these years. It wasn't the time or place for the kind of conversation he ached to have. Social chitchat seemed absurd.

Before he could utter another sentence, Lavinia put her hand on her mother's arm. "Come away, Mama. They want us in the drawing room."

His mother shot Lavinia a worried glance, then smiled deprecatingly at him. "I'll just . . ."

He felt the cynical hardening of his face. "Yes, do go in." *Away from my contaminating presence.*

"Constantine?" Her voice came from above. All three Blacks turned to look at her, poised up there on the stairs.

He barely heard his female relatives gasp.

Constantine swallowed hard. He had never seen anything like it, not in all his misspent days. Slowly, Jane descended, a bird of paradise floating down from the heavens, a flame to set him burning for eternity.

She wore red.

Her eyes sparkled; her skin glowed with a sheen that transcended even the magnificence of the color she wore. The vivid color picked out tawny highlights in her hair. The gown was perfectly plain, except for the graceful drape of fabric that cupped her breasts. Not many women could carry off a gown like that, but she . . .

The swell of her bosom made an enticing appearance above the low, unadorned neckline. Diamonds sparkled at her throat. He recalled with aching intensity that first night they'd spent together, when he'd kissed her there, the way she'd melted against him . . .

Fury ripped through him. What was he doing, letting himself get caught up in daydreams? They were finished. Over. Forever and ever, Amen.

He realized it was some moments since anyone had spoken. Jane paused like an actress on the stage to allow them to look their fill. Then she lifted her chin and paraded down the stairs.

Here was no princess. Tonight, Jane was Queen.

"How delightful." She smiled graciously, oblivious of the ladies' shock at her scandalous dress. "Constantine, this must be your mama. Do introduce us. I've been dying to meet her."

Hoarsely, he performed the introductions. His mother fluttered. "How happy we are to make your acquaintance, Lady Roxdale. I don't come to Town very often but I was most charmed to accept . . ." She looked about her, clearly discomfited. "What . . . what an elegant house this is."

Jane took her hand and shook it, smiling warmly. "Mrs. Black. You must be very proud of your son."

Lavinia sniffed. His mother merely looked confused. Constantine sent Jane a warning glance. What was the minx up to?

Jane turned to Lavinia. "And you, Mrs. Worth, are most welcome."

"Did I hear correctly?" asked Lavinia. "Do you really intend to marry my brother?" She sounded as if she'd never heard of anything so ridiculous.

Jane sent him a glance under her lashes. "Ah, you are impatient as I to know the answer to that question! Now do, please, go in to the drawing room. You will find His Grace there."

She waved her hand like a conjurer and, accordingly, Constantine's relations disappeared.

He was left standing there, glaring at her.

She raised her brows, all elegant hauteur, except for the slightly pugnacious set to her jaw. A warrior queen, riding into battle.

He spoke softly, but his voice seemed to echo around the hall. "What in God's name are you doing in that getup?"

"This?" She gestured down at herself, and the movement drew his eyes down the delicious curves of her body. His groin tightened. His jaw clenched.

Think of something else. Anything.

Remember how she betrayed you.

But his mouth was dry and his breathing rapid and the blood in his head was rushing south. He wanted her more than he'd ever wanted anything or anyone before. His eyes flicked to the stairs, and his animal brain began to calculate whether they could make it up to a bedchamber before he ripped that stunning dress away from her body and made love to her against the wall.

It was torture to look at her, but if he dropped his gaze she would have won. He didn't want to show her by word or gesture how crazed he felt. He'd already gone against Montford's wishes and his own good sense by speaking to her at all.

A slow smile of those red, red lips made him shudder inside. She lifted one slim shoulder in a shrug. "I was so tired of dreary old black."

What the hell were her lips doing now? Was that a . . . a pout?

Jane. Pouting. Good God, where had she learned all this?

She took a sultry step toward him. In a low, husky voice, she added, "You always said you wanted to see me out of mourning. Well, here I am."

Take me.

Her eyes said the words, even if her mouth did not.

That mouth . . . Hot chills began again when he thought of what that mouth could do to him, had done to him. She was a siren, and he'd need to be blind and deaf to resist the call.

Remember what she thinks of you.

A fresh wave of pain gave him the impetus to break her spell. He bowed. "My lady."

As he turned, her fingertips grazed his arm.

"Don't!" He ground out the word. "Don't touch me."

But her hand closed around his bicep. A catch in her breathing told him she was as affected by that small contact as he. "Won't you give me your arm, Constantine? Shall we go in together?"

He looked down at her. "No."

Shaking off her hand, he strode away in the direction he'd seen the others take.

A hush fell over the drawing room when Jane walked into it. She kept her head high, greeting guests left and right as she moved toward the duke. It took every ounce of courage and determination to appear oblivious to their shock and disapproval.

When she saw Beckenham's quick frown, her steady pace nearly faltered. But with a nod, she moved past, sending up a silent prayer that he'd say nothing to spoil the effect she was trying to create.

And now, the real test of her mettle. The duke.

When she reached his side at the far end of the room, Montford took her hand and bowed over it. As Jane rose from a deep curtsy, she scrutinized his features. They evinced no sign of the fury or disgust she'd fully expected.

After a silent moment, His Grace said clearly, "Ah, Lady Roxdale. I've never seen you look so well."

His voice carried so that everyone in the room must have heard it. Inwardly, Jane staggered at the amusement in his eyes. Was this the proper, stiff-rumped duke she'd held in such stricken awe?

Of course, she'd known that whatever his private opinion, Montford would never rake her down in public over her transgression. In her wildest dreams, she hadn't expected his support. Now she had it, she was so grateful she could have hugged him.

Where the Duke of Montford led, society would be sure to follow.

One by one, conversations resumed and Montford made Jane known to various guests she did not recognize. In all, it was to be a cozy dinner. No more than thirty at table was modest by Westruther standards.

The butler announced dinner. The crowd shifted, and as her dining partner took her arm, Jane gasped.

Adam Trent.

In consternation, she glanced at the duke. What on earth was Trent doing here? She must suppose Montford had invited him before he'd begun to make such a nuisance of himself. How unfortunate! She hoped he wouldn't have the bad manners to make a scene.

The hope was short-lived, however. She saw Trent sway a little as he leaned down to speak with his partner. The lady did her best, but she couldn't hide her recoil at the smell of his breath.

Jane looked around. Perhaps she ought to have a footman escort Trent from the house.

But it was too late; she couldn't have him removed without creating a scene.

At the dinner table, she found herself seated opposite Constantine. Dishes were served all around her, fragrant, elegant, sumptuous. She didn't eat a bite, simply devoured Constantine with her eyes.

She made awkward, desultory conversation with her neighbors at the table. It was too much to expect she'd become adept at small talk overnight. She did her best, however, managing the social niceties with a small part of her brain while the rest of her mind went over and over what she intended to say.

Soon, the moment she'd been awaiting arrived. Toasts were drunk. To the King, to the Queen, to the Regent, to the nation, to the host. They went on and on.

Finally, the formal, obligatory toasts ended.

Jane rose to her feet.

In a clear, carrying voice, she said, "My lords, ladies, and gentlemen, I have a toast of my own to make."

CHAPTER TWENTY-SEVEN

Hell and the devil confound it! What was she up to now?

Constantine had been studiously avoiding that intent, gray gaze all through dinner. Now, he couldn't take his eyes from her as she stood there, so regal, so poised, with a liveried footman standing like a guard behind her.

When she spoke, it was in a clear, low voice. "You will have heard the news, no doubt, that I and Lord Roxdale—the present Lord Roxdale, that is—were engaged to be married."

Her color heightened a little, but otherwise she remained calm. "I say we *were* engaged, because we are betrothed no longer. However, I wish to make it clear to you all that this rift between us is not Lord Roxdale's doing. It is mine. I made a terrible mistake, one I bitterly regret. I misjudged him." She flashed a look around the dining table, and her gaze rested for a significant moment on his mother. "I think many here are guilty of that. Guiltier than they will ever know."

She took a deep breath. "If his lordship could find it in his heart to forgive me, I . . ." Her voice suspended here, and she gave a tiny shake of her head. "I love him," she said, with a hint of defiance. "And I'd give anything to be his wife. If he'll have me."

Jane, Jane, what are you saying?

Resolutely, Jane met his gaze and lifted her glass. "So . . .

A toast. To the finest, bravest, most *honorable* gentleman I've ever had the privilege of knowing."

The room fell silent; no doubt the guests were as shocked and disbelieving as he was. Something hard and sharp lodged in his throat. She said those things as if she meant them. And she said them publicly, for everyone to hear.

Suddenly, from farther down the table came a feminine voice, "Hear, hear!"

Lady Arden, of course. He sucked in a ragged breath. He'd feared she'd given up on him entirely after yesterday's confrontation.

Then the strangest thing of all happened. Montford said, "To Roxdale!" He raised his glass in a salute and drank.

With an echoing murmur, others began raising their glasses, clearly following the duke's lead. The tightness in Constantine's chest seemed about to crush his lungs. He saw his mother, her mouth working with emotion, lift her glass, too.

The murmur around the table grew to a rumble. Montford's guests clearly ranged from confused to titillated to rampantly curious. But if the Duke of Montford gave his imprimatur so wholeheartedly and in public, who were they to cavil?

Only his sister Lavinia sat, still and unmoving, two hectic spots of color flying on her cheeks.

No, she would never forgive him. And judging from the lines bitterness had carved into her face, he began to think that was Lavinia's loss, not his.

Unable to keep his gaze from Jane's any longer, he looked up. Tears glittered in her eyes; the hand that held her glass aloft trembled. For someone so averse to calling attention to herself, she'd given the performance of a lifetime tonight.

The wound she'd dealt him back at Lazenby seemed to heal over in that moment. All of a sudden, his heart expanded with love for Jane until it all but burst from his chest.

She loved him. Before all these witnesses tonight, she'd

told him so. Not only that, but she'd risked her own reputation to salvage his.

The dowager beside him nudged his ribs with her bony elbow. "Go on, boy. You must reply."

He must. Yes.

Slowly, Constantine rose to his feet. His eyes locked with Jane's as she sank down to her chair, giving him the floor. A hush fell over the room again. Tension thickened the air.

It took him some moments to find his voice, and when he did, it came out rustily. "Lady Roxdale does me too great an honor. I—"

"Stop right there!"

Knocking over his chair in his haste, Trent strode down the long line of chairs at the table to Constantine, shoving a hapless footman out of the way. "I don't know what lies you've been feeding these people, but I'm here to tell the truth about you!"

Between gritted teeth, Constantine said, "Sit down, you ass."

Rage flushed Trent's cheeks and narrowed his eyes to slits. Breathing hard through his nostrils, he said, "No, I will not be silent! I've held my peace too long, it seems." He curled his lip in disgust. "You cannot marry Lady Roxdale. Why, you are not fit to lick her boots."

Constantine smiled. "Well, there is one thing we agree on, Trent." He turned to Jane. "But if my lady will have me, I am not so noble as to refuse her."

"You blackguard!"

Trent grabbed Constantine's shoulder to spin him around. Constantine ducked the fist that flew at his head, caught Trent's flailing arm and wrenched it behind his back, pinning him in a wrestling hold.

In Trent's ear, he said, "You are making a fool of yourself and a spectacle of Lady Roxdale. Get out of here, before I give you the thrashing you deserve."

DeVere's voice boomed down the table. "Be damned to you, Trent! Roxdale's worth a dozen of you, you sniveling little worm. You, there!" He gestured to the bank of footmen that lined the wall. "Take him out of my sight! Turns my stomach to look at him."

Trent stopped struggling, his jaw dropping in surprise. Clearly, he was staggered by his kinsman's disloyalty.

Constantine was similarly dumbfounded. Despite his seething anger at Trent, deVere had paid him a compliment he couldn't ignore.

Jane's reckless declaration had made an ally of everyone at this table. Constantine had never looked for Montford's approval, but he'd be lying if he denied it meant something. Lady Arden's support, he'd learned to count on, but deVere weighing in like that . . . Well, that was unprecedented. A deVere defending a Black against one of his own? Who would have thought?

Bemused, Constantine glanced around at Montford's dinner guests. Jane's bold maneuver had seen Constantine not only accepted but publicly embraced by three of the most powerful figures in society. The prodigal son had returned, and he'd been welcomed with open arms.

She'd achieved the impossible. She could have made herself a laughingstock, admitting her fault, announcing her love for him so boldly. Yet, for his sake, she'd braved all that.

For him.

She'd believed in his honor and defended it, even when he hadn't.

Roxdale nodded to a couple of the footmen and shoved Trent toward them. "Show him the door."

Wooden-faced, the liveried servants looked to their master. Montford inclined his head. Then he turned to his neighbor and resumed his conversation as if nothing at all had occurred.

"You'll meet me for this!" Trent spat out the words, his voice spiraling higher as he lost all control. "You've bewitched her. You've beguiled them all, but I know what you are, you jumped-up mongrel cur!"

The world seemed to slow as Trent ripped his glove from his pocket, lurched away from his captors, and slapped Constantine's face.

The hot blood of rage roiled in Constantine's body, suffusing his brain. There was no escaping such a challenge. This time, Constantine had little desire to refuse it.

He'd nearly killed a man once in a duel over Amanda all those years ago. He'd vowed that never again would he allow himself to be goaded into such foolish and deadly posturing. No matter what, he'd always kept his distance and his head. No matter what the provocation, he'd never allowed anyone to tempt him to repeat the experience of that awful morning on Hampstead Heath.

Until now.

Suddenly, a voice came back to him from long ago. His father's. *Your honor is your most precious possession, Constantine. Guard it with your life.*

He'd never taken the chance to reclaim his honor while his father lived. But it was not too late to defend it now.

A slow, dangerous smile spread over his face.

"Constantine, no!" Jane's fearful voice came from across the table.

Ignoring her, Constantine straightened his coat and twitched his ruffled cuffs back into place. "Since you put it that way, Trent, what can I do but accept?"

The room fell into dead silence around him. A glance at Jane told him her face was white, stark with fear.

Languidly, the Duke of Montford spoke. "If you two gentlemen have finished your . . . ah . . . enlivening conversation, perhaps we might all get on with our dinner."

Jane was hardly aware of Rosamund's voice inviting the ladies to leave the table.

No. No. No. Denial beat in her brain until she could scarcely think around it. How could he do it? How could she let him fight? Trent was maddened enough to make this a duel to the death. She didn't think his fury would be satisfied with a nice pink on the arm.

And what if Constantine killed Trent? He'd have to leave England. Oh, God. She'd held out such hope for this evening and now it lay in shards at her feet.

She watched Constantine eat with a heartier appetite than he'd displayed for the first part of the evening. Every now and then, he bent his dark head toward his dining companion, smiling as if he hadn't a care in the world. He didn't meet Jane's gaze. Not once.

She needed to speak with him privately, but would he leave before she had the chance? If he had a meeting at dawn tomorrow, he was unlikely to stay for the ball.

A gentle hand came to rest on her shoulder. She gave a start and looked up to see Rosamund's mouth forming words, but she couldn't seem to make out what they were.

Then she glanced around. Besides Rosamund, she was the only female left in the room.

"Oh." Taking Rosamund's proffered hand, she rose and turned to go.

Suddenly, she looked back to see Constantine's gaze burning on her, a fierce longing written there, plain for her to see. But there was grim determination in the hard line of his jaw, in the set of that stubborn chin. It showed her without words that he would not be dissuaded from meeting Trent.

She wanted to go to him, to try to make him understand. She tugged at Rosamund's hold.

"Jane!" Rosamund whispered sharply. "Come away."

She would have ignored her but Rosamund tightened her grip. Jane had enough presence of mind left not to struggle with her cousin in a room full of aristocratic gentlemen. She lowered her gaze and allowed Rosamund to lead her from the room.

When they gained the hall, Rosamund pushed her into the empty bookroom and shut the door behind her. "What did you think you were going to do, Jane? Leap across the table to him? Jane, I've gone along with all of this for your sake. The ball, the gown—all the things you might get away with. But making a spectacle of yourself like that! How *could* you?"

Jane bit her lip. "I was desperate. I love him!"

Rosamund stared at her. "You risked your reputation on a gambit. Do you know how serious that is? Jane, your reputation is your life! Cecily is to make her come-out next Season. What if she were to be tainted by your actions tonight?"

"She won't be. Besides, he said he'd marry me, didn't he?"

"After you'd bludgeoned him into it. Take care what you are about, Jane. Men don't like being trapped."

Silently, Jane shook her head. Bludgeoned? Trapped? Was that what she'd done to him? Was that how he'd feel?

Rosamund studied Jane for some moments. Her expression softened. "Poor darling. You're in no state to come to the drawing room. Why don't you go upstairs and prepare yourself for the ball?"

The ball. Oh, God. This evening was a very long way from being over. "Yes," said Jane. "Yes, I'll do that."

She watched Rosamund drift out of the library, so graceful and elegant. Unlike Rosamund's innate poise, the confidence Jane displayed earlier in the evening had been assumed. Now, it seeped out of her like air from a balloon, leaving her anxious and sick.

On reaching her bedchamber, she rang for Wilson to attend her. How could she contrive a private conversation with Constantine? Would he go home after dinner? If he did that, she might have to sneak out at some point during the night. Cecily would help her, of course, though the thought of borrowing Diccon's livery did not appeal. Surely there was some other way . . .

Wilson tidied Jane's hair and arranged a filmy red shawl to drape artfully over her elbows. Jane touched a little more rouge to her lips. Then she smoothed on her long white gloves, picked up her fan, and surveyed herself in the cheval glass. Looking one's best always seemed to bolster one's courage. She'd need every ounce of fortification she could dredge up tonight.

Jane turned to go down and rejoin the ladies, but a rumble of male voices and footsteps tromping up the stairs made her pause. She opened her door a crack to see the gentlemen from dinner filing up the staircase and turning left, heading away from her bedchamber in the direction of the long gallery.

Something told Jane they were not going to view Montford's art collection.

"What is it, my lady?" Wilson asked.

"Hush!" Jane made a shooing motion behind her with her hand.

Her heart thumping with fear, she watched until there was no one on the stairs and the landing was clear. Then she stole out of her bedchamber.

"Jane!" The whisper came from Cecily, down the corridor a way. "What's happening? What are they up to?"

"Nothing good," Jane said grimly. "Let's go and see."

The long, narrow salon was a two-story affair, with a gallery above. Jane grabbed Cecily's hand and they flew up the stairs to the next floor, where they might observe the proceedings unnoticed. On the way, she gave a brief explanation.

"What are you going to do?" whispered Cecily. "My goodness, Jane, for someone who has led a quiet life, you are getting excitement in spades now, aren't you?"

"What *can* I do?" Jane wasn't stupid enough to try to stop the duel. Men never listened to reason when their blood was up, and Constantine's honor was at stake now.

However stupid she might think it, men set a lot of store by how well a fellow conducted himself in a fight. If Constantine tried to be conciliating now or refused to go through with the duel, he would lose every bit of ground he'd gained tonight.

Of course, he would still be alive, but that consideration would not weigh with him.

"Men!" muttered Jane in disgust.

"Say something!" Cecily hissed. "If it were me, I'd go down there and pink him myself so he couldn't fight."

"No, you wouldn't, Cecily." Jane gripped her hands together. "You would let him go through with it. You'd allow him to defend his honor."

As she was going to do.

If Constantine knew she watched, it might affect his concentration, so she remained silent, straining to see what was happening without letting anyone catch a glimpse of her.

The men seemed to have divided into camps, the deVeres ranged firmly on Trent's side against the Blacks. Oliver, Lord deVere, was acting as second to Trent despite his earlier condemnation. Montford acted for Constantine. Jane took some small comfort from that. The duke would ensure there was no foul play.

Constantine must have chosen swords, because a pair of gleaming, deadly-looking rapiers was brought for the seconds' inspection, while footmen helped the combatants remove their coats and boots.

Without his coat, Constantine's muscular body seemed even larger. His frame was relaxed and loose. A smile touched his lips as he made some remark to one of the bystanders. One might have thought he engaged in a friendly bout at Galliano's rather than a treacherous duel with a man who wanted to kill him.

Trent might be half mad with self-righteous fury, but there was no denying his physical fitness. He had the look of a swordsman, lean and limber. His sandy hair gleamed angelically in the candlelight but his face had lost none of its fury.

Jane's stomach clenched. She couldn't make herself believe that Trent would show restraint.

The word was given; the duelists saluted. Jane jumped as their blades rang together.

* * *

As they readied for the fight, Montford muttered to Constantine, "I thought you said you were no swordsman."

"What I said was that I don't fence."

"I happen to know that Trent *does* fence. Why the hell didn't you choose pistols, man?"

"Because if I chose pistols, I'd have to kill him or risk death myself. This way, he stands a chance of survival."

Montford narrowed his eyes, but said no more.

Constantine was rusty from lack of practice these past months, there was no doubt. It took him almost too long to find his feet. A skillful pass from Trent and the blade flashed up Constantine's arm, ripping his shirt and searing like fire into his flesh.

It was his sword arm, but no matter. The pain seemed to jolt his senses, sending the message to his body to find its pace damned quick or he'd wind up dead in a pool of blood on Montford's highly waxed floor.

He knew Trent for a swordsman; the fellow had been mad over the pastime when they were youths. He fenced in the French style, where Constantine favored the Italian. They were fairly evenly matched in skill, but Trent was a little drunk and very angry; he made mistakes. Constantine kept a cool head, played the long game, intent on tiring his opponent.

He fought on, his mind divorced from the blood that soaked his shirt, the pain, the rage. When any thought of Jane intruded, he banished it. He needed all of his mind, all of his will to survive.

And he needed every ounce of skill to find the right opening in Trent's guard, the exact moment where he could disable the man's sword arm without killing him.

It was much harder not to kill Trent than he'd thought.

Luckily for Constantine, Trent's stamina didn't match his skill. Soon, Constantine's eagle eye picked up a misstep, a slight falter here and there.

It was time. He stepped up his own pace, drove Trent harder and harder, until he'd retreated half the length of the gallery. Trent's guard faltered for a bare moment, but that was all it took. Constantine thrust in a powerful lunge straight through to Trent's shoulder.

Trent's rapier clattered to the floor. He stumbled back, clutching his arm, his eyes startled, his face draining of color.

A shout went up. DeVere strode forward to tend to Trent's wound.

Constantine threw down his sword and turned to collect his belongings. He did his best to suffer the congratulations of his peers with grace, but he seethed inside. He hated senseless fighting. Something in his nature would always rebel against such meaningless ritual; yet, sometimes it was necessary to teach a man like Trent a lesson in language he'd understand.

Having donned his boots, Constantine draped his coat over his good arm. Untying his cravat, he wadded it up and pressed it against the wound that was sluggishly dripping on the floor.

He walked over to the couch where Trent lay, chalk-faced and bleeding.

Quietly, Constantine said, "You'll live this time. But if I ever hear filth about me or a certain lady from you again, you *will* die."

He bowed to the duke. "My apologies. I must return home to change."

When Constantine reached the landing, he saw Jane flying toward him.

"Take care," he said sharply, before she had the chance to fling herself into his arms. "I don't want to get blood on your dress."

She halted, her eyes searching his face. "You haven't forgiven me."

"Yes, of course I . . ." He closed his eyes. Suddenly, he felt exhausted, as defeated as if Trent had run him through.

He *had* forgiven her, somewhere in the middle of that brave, reckless speech she'd made in the dining room.

She touched his good arm. With a tremor in her voice, she said, "At least let me bind your wound. I've sent Cecily for supplies."

She drew him into a spare bedchamber off to the right of the stairs.

"It's barely a scratch," he muttered, but he went with her, longing to be near her after starving of her company for far too long.

"Well, then, you must let me make you look more presentable. You can't attend the ball looking like that, can you?" she said briskly.

"I wasn't going to." More than anything, he wished to go home to bed and take her with him. But no, he had to attend the ball, didn't he? For Jane's sake. And for his own pride, of course. Constantine Black would never fight a duel and then tamely go home.

"I'll have to send for a new shirt." He looked down at the wad of bloodied linen in his hand. "And a new neckcloth, too." His waistcoat had suffered a little down the side, but his coat would hide that.

"Yes, I've already done so. One of Beckenham's shirts will be bound to fit you." With quick efficiency, Jane took the basin of water and cloth from the maid who brought them and set them on the dressing table.

"Sit here, if you please." She indicated a low, padded stool.

He obeyed her, smiling a little at the way she took charge of him. A warm feeling spread in his chest, a feeling of coming home.

When Cecily arrived with bandages and fresh linen for Constantine, she was clearly agog. "I saw the surgeon go up to the gallery. You truly are the Wicked Baron, aren't you? I hope you have not killed Trent or you'll be obliged to kidnap Jane and fly the country."

"No, he'll live." Unless an infection carried him off. Best not to think about that.

"Thank you, Cecily." Jane's tone dismissed her cousin.

With a pert curtsy and a speaking look, Cecily whisked herself out of the room.

Jane laid out bandages and basilicum powder on the dressing table, then dipped the cloth into the water.

She undid his waistcoat buttons and carefully slid it off him.

"Now for your shirt." Her manner was businesslike, but he was too experienced not to catch the husky note in her voice.

Ordinarily he'd make some warm remark, but he didn't feel equal to witty innuendo at this moment. With her help, he peeled off the bloodied garment, hissing when the sodden linen tore at his wound.

"Ah, yes, merely a scratch." Relief colored Jane's tone.

Carefully, she cleaned the blood from his arm, then dabbed at the six-inch slash that ran down his bicep. "I have definitely seen worse. My cousins," she added, on a note of explanation. "They were always getting into fights."

He squinted down at himself, and was relieved to see that the wound was not at all serious. He was acutely aware of her closeness, of her scent, of that soft, sensitive skin behind her ear that always begged him to kiss it.

"Brandy," she murmured. She doused the wound thoroughly, making him wince.

Glancing up at him, she smiled a little. "You are very stoic."

"Will you give me a sweet for being so brave?" The teasing words were out of his mouth before he could stop them.

Her gaze flew to his, her lips parting in surprise. For a moment that seemed a small eternity, she hesitated, then her gaze lowered. She reached for the basilicum powder and dusted it over his torn arm, then bandaged the wound.

"There," she said, a trifle breathlessly. "Not so thick as to spoil the set of your coat."

"Thank you."

He was silent for a moment. Then he said, "There's been

no one else for me since I left Lazenby." Best get that out of the way at once.

"No," she said. "There has been no one else for me, either."

The speed and violence of his fury at the mere thought of her with another man nearly knocked him sideways. He tried to hide it, but he wasn't sure he managed too well.

Then he looked up, to see a teasing light in her eyes.

Ah. He deserved that, he supposed. He rose to his feet and took her hands in his.

Sobering, Jane said, "There never will be anyone else. Not if I live to a hundred. Not even if we part tomorrow."

He drew her to him. "Well, my lady, that is a very good thing because I meant what I said about killing any man who touches you."

And there it was, that rush of emotion so powerful, he thought she must see it reflected in his eyes. They'd been the hardest words for him to say. Now, it was as if he couldn't exist a moment longer without saying them.

"I love you, Jane."

The sheer brilliance of her smile suspended his breath. She flung her arms around his neck and tilted her face up to his.

He closed his eyes and found her lips and kissed her with a deep, animal hunger that knew no limits, no constraints. Under his ravishing fingers, pins fell from her hair and scattered with little clacks on the floorboards. Her scent rose to meet him and he breathed it in as he devoured her. He was desperate to instill this moment in his senses as well as in his heart and mind.

Her hands explored his chest, his shoulders, his waist, firing his blood and sending it racing to his loins. She gave a frantic, choking noise in the back of her throat that made his groin throb with need.

Music floated up from below. She drew a shuddering breath. "We have to stop."

Yet her hands caressed him as if they disagreed heartily

with their owner's sentiments and her lips continued to feather kisses over his chest.

He gasped, then nodded. "Yes. Stop. In a minute or two." He drove a hand into her hair and gently tipped her head back so he could kiss her, then maneuvered her toward the bed.

"Turn around," he murmured, his fingers deftly working through buttons and tapes. "This, we must preserve."

"It is a stunning creation," she sighed.

"It's a damned work of art when you're inside it, princess."

He undressed her with the skill of a seasoned lady's maid and laid the gown carefully over a chair. Next came petticoats, corset, shift. He unwrapped her soft, silky flesh as if it were the most precious, desirable gift in the world, murmuring his appreciation as he went.

The ball might be in full cry below, but now was likely the last time he'd have her like this before their wedding night, and he wanted to wring every last ounce of enjoyment from it.

When she was finally naked, all pink and white and deep, glorious auburn, he picked her up, laid her on the bed, and simply gazed for a moment. She stared back at him, flushed and trusting, completely open to him.

Love and gratitude for such a gift flooded his chest. He turned from Jane to lock the bedchamber door and shuck his own clothes. When he came back to her, he was fully naked, as vulnerable as she'd made herself. He stretched out on the bed beside her.

They lay face-to-face on their sides, staring into one another's eyes. There was a smile in her gaze, a questioning tilt to her brow.

No games, no tricks this time. With a slight shake of his head, he leaned in and pressed his mouth to hers. He savored her lips with soft, clinging kisses, while he stroked his fingertips lightly down her spine. After a while, he let his hand wander lower, cupping the globe of her bottom, then smoothing over the back of her thigh. Without flourish or fanfare, he hooked her knee over his hip and guided himself inside her.

Their sighs mingled as he slid home. With slow, easy thrusts, the tension built and built, until his entire body trembled with the effort of holding that steady rhythm. Jane's eyes fluttered closed, but he watched her face. He gauged every nuance of her reactions, every fleeting change in her expression, until with a final, deep surge, he sent her spilling over into a sweet, shuddery climax.

With a guttural groan, he let himself follow her, falling into the deepest, most resonant pleasure he'd ever known.

They remained silent for some time afterward, but the hubbub of the ball soon became difficult to ignore. Constantine traced a pattern over the swell of Jane's breast. "We must go down or we'll be missed."

"Mmm." Her lips drifted over his shoulder. "Wouldn't that be a scandal? You'd have to make an honest woman of me."

He gasped a laugh. "I believe I've rather made a wanton of you, but you won't hear me complaining."

He put a finger to her chin and tilted it upward, stared down into those silvery eyes. "Tonight, my darling Jane, you will waltz only with me."

She made a face. "I would, but I don't dance."

When she reached up for another kiss, he murmured against her lips, "Princess, you *will* dance at the ball. Trust me."

CHAPTER TWENTY-EIGHT

Montford never danced, but he appreciated music and he admired the ease and grace of the waltz when performed adroitly. Indeed, the dance was quite instructive to an observer: there was very little men and women could hide about their emotions when they moved in such close physical proximity to one another.

Rosamund twirled gracefully down the room with her cavalry officer. A fine figure of a man, he gazed down at her with a worshipful look on his face that reminded Montford somewhat of a spaniel pup. Those sad eyes. Ah, to be young and thwarted in love.

Rosamund herself looked troubled. Despite her partner's obvious absorption, she kept darting glances around the floor. Looking for Jane, perhaps? Well, he'd not deny that he was anxious, too.

"What a stirring evening it has been," said Lady Arden, at his side. "One feels quite invigorated!"

Her ladyship trusted in a happy outcome. He was not so sanguine.

"Rosamund is in great beauty this evening," Lady Arden commented. "Captain Lauderdale is like to devour her with his eyes."

Montford's mouth hardened. "Unfortunate, that. But I shall deal with it."

"I've no doubt." A slow smile spread over her face. "If

your delicate rosebud cannot stomach that great brute deVere found her for a husband, I assure you I have picked out the very man for her."

"Oh, Lady Rosamund will go ahead with the match, never fear," returned Montford. "I did let you have one Westruther heiress. Don't be greedy."

"I wonder shall I have her a second time?" murmured Lady Arden, craning her neck to peer through the crowd. "Where can the two of them be?"

Then, it came. A glimpse of red, flickering through the crowd.

Montford's eyes widened. Jane, *dancing*? Waltzing, no less, in Constantine Black's arms.

They whirled toward where he and Lady Arden stood. Jane gazed up at Roxdale with her heart in her eyes, a pretty flush mantling her cheeks. The awkward, shy girl had vanished forever, and a confident, loving woman stood in her place.

Constantine smiled down at her with such tenderness, Montford felt vaguely embarrassed by it. Yet, he couldn't take his eyes off the pair of them.

"Oh!" cried Lady Arden, clutching his arm. "*Oh!* I think I'm going to weep."

He took out his handkerchief and passed it to her. "My lady, you grow sentimental."

"I do not!" She snatched the monogrammed linen from him and carefully wiped her eyes. She sniffed and blinked rapidly. "Only, don't they look so *marvelously* happy together?"

Yes. Indeed. Montford was forced to admit they did.

"Well, princess?" Constantine whirled Jane in a powerful spin that nearly lifted her feet from the floor. "Didn't I tell you you could waltz?"

With him, she felt as if she might fly. "I can tonight," she said breathlessly. "I'm floating on air. I cannot believe that *finally* we are together."

She sighed. "I wish we could be married this very minute. I don't want to spend another second apart."

He pulled her scandalously close. "What, and miss a society wedding?"

"You know I don't care for society." She moistened her lips, tasted a hint of rouge. "In fact," she said huskily, "I believe if you were to kiss me here, now, during a waltz, in the middle of a ball, I should not care a button."

His gaze snagged on her mouth. His hold tightened on her hand. "Oh, wouldn't you?" he said softly. "Well, I should care. My wife shall be like Caesar's—above reproach."

"That sounds horridly dull."

"Nonetheless."

She pouted.

"Where did you learn to do that?" he growled.

She fluttered her eyelashes. "Do what?"

"Don't play the innocent with me. What did you do, attend a school for wayward temptresses while I was gone?"

She slid him a sideways glance, brimful of triumph. "It's working, then?"

On a muttered oath, he danced her down the ballroom, through the open doors, and onto the terrace.

Without breaking stride, he swept her into his arms and kissed her. Deeply, passionately, for so long that the rest of the world fell away, left them melded together with the night. Tonight, Constantine truly claimed her as one who had the right.

"I love you, Jane." He rested his forehead on hers, his breath warm on her lips. "I was going mad without you."

She reached up to take his beautiful face between her hands. Softly, tenderly, she kissed him again. "And I love you. Let's get married tomorrow."

He smiled. "Why not?" Then he threw back his head and laughed and swung her around in a circle. "Shall we go up and tell Luke the news?"

Her happiness filled her heart and flowed over. "Yes! By all means. Yes."

EPILOGUE

Haven't Jane and Constantine left yet?" said Rosamund. "They said their farewells half an hour ago."

Cecily stood at the sitting-room window, her hand resting on Luke's shoulder.

Rosamund moved to join them. She gazed out into the distance, beyond the winding gravel drive.

"They're probably off kissing somewhere," said Luke, rolling his eyes. "They're always kissing and cuddling these days."

Cecily sighed. "He's right, of course. They are the most nauseatingly happy couple. The sooner they get to Scotland for their wedding tour, the better."

A wistful ache took up residence in Rosamund's chest. Constantine and Jane were blissful together, it was true. Their wedding reception had seemed more like a public day than the traditional breakfast; Lord and Lady Roxdale were as eager to share their joy with their tenants as their tenants were to join in the celebration.

While Rosamund was deeply thrilled for Jane, such a surfeit of good cheer had been a little difficult to bear. Her own marriage would be nothing like her cousin's. The prospect of that union hung over Rosamund's head like the dreaded Damoclean sword.

"There they go!" Luke cried, clapping his hands in his excitement.

"At last!" said Cecily.

Rosamund dipped her gaze to the front of the house. She saw not only the traveling carriage with baggage piled high on its roof, but Constantine astride his big white stallion. Jane was draped romantically across the saddle bow before him, her head nestled against his shoulder.

"They're not going to ride all the way to the border!" said Cecily.

"Heavens, no," said Rosamund. "I expect they'll continue in the carriage after the first stage."

The stallion pranced and shook his head as Constantine wheeled him around. Constantine tossed a laughing remark to Jane and they both looked up to where Rosamund, Cecily, and Luke now stood.

"Good-bye!" Luke yelled, though there was no chance of them hearing.

Cecily waved madly. Rosamund, blinking back mawkish tears, raised a hand.

Her face bright as a burst of sunshine, Jane waved back. With a military-style salute and a flashing grin, Constantine turned his horse and spurred him into action. The stallion leaped forward, and they galloped off down the drive. The horse's white tail streamed like a banner in their wake.

Moving away from the window, Cecily took Rosamund's elbow companionably. "Well, it's just us again, old thing. Shall we take Luke back to London with us directly, or stay here for a bit?"

"Back to London, I think," said Rosamund. At least Philip Lauderdale would be there.

"Oh, *no!*" said Luke from the window.

Rosamund raised her brows. "What is it, my dear? Don't you wish to go back to Town?"

"No, that's not it." He turned back to them, his face filled with scorn. "They've stopped and they're kissing again. In the middle of the drive! They'll never get to Scotland at this rate!"

Read on for an excerpt from Christina Brooke's next book

Mad About the Earl

Coming soon from St. Martin's Paperbacks

B *eastly man!*
    Rosamund's first sight of Griffin deVere would have caused a maiden with a less valiant heart to quail. Shirtless, dirty, sodden, and glaring, he presented a spectacle to strike terror into any gently bred lady's soul.

His massive body gleamed wetly in the sunshine: acres of hairy muscled chest, miles of long, strong legs. Hands as big as plates shoved a shock of black hair from his eyes, plastering it back over his skull. The movement made the muscles in his biceps bulge with latent power.

Her fascinated gaze snagged on the tufts of dark hair beneath each armpit. Oddly, the sight was the opposite of repulsive. A hot shiver burned down her spine.

But it was the brooding, angry look in his eyes that made her insides melt and slide and sizzle, like butter in a sauté pan.

Rot the man! Why did he have to be even larger, more intensely alive, more masculine than her wildest imaginings had painted him? He was colossal, and not only in stature. The powerful life force within him seemed to blaze from that lightning gaze.

She ought to be disgusted by the state she found him in, particularly in the circumstances. The least he could do was make himself presentable on this, of all days!

Ah, how she wished she *were* disgusted. Her fury fired anew that he should have such a cataclysmic effect on her. He was rough and dirty and in a shocking state of undress, so far from the gallant prince of her imaginings it would have been laughable had she not been consumed by disappointment.

Well. If he wanted to behave like a groom, she'd treat him like one.

But her heart obstructed her throat as she opened her mouth to teach him a lesson. Her voice wavered on the first attempt; she was obliged to repeat herself, and that only honed her temper to a sharper point.

Still, the brute made no answer.

"A horse, if you please," she said again. "I presume my saddle has been sent down by now."

A snicker sounded behind Griffin. His jaw hardened.

"Back to work." He tossed the growled command over his shoulder, not bothering to check whether it was followed. The men scattered, leaving Rosamund and her beastly betrothed alone in the stable yard.

He tilted his head, surveying her as keenly as a predator examined prey. She half-expected him to sniff the air, bare his teeth . . . and pounce.

Instead, he crossed his massive arms in front of him. "Your mount hasn't arrived yet."

The deep rumble of his voice set parts of her to trembling. His pale, penetrating gaze traveled slowly over every inch of her, making those trembles multiply. If he *were* a servant, she'd reprimand him for such insolence.

More heat washed over her, wave after wave of it. "S— saddle me something from here, then."

Oh, she could have killed herself for that betraying stammer. Besides, she was never so autocratic as this in her dealings with servants. *He* put her all on end. She couldn't seem to come to grips with restraint.

He shrugged. "Nothing fit for a lady in these stables."

Her lips pressed together. "I'll be the judge of that." She nodded and started toward the stalls. "Show me."

She tried to sweep past him, but he caught her elbow and tugged her to a halt. "No, you don't."

Rosamund gasped. He wasn't rough, but his grip was firm enough to prevent her escape. She whipped her gaze up to meet his. "Let go of me."

"You can't ride the horses here. I forbid it."

She tried to pull away, knowing it was futile. His hold was as strong and uncompromising as a steel manacle. "*You* forbid it? And why should I obey your commands?"

He showed her his teeth in a grimace of a smile. "Ah, my sweet, innocent angel. Didn't you guess? I'm Griffin deVere."

Griffin waited, bristling with anticipation. *Now* she'd shriek and run away.

"But I know who you are," she answered, widening those impossibly blue eyes. "You sent me a miniature of yourself, don't you recall? Though you have a point. I should hardly recognize the grandson of an earl in such a guise." An impatient grimace crossed her face. "Oh, do let go of me. You'll soil my riding habit and it's new."

He dropped her arm as if it burned him. Astonishment was an inadequate word for what he felt. This . . . this slip of a girl stood up to him as if he weren't some ogre who ground children's bones for bread. No woman other than his sister had ever reacted to him like that before. And she *knew?* She knew that he . . . that they . . . And yet, she stood her ground.

Aware that his jaw had dropped, Griffin hastily shut it.

Wait. "Miniature?" he repeated, frowning. "What miniature?"

Her cool gaze flicked over him in a dispassionate inspection. How old was she? Seventeen? Eighteen? Yet she displayed all the poise of a matron in her prime.

Her lips quivered with impatience. "The portrait you gave me. I sent you my likeness and you sent me yours."

He felt himself redden around the gills. Damn his sadistic grandfather! Gruffly, he cleared his throat. "The earl must have sent it. I would never . . ."

He broke off. He'd almost said he'd never voluntarily inflict the sight of his face on anyone.

The lady's features relaxed. "Oh, I see. The earl appears to have kept you in the dark about all this." She tilted her head, her gaze softening. "Do you not know why I'm here today?"

Griffin gave a clipped nod. "I know."

His answer didn't please her. Coldly, she said, "Then why, might I ask, do I find you thus? Any gentleman with an ounce of courtesy would have awaited my arrival." Her gaze wandered over him. "And dressed appropriately for the occasion."

He snorted. "I had more important things to do."

"More *important?* What could be more important than meeting the person you're going to spend the rest of your life with?"

Griffin nearly laughed. She didn't seriously expect they'd go through with the betrothal? What a travesty that would be. Though every cell of his body urged him to take this perfect, virginal sacrifice, drag her back to his lair, and defile her in every way known to man, he knew better. Such an act would be a desecration.

This bright angel was so far above his touch she might as well have dwelled in Heaven itself. How could the Duke of Montford even consider someone like Griffin an appropriate match for such a delicate maid? Lady Rosamund Westruther ought to take a handsome knight to husband, not a monster like Griffin deVere.

He reached for his shirt and used it to towel off his body in large, efficient swipes. "You needn't worry. I'll explain to the duke that we won't suit. Come on."

Snatching up the rest of his garments, he strode out of the stable yard, leaving her no choice but to follow.

Refusing to match his strides to hers, he obliged her to run to keep up with him. Even then, she soon fell behind. Rounding the rose garden wall, he heard her cry.

"Wait!"

With a curse beneath his breath, he halted. Turning, he watched her hurry toward him up the lawn. Despite her haste, she still looked unruffled and elegant. It made him want to muss her up good and proper.

Hell, he needed to nip those kinds of thoughts in the bud.

She finally caught up to him, and he noticed that the exertion had made a slight alteration in her appearance after all. A flush pinked her cheeks, and her eyes glowed like sapphires. If anything, her beauty deepened with exercise. It made him wonder what she'd look like after a prolonged bout of lovemaking.

He dragged in a shaky breath.

"Do you mean to say you don't wish to marry me?" Her surprisingly low voice betrayed no emotion.

A harsh bark of a laugh burst from him. "Oh, come now, my lady. You cannot pretend *you* want to wed someone like *me*."

He refused to spell it out for her. If she chose to maintain the polite fiction that she didn't find the idea repulsive, more fool she. He ought not to marvel at how well disciplined she was. He knew something of her guardian, the Duke of Montford, after all. The man was famed for his ruthlessness and his insistence on the paramount importance of duty to one's family.

Were Griffin's prospects of wealth and position so attractive to Rosamund that she'd refuse to be swayed by his ugliness? Rich, heart-breakingly beautiful, well-connected. . . . Surely, this girl had her pick of titles and estates the length and breadth of England. She didn't need his.

She swallowed hard. "I don't follow you, sir. Before we undertook this journey, the earl gave us to understand all was settled. Is . . ." She faltered and bit her lip. "Is there something about me that does not please you?"

Oh, for God's sake!

Pairing such an exquisite creature with him must be someone's idea of a joke—his grandsire's most probably. The question was, why the hell did she play along with it?

He stared hard at her. "Do *you* wish for the marriage, then? You are prepared to obey your guardian in this?"

She averted her gaze. "I—I never thought . . . I never considered doing otherwise."

Fury burned through him, the same kind of frustrated anger that ultimately crashed in after an encounter with a willing bit of muslin. Those women never cared what he looked like as long as he paid handsomely for their favors. This marriage was no less a business transaction than a punter taking a whore, though it was dressed up in the trappings of wealth and respectability.

Did Lady Rosamund have the slightest inkling of what she'd be called upon to do as his wife? He'd wager if she did, she'd turn tail and run. He couldn't imagine this cool goddess *accepting*, much less *enjoying* his touch.

Yes, he wanted her so much he was near crazed with it. But he hated the feeling. The hurt and resentment of it tangled inside him until he couldn't see straight.

And that same impulse that made schoolboys pull pretty girls' hair made him step toward her, boxing her in between his body and the stone wall behind her.

She didn't shrink back or cry out or weep. She simply looked up into his face. Her eyes were wide, pink lips slightly parted.

What the devil was wrong with the chit? Why wasn't she screaming?

His breath quickened. Brutally, he said, "There'd be no ordinary marriage of convenience between us, you understand? I'd want you in my bed. In mine alone."

Her color flared. When she spoke, however, her voice was cool. "Naturally," she said.

Naturally? Was she touched in the head? Did she not understand what he meant? He sucked air through his teeth. "You don't know what you're talking about."

With a frown of impatience, she said, "I'm not a simpleton, Mr. deVere. I know what marriage entails."

The directness of her gaze threw down a decided challenge. Images of her tumbled naked on his bed flooded his brain, strangled the breath in his lungs.

No. No, she couldn't mean she'd willingly suffer his advances. It was all a ploy to get him to the altar. She'd do her duty and marry him, then wait until the wedding night to reveal her revulsion.

The tangles in his belly drew into tight knots. Were his prospects so attractive to her? No other woman had been willing to risk herself in pursuit of his worldly expectations.

As he stared down at her, a smile trembled on those plump, pink lips. Gently, as if speaking to a child, Rosamund said, "I'm not afraid of you."

The bottom seemed to fall out of his stomach. Apart from Jacks, he scared the living daylights out of every female he met.

Unreasoning anger filled him. Suddenly, he wanted to scare her, to make her admit her fear. Otherwise, what chance did he have against her?

With a strangled groan, Griffin gripped her waist and lifted her up and planted his mouth on hers.

Fire surged through his veins at the first touch of those soft, warm lips. He ravished her mouth, hardly registering whether she responded. He wanted to punish her, to show her how much she'd loathe suffering the intentions of a man like him. To strip away her veneer of acceptance and make her admit her disgust.

But her soft, fragrant femininity called to him, a siren's song that drew him, stirring not only his body but shaking him down to his soul. With a hoarse groan, he wrapped his arms around her waist and angled his head to delve further into her mouth.

S